DEADER BY THE LAKE

DEADER BY THE LAKE

A Reno McCarthy Thriller

By Doug M. Cummings

iUniverse, Inc.

New York Lincoln Shanghai

DEADER BY THE LAKE
A Reno McCarthy Thriller

iUniverse, Inc.

For information address:
iUniverse, Inc.
2021 Pine Lake Road, Suite 100
Lincoln, NE 68512
www.iuniverse.com

Cover Photography by David H. Lasker

Cover Design by Meg Gruchot

ISBN: 0-595-29359-X (pbk)
ISBN: 0-595-65992-6 (cloth)

Printed in the United States of America

This is for Marilyn, Lily, Mandy and, of course, Socks-Monster,
the feline super-hero.
As always, have a *whole* good one, buddies!

Acknowledgments

Those who say that writing is a solitary pursuit are correct. The process of putting it all together afterward, however, requires team effort. Tess Schmieg, my editor, understood Reno from the beginning. Linda Mickey "walked point" for me through the publishing labyrinth and provided inspiration, support and, friendship. David Lasker, is a good friend and one of the best "reporter-people" I know. Tom Gancarz fed the monkeys that run on wheels inside my computer. Meg Gruchot created wonderful cover art. Lyle Dean kept me focused on days I was supposed to be working at my "other job." Ken Herzlich helped with geography lessons. Cisco Cotto, preacher-to-be, kept me laughing. Henry and William's dad and mom contributed essential television news lore and great friendship.

Good sources are the essence of a reporter/writer's life.

John Drummond and Mike Sliozis offered exceptional insight into the Chicago"Outfit." Thanks to David Bayless, Pat Camden and the officers of the Chicago Police Department News Affairs Section for making both of my jobs easier. Mike Waller, Barbara Richardson and Jim Wipper each helped me figure out various intricacies. Thanks to numerous other active and retired police chiefs, deputy chiefs, officers, deputy sheriffs, detectives, evidence technicians, crime lab personnel and states attorneys who contributed their wisdom and anecdotes. Agents of several federal agencies also went out of their way to share their knowledge of Russian organized crime. They asked not to be identified.

Any errors are mine, alone.

"…and at 7:05 in the morning, a look at Chicagoland weather. Another scorcher in the forecast, with sunny skies and a high of 97 inland…but cooler by the lake…"

—Reno McCarthy, on the *A.M. Driver and Goofy Show*

CHAPTER 1

▼

There's a popular axiom in the broadcasting business. Maybe it applies in yours, too.

"You haven't paid your dues until you've been fired at least once."

I was all paid up that afternoon in early June when I sat under the blue and yellow striped awning at Riva at the end of Navy Pier and watched all the pretty boats and pretty ladies on parade. The guy who had fired me was sitting across the table and ignoring everything except the three sticks of Wrigley's Doublemint he was stuffing into his mouth. He'd bummed them off me the way he'd borrowed cigarettes back when I worked for him and we both still smoked. That seemed like a half century or so ago but, when I counted it out on my fingers, only amounted to two years.

Prisoners in lockdown don't feel time crawl by any more slowly than I had for those two years.

"Who would have ever thought that this junk pile could look so good?" Frank Hanratty, Vice President and Director of News at Chicago's Channel 14, said, swiveling his head to take in the sights. "I remember when all that filled up these buildings on the pier were bums and rats and piles of bird shit."

"Amazing what a few million, minus the kickbacks, will do, isn't it?" I said.

Frank's mouth moved but didn't quite slide into a smile. That was classic Frank, the sort of boss who even limited his compliments on a kick-butt story to a nod or a few muttered words, if he offered any praise at all. He was a low-built guy in his late fifties yet still had the thick shoulders and powerful arms that helped him wrestle his way through college. Age had sagged his waistline a bit and there was twice as much salt as pepper in his hair than I remembered but somehow it was just the right look for a respected major-market television news boss. In the two years since I'd last seen him, he'd also changed to contacts from what had been trademark black-framed Coke bottles. The thick drinker's veins in his nose and cheeks seemed less obvious, too. I wondered if he'd let a dermatologist do some laser etching.

Frank had been one of Chicago's most dynamic newspapermen, a colleague of Royko's in the school of Making Them Sit Up and Take Notice. His stories sparkled with unusual angles and facts that others seemed unable to find. Frequently, information he unearthed changed the outcome of the events he reported. When he decided to trade his barstool at the Billy Goat Tavern, where decades of Chicago print reporters have gone to let alcohol wash the city's sins from their pores, for the News Director's chair at Channel 14, his colleagues were shocked. Gradually, they came to understand his reasoning. Everybody knew Frank Hanratty welcomed a challenge and the owner of Channel 14, Chicago's upstart independent station, had offered him one. Within months of his hiring, critics noted how the station appeared to have shifted from building its newscasts out of stories in the morning papers, to producing accurate and in-depth enterprise pieces of its own. A ratings jump followed. Though he handed off the credit to others, everybody knew Frank was the drill-sergeant whipping the troops into line.

The perky waitress came to ask if we were ready to order. I picked a sandwich off the menu and asked for a beer. Frank grunted that he'd stick with iced tea. The order didn't surprise me but the attitude he gave with it did. Channel 14's owner and general manager, Charles "Chazz" Bascomb abstained from alcohol and quietly expected his managers to do the same. Frank had ridden the wagon since the day he arrived to run the newsroom. While he'd never cheerfully embraced the forced sobriety, I'd never seen him get ticked about it. I'd also never observed quite the same coldness in his eyes as when he suddenly brought them to bear on me.

"Let's get something out of the way. You agreed to meet because you thought I was going to offer you a job, didn't you?"

"Nah. Just the free meal. I don't make as much money as I used to when I worked for you." I figured one zinger couldn't hurt.

"I can't make you the offer you're hoping for, Reno. If you want to take your sandwich and leave, that's up to you. But if you stick around and hear me out, it'll be beneficial for both of us."

"As we say in the broadcasting business, 'good tease.' Beneficial, how?" I fixed my eyes on a blonde in a halter and shorts. She gazed my way, saw me kicked back in the chair in khakis and short-sleeved shirt, beard neatly trimmed, hair recently barbered, and made a little movement with her mouth. It could have meant just about anything. Before I could decide whether to call out something snappy, a crewcut guy the Bears should have picked up as a tackle in the last draft swept past, latching on to her arm and pulling her with him. She smiled at me over her shoulder as they winged away.

Frank said, "I want to hire you to handle something for me as a freelancer. It works out into a story, like I think it will, I'll tell Chazz what you did. Being honest, I don't know whether I can talk him into taking you back. You help me with this, I'll give it a shot. Bringing in this story wouldn't hurt."

Like the credit card ad used to say: Dollar signs. A good thing. Getting the job back? Priceless.

"I'm listening," I said.

He waited a moment, and then nodded as though confirming something for himself. That I was a sucker, probably. I headed Channel 14's Investigative Unit or "I-Team" for five years before he dumped me. I hadn't been able to find a TV job since. He knew I'd take whatever bait he dangled.

"I need you to identify a call girl," he said. He might have read my reaction from the look on my face but I kept my mouth shut for once. He kept going.

"This gal seems to have the goods on a very upscale, very expensive escort service. You remember the 'Mayflower Madam' in New York?"

"Sure. The woman with all the Social Register friends and a string of rich twenty-year-olds she ran out of her apartment?"

"We could be looking at the same thing here. I've been hearing rumors for probably a year. You know how people drop hints, they want you to think they're giving you a big tip but they don't want to go on the record? Over the past week, I've had a couple conversations with a gal who sounds like she's been part of a high class operation. Maybe in her twenties but she's got that same kinda refinement the gals in New York had."

"How do you tell how refined someone is over the phone?"

He made an impatient gesture, mouth curving into a grimace. "What I'm saying is, she's not giving blow jobs for ten bucks on North Avenue. She says to me she wants to tell us all about how this service we got here in town works. According to her, it's Gold Coast all the way. Heavy clients, politicians, a few judges. Charlie Bridges' name came up once. Some ballplayers we all know."

"And she's tattling why?"

"Tell you the truth, I don't much care why. But it sounds like somebody pissed her off. She also sounds a little, I'm gonna say, shaky. Like maybe this outfit has some muscle after her."

"Muscle?" I grinned. "C'mon Frank. Maybe if you want to leave the Latin Kings, even give up your country club membership, they'll send somebody after you to break your legs. Not an escort service. You know that. They just run down to the bus station and find another fresh face from Topeka or Minneapolis. How much did she want you to pay for this expose?"

"You know Chazz wouldn't part with it and I wouldn't pay for a story anyway." He leaned forward, intense. The way I remembered him. "My years in the business, how many nut-jobs you figure I've listened to? Give me some credit. She says she wants to talk. No mention of any dough. Could be she's afraid of one of her clients and wants to split town. Whatever. I think she's legitimate."

I shrugged. "Fine. What do you want me to do?"

"First, you're gonna have to find her."

"She's lost?"

Irritation rippled across his face. "Like I said. We've been talking. It's been informal and only on the phone. She calls me. She was supposed to get back to me a week ago Monday so I could set her up with Marisa Langdon for an interview. I told her we'd protect her, do the Q and A with her in silhouette, the works. Told her we'd come to her, the place of her choice, whatever she wanted. She seemed to go for it. I haven't heard word one from her since."

"She changed her mind."

"I don't think so. She came forward. We didn't go looking. Talked my ear off on the phone. Believe me, she wanted to do whatever to bring this shit to light. She teased me with a great fucking tip and now she's in the wind. I want her back."

A couple of things occurred to me. The Frank Hanratty I'd worked for had never led me wrong on a story. He'd get a call from a source or come up with an idea and he'd worry it alone for a few hours, or even a few days. He'd strip it down, look at it from every conceivable angle, reassemble it as precisely as a watchmaker, and then, when he'd decided it was worth pursuing, he'd call me in and we'd go over it again. This had the feel of something that hadn't gone through his typical refinement process. It sounded like goofiness that had come off the top of somebody's head.

I leaned back farther in my chair and looked west beyond the end of Navy Pier at the tall brown building that sat up like a unicorn from the body of the old cartage docks that were called North Pier Terminal. Up to a few years ago, North Pier was the entertainment and shopping center of the lakefront. It fell onto hard times, as everybody expected, when the city poured millions into constructing its own tourist trap on the water a couple of blocks away. Chazz Bascomb bought up space in the high-rise and turned it into Channel 14's new headquarters and a world-class television production facility.

I counted up the appropriate number of floors to where the newsroom would be. Behind one of those windows was Hanratty's office. It wasn't much, but it had a lake view. It also had walls heavy with a museum-load of plaques, photos and awards. The name Reno McCarthy was on a few of them. The Edward R. Murrows. The Sigma Delta Chi's. My face showed in a few of the being-hugged-by-the-politician pictures, too. I was the husky, bearded guy with one hand holding tight to his wallet. I was also the only one missing a professional get-along smile. In the later photos, even Frank wore one of those.

The waitress came back with our drinks. I watched her depart, then said, "What's the rest of the story?"

"What's that supposed to mean?"

"For one thing, it's a sweeps piece and a cheap one at that. It's something the people over at Fox would do, right along with World's Bloodiest Home Videos or whatever they're showing now. Hookers in Chicago. Hoo boy, now there's a surprise. For another, you've got a whole newsroom full of reporters to send after something like this. Why me?"

He took the straw from his glass and concentrated on bending it into a triangle, sticking one end into the other and propping it up next to his glass of iced tea. It was one of his hand occupiers for when he was nervous or pondering what to say. Straws, pipe cleaners, anything that he could shape with his fingers. He told me once a doctor had suggested it as a way to slow down his words which, when he was drinking, occasionally got him into trouble. After a moment, his mouth twitched again.

"I can see that world-class radio job you got hasn't changed you, has it? Still rude as hell."

"I believe *you* told me that the question you don't ask is the answer that comes back to bite you on the ass."

He went back to fiddling with his straw but that tiny sprig of a smile was back. I noticed for the first time his blue blazer wasn't the same old ratty one I was used to seeing on him. No broken buttons or hanging threads. And his tie, if I wasn't mistaken, was from Brooks Brothers. Odd for a guy who had shopped most of his life at JCPenney. But then, as my mother used to say, Frank Hanratty had "married up."

Without bringing his eyes to my face he said, "Cards on the table. She called Chazz first. It set him off."

I waited. Sometimes that's the best encouragement you can give.

"Chazz tells me he has this story he wants checked out. I said to him what you just said to me. It's bullshit. It's not news. Then he has her call me. What can I tell you? She convinced me. There's sweeps trash and then there's real meat. The kind of operation she's talking about has to be a major setup. It may even involve kids. She hinted at a whole lot."

"And Chazz wants it on the air yesterday, right? Chazz the Crusader. He fixing to run for office or something?"

That brought a stare.

"I think owning the place gives him the prerogative to suggest a story once in awhile, don't you?"

I stayed away from that one. An honest opinion from me about Chazz Bascomb's management techniques would have led to the same argument Frank and I had several times in the days before he fired me. We both detested the man but the difference between us was, he couldn't admit it. He'd married the creep's daughter. Ask me why and I couldn't tell you. I'm not sure he could, either.

For most of his career, Frank had lived by himself and his social circle was limited to those colleagues who could keep up with his drinking, his other bar buddies and his mother who was in a nursing home. He told me once that mama allowed him to visit her only because she thought he was her long-dead husband. He said she often talked about her only son as "that bastard I should have aborted."

Both of us watched a guy in a wide-brimmed hat, Hawaiian shirt and shorts that hung below his knees taking pictures of a woman and two little girls with the lake as a backdrop. The woman looked tired but the kids wore big smiles.

After a moment, Frank gulped down the rest of his iced tea and then said, "You interested or not?"

"Why me?"

"No matter what I gave you to do, you always came back with the story."

"Except when I gave one away."

"I told you at the time and I'll tell you again now. You were wrong the way you handled it but I might've done the same in the old days." He watched his tea glass move as he slid it back and forth between his large hands.

"You *might* have?"

And here I thought I'd worked off all of the residual anger from back then.

He sighed. "Chazz signs the checks and he made the decision. I work for him and I did what he told me to do. It ripped my heart out. You know it did. You're the second best goddamn investigator I ever saw in this business, Reno. Fearless. I can't say that about myself anymore. Spitting into the tiger's eye has...consequences now. Used to be you just had to worry about the tiger. Now you don't know what's coming out of the jungle behind him. Or behind you."

Frank suddenly seemed embarrassed by the admission. He got very busy patting his pockets. He came out with a worn, free-form briar pipe which he laid on the table. For a moment, he focused on picking lint from the outside of the bowl. When he spoke again, it was in a lighter tone.

"I've got some good kids in the newsroom. You ever watch?"

I shook my head. I hadn't seen a moment of Channel 14 programming since he and his father-in-law booted me. Even set my remote to skip past it when surfing the dial.

"I have no problem with their work. I tell 'em to go out and do this, do that, ask about this, ask about that, they do it. Most of 'em are even pretty good writers. Fine, even. Marisa Langdon is the best of them. Three years out of J-School and she could go network any time. Talk about tigers? She'd bite one on the ass. Jennings' people, a couple of headhunters for CNN, they've all been sniffing around her."

"Sounds like she could handle chasing down a hooker."

"I've got her on something else. I don't want to pull her off."

The fact he didn't spell out the nature of that "something else" made clear more than anything he could have said that I was only being granted limited access to my old world. In and out, a specific task. I was not a member of the team. What if I never was allowed back? The thought jarred me as much as his moment of candor had startled him.

The waitress chose that moment to arrive with my sandwich. He growled for her to leave the check and paid in cash when she slapped it down in front of him. As she scurried off to find friendlier customers, he started talking again.

"Say you're right. The gal just changed her mind. I don't think that's what happened but, yeah, sure, it's a possibility. I don't want Marisa to lose time on the story she's working now to check it out. And, frankly, I'm not sure any of the others in the shop could do it. They're fine with the official sources but this kind of thing can't be done by somebody who thinks they're headed out to defend the First Amendment every time they stick a notebook in their pocket. It's going to take a snoop. That's you. No offense."

I shook off my surprise at what, coming from him, actually sounded like a compliment.

"What do I do when I find her?"

"I want your read on whether she's the kind of broad who's gonna have the information she claims she does. Is she a hooker or just," he waved a hand, "some goofball. If you figure she's legit, you tell me where to find her. I'll try to figure some way to get her to come in. You think she's running a scam, then she's history. I'll tell Chazz you helped us duck some embarrassment."

He slid a leather pouch out of his inside jacket pocket and laid it next to the pipe on the table. His monogram was etched into the supple calfskin. When I'd worked for him, he'd kept his tobacco in the store's bag. He saw me notice the up-scaling.

"Old lady's idea," he said but there was no approval in his eyes. I suspected it was not the moment I should choose to ask how the little woman, Elise Bascomb Hanratty, was doing.

"Tell me the girl's name."

"Stacey DuMount."

I smiled. "I'll bet she do."

"Don't laugh. She actually asked if I'd heard of her."

"Had you?"

"I figured it'd be more likely to ring a bell for you."

"Is that why you're asking me to do this? You think I have some sort of special connection to the escort business because of my history with Megan?"

"Jesus. Loosen your shorts, Reno. I'm asking you 'cause if I wanted to know what kind of teddy bear the Cardinal sleeps with, you're the guy who could find out. That's the only reason."

I sighed and let it go, despite the flare of anger in my chest. Meg was history. This conversation held a glimmer of my future or, at least, I could hope it did, anyway. I pushed away my hostility and asked, "What else did she tell you about herself?"

He'd started dropping tobacco into his pipe, but my question prompted him to lay it down and reach inside his jacket again. This time he came out with a reporter's notebook and flipped to a page he'd marked with a paper clip.

"Said she's done a couple of those web porn videos. Been in the business since she turned 19. But I wasn't talking to some street urchin. I put her in her early to mid-twenties. She's had college."

"Why?"

"She speaks well, chooses her words, thinks on her feet. And if she's from around here, she's not a South Sider. No accent, proper articulation. Quick sense of humor but it's very dry, almost like one of us cynical reporter-types."

"What else?"

He closed the notebook. "The couple of times I talked to her, I thought I could hear the El in the background. Not in the Loop, or at least I couldn't hear other traffic noises. Out in a neighborhood somewhere. Not near a stop, though. I never heard any announcements being given. Just somewhere along the tracks."

"And you peg her as mid-twenties, tops?"

"Mid-twenties, white. I think she smokes and might be heavy into the sauce, too. At least at one time. She has that kind of voice you hear down the bar asking for a shot and a beer. And then a few more shots." Given his own history, he'd know something about that.

"What gave you the impression she's scared?"

He touched the mouthpiece of his pipe. "I can't tell you exactly. Like, if she was going to do an interview she wanted to get in and get it over with in a hurry. She also told me she doesn't plan to stick around town much longer. I asked why. Never got an answer."

I scratched the side of my head and looked out over the water. A girl in bikini bottoms and a t-shirt was mopping the deck of one of the big day-cruiser sailboats tied up on the other side of the pier. There was a slight breeze and the smell of marine diesel mixed with eau de dead fish. The blonde and her bear of a boyfriend who had skated by earlier were now at the ice cream shack across from the restaurant. Each held a cone and stood watching two bicycle cops pedaling slowly toward the end of the pier.

Hanratty scooped more tobacco into the bowl of his briar and tamped it down. He used to tell me that fiddling with his pipe was one of his "relaxers," too. It didn't appear to be working. When he finally slipped the stem into his mouth his teeth settled around it like a rictus.

"Tell you what. I'll give you a grand. I figure two days work, max. You don't find her by then, I'll believe she's skipped and forget the Pulitzer."

I leaned back in my chair, aware of the hard bar of tension between my shoulder blades.

"Let's see if I have this straight since I'm not crass enough to carry a tape recorder around in my back pocket. You want to pay me a thousand bucks to try and find a phantom who may or may not have information on a major call girl operation. She uses the street name of Stacey DuMount. She might be in her mid-twenties. She sounds like she smokes, probably drinks, but, in any case, has a deep voice. If I find her, I'm to call you and you'll take it from there. If it turns into a story, you'll give ol' Chazz the warm and fuzzies about me."

I raised an eyebrow.

"That about sum it up?"

"Could you talk any louder, Reno? Maybe the folks down at the Aquarium didn't catch all that."

"I'm trying to see if the idea makes any more sense coming from my mouth than it does from yours. Chazz is really pushing this down your throat, isn't he? There's some reason he especially wants this story done."

"That's not something I'm privy to. He wanted it checked out…"

"Of course you're 'privy' to it. The Old Man's out to get somebody. Whose name did this gal drop on him, anyway? The Mayor? Governor?"

I wasn't expecting an immediate answer but he yanked the pipe out of his mouth and said, in a very soft voice, "I give you the name, you are not, and I mean not to approach this guy. Him or anybody connected to him. He is not a lead you can use to track the girl down."

"So? Who is it?"

"No, Reno. The guy is off-limits. I don't want anything shaking him up until we have whatever story there is in the can. Agreed?"

I nodded. "Fine. Your turn."

He looked like a refugee from a Jimmy Cagney movie as he leaned across the table and spoke barely loud enough for me to hear.

"Ferguson."

And that, my friends, was the other shoe going ker-plunk.

Senator Brian Fahy Ferguson was from suburban DuPage County where they damn near stamp "Republican" on birth certificates. An ex-FBI agent and former federal judge, he'd stepped away from his lifetime appointment to the bench and gotten himself elected to the U.S. Senate several years ago on a platform of family values and a hard nosed attitude toward crime and terrorism. Just re-elected and with the Republicans holding a tenuous one-member majority in the Senate, he'd won the coveted Chairmanship of the Foreign Relations Committee.

A lot of politicians hang with prostitutes. Ferguson, however, was more than a guy with a Family Values tag. He was Mr. Rogers Goes To Congress. He was Jimmy Stewart without the cowlick and "aw shucks." If the woman who had come to Hanratty was telling the truth and Channel 14 ran with it, Ferguson would have to resign from the Senate and move out of DuPage before they fire-bombed his house. And were he to quit, our esteemed governor would be the one to name his replacement. Our Governor was a Democrat.

If I remembered correctly, so was Chazz Bascomb.

"I'd like to think that, at some point before we got up from this table, you were going to spell all that out for me, Frank. Even if I hadn't asked," I said.

"You asked and I told you. Leave it at that." If the money and the offer to go to bat with Chazz for me had been the carrot, this was the stick.

"Senator Charles "Chazz" Bascomb. Bet the old man gets a woody just saying that to himself in front of the mirror at night. What do you get out of it? Chief of Staff? Press Secretary?"

"I'm looking at a damn good story. That's my only focus, you self-righteous prick. In fact, I'm looking at two great stories, with the one Marisa's working on. We need to kick ratings in the ass. This sweeps period, we might even be able to."

"Oh, I'd say potentially changing the makeup of the U.S. Senate could qualify as a ratings chart-buster. Pulitzer material, probably. Then again, we know King Chazz has no problem nailing a guy in the career because he doesn't like the fellow's choice in girlfriends."

Hanratty colored a bit on that one but he didn't say anything, just clamped down a little tighter on his pipe stem. One of the unmentionables about my firing had been that I'd brought my now ex-girlfriend to Chazz's Christmas party that year. At the time, Meg had been a high-dollar, independent call girl. Not an escort, mind you. Escorts work for a couple of hundred a throw. Meg's bottom line was fifteen hundred dollars, and that was just for a first dinner meeting without sex. She'd size the client up there, and if he acted like a gentleman, the next date might win him her favors at double the rate. No one would have been the wiser about her profession except that one of the other guests at the party recognized her. She ignored him all evening. Feeling slighted, he had whispered in Chazz's ear.

The irony of what Hanratty was asking for wasn't lost on me.

If I found the girl and she spun her story for the cameras, I'd be setting Ferguson up for the same kind of abrupt career change I'd had, with the humiliation factor a hundred times greater. It wasn't something I was breathing fire to do. I was making a halfway decent living as a morning news anchor for one of Chicago's popular FM music stations. Then again, as far as I could tell, none of LaSalle Street's bankers were lining up offering to finance the new roof I needed on my house in Evanston. And there was, of course, the ridiculously unlikely possibility of getting my old job back.

"Chazz is footing the bill?" I asked.

Frank nodded.

I finished my beer. It wasn't strong enough to cover the taste from swallowing my self-esteem.

"I'll do it for twenty-five hundred."

*   *   *   *

We walked back to his car in Channel 14's garage. The fact that it was a snappy, new, black Lincoln LS instead of his trademark Taurus with the sagging suspension made me smile. He didn't notice. I kept my mouth shut. When we'd worked together, I could've razzed him. Now the hard ass veneer he'd always adopted appeared to have thickened to the strength of bulletproof glass.

Frank paid it all up front and in cash. He'd known I'd agree to do his scut work and had come prepared. Figuring the angles had always been something Frank Hanratty excelled at. He took a bank envelope down from above the visor and counted hundreds into my hand. They had that sandpapery, just-popped-from-the-teller-machine feel. It annoyed me that there were exactly twenty-five of them in the folder.

"Don't think this is vacation money, Reno. I want an update from you before we go on the air tomorrow night."

"What's the rush? You said your star reporter's tied up on something else anyway."

"Marisa will make time for her. If this chickie has what she claims, I want her interview in-house before anybody else gets a whiff."

I'd had the same thought. Stacey DuMount might not have disappeared at all. She could just be a couple of blocks away, peddling her tale, so to speak, to another station. TV news in Chicago redefines the meaning of competition. The distance between Channel 14 and its nearest competitor for advertising dollars was as narrow as an anchorman's tie. If Channel 9, or any of the network stations, sniffed out the piece and ran with it before Hanratty could put it on the air, the delicate balance holding Channel 14's amazing third place in the ratings might shift and a few sponsors could choose to buy time somewhere else. News Directors' careers rise and fall on such measurements. Even more so if they're the boss's son-in-law.

"Tomorrow it is," I said. He looked as though he might've wanted to shake my hand and then decided against it. Instead he jiggled the knot of his club tie, grunted and shuffled off toward the elevators. I thought about where he was going. Back to a newsroom that would be in the midst of preparations for The Chicago Beat, Channel 14's six o'clock news program. I could see it as though I'd left for the last time just moments ago instead of two years. Desks pushed to face one another. Newspapers, stacks of old scripts and video tapes all crowding each other for space on shelves. The assignment editor's carrel sitting in the midst of the frenzy like a control tower at O'Hare. Scanners buzzing and the chatter of people on the phone. Maybe the room would be smaller and less crowded than I remembered it, the difference between memory and reality. Marisa Langdon would be occupying the closet that had been my office which was always cold enough to store racks of meat.

I slapped away those thoughts and trudged toward the exit. As I stepped into the sunlight I saw, coming toward me, someone I'd half-hoped, half-feared I'd run into while I was in the station's vicinity.

Andy Nunez had been my producer on the I-Team, a guy with pockmarked features, early gray in his full head of hair and whose weight problem was now manifested by a belly so perfectly large and round it could have been a medicine ball hidden under his shirt. As usual, he was smoking, walking with his head down, and didn't see me until the last moment. He pulled up short, a look of surprise and then a smile crinkling his features.

"Man. There's a guy who has *got* to be lost," he said. Like Frank, he doesn't smile much and when he does, it's usually fleeting. This one disappeared quickly as usual but his eyes showed true pleasure. Made me feel good but also a little guilty that I had not made any effort to contact him since being booted.

We shook hands.

"I'm glad to see you hide out on your current boss like you hid out on me."

"This one doesn't come looking very often. How you doin', Reno? Don't tell me Chazz Moneybags got some sense in his head and is going to bring you back?"

"No such luck. Frank found me sleeping in my Dumpster on Lower Wacker and took me to lunch."

"Well he certainly can afford it now, can't he?"

"It appears so. Nice ride he's got."

That produced another chuckle. "He probably didn't tell you the story about that, did he?"

"The old man order him to spiffy up his corporate image or something?"

He took the last drag off a butt not much bigger than the end of my little finger and pitched it into the street.

"Nah. You know how he drives? The original Kamikaze News Director? 'Bout a year ago, he's tooling around some street up there in Winnetka and he smacks into some society broad. Now her car was a Benz or a Beemer or some such. Hardly hurt it. But that Taurus of his, it was all rusted out and dyin' anyways. It just fell apart."

"So he bought a Lincoln to replace it?"

"C'mon, you know him better than that," Andy scoffed. "He wanted another Taurus. Miss Ice Princess bought the Lincoln for him. He's still bitchin' about that. Even asked me, bring my mechanic brother-in-law and come up to the gas station where they towed the Taurus, see if it could be rebuilt. My brother-in-law told him God's the only one can create something from dust. Mind if I smoke another one while we're out here?"

I shook my head but he still looked nervous as he lit up. His eyes don't settle when he talks. They move like those of a just released convict who's afraid someone is coming to haul him back to the slammer. Or, at this particular moment, like the ardent non-smoker Chazz Bascomb is going to find him with a cigarette and fire him on the spot.

"You know what else? Ever since we told him that old Taurus was DOA, he's been walkin' around lookin' like he's carryin' that new Lincoln on his shoulders. Only guy I know drivin' forty thousand dollars worth of car and feeling guilty about it." He took a hit and then held the cigarette cupped in his hand down along his side and kept talking.

"I hear you on the air some mornings when I'm coming in to work," he said. "Bein' over there is like a broadcaster's version of hell, ain't it?"

"There are drawbacks." I wasn't going to lie. One thing about Andy. He's all producer, all the time. When he asks a question, he'll work you until he gets the answer.

"Come on, Reno. Since when was Britney's new bra size a news story? J-Lo's latest affair? You got to come back, man. There are guys at every station in town who'll step up for you if you want to make the move."

I hoped my expression stayed as bland as I tried to make it. "Someday," I said.

I didn't tell him I'd already tried to make a return. Right after being booted, figuring my highbrow ethics would give wings to my resume, I told my then-agent to market me to the other Chicago stations. Six months, and no takers, later he sat me down in his cherry-wood paneled office in the Aon Building and gave me their response. Yes, he said, my fellow reporters might admire me for turning a bribe-taking story, hidden video and all, over to a competing station because Chazz hadn't wanted to embarrass one of his fellow church members by running it on Channel 14. But my fellow reporters' bosses, meaning every TV general manager in the city, regarded me as an uncontrollable hothead.

The radio job had been a gift. One of his other clients owed him a favor and he was willing to pass it along to me, as long as I promised to keep my head down and read drivel.

"We'll try again in a year or so, Reno. And a year or so after that if we have to. The climate'll change. These tight asses'll move on. You know how it works."

I don't doubt he would have been true to his word, too, if he hadn't keeled over on the 15th tee one afternoon about six months later.

So I was still reading drivel.

$$*\qquad*\qquad*\qquad*$$

Andy and I talked for another few minutes, catching up. I was tempted to ask what the hush-hush project was that Marisa was working on but knew that would make him uncomfortable. I wasn't sure I wanted to know anyway. He showed me pictures of his two young sons and another of his wife, pregnant with their third. He told me we should have a beer sometime and to call him if I ever needed anything.

"I mean that, Reno. I'd probably still be a Desk Assistant in Sports if you hadn't brought me over to the I-Team. It's not as much fun now, with Marisa, but it still beats the hell out of chasing down high school ball team scores and setting up coach interviews."

"Why no fun?"

Andy shook his head, took a drag off his cigarette. "She's got all the moves, you know? I'm not knocking her. For a kid just a couple years out of college, she's way ahead of most of the people we got working here. Good looking, asks the right questions. But she comes across so blasted serious on the tube. Never lightens up. And, you can tell when you're talking to her, giving her an idea, she's sort of listening but part of her is never there. An I-Team of one, you ask me."

He ground his cigarette out on the sidewalk then picked it up and threw it into a curbside trash basket. "Hey, back to the grind, man. Don't be such a stranger, huh?"

When I walked away, I felt better for having talked to him, glad in a somewhat snotty way that Marisa didn't seem to have the people skills people credited to me. Glad to be missed.

Overall, though, what he'd said had me kicking myself. Frank Hanratty might be carrying around the burden of marrying into wealth but he'd laid a load on my shoulders, too. I wanted to be rid of it, soon.

*   *   *   *

I had hoisted my misgivings onto a shelf in the back of my brain by the time I got to my car. It doesn't get much better on an early summer afternoon than pointing my '67 Mustang convertible north along Lake Shore Drive while the breeze is blowing cool off the blue waters of Lake Michigan. I watched the sailboats and power craft negotiating the swells just beyond the breakwaters. Rollerbladers and joggers filled the blacktop paths along the beachfront and the sand, as far as I could see, was dotted with reclining bodies, their bathing wear a colorful kaleidoscope against a backdrop of waves and sun.

The forecast I'd tagged onto my newscasts all through morning-drive called for a saturating, hard rain by early evening. I always feel like a jerk when I read those things and then none of the predictions come true. The weather folks had been calling for measurable precipitation for a week and we had yet to see it. Right now, the sky was so clear it looked like you could run your thumb across it and hear it squeak. The only things needed to convince me I had somehow stepped into a time warp and been transported back to my childhood would have been an 8-track tape player under the dash kicking out the Beach Boys and the Edgewater Beach Hotel sitting like the dignified lady it had been for so many years at what's now the north end of the Drive at Hollywood.

I spent the better part of my drive toward home in Evanston on the cellular, excusing myself from work the next morning and lining up a replacement. When you're the entire news department and morning anchor of a music radio station that leans on its morning drive programming, taking a day off without several weeks advance notice doesn't endear you to the bosses.

I first had to clear my absence with the Program Director. Rudy's an amiable sort but one who lingers over decisions about where to go to lunch and whether to make daily changes to his outgoing voice mail message. However, when I told him I had the per-diem news anchor I use occasionally all set to take my place, he agreed to my time off without argument. He's been seriously in love/lust with Sunny Dee ever since she brought the station's computer system back to life after we all thought a Com-Ed power surge had fried it a couple of summers ago. If she'd accept it, I'm sure he would give her my job without even a thought about the lawsuit I'd shove up his ass for doing so.

More challenging was Asa Michael Driver, the senior member of the duo of A.M. Driver and Goofy, the station's moneymakers who run amok on the air for four hours every weekday morning. Asa claims his name is as real as the framed copy of a birth certificate that hangs on the wall of his office. Just happenstance, he says, that a guy with a moniker like that ended up in morning radio or, as a shift like ours is known in the business, AM drive.

Asa and I signed a non-aggression pact my first day on the job. He thinks I come off as a grump because I don't go along with what a generous radio critic once called their "madcap antics." I think abusing people on the air, setting up gags that often make police officers the fall guys and announcing that various famous people have died when they're very much alive make us radio folks look like stooges. We've agreed to disagree.

Sunny, however, had to handle Asa a bit differently. One morning, after the show, he caught up to her at the water fountain. As she leaned to get a drink, he reached around from behind and grabbed a breast. Her reaction was instantaneous. She reached up and locked his hand in a come-along hold, one of those that nails the nerve and sends an electrical shock of pain straight up the arm. Then, without letting go, she walked him down the hall, through the offices of the mostly female sales staff, and into the General Manager's suite where she announced his transgression and asked the GM what he planned to do about it. Her fill-in work for us suddenly became more lucrative for her.

Asa apologized in writing as soon as his hand was able to grip a pen. Sunny wasn't surprised. She told me how she explained to him while they were strolling the corridors just how easily she could have turned the bones in his fingers to confetti.

Asa and Goofy's on-air banter with her changed pretty drastically after that, going from crude and sexist to gentle joshing.

When I'm working, their handoffs to me are totally professional as well.

I reached Asa on the phone but, before I could tell him what I wanted, he allowed as how he was out by the pool and why didn't I just stop by and join him? Since I would drive right past his building on Sheridan Road on my way home, I agreed. I also let him talk me into it because it occurred to me there were a couple of questions I could ask him that were better thrown in person than over a cell phone.

He okayed me for the desk man in the lobby and I followed the guard's directions up two floors and out of the elevator. I could smell chlorine even before the doors opened. He had his feet propped up on a pool-side table and was reading a copy of The New Republic with a handful of other magazines splayed out fan-shaped on the concrete deck next to his chair. Asa goes through the four Chicago papers front to back every morning before he takes the air, scans some of the other biggies on-line during breaks and subscribes to a dozen weekly publications. While I'm the first to say he and Goofy normally sound like a couple of testosterone-addled frat boys, if they get a politician or bureaucrat in their sights, they can cross-examine as deftly as a divorce lawyer going after hidden assets.

When Asa saw me, he raised a substantial schooner of liquid that could have been iced tea. He wore long Hawaiian swim shorts, no shirt and wrap-around sunglasses. His dark hair was slicked back flat to his head and I could see a trail of watery footprints leading from the pool to his chair.

"Hey. There's extra swimsuits in the changing room."

"I'll pass. The exercise might be good for me."

He took his feet off the table and gestured again with his glass. "If you want to wait five minutes, I'll run up and mix you one of these."

"I'm fine, Asa. Thanks."

"That's right. You're not much of a drinker, are you?"

"On a real hot day, after I've been working in the yard, maybe a Corona or Carta Blanca."

He swallowed and put the glass on the table. He claims he keeps in shape with weights and club-level rugby but there's a doughy roll around his midsection and his eyes are perpetually bloodshot. I've never seen him outside without shades and sometimes, away from the muted studio lights, he even wears them inside.

"You see the letter of censure this morning?" he asked. "Feds came down against us."

"Damn, Asa. You mean they took offense at you taping yourself having sex and then playing it on the air? Imagine that."

"It was a joke, for chrissakes! She was a damn hooker in the upstairs bar at Sensation. All I did was get her to moan a little for me. Fucking FCC tight asses probably got boners listening to it, too."

"Well it's obvious they have a hard-on but I think it's against you, not with you."

"Freaks. So what's the special occasion, m'man? You never call me at home." He smiled the way he does in front of the crowds at his personal appearances. Not for the first time I noticed he had a good start on a set of jowls.

"I have to do a favor for a friend the next day or so. I need tomorrow morning off. Rudy's cleared it. I just thought I'd run it by you."

"No problemo. Leaving us with ol' Sunny Side Up? Speaking of boners…"

"I'll tell her you were thinking about her."

He waved away that idea. "Nah, not necessary."

I looked at the lounge chairs and tables carefully scattered pool side and the exquisite view of Lake Michigan. While we'd been talking, a young woman had shepherded two little boys out of the building and was now affixing their water-wings on the other side of the pool. I lowered my voice.

"Actually, let's talk about hookers for a minute."

He put a hand to his ear. "Hello? What's this I'm hearing? Mr. Tight Ass McCarthy needs a little nookie and ol' Sunny Delight won't give it up?"

"I keep hearing rumors about a chick who calls herself Stacey DuMount. I'd like to know where to find her."

"And I'm the Answer Man?"

"You hang out. You meet people. You get women to moan for you on tape."

He kept his dark glasses aimed at my face longer than I could ever remember him doing, the way someone might if they ran into you unexpectedly and were trying to come up with your name. His eyes stayed hidden in the filtered darkness.

"You rip my show in staff meetings. You never chill with us after. You won't even let me mix you a drink when you come to my home. Then you're not here five minutes before you basically call me a pimp. How'm I supposed to take that, Reno? You wouldn't be some kind of snitch for Doctor Ducat would you?"

Dr. Ducat was his pet name for the station's general manager, a shill for the New York-based media conglomerate owners.

"He doesn't need a snitch," I said. I could have added more, about the illicit favors Asa had done for Dr. Ducat and the transgressions that had been smoothed over in return, but I gave him my patented "the reporter knows all" expression instead.

"Stacey DuMount? A name like that, she calls him up, I bet Howard Stern'd use her no problem. I never heard of her."

"She supposedly cut some porn videos a few years ago. She's maybe mid-twenties, smoker's voice…"

"Reno, Reno." He held up a hand. "Lemme tell you something about escorts, hookers, whatever you want to call 'em. They're all mid-twenties, or say they are, anyway. And, c'mon, who watches the credits on a fuck movie? Now, the one you really want is this one I used for the tape those FCC turds didn't like. Julia. She's twenty-two, looks about sixteen, and I guarantee she doesn't leave any chrome on the trailer hitch if you catch my meaning."

"Actually, I'd like to find this other one, Asa. The fact she's been on video is sort of interesting to me."

He smirked. "Right. Interesting. What is it, you figure you've been on TV, she's been on video, you'll find some kinda karma?"

"I figured if you didn't know her, you'd know someone who might."

He took another swallow of his drink. "I can't believe I'm having this conversation with you, of all people. OK. Got a pen and paper?"

CHAPTER 2

▼

Asa swirled the ice in his drink. "Now, I'm not saying he'll know her but this is a guy who occasionally makes the sort of movies you're talking about."

I scribbled the name and number in my notebook.

He wasn't finished, however. "So, gimme the skinny here. You want tomorrow morning off so you can fuck all night or what?"

"Asa?" I said. "Let me say this one time. I don't want to hire the girl. I just want to talk to her."

He sat back in his chair, grinning. "Talk. Sure. Well if you can't find her to, ah, *talk* to, you keep Julia in mind. She'll talk your brains out."

I had already turned to go so I waved acknowledgment without turning my head. Out of the corner of my eye, I could see the young woman with the kids staring at Asa, disgusted by his offensive language.

I thought about the name he had passed along as I rode down in the elevator and kicked myself for not thinking of Eddie Marn on my own. Proof of how mental reflexes get rusty when not used. When I got home, I cross-referenced his phone number on the computer and turned up an address not far from O'Hare Airport, near the Mannheim strip. Then I went to the disc file in my study where I keep copies of the notes and scripts for all of the investigations I put together at Channel 14.

I don't bump down that part of memory lane too often. When you get canned from a job you love, it hurts like hell to go back and look at the work you used to do. I found the reference in a story we'd done right after I started the I-Team.

Two teenage sisters who appeared to be closer to their twenties than 13 and 16 had disappeared from their home just over the Wisconsin border in Kenosha

County. Given their ages, the missing girls became a media sensation during the middle of a very slow news summer in the Milwaukee and Chicago TV markets. Their father thought that publicity about them might somehow materialize into bucks for him somewhere down the road. He supplied pictures taken at a church outing to emphasize their youth and downplayed the fact both had been picked up several times for truancy and drug violations and that the older girl was a chronic shoplifter.

One of the deputies who knew the girls took me aside during the father's first news conference on the steps of a church he never attended but where his wife was a regular. While papa worked himself into a frenzy for the cameras, the deputy filled me in on the teens' backgrounds and his suspicions. I followed through with a contact at the FBI.

Four days later, my cameraman and I rolled tape from inside a rented panel van at San Diego International Airport as the girls left the terminal in the company of a convicted pedophile named Keller Washburne. They were dressed in the casual beachwear and sunglasses that are the uniform of Southern Californians and moved with the grace of the actresses Washburne had promised them they would become. Neither looked remotely like the pictures their father had been circulating.

We learned later that Washburne had driven the two of them to Kansas City and, after bedding down with both of them in a motel for three days, had turned them into pseudo-Baywatch babes with the help of some clippers, hair dye, rub-on tanning solution and the nifty new threads. Washburne told them he had contacts in Hollywood and that the two of them together would be just the sort of girls his director/producer/writer friends were looking for. In truth, he planned to sell both of them to a skin flick producer operating just south of the border.

We kept rolling tape as a brace of FBI agents surged out of an SUV and two cars and surrounded the happy trio. Not surprisingly, the girls put up more of a fight than Washburne. After all, they'd thought it was only a matter of hours before they'd be in show business.

I took the archive videotape that contained all the pieces I'd done on that story and set it aside. Then I slipped the disc with my scripts and notes into the computer and scrolled through the file looking for Marn's name. It popped up almost right away. He was Keller Washburne's half-brother and it had taken us two days to find him but, when we did, he snitched off his sibling without even a whimper. Told my crew, and then the FBI agents who followed on our heels, that Ol' Kell was a store security guard and had expressed a few salacious opinions about a leggy 16-year-old he'd busted and had even offered the thought that he'd try to hook up with her. Then with his eye on helping himself with a felony check charge, Marn pointed us toward one of Washburne's kiddie-porn loving former cellmates who owned a body shop in Kansas City.

We found the body shop and then the motel where Washburne had taken the girls two blocks away.

I smiled, stretched, then carefully put my files back where I'd found them.

It's always nice to have leverage when you try to get information from a low-life. Cops can hang all sorts of stuff over the head of a reluctant witness. Grand jury subpoenas. Threats of charges being filed. Even a smack upside the head. As a reporter, leverage is sometimes hard to manage. But Eddie Marn had ratted out his brother to save his own ass and I was one of only three people who knew that. The other two were Feds who are required to tape their mouths shut at night so they don't talk about cases in their sleep.

It was closing in on three o'clock. The rising swell of afternoon rush hour would be clogging traffic between Evanston and the rest of the world for at least the next couple of hours. I locked up the house and launched myself toward the highway.

Mannheim Road runs north to south as the eastern perimeter of O'Hare International Airport. In the not-so-old days, the area was a home to strip joints, massage parlors and hot-sheet motels, a living testament to the Mob's ability to infiltrate the suburbs even as their influence in the city was on the wane. A couple of recent Cook County Sheriffs have made it a target for their vice efforts and now airport satellite parking, car rental operations and mid-size chain motels have helped drop the sleaze factor considerably. There are many, however, who would say it's just moved out of sight. They could be correct. Tavern poker machines, for example, seem to have replaced smoke-filled back rooms and guys in hard hats play the electronics with the same fervor as the boys in fedoras and suspenders who used to sit at tables with green felt tops. No bodies have been found in car trunks for awhile, however, and the still-flowing juice keeps the politicians happy.

I found the address where Marn's phone was registered a couple of blocks off Mannheim, across from the Metra commuter tracks and sandwiched between a small freight-hauling operation and a cinder block tavern with a cracked Old Style sign in the window. His place looked like a city two-flat set back from the street by a double-wide blacktop driveway. A set of concrete steps led to the front door. A Caddy, not much smaller than the trucks in the next yard, was parked in the drive and a Jeep Sahara with the canvas sides and top removed sat behind it.

Cruising by on the street, I saw my only option was a frontal approach and in making it, I'd be visible from the moment I left the sidewalk. I told myself that kind of paranoia was irrational. The porn makers know how the system works. They know how unlikely it is that the cops, even the Feds, will dedicate the time or the manpower to raid their operation. They aren't like dopers, where anyone moving through their perimeter is seen as an attacker. I started down the driveway. I could smell the cakes and rolls baking at the Entenmann's plant a mile or so away and felt the rumble of a Metra commuter pulling out of the station.

The front door opened before I even got close to the building and a young guy stepped out on the porch. Wide shouldered, with a blond burr-cut that was almost white, he wore a black baseball cap turned sideways on his head, skintight t-shirt, and oversized painters' pants slung low enough to his hips that the top of his boxer shorts became part of his haute-couture. He made no move toward me, just slouched against the wall watching until I reached the bottom of the stairs.

"Whattya want, man?" He was as white as me but the words came out in a ghetto wannabe drawl.

"Eddie Marn."

"Who's that?"

I leaned back to look at the front facade of the building, paying particular attention to the shadowed corners under the soffit. I could barely make out the lens of a mini-surveillance camera pointed my way. I gave it a little wave with my right hand. I wondered if there was a microphone attached.

"If he doesn't remember my name, tell him it's Reno McCarthy."

"I'm not telling nobody nuthin' man," the kid said. "'cept you. You, I'm telling to book." He pushed away from the wall and halfway down the stairs, looming over me. His shirt accented tight abs and biceps but his eyes were of more concern. He was in the stratosphere somewhere.

"Eddie? You remember the folks I brought along the last time we chatted?" I kept my voice conversational, now talking for the benefit of the hidden microphone. "I leave and you'll see them again."

"I told you to beat it, man!" The kid came off the steps.

I smiled at him. "Why don't we let Eddie decide this?"

He was pretty fast, but a defensive tactics instructor I had back in Kansas City told me he'd never seen reflexes like mine. Maybe they are the natural result of having an alcoholic father who occasionally liked to take a belt to me without warning. Maybe I was just born quick.

The kid dipped his hand behind his back. Before he could grab what he was reaching for, I snap-kicked my right foot into the side of his right knee. If you've ever crushed a chicken bone under your heel, you know the sound cartilage makes when it's cracking. He dropped hard on his side, trying to scream but so overwhelmed by the sudden onset of pain that all he could do was open his mouth. I followed him to the ground as, behind him, the screen door slammed open and two men charged onto the porch. Before they reached the top of the stairs, I had the kid's Beretta 9mm in my hand and extended. I snapped the hammer back.

"Hi Eddie," I said.

Eddie Marn's face turned white and he tried to shrink sideways behind the white-haired man who had emerged in front of him. "McCarthy! Jesus, man. Lighten up! Don't…do anything…"

"I don't know your friend in the fat suit but he's going to eat one of these rounds if he doesn't drop his hands to his sides," I said. Guns, coupled with an adrenaline bump, always make me sound like a refugee from a Clint Eastwood movie.

The guy had a ring of flab where a neck once might have been. He also had a smear of barbecue sauce on his flower-print shirt just below one of his chins. Another spotted the massive right thigh of his gray slacks. He'd been trying to pull back enough of his belly to get at a chrome pistol stuck in his waistband. What was with all these guns, anyway?

The kid behind me finally sucked in enough air to let loose with a bull moose roar.

"McCarthy, he needs a doctor, man," Marn said.

I beckoned the fat man down the stairs. He held to the iron railing as he descended and when he was close enough, I shoved the barrel of the nine against his forehead. He was wheezing slightly.

"I know this is rude as hell since we haven't been properly introduced…" With some difficulty, I lifted what felt like a .380 automatic out of his pants. It was soaked with sweat. "…but wasn't it good for you, too?"

"You are very fast," he said.

He had a slight accent I didn't recognize. Polish? For a guy who now had a red indentation from a gun barrel in the middle of his forehead his voice didn't falter and his eyes hadn't left my face. I put the .380 in my pocket, let the nine fall to my side and half-turned.

The kid was crying and grasping his knee with both hands.

I looked back at Eddie. "Who has the keys for the jeep?"

"It's Archie's." He indicated the kid.

"Get the keys," I said to the fat man. "Get him in the jeep and get him out of here."

"Where do you suggest I take him?" Yeah, he had an accent. Eastern European at least, maybe Russian. And those flat eyes.

"Flag down a cop, find a fire station, go somewhere and dial 9-1-1." I gestured with the Beretta. "But get gone."

It took some exertion on his part, and left him wheezing and with a face the color of a tomato, but the fat guy did what he was told. The kid made enough noise you'd think I'd amputated his leg. Surprisingly, no one came out of either the bar or the truck yard to see who we were torturing. As the fat fellow backed out of the drive, he did a peculiar thing. He didn't look over his shoulder as most people would. Instead, he kept his eyes on me until he was almost to the street. Only then did I see him angle his head to check the rear mirror.

Marn sat down on the front steps and wiped his forehead with a handkerchief. "Good Lord," he said. His hand shook as he stuffed the cloth into the front pocket of his shirt.

Eddie wears his hair parted in the middle and a peace medallion on a chain around his neck. What was no doubt an acne problem of his youth left his face cratered and during one or the other of his jail visits, someone had mashed his nose almost flat. It was the only thing changed since I'd last seen him. He smelled of marijuana and looked like he'd eaten the roach.

"What's with all the artillery?" I asked him. I felt a little silly with the Beretta in my hand so I took both it and the .380 and laid them on the top step next to him. They'd go off by themselves before he'd pick one up.

"It's a lousy neighborhood at night. Spics mostly."

"Sun's still out and I'm not Hispanic. Try again."

"I didn't recognize you! Just leave it be, will ya? Come in here, busting people up like that." He shook his head at the injustice.

"Who's the fat man?"

He looked up at me. "If he's pissed, you'll find out. You can believe that."

"Eddie, you disappoint me. Last time we chatted you were driving the ladies around to their sessions and trying to get them to cop your joint as a tip. Now people tell me you're the new Steven Spielberg of the sicko set. Come on. Brag on yourself a little bit. And tell me about your friends."

"Fuck off." He said it without much heat, like I was his last and least significant problem of the day.

"OK, showing is always better than telling. Let's take a look inside."

I started up the stairs. He reached and caught my leg. I grabbed his ear and twisted, lifting him to his feet as he wrapped both hands around mine. I pushed him through the front door.

"Ow! Man, what IS it with you? Leggo my damn ear..."

I put my face in his. "If you'd played straight, I'd already be gone. But you've got me thinking I've stepped in something that's going to have a comeback on me and I want to know what it is. We on the same frequency now?"

I let him loose. He grabbed at a chair and sank into it.

We were in what once had been a living room but now was decorated to look like a unit in a cheap hotel. I looked around. The dining room across the hall had been turned into another kind of bedroom, this one with teddy bears on the queen-size bed and college pennants and Ricky Martin and Eminem pictures prominently displayed. Each set had mirrors in faux walls at the head and foot of the bed. I went over and peered behind one of the walls. A broadcast-quality Sony video camera was mounted on a tripod, pointed at the bed through the mirror. I glanced up. Track lighting ran across the ceilings of both rooms and, attached to the track, I saw a tiny spy cam with a remote transmitter. We'd used similar devices on the I-team.

Marn watched me. "Yeah, ok, ok. Yeah, whatever. I got some cameras, we're shooting videos. Or we were until you mashed up my cameraman just now. That's the shits."

"Interesting layout," I said.

"You think so?" He suddenly smiled. "It's one of the trends in the industry right now. Customers like the voyeur effect. Like they're watching in secret, you know?"

"Whatever." I stared at him until his smile curdled. "Where are the girls?"

"They'll be here later. I was just, you know, laying out the scene for Archie."

I waved a hand at the equipment. "This is your operation?"

"Yeah, mainly. Hey, I ain't stupid. You think I'm stupid? You think I'm just some goof? I got some good people. I got an art director from one of the ad agencies doing the sets. You gotta admit this is sweet."

"And 13-year-olds on the beds like your big brother?"

"No, dude." He had one hand on his ear, rubbing it. "Kell was a dumbass. Law's always after you on that kiddie shit. County, The G, Postal Inspectors. Every one of my girls is 21. They may not look it but I got every driver's license, every birth certificate. They're old enough, believe me. We just make it look like they ain't."

"Oh yeah, I believe you, Eddie. You're the cat's ass of believability. So who's the fat man?"

He stopped rubbing and seemed to sag some more. "He's just a guy, ok? Money guy. He came in, wanted a piece of the operation, said he could get me some better quality equipment and stuff. And he did everything he said. High-end Betacams, all that shit."

"So why's he so scary?"

"I was just…you pissed me off. I was, you know, scamming you. He's just the wallet. It's not like he's mobbed up or anything."

I could tell he was lying but we were a couple of miles down the road in the opposite direction from what I'd come here to talk about. This was none of my business. What can I say? Just because I don't do real reporting any more doesn't mean I'm not curious. I sighed.

"All right Eddie. There's one thing I'm interested in. Not fat guys with bad table manners, not pseudo-kiddie porn."

I described the girl who called herself Stacey DuMount. His eyes flickered when I said the name then, when I suggested she had a booze and cigarettes voice, he looked down, maybe afraid he'd given something away.

"You came here, pissed off Sergei and fucked up my cameraman looking for a hooker? That's so fucking lame!"

"I did you a favor. You might have had a little more explaining to do if I'd let Archie shoot me. I press charges against him for aggravated battery, you'll get all sorts of attention you don't want. Tell me about the girl."

"I don't know all the whores in the city…"

"How about I bring in the cops plus I hang around and give your friend Sergei the history lesson on you and your loyalty to your brother?"

His eyes crinkled and he looked hurt. "What is it with you, dude? You wake up this morning and decide it's Fuck Eddie Day or what?"

I didn't say anything. I suspected he had days like that 52 weeks a year. When he spoke again he aimed his remarks at the floor and not at me.

"The one I'm thinking about, she was maybe twenty when I seen her. Maybe three years ago. Looked like a rich girl. Blonde. Probably the real goods but we never got to the point of me checking her snatch. Good rack on her, too. She's a full 36-C, maybe a D but she definitely don't need no bra for 'em."

"Assuming she's not topless when I see her, how about a height and weight?"

"Hey, you got things you look for, I got things I check out. She'll go five-five, five six and she ain't fat. That's a hardbody for sure. But you say the one you're looking for works for an agency?"

"Yeah."

"If this chick's the one I'm thinking she is, she didn't strike me as the agency type. Maybe she changed." He shrugged, looked at me, flashed his teeth. "Don't think so."

"What's that mean?"

"She was one badass bitch. Not the get-along type at all. Tried to tell me how to run things, how she'd fit in, what kinda cut she wanted. Plus, she talked like she was into some serious leather, S and M shit. I mean, there's all kinds of agencies but the ones I worked for in the old, old days? She woulda been too heavy for them. Their johns don't want to be marked up. My guess was she seriously liked to hurt folks. Men, anyway. Just from how she talked."

"What's her name? Her real name?"

"Beats me, dude," he said. "No reason to get an ID. I only remember she used that Stacey DuMount cause I joked about it and she got all bent. No way we could'a worked her into our story lines. I told her the age thing was the problem, being a little honest anyway y' know? I remember the way she reacted. She was frosty. Never had one take it that way before. Never one since. Frosty cold. Then she just walks out. Not a word."

"If you didn't hire her, why do you remember her so well three years later?"

He didn't answer right away. I let the silence stretch.

"Oh, fuck it. I found my tires slashed when I went to go home that night, ok?"

"Not a coincidence?"

"Yeah, yeah. Could be. Maybe she came across pissy 'cause she had that PMS or something, too. Maybe she's a Sunday School teacher. I'm just telling you the read I got."

"Where'd she come from, Eddie? Who sent her over?"

"Man, this is years ago. How the hell am I remembering that?"

"Because she scared you. Because she slashed your tires and you probably thought she'd stick a blade in you next, so you called whoever referred her, didn't you?"

He started to shake his head again but then he snorted a laugh.

"Yeah. Yeah, she had me crapping my pants. And her dicking with my car is the only reason I'm talking to you. She cut all four tires, right at the stems, cost me seven hundred-eight hundred bucks to fix. The gal who passed her along is an indie, used to send the young looking ones by for a couple hundred worth of referral fee."

I waited again.

"She went by Lynn Robin. Real name, street name I don't know. That's all I ever knew her by."

If it was the same Lynn Robin, and I suspected it was, it was her street name.

Small world, I thought. Her real name was Lynn Robinette and, once upon a time, she had been Megan's best friend.

I headed for the door. I wanted to slide my jacket down over my hand before I used the knob. A thought struck me before I reached for it, however, and I turned back.

"Where did she end up going to work?" I asked.

"Beats me. How would I know that?"

Still no eye contact. I took a step toward him and he stood up fast.

"Because you're a slime dog, Eddie. Because you and your slime-dog friends all have private web sites and chat rooms where you talk about your slime dog stuff. I'm betting you kept track of her."

He was shaking his head like he had palsy. "I don't know, OK? I don't know."

I didn't pull down my jacket sleeve but I used a alcohol-wipe first thing when I got back into the car.

*   *   *   *

A history lesson.

I first met Megan Kelly at Ravinia, the suburban outdoor music park which is the summer home of the Chicago Symphony Orchestra.

It was a few years back, when the board of directors, and the rest of us, still assumed June would always be the beginning of summer instead of a waterlogged afterthought to a schizophrenic spring. They'd set up two weeks worth of jazz featuring a sparkling list of performers sure to attract a wide spectrum of fans. One of Channel 14's biggest advertisers sponsored a big, tented cocktail party on the lawn before one of the shows. I attended solo, planning only to put in the required appearance and then escape to a blanket, a folding chair and a box of the Colonel's finest way back under the trees and near the parking lot for easy access to my car.

I'd said my goodbyes, in fact, and was trying to shake hands and get out of there, when a leggy and athletic brunette put her hand on my arm. Widening her eyes, her mouth set in a playful smile, she said, "Haven't I seen you on television? Aren't you one of those crusading investigative reporters who run up and bushwhack the bad guys with your big microphone?"

It cracked me up, just as she'd intended. As it turned out, she was a nurse who wanted to thank me for a piece my investigative unit had done about a surgeon with a long record of mistakes, none of which had ever resulted in a single censure from the state healing arts board. The story aired in three segments, Sunday night through Tuesday. By Friday, the good doctor had not only been ordered to appear before the state board but was notified that the U.S. Attorney was opening an investigation for Medicare fraud. The following Monday, citing the high cost of malpractice insurance, he voluntarily gave up his license to practice medicine and announced he'd be retiring to Arizona within the month.

"I used to see him in the OR before I went to work in CCU," she said. "He treated his nurses like servants."

We chatted a bit about the doctor, about her hospital, about medicine in general. Part of me waited for a boyfriend or husband to return and claim her, though she wore no ring. She was the toned and tanned essence of North Shore grace, from the airy print skirt and short sleeve top to the pearl necklace and white cashmere sweater tied around her shoulders and I couldn't shake the feeling I'd seen her in the society pages. She seemed totally assured in her surroundings, yet the longer we talked, the more I realized she was somewhat of a phantom. Folks would come by and say hello to me yet none of them addressed her until I made the introductions.

I wouldn't have brought it up but she did, grinning. "You know I don't belong here?"

"I think you probably belong here more than most," I said.

She drew close enough to me I could tell even her fragrance was understated. Obsession.

"My date showed up drunk. I left him with his friends and wandered over here for something to do before the show. That means we could find a better dinner than what's in that KFC box. If you'd like to, that is."

In the middle of eating at one of the lawn-side restaurants, and shortly before Dave Brubeck and his group were to take the stage, Meg looked past me and stiffened. I noticed only because I was watching her with the intensity of a kid at his first prom. I turned to see a statuesque blonde, her arm linked through that of a tall, dark-haired man, pause outside the hedge that separated the restaurant from the blacktop path circling the grounds.

"There you are, sweetie!" the blonde called. Her accent suggested mint juleps on the veranda of a white-columned mansion and was as phony as a Confederate dollar. "Don and I wondered where you had disappeared to. I see you found your own foxy man."

"Lynn, you made it. Why don't you guys go on ahead," Meg said and smiled. "We'll catch up to you later."

"Oh, once we get started there won't be any catching up." The blonde grinned and hugged the man's arm to her breast. She winked at me. "But you could sure try."

Her companion grinned in a slightly offbeat way, eyes glazed by alcohol, and as they strolled off across the lawn I saw him stumble once, prevented from falling only by her arm around his.

"My roommate. My date, too," Megan said and busied herself with her salad.

*   *   *   *

I don't think she planned what happened later. Not any of it.

We ended up in bed at my place. But in the midst of our lengthy and energetic foreplay, while we were still mostly clothed and breathing as heavily as two teenagers fogging up the windows of a family car, she suddenly pushed my hands down to my sides and climbed atop me, her strong legs trapping my arms and one finger brushing my lips in a shooshing gesture to silence my protest.

"Quiet down, big man. Quiet."

I stopped laughing and trying to speak and felt my chest rising and falling as I sucked in air. I nodded against her finger and she took it away.

"There's something we have to talk about…that I have to tell you. I don't want the lights on and I don't want you to look at me while I'm getting this out, OK? I just want to lie like spoons side by side and you be quiet while I talk."

"OK," I said.

The refrigerated air suddenly felt chilly. I hadn't noticed it until then.

She shifted down along beside me, fitting her long form into my chest. My physical want of her had not subsided but she ignored it and pulled my arm across her breasts like a hug-toy.

That was when she told me she was not only a successful CCU nurse with a masters degree and hours toward her doctorate. She described her alter-ego, a professional escort named Janelle.

That was when we began what turned out to be a nearly three-year affair.

*   *   *   *

I left Marn's and immediately got stuck in a mile-long traffic jam, courtesy of a jack-knifed semi-trailer at Irving Park and Mannheim. By the time I extricated myself from that and made it back to the Kennedy expressway, it was past six. I hadn't eaten since I nibbled on the sandwich Hanratty bought for me on Navy Pier. I detoured to Superdog, always worth the trip, then headed south again to Lincoln Park. Humidity and some high clouds had moved in from the western 'burbs and the fumes from the big trucks hung in the air around my convertible and turned the sun an unhealthy mustard color.

The drive was useful. I knew where I was going but not eager to get there. Lynn Robinette, I had learned during my years with Meg, was a head-case. She was a reminder of Meg, something I didn't need right now. Unfortunately, she might have useful information and I couldn't ignore her.

Meg became a call girl for the money and the control it allowed her to have over certain types of men. She left it when she realized she no longer needed either. She left me when her discoveries about herself led her to the conclusion she would never be rid of the stain on her heart as long as she and I continued to see each other. We agreed neither would contact the other. I reminded her too much of what she'd been. Talking to her, knowing that, would have been excruciating for me.

Lynn, on the other hand, got into the business because she was the type of person who would encourage an alcoholic to drink up and have another or suggest to a pedophile that he drive past a schoolyard at recess. She had dangled the high six-figure income in front of her best friend and Meg had willingly bought the package.

Lynn Robinette liked the game and the lifestyle it afforded her. The day she learned Meg had moved to California, she called me to offer her companionship at substantially reduced rates. Not free, she stressed. Nothing personal, but her accountant had told her she had to pay down the mortgage on her three-quarters of a million dollar condo overlooking Lincoln Park.

In the three months since Meg moved, Lynn had received two notes from her. She called the days both arrived to read them to me, though Meg had expressly asked her not to do so. She'd known I would be dealing with her absence in my own way. I hung up on Lynn the last time she phoned.

It was nearing 7:30 when I circled the block near Lynn's condo building and tried her on the cell phone. She had two quirks that worked in my favor. She hardly ever left town during the summer, saving her travel for the snowy months of December through March. She once told me she had too many nice friends with nice boats to need to go anywhere else when it was warm in Chicago. I also knew she seldom went out for the evening, any evening, before eight or nine o'clock at night. She regarded any bar or club during the hours before midnight the province of amateurs and suburbanites and chose not to spend time around them. Thus, if she had a date, she insisted it begin about the time the light drinkers and the occasional partiers would be going home.

She might have company, I reasoned, but that was unlikely. Lynn was an interesting study in personality disorder. Meg told me several times that she had few women friends, and allowed virtually no one, man or woman, to visit her at home. She maintained a suite at one of the city's five-star hotels for business purposes but she preferred men who would take her home with them.

She answered in a voice more businesslike than sensual. I suspected that was closer to her real personality.

"It's Reno. Company?"

There was the briefest of pauses.

"I should ask 'Reno who?' No, I don't have company. I never answer the phone with my mouth full."

"I'm downstairs. Can I come up or do you want to meet somewhere?"

"Well that depends. Is your libido bothering you?"

"Not my libido. Just my curiosity."

"You're so subtle. And what kinky l'il thing are you curious about?" she asked.

"I'll be in Cleary's," I said, naming a tavern just up the street from her building. "Come find out."

"Oh, you man of mystery you. My heart's pounding already. Let me just freshen up."

I settled into a back booth that had high slatted dividers and a scarred wood table with a stack of Heineken coasters and a small bottle of Tabasco on it. It was a good joint. Sinatra belted "Mack the Knife" through speakers scattered throughout the place and several faces of John Wayne watched me from the walls near the pool tables. How can you not love a place that plays The Chairman and hangs the Duke on the walls?

Early as it was on a week night, there were five or six couples eating dinner and three men and a woman sitting at the bar playing an electronic trivia game with the bartender. I told the lone waiter to bring me a Dr. Pepper with crushed ice and a couple of cherries. He paused after I spoke as though waiting for me to give him my real order, then turned away suddenly and went to the task. Lynn walked in five minutes later and came directly to my booth without even a glance around. As she sat across from me, the first thing I noticed was her fragrance. It had been Megan's favorite. I had no doubt that's why she wore it.

Tonight, she was a yachting queen in long Bermuda shorts and a blouse that showed just enough tanned skin and a hint of cleavage. She could have been an upscale model or a Fortune 500 executive but with her looks and body and the way she sucked the air from every room she entered, she would never be mistaken for anything less than successful and, depending on her mood, inordinately sensual or cool and remote.

"There you are, Mr. Gunfighter-with-his-back-to-the-wall. You're so predictable. The standing to greet me was so gentlemanly but the lack of a kiss was rude."

"Cheek or ring?" I asked.

She rolled her eyes. "Oh please. It's not like I intimidate you."

The waiter brought my Dr. Pepper and Lynn ordered a double Stoli collins with a lime twist. That seemed to satisfy the waiter.

"Heard from Megan?" she asked sweetly.

"You know the answer to that," I said. I wasn't interested in verbal jousting so I pushed on. "I need information about someone in your line of work. I'll pay for it. You tell me how much."

"Enough with the small talk, off with the clothes? That's so unlike you."

I gave her the name and watched her eyes. She was as good an actress as you would ever see on stage or in the movies, self-trained over a lifetime in keeping her emotions and reactions out of public view. However, there is some thinking, and I've read it in more than a few psychology and even police journals, that when men lie they glance to their right, women to their left. She looked away to the left, studying the knotty pine paneling.

"Stacey DuMount. How cute. Who is she? Some little suburban daddy's girl? Are you trying to rescue her the way you 'rescued' Megan?"

"Meg rescued herself."

"Ooh. Sharp. You should do something about those angry feelings. I can recommend a wonderful therapist."

"Eddie Marn says you sent this girl to him. Does that help jog your memory?"

"How is Eddie? He's such a suave, erudite little fellow." The waiter brought her drink. She took a sip, then another bigger one and pronounced it acceptable. He beamed as though she had complimented his sexual prowess.

"He's still pissed because your referral did a number on his tires."

She shook her head, stretched her arms over her head so that her large breasts thrust against her blouse, and smiled at me. "Oh, Reno. Why haven't we ever gotten together? Do you really find me so repulsive?"

"Repulsive, no. Voracious, yes."

"Voracious! You *do* know me well. Or did someone tattle?"

"Tell me about the girl. Who is she?"

"Just someone new I was trying to help. I used to do that a lot. Now, all the young ones…" she sighed and put her arms down. "It's all competition. All those tight little bodies, those unlined faces. All those plastic boobs. I'm ancient at 35, can you believe that? But still all natural."

"Two hundred for a name, address and/or phone."

"Oh come on! Do you think we have business cards to exchange? 'Let's do lunch,' that sort of thing?"

"I think you remember her."

"Why on earth do you want to find her so badly?"

"A favor for a friend." I decided to go with part of the truth. "He thinks she's in some kind of trouble. The kind you don't walk away from without help."

She studied me as she sipped away at her Stoli then ran her tongue along the rim. Her eyes were bright with amusement. "Forget about the money. What kind of favor are you willing to do for me if I tell you? Will you take me upstairs and ravish me?"

"No. But I've got a buddy in the Bears' front office who handles skybox tickets."

"Skybox tickets?"

She barked a laugh that turned every head at the bar.

"Reno, you are a trip, I'll give you that. Such a straight, lovely man." She paused. "I don't know her name. I thought she looked young enough for one of Eddie's movies. He paid very well for referrals so I suggested she call him."

"How did you know her?"

"We met at work. What do you think?"

"I think you normally don't work with someone unless you've checked them out." Meg had always been adamant about that. "So…"

"That's true," she said in a patient voice. "I don't normally do threesomes with strangers, no, but the client was a semi-regular. He vouched for her. She was freelance, too."

"If she didn't work for an agency, how did he meet her? She have a pimp?"

"You're so retro. It's cute. He just…" She smiled. "Let's call him one of the Springfield contingent. He comes to town once in awhile so he's familiar with the menu. Usually, he calls me. Occasionally, he decides to sample something different. He'd seen her several times. He thought she and I would enjoy each other. I met the two of them in the lobby bar at his hotel. We talked for awhile. There was some chemistry so…we retired to the boudoir."

"Who was he?"

"Reno!" She shook an exquisitely manicured finger at me. "You know better. It would never have gotten to be the world's oldest profession if we talked about our clients, now would it?"

"What kind of different was he looking for?"

"Oh you like hearing the juicy details, do you? You *are* normal. All he wanted me to do was tell him what a bad boy he was while she did her thing with a whip. And not a nice little velvet one either." She wrinkled her nose. "She brought bandages and Lidocaine and even a few hits of codeine for afterward. And he needed it. It was all I could do to keep away from the blood. I'm sure he stood up to cast his votes for the next few days."

"She was that vicious?"

"She was *very* ferocious. Oooh it still gives me goose bumps thinking about it." A shiver went through her. Acting or not, her eyes went slightly out of focus as she recalled the moment. "But she was a very sweet little girl in…other circumstances."

"What's that mean? You seduced her?"

The sexual heat left her voice and her eyes looked as if I'd slapped her.

"So judgmental. What if she seduced me? Either way, yes. We had a lovely evening together."

"You slept with her, she turned you on, you thought enough of her to refer her to Marn but you don't remember her name? C'mon."

She blinked at me. I guessed she wasn't trying to remember the name as much as she was trying to decide whether to reveal it.

"You are *such* a forceful man. Her name was Brooke. With an E. Yes, it was her real name. I don't know her last name. She's quite private, your little daddy's girl. And quite confused I think. I also think she would be very angry at me if she knew I had told you any of this."

"What else do you know about her? Out of bed."

"Let's see now. She was quite North Shore fashionable. Oh yes, and she's very direct. For her age, she was remarkably intelligent and seemed to know a great deal about our business. She wouldn't talk about her other clients but I got the impression she knew a number of men like the gentleman who introduced us."

The longer she spoke about the girl her face softened, the tension I'd noticed in her jaws relaxing.

"When did you see her last?" I asked.

"I have a beeper number for her. That's all I have. If you'd like, I'll call you with it when I go back upstairs."

"I'd like you to answer my question. Have the two of you stayed in touch?"

Now she tapped her long fingernails on the tabletop and looked to her right. The waiter caught the glance, thought it was meant for him, and eagerly started over. She waved him off.

"Two weeks ago. She was in the Sports Bar at the Marriott by O'Hare. She was a little drunk, a little depressed." Lynn's expression turned inward, as though she was contemplating whether she'd ever find herself in those circumstances.

"Seeing her there was very odd. Out of context. I wanted to find out what was up and give her a chance to talk about herself but I was with a group of people. If I'd stayed to chat, it would have attracted attention and that was quite obviously what she didn't want."

"What do you mean??"

"I watched her for a little while, just sitting there by herself. Four different men tried to move on her but she shooed them away."

"Could she have been waiting for a john?"

Another smile, this one with less wattage and more uncertainty than the others. "Not a client, no. Hotel bars aren't her style. A special friend, though? That's possible."

"Did you try to page her afterwards?"

"Why would I?" She widened her eyes.

"This was a girl you had some affection for. You were concerned about her," I shrugged. "Maybe you thought she needed comforting."

"No, dear," she said. "You're confusing me with dear Megan. She was the nurse. I just take care of me."

I would have believed her if she hadn't closed her eyes and glanced away just as she finished speaking.

*   *   *   *

She offered no objection so I rode up in the elevator with her when we left Cleary's. I chose not to meet her glances in the mirrored walls. I asked her for a better description of Brooke and she told me the only difference in her appearance between two weeks ago and the last time she'd seen her was that her hair was short, not quite shoulder length, and more blonde.

At the door to her unit, she invited me in but I told her I'd be just as happy waiting in the hall. I wondered, briefly, if she'd stiff me. She didn't. She came back to the door a moment later and handed me a slip of paper with Brooke's pager number written on it in a flowing script. As I took it, she let the back of her hand brush mine.

"You know, we could renegotiate what I suggested after Meg left. My accountant wouldn't have to know." Unlike her earlier flirtation, she now sounded wistful.

"It'd never work, Lynn," I said, surprising myself at how gently I spoke the words.

"You're still in love with her aren't you?"

I didn't respond.

She drew her hand along the side of my face. "I miss her, too. But if you invite me to dinner someday, I promise we don't have to talk about her."

"Sure," I said.

CHAPTER 3

▼

Even in late evening, it can be tough getting to the Kennedy from Lincoln Park. I flipped on WGN to catch a traffic report as I cruised out North Avenue, thinking about how i might go about tracing the beeper number Lynn had given me. If I hadn't gotten my friend Sunny to fill in for me in the morning, I could have called her. She spends her days, when she's not substituting for various radio news anchors, as a private detective and skip-chaser for bail bondsmen, something Asa didn't know when he tried to cop a feel. Her computer hacking skills would make Bill Gates nervous.

Knowing her habits, however, I was sure she had already shut off her phones and gone to bed. She's not what you'd call a morning person under the best of circumstances and to sound perky on the air at 5 a.m, she needed a solid nine or ten hours of rack time. I've never figured how someone who drinks three cups of coffee just to get their eyelids unstuck could run a twenty-four-hour surveillance to track down a bail skip, but she pointed out she doesn't have to act human for something like that. Quite the opposite, in fact.

With Sunny unavailable, I remembered the offer Andy Nunez made while we chatted in the Channel 14 garage. It made more sense for me to get him involved since he'd likely be working on the story soon enough. I rang him as I waited in another line of stalled cars near the expressway on-ramp. He wasn't in the office so I had the operator page him. He answered out of breath.

"In the middle of something?" I asked.

"Got a little editing problem." I heard him turn away from the phone and say something to someone else about an in-cue on a sound bite and then he came back. "What's up?"

"What are the chances of getting a name and address off a beeper number?"

He humphed and thought about it. "Good question. Each paging company's computer has the information. Yeah, I suppose it's possible. You'd need to know the service provider first."

"Couldn't you track something like that down with the phone number?"

"Damn, Reno, I don't know." The sound of a taped conversation going to fast rewind came through the phone and brought an image so tactile I could almost feel the digital editing computer's keyboard. "The master list of numbers allocated to paging services and cellular companies is public record. I could go in there, match the number to a service and try to come up with something. Sure. Probably not tonight, though. Big time urgent?"

"It could be."

"Hang on." He put a hand over the mouthpiece and I heard muffled conversation. When he returned, he said, "Gimme it. I'll do what I can."

Had I been a smart guy, I would have waited for his callback.

Instead, I let the wind blow in my face for a few minutes while I took advantage of a break in traffic and gunned the Mustang into the left lane, headed out to the O'Hare Marriott hotel. The needle was doing a nice dance at seventy when I slipped the Three Mo' Tenors Greatest Hits album into my CD player. They're three classically-trained black guys who do everything from opera to Motown to blues and gospel. I especially like it when they open with "La Donna E Mobile" from *Rigoletto* and then slide effortlessly into "Let the Good Times Roll." Even a musical hack like me who likes to use an old chopstick as a baton and conduct the Chicago Symphony from the lawn at Ravinia can appreciate that kind of versatility.

The Marriott's parking lot was just full enough and the sports bar doing enough of a week night business that there was obviously a sizeable convention in the hotel. A guy with blow-dried hair collected a cover charge and I stood just inside the doorway to scan the room. It was noisy and had all of the toys you'd expect in such a joint: basketball hoops, video games and even a small raised putting green. A joke of a Cubs game showed on four plasma-screen TV's, the sound competing with the shouts of some of the game players and the general level of conversation. A couple of ceiling fans strained, without much success, to move the smoke.

I slid onto a stool near the middle of the room-length bar and waited for the bartender to notice me. He was either a twin of the guy at the door or they used the same stylist. He wore an earring in each ear and a Bulls' t-shirt with Michael's old number on it and, when he came to stand in front of me, his smile was as genuine as his capped teeth. He lifted his chin as a signal he was ready to hear my request but his eyes roamed vacantly somewhere over my left shoulder.

"Looking for a girl," I said over the noise. I described her. "A buddy says she hangs out here sometimes. Her name's Brooke."

I didn't rate his eyes, or his interest, yet. "We got a special tonight, 'cause of the game? The Sosa Souser. It's like a Kamikaze."

"Heineken," I said. He tilted a beer glass under the spigot and filled it but some of the phony pizzazz went out of his expression.

"I've got my hands full just pouring the booze, man. Y'know? I don't have the time to watch who's doing what to who." He slapped a Bud coaster down in front of me and planted the glass atop it.

"That's four bucks," he said.

I laid a crisp new twenty on the bar. "Give it some thought, why don't you? My buddy says this little blonde's worth the effort."

His eyes stopped moving now and he just stared beyond me like a recruit whose just been chewed out by his drill instructor. "You got exact change? I'm a little low on ones."

So much for good old Chicago-style memory enhancement. I paid him. He wandered down the bar. I sipped the brew thinking that it wouldn't be good to knock 'em back too fast. I might lose whatever subtlety I had left. Pretty soon a table opened up where I could watch both the door and the bar and I carried my beer over there.

A deer hunter couldn't have had a better blind. The place was nearly full, median age my side of forty. Over the next thirty minutes or so the noise level rose appreciably as a table of mostly chunky guys in lame sport shirts and polyester golf slacks tried to out-putt and then out free-throw each other while sucking down at least two serious-looking cocktails apiece. One of them dropped twenty baskets in a row, missed one, then hit another ten.

The cigarette smoke was strong, undercut by the smell of alcohol and joined by the sexual tension of any meat market where the idea of making the trip back to the ol' hotel room alone becomes more bleak as alcohol dulls the receptors and midnight approaches. At mixed tables, the guys leaned over the women as though imparting some special kind of knowledge. Some of the women appeared interested. Most, however, remained upright in their chairs, arms gathered in front of them, sure in the knowledge that the beds they slept in tonight would have only one occupant.

If Lynn had told the truth about her recent meeting with Brooke, I thought, what did it mean?

Here's a girl who starts out wanting to do porn. She's turned down by one guy because she appears to be too violent for his kind of flicks. Possibly she gets her shot somewhere else. Possibly she persuades him to take her on by threatening something worse than slashed tires. She also channels her anger into the outcall prostitution business where she has a niche, servicing those clients who like to tap dance on the razor's edge between real pain and perceived pleasure. Then, if I could believe what she told Hanratty, she takes up with some kind of service. There are agencies that handle the sadomasochism scene, just like there are places one can find German Shepherds in G-strings. No doubt some of them have web sites, e-mail and little old ladies to answer the phone for them. Finding one of them might have to be my next step.

I segued from thinking about that to thinking about the good senator whose name Hanratty had dropped. Was he patronizing that kind of an outfit? Had he and Brooke, in fact, shared an intimate moment or two or was she just slinging hash to get Hanratty interested?

I took another sip of my Heineken. I'm not a big drinker. It may come from the fact my old man died a falling down drunk after a pretty shiny thirty years as a Chicago cop. I say died a drunk but what he really did was wait until I was just about ready to graduate from high school, when he knew I was old enough and tough enough to take care of my mother and myself, then went to a field across from the house he'd bought and remodeled by his own hand in Evanston and stuck the barrel of his old .357 in his mouth. It was the way he'd seen plenty of street mopes do it and he knew, without exception, it had worked for them. Worked great for him, too.

The main reason I don't drink much, however, is because, at best, alcohol just tastes like a bunch of chemicals to me. At worst, when my overactive imagination gets cranking, booze of any kind has the flavor of gunmetal and blood.

That's why half the Heineken was still in my glass when I scanned the room for the thirtieth time and noticed a young woman, who looked very much like the one I'd been hired to find, standing just inside the doorway talking to the bouncer.

A shiver started at the top of my spine, as though someone had slipped an ice cube inside the back of my collar. I wanted to shout "Yes!" and pump my fist in the air. Then I got cautious. The girl at the door matched the description, but was she Brooke?

If I measured her against the height of the door, as they now train convenience store clerks to do so they can approximate the height of the gunman who has just robbed them, she would be 5'6 or 5'7 with no suggestion of fat. She wasn't a knockout but her linen skirt and sleeveless blouse showed off a good build with muscular definition in her shoulders and legs. Had we met at a country club, I'd say she was tennis, not golf. Her short blonde hair played well against what looked to be a genuine sunshine tan.

Not every head in the place turned as she passed but her entry caused a definite ripple. She seemed oblivious. She wedged between two couples at the bar and I realized if the bartender knew her, he'd probably point me out. She stepped away a moment later carrying a glass of something but without looking my way. Instead, a couple left a table along the far wall and she slid in behind them to claim it. When she sat down, she surveyed the room, her expression bland. I became very interested in my drink so she wouldn't catch me watching.

I realized I was comparing her to Megan. They were different physically but might have come from similar backgrounds. Meg's dad had been a top international lawyer; she'd grown up in the old-money Saint Francis Wood neighborhood of San Francisco. I would have pegged Brooke as North Shore even without hearing Lynn describe her that way. Another similarity was in the attitude both exuded. "I'm available," it seemed to say, "If you prove you're man enough." It's not arrogance. It actually hides the fear of a business where any appointment, no matter how well researched, could end with a sizeable cash tip or a knife slash across the face. Meg learned to take control early and walk out if she detected any hint of deviancy or even just a significant personality clash. She told me once she had probably turned her back on thousands of dollars in her several years as a call girl. I wondered if Brooke was as careful. After all, her specialty was deviance.

I had to crane my neck to see her and I didn't want to keep doing that. She'd given the room a pretty thorough casing. Two girls moved away from an old-time video game table that faced her part of the room. I went for it. I immediately fed quarters into the game and made as though I was having fun chasing the little critters around the board, chomping all the way.

Over the next hour or so, several guys hit on her. She reacted the same way each time. A look that could have flash-frozen meat and then a dull, almost afterthought shake of the head. She finished her drink, went to the bar for another, came back and went through the routine twice more with newcomers. Exciting stuff.

I was pretty certain I'd found "Stacey DuMount." Hanratty wanted me to observe and report. Much as I would have liked to go home and shower, I needed to watch her until she either met up with a john or went home herself.

If she called it quits for the night, and I could discover where she lived, I'd stake out the place, get some video of her in the morning or whenever she went out again, and have both Lynn and Marn ID her from it. If she took on a client, well, I'd just have to think out what to do then. I wanted the visual ID. Probably didn't need it to convince Hanratty but I'm sort of a stickler for nailing all the corners of a story before presenting it to the audience. Even if, this time, it would only be an audience of one. Or maybe two if, as promised, he followed through with Chazz.

It was sometime during the review of my alternatives that I began to feel the effects of the day. I've waded through the depravity of the street for the past twenty years, first as a prosecutor's investigator and then as a reporter on the crime beat. There aren't too many things one person can do to another that I haven't seen. I've done jailhouse interviews with a man who cut a woman's throat so he could steal the fetus from her belly, with a woman who suffocated her three children because she was convinced the devil inhabited their bodies and even with a cold-eyed 13-year-old who calmly told me he had disemboweled his grandmother because she wouldn't take him to an R-rated movie. You can still surprise me but I long ago lost the ability to be shocked by any sort of human behavior. Saddened, yes. Even depressed by it sometimes.

Right now I just felt unclean. I was sitting in a hotel bar, surrounded by mid-dle-aged conventioneers well on the road to a morning hangover while I watched an attractive woman prospecting for some poor schmuck who would pay her to beat him up. Or whatever her specialty was these days. I couldn't quite tell where she'd hide a whip in the outfit she was wearing but, for all I knew, someone had come out with The Fetishists' Handy Collapsible Cat-O-Nine Tails and she had it stowed away in pocket or purse ready for just the right intimate moment.

I caught one of the women at the next table looking at me and smiled at her. It must have been an unpleasant sight because her shoulders dropped and she jerked her head away, as though afraid I was another one of "them" and she real-ized she was surrounded. Probably should have bared my teeth and shot her the finger. The thought of how she might have reacted to that cheered me for an instant, until I saw Brooke passing through the doors to the lobby. I dodged a guy bringing two drinks back to his table from the bar and went after her at as nonchalant a pace as I could muster. When you're following someone, you want to blend into your surroundings. I moved like a guy who was headed to his room, not really eager to go but tired enough to know he should.

She didn't catch my act. She reached the revolving door to the parking lot just as I entered the nearly deserted lobby. I quickened my pace a bit. Losing her would mean I'd endured the last couple of hours for nothing. I followed her through the door, watching as she crossed the driveway into the parking lot.

Brooke appeared to be the only person on foot in the lot and she was moving at a pretty good clip between the cars. I heard the double chirp of an auto alarm being turned off and assumed it was hers. I took my own keys out and began to whistle softly as I walked with a bit more speed in her direction. All I wanted was a glimpse of her car and then I'd sprint for mine and try to get into position behind her as she left the lot.

A few low-voltage light cans aimed at the trees provided the bulk of illumination but they enhanced rather than eliminated the shadows. I stayed about a row behind her, scanning left to right, like a constantly moving security camera. The too quiet *snick* of a car door latch caught my attention. I sought out the source of the sound. It came from my right, about four rows away. I watched a man move toward Brooke from the driver's side of a Toyota Land cruiser.

I wasn't the only one who spotted Mr. Toyota. Brooke stopped walking, body going rigid, and I knew she'd seen him, too. He was a couple of inches over my six-two and powerfully built through the chest and torso with forearms as thick as my thighs. Brooke looked ready to turn and run. Instead, she stood her ground as he approached. He reached out and clamped a hand around her upper arm. I stopped where I was and made like I was fiddling with a car door. If he hadn't seen me yet, I didn't want him to notice I was watching.

Brooke tried to free herself.

"Goddamn it Yevvie, get your hands off me!"

"We must talk. Just talk," Mr Toyota said. He had one of those voices that was probably loud even though he didn't want it to be.

"Go talk to Michael! Tell him I'm leaving. Tell him he can kiss my ass."

"Leaving is not for you to decide. He wants you."

He had an accent that was, at the very least, Eastern European, if not Russian. The second one I'd heard within hours.

"You don't get it, do you?" Brooke said hotly and yanked her arm from his grip. "I'm not his whore anymore."

"You will speak with him. That is all he wants. We go to my car. I have cell phone…"

"Fuck your cell phone! I'm not getting into any car with you. Call him and tell him fuck him, too."

She turned away but Mr. Toyota reached for her arm again. She spun out of his grip. He lunged for her.

"God DAMN you!" she screamed. Her hand flashed up and I heard the distinctive hiss of a Mace or pepper spray container. The big guy grunted but punched out at her and she went down as though she had been slammed behind the knees.

The hell with subtle, I thought. I had no idea what this was all about but I was going to feel mighty guilty if Mr. Toyota Man beat her to death right in front of me.

It took four long strides to reach him. He'd knocked Brooke down but she had apparently dodged the force of the blow. Flat on her back, she tried to kick free as he bent to grab her. He was so focused on the pain in his eyes and the woman he was trying to control, he never heard my approach. Leaning over, feet about shoulder width apart with his back to me, he provided a perfect target.

I could have kicked him in the knee but, what the hell. I wanted him down and out with no opportunity for comebacks. I took a quick two steps and drove my foot into his testicles.

I read somewhere that it actually takes about a second and a half for the brain to process a kick to the nuts. In Mr. Toyota Man's case, I'd nailed him so hard that the impact lifted him off his feet. No doubt he was moving before the pain walloped him. He stumbled past Brooke to land with a WHUMP! in the middle of some shrubs behind her. I watched him try to get his feet under him. Brooke was quicker. She scrambled up and emptied the rest of her container of magic dust into his face. He moaned and lurched onto his side, swiping out at her. She danced back out of range then redefined the act of adding insult to injury by kicking him in the groin again.

"Whoa," I said.

Given the way he flopped over onto his back and didn't reach for Ground Zero with both hands, I suspected he was unconscious or paralyzed with pain. I stepped between them and blocked her from taking another shot.

"Fucking assHOLE!" she shouted, bouncing in agitation trying to see over my outstretched arms. She threw the empty container and it bounced off his chest. Then, like her threat alarm had gone off again, she bared her teeth and came after me. She tried first to gouge out an eye, then hooked her fingers and went for my face with her nails. I managed to parry her hands and turn fast enough to take a knee to my thigh instead of her intended target. She stumbled backward but this time kept her balance. Tears streamed down her cheeks and her chest heaved.

"Easy, easy, easy," I said. "I think between us we've gelded him."

I put out a hand in a placating gesture but she slapped it away.

"I don't give a shit. The prick. The absolute prick! Fucking Russian asshole!"

"Come on. Cool it."

She wrenched away from me. "Who the fuck are you? Did Michael send you to play the nice guy or something?"

"If he did, he's gonna be pissed as hell at what I did to the one playing bad guy."

She blinked, then after a moment seemed to realize I wasn't another attacker. She wrapped her arms around herself and cupped her elbows. We stared warily at each other until the lump on the ground began to grunt.

"You have your keys?" I said. "I don't think we want to be here when he wakes up."

"Yeah. Yeah." She dug them out of her purse and looked at me still standing there. "What? You want a blow job in gratitude?"

"Um, that's not quite what I was thinking. Maybe a 'thanks, see ya around' would be cool though."

She started walking away. Over her shoulder she said, "Whatever. Thanks. But you sure as hell won't see me around. No fucking way."

My car was on the other side of the lot so I let her go. Once she got into a black Mercedes, I took off running, watching as her brake lights came on and then her headlights. By the time I reached the Mustang, she'd gunned across the driveway and was waiting for traffic to clear at the exit to River Road. I blasted out after her, nearly sideswiped an airport bus and blew the red light just to keep her in sight. I didn't get close enough for comfort until she slid into inbound traffic on the Kennedy. Even then, she played the lane-darter game for a few minutes, working off her adrenaline buzz. When she settled down, I laid back a couple of car-lengths and tried to keep a semi or two between us.

I hoped she was headed home and wasn't just out for a calm down drive. I'd been up since 3 a.m, my normal hour to rise and shine for the shift I worked, and I was maxed on the amount of time I wanted to spend behind the wheel. If she was going to cruise aimlessly for a couple of hours as she tried to decide where she could settle so the bad guys wouldn't find her, I wasn't sure I could keep up.

Seemingly unaware of being tailed, she left the Kennedy, cut across to the Edens and took that to Touhy eastbound. It got a little tougher to stay behind her at that point. I was glad I'd put up the top on the Mustang. I didn't want her to glance in her rear view and see me plus I could smell rain packed into the dense air.

Drive to the far end of Touhy, as far east as you can go, and you hit Rogers Park, the last North Side neighborhood along the lake before you run out of Chicago. It's as eclectic as anywhere in the city, from its quaint Swedish grocery stores selling limpa bread to a strong Hasidic community to Black and Latino street gangs and a campus of Loyola University. Years ago it was considered a fashionable area, a suburb for the upper middle class. Its personality has steadily eroded since the '50's and now you see cops breaking up any group of more than four or five young people on street corners and gunfire isn't an unfamiliar sound.

Traffic tightened up the closer we got to the lake. I suspected Brooke was headed home. She crossed Clark and turned down an alley, then went east on Grove under the El tracks. I considered the train rattle Frank had heard during their phone conversations. Home. Yup. While she used the driveway next to a five-story courtyard brownstone as a turnaround, I zipped into a church parking lot that fronted the brownstone and killed my lights. She cruised back the way she'd come, spied a space on the street near the building and backed in. As she stepped out of her Mercedes, however, I saw the dome light come on in a BMW parked on my side of the street and watched a guy pop out and call her name. What was going on here? This woman had more drivers after her than a carhop in a Fifties beach movie.

I reached to open my door but gave it up when I saw her stop, turn, and then wait as the guy hustled across the street. In the spill of the streetlights, he looked to be in his mid-twenties, a moderately tall, chunky guy who moved without grace, one hand running through a thick mop of hair. Who the hell was he? A client looking for a midnight quickie?

She embraced him hastily, as though to ward off a more physical approach from him. A short conversation followed, during which he seemed to shrivel into himself every time he stopped chatting long enough to listen. I guessed he was no threat. Whatever she said convinced him to leave. He handed her a thick envelope and then, head down, trudged back to his car. She headed across the courtyard to the brownstone.

I waited for him to pull away from the curb, then got out and jogged after her. Just as I reached the courtyard, I saw her through the door glass getting her mail. She went through another door that was propped open with an old Yellow Pages. I followed, closing the outer door quietly behind me. Her footfalls thudded on the stairs. I pondered my next move. "Talmadge" was printed on a piece of paper taped to the box from which she'd taken her mail. Now I had a probable last name and her address. No apartment number, though. I wanted that. Frank was the sort of guy who would ask for it.

I left my shoes in the foyer and went slowly up the stairs. I could still hear her climbing above me. Cooking smells clung to the worn wallpaper like bad memories. Music played somewhere in the building but it was muted and I couldn't identify the tunes. The sound of her footfalls faded and I took the steps two at a time, afraid I'd lose her. At the third floor landing, I peeked around a corner. She was at the end of the hall. She put a key in the lock of the apartment farthest from the stairs. Bingo!

I eased down to the lobby with as little noise as I'd made going up and slipped back into my shoes. I was wondering whether to call Frank as soon as I got to the car. Would he think I was bragging? It was almost one o'clock. Probably not a good idea. Fun to consider though.

A strobe of lightning lit up the courtyard as I stepped to the door. I waited for the thunder, counting slowly to see how far away the storm might be.

Brooke's scream beat the storm's roar by a nanosecond. Though muted by the building's walls, there was no mistaking it. The thunder erupted in its wake and then I heard another shriek, louder. Not the sound of passion but the full-throated noise a mortally wounded animal makes.

I cleared the third floor landing before I was aware I'd run up the stairs. Steaming down the hall, I heard her scream again. The screams stopped. Something crashed to the floor. Hard.

Brooke's door was locked. Pain seared down my arm as I tried to shoulder my way in. The wood held. I backed off across the hall, launched my full 210 pounds, foot-first, at the latch. The door crashed open. I stumbled forward into darkness. I tripped over something that felt like a foot. It dropped me to my knees.

What happened next was like seeing the last few frames of an old home movie as they flap through the projector's gate, brightness distorting the images that flash across the screen.

A stunning glimpse of Brooke Talmadge on the floor, eyes fixed and staring.

Something rushed out of the darkness at me low and from the left. I jerked my head in that direction. I was still disoriented from blasting though the door, horrified at what I'd just seen. Something square and white and hard slammed into my face with the impact of a thunderclap. Pain exploded through my skull as lightning flashed again. The last thought I remember was that the rain had come late and so had I....

*   *   *   *

...and my father spoke through a phone to me.
"You don't want to talk to your own dad?"
I was seventeen.
"I don't want to talk to you when you're drunk." My voice, petulant.

"I raised a few with the boys from the District," he snapped. "I ain't drunk. Just a little misty."

He'd tracked me down at a girlfriend's place.

What was her name? Angie. The older one. The one with her own apartment.

He was a cop. He could find me anywhere.

"Dad, no. That's why mom has that court thing against you. You're not supposed to come around."

"Am I comin' around, boy? You see me standing there? I just want to talk to my son. That ain't allowed now?"

"Reno?" Angie asked. She was on the bed next to me, her voice soft in the darkness, just like her skin. She took my hand.

"I wanna go fishing. You wanna go fishing? Why don't I call, get that cabin up in Eagle River? Remember that first cast last summer? You about passed out, I brought in that 18 inch bass."

"It's almost October. They probably have snow up there or something."

"Nah, they don't have snow. I checked. Whaddya say? You, your mom and I. You can even bring that little girl you're staying with, how about that?"

"We're not supposed…"

"Fuck supposed! Judges aren't nothing but lawyers that paid somebody off to get regular work. I know a few judges, too. I can smooth it over, trust me."

I felt a thickness in my throat that swallowing wouldn't dislodge.

"No. Not while you're drinking. If you stop…then we can talk. Mom's right about that. You stop drinking, ok?"

"It's too dark. Did I ever tell you I was afraid of the dark? All the time you were little and would cry at night because you thought the tree outside was a monster, I knew what that was like. There are monsters in the dark, Reno. Don't you ever forget that. Monsters in the dark places…"

*   *   *   *

…and a blaze of pain melted the scene. My face was on fire. I was lying curled on the floor, no longer on the bed with Angie. As hard as I tried to smother the blaze with sheer willpower, it burned until my nose scraped the carpet. Another bolt of lightning fried my brain and when it winked out, so did I….

*   *   *   *

…*the gunshot broke the night's stillness.*

I awoke, disoriented. For a moment, I thought I was in Northern Wisconsin…the deer hunting weekend with my dad and his partner from Violent Crimes.

Maybe they'd started into the woods without me.

No. No. I was home. I recognized my room, the one in the house Dad bought for Mom and me in Evanston after the divorce.

Dad had called me at Angie's. I'd hung up on him and called Mom. She asked me to come home.

The clock on the bedside table read 3:30.

I struggled up in my bed. What was the noise that woke me? I listened. Whatever it was might repeat. A door closing? A car backfiring?

Something drew me to the window. My legs felt weak. The darkness was there. Tree branches scraped the siding, fingernails on the blackboard.

I looked through the screen.

I sniffed.

A faint metallic odor rode the breeze. It made me think again of our hunting weekend. The chill of that day crept along my spine. There was no forgetting the look of the buck's torn open chest, the dark of the cavity and the black blood turning crimson as it pumped into the snow.

A metallic smell. Blood. "There are monsters in the dark, Reno. Monsters in the dark places…"

*   *   *   *   **

My second return to consciousness was easier than the first. Some primitive process told me to move very, very slowly. I lay on my stomach now, cheek pressed into the hardwood floor. I brought my hands to my sides and tried a feeble pushup.

Never up, never in, pal. My dad's voice in my head, stronger, more commanding than in the dream. He sounded exasperated.

I pushed with my hands and feet, very conscious of and very careful of my nose. I made it to my knees. Rested. My nose felt as if a weight were attached to it.

About a year passed. I eased back into a sitting position, felt the wall behind me and leaned against it.

I was in a corridor where I faced a Pullman kitchen. The door I kicked in was to my left and still open about three inches. The light filtering in showed shapes of living room furniture to my right. I could hear querulous voices in the hall. I tried to say something but the pain from opening my mouth was so intense I could feel knives poised to thrust in through my closed eyes. Bile rose in my throat. With effort, I swallowed it. If I puked now, I'd pass out.

Rain lashed the windows and thunder rolled, a dull faraway sound as it moved out over the lake. Sirens came near, went silent.

I turned my head. Brooke Talmadge's lifeless form hadn't gone anywhere, a sad huddled lump in the gloom.

Check for vital signs, son. Only the medics can pronounce her dead and you don't have an MD after your name, do you?

I didn't want to move. I didn't want to leave the security of my wall and take the chance of smacking my nose into something. Pain radiated from the center of my face. The fire had died but the embers smoldered brightly, ready to flare.

Move it.

My dad again. Demanding.

Footsteps and the flat, hard voice of a police radio sounded in the hall before I could comply. More voices, human ones, louder, commanding. The door swung open and slammed hard into the side of my leg. The light revealed Brooke more clearly.

One hand stretched toward me, fingers slightly curled. The ferocity in her face when she kicked Yevvie in the balls, the furious light in her eyes as she looked at me after we put him down…gone. Eyes open, mouth open, as if all that light and energy had drained away.

A blue-shirted patrolman with no discernable neck swiveled around the open door and pointed his automatic at me in a two-handed grip.

"Don't move," he snapped. Then to his partner, "Guy back here, banged up some."

I left my palms flat on the floor.

"The girl's banged up worse," came back a dry voice. An older, taller cop followed him through the door. Both were hatless, hair plastered to their foreheads. The second cop wore a gray rain slicker. Rain dripped from it to form puddles on the floor.

"Cuff him," he said.

"Down on your face!" The first cop grabbed my shoulder and hauled me forward. I caught my weight on both hands as I toppled. The pain shot straight through me when he scooped my arms back. I didn't pass out but the world went gray around the edges.

"Girl's done for," the older cop said.

"My nose…" I began.

The cop lifted my arms as he snapped on the cuffs.

"Fuck yer nose," he said.

*   *   *   *

In the old movies, when cops walk the suspect from the crime scene to a waiting car, it's always done amidst bursting flashbulbs and turning newsreels. Reporters crowd around asking questions and they all have little cards with 'Press' stuck in their hatbands. Everyone wears narrow lapel suits, the detectives are all impossibly skinny and the uniforms fat and Irish-looking. When the detectives talk, they call the reporters by their last names and then the reporters run to a phone and snap, "Stop the presses. And gimme rewrite, doll!"

That's not how it works any more.

Most of the time, if the cops are lucky enough to find some dummy standing around with a smoking gun, the cops sneak him out the back door, well away from the cameras. They haul the body that way too and, depending on the shift commander's mood, get the uniforms to hold up a tarp so as to further screw with the news photographers. Any reporter who asks a question will get a curt "No comment" in return or, if the officer he's asking has had run-ins with the news media before, he may be threatened with arrest.

Then again, there are always exceptions.

I saw Marisa Langdon and her cameraman before I was two steps into the courtyard. I still wore the cuffs and my two new best friends, the coppers I'd welcomed to the scene, each had a hand on me. It was clear the three of us weren't going bowling. The camera swung up in my direction, light flashing on, and I had to resist the urge to duck my head. This sure wasn't the way I wanted to get back on Channel 14.

My two buddies walked me close enough to the camera that if he zoomed in he'd have a nice close-up of my nose hairs. Marisa did exactly what they teach in TV Reporting 101 and what I'd done probably a hundred times. She extended her microphone and asked, "What happened in there, Reno? Did you kill someone?"

My nose throbbed and felt as though it were spread out across my face. I was tired of answering questions. I couldn't say anything that would help myself so, like most people put in that situation, I kept my mouth shut and walked right by her.

"C'mon, Reno. What were you doing in there? What's going on?" she persisted.

She was still pitching questions as the cops put me in the back seat of their squad, pulled out around the station wagon from the crime scene unit and the two unmarked detective cars and accelerated toward the hospital.

CHAPTER 4

▼

"Do you need me to tell you it's broken?"

Dr. Lauren Goddard was everything I thought a physician needed to be. Skillful though gentle. Polite. She was also quite attractive in a harried, tuckered-out sort of way. Wearing no makeup, her blonde hair swept back in a clip, she could have been a college senior interrupted while studying for an exam. I knew she was a real doctor because MD was stenciled after her name on the left breast of her gray lab coat. Besides, we had history. We had crushes on each other, at different times, in high school.

"After the first couple of times you get so you know what it feels like," I said. "But this time it feels a little more broken than before."

"Bet you've never had it broken in two places. That's why it feels different. I'm just going to pack it for now and get the bleeding stopped." She picked up a long roll of gauze tape sticky with ointment. "We'll wait to set it in the morning, give the swelling a chance to subside."

We were in a treatment room at Weiss Hospital along with a male nurse in rumpled whites who absently picked at a large zit on his nose. He watched Lauren's profile with the intensity of a med student studying surgical techniques. Every couple of moments his tongue came out, ran across his lower lip, and disappeared.

"I think I can handle this alone, Kenny," she said without looking at him. She laid out her scissors, forceps and gauze on a sterile pad. He didn't move.

"I dunno, doc, the cops brought him in, you know? I think I better stick around."

She turned and gave him a tight little grin. "I said I can handle it."

The nurse started to reply, rubbed his nose instead and slouched out of the room.

"Hard to get good help nowadays?"

"We have candy-stripers who are half as horny and know twice as much about medicine as he does."

She brought her black-framed glasses down from the top of her head and looked in my eyes.

"Now. About your head. Are you going to be our guest tonight or is there someone unwise enough to be dating you who will keep an eye on you at home?"

"Much as I'd love to stay here and have Kenny waking me up every ten minutes, something tells me I'll have plenty of people watching over me. No dates, though. If you didn't have that husband…"

"You had your chance, bucko. Reno, I'm serious. I'm worried about intra-cranial bleeding. If you start to feel weak, dizzy or a little sick to your stomach, get back here. If you have to be with the cops, make sure they know that."

I opened my mouth to respond but stopped as a burly, rumpled looking guy whipped back the curtain cocooning the treatment area. He wore a blue police ID clipped to the breast pocket of his corduroy jacket and carried a Motorola walkie-talkie and note book.

"'bout wrapped up in here, doc?"

Charley Kinsella had thick, dark hair just starting to show some salt. The slight paunch was new since the last time I'd seen him. He knew how my nose felt because his has been broken several times. The rest of his face is lumpy, too, as are the knuckles on both hands, from breaking his own share of noses and other various parts. When I worked the police beat, Charley and I crossed paths several times. He makes it clear he has no use for reporters and feels the First Amendment is as useless as the rest of the Bill of Rights.

Given all that, he's the kind of guy other cops like to slam behind his back. He mostly works alone, drinks alone, and God help anyone who ever seeks him out for contributions or membership in any police fraternal organization. A woman I knew slightly dated him once. She told me he writes poetry and has, as wall art in his home, framed photos of crime scenes he's worked. She said she didn't date him long, despite the poetry.

Lauren's reaction to him was instantaneous. Red-faced, she said, "I am working on a patient, Detective. Hospital rules say you wait outside and I'd appreciate it if you'd do that."

"C'mon, doc. He's a murder suspect. And it's not like you're doing brain surgery."

"He may be in your custody but he's still in my hospital." She stepped to the curtain, snapped it like a lion tamer's whip and held it open for him. "There's only one door out of here and he'll have to pass you to reach it. If you'll wait out-side, we'll both get our work done a little sooner tonight."

Kinsella didn't move. "How long?"

"If you let me work, about ten minutes."

He nodded once and went through the curtain, then shambled out through the door that led into the hall. His expression never changed. Lauren swung the curtain closed again, then picked up a forceps.

"That man needs a long ride on the silver horse," she said.

"Huh?"

She nodded at the 12 inches of steel proctoscope hanging on the wall and smiled brightly.

*   *   *   *

When Lauren finished packing my nose, I found Kinsella had dismissed the two uniforms so he could drive me into the area detective headquarters himself. The rain had stopped, but the humidity hung on like the limp vestiges of a bad dream. Fog haloed the street lamps in the parking lot but across Lake Shore Drive from the hospital, I could see the running lights of a boat traveling north near the shore. We walked, without speaking, to Kinsella's unmarked black Ford. He opened the passenger door for me and started around to the driver's side.

"What, no handcuffs?" I said.

"You feel a violent spell coming on, let me know and I'll shoot you, ok?"

I got into the car. It stank of the hand-rolled cigarettes he smoked and the windshield was gummy with their emissions.

"Gee, if you're going to be the good cop, I'd hate to see who you've picked to be the bad guy."

He grunted as he levered in behind the wheel. Then he turned in the seat and regarded me sourly.

"You listen to me, smartass. I saw that girl before they carted her off. She may not have been Rebecca of Sunnybrook Farm but you think she deserved to die that way?"

I shook my head.

"So shut the fuck up until I ask you a question."

He started the car and jammed the gear shift into drive. As he swung out of the parking lot, he cut off a Jeep. They flashed him the finger. Fortunately, he didn't shoot them.

Area Three detective headquarters sits over the 19th District station house on the site of the old Riverview amusement park at Belmont and Western. A branch of the Circuit Court is next door. I have fonder memories of the park. The Blue Streak and even the Roller Rink were a hell of a lot more thrilling than the brick police building with its radio tower in the backyard. I've been in the cop shop maybe seven or eight dozen times more than I ever got to Riverview, however. My dad hated taking me to places like that. Too many hooligans and grifters, the games were fixed, and the concessions didn't sell Jack Daniels.

A desk officer nodded to Kinsella as he led me through the back door and toward a flight of stairs. A sign announced that the Detective Division, Youth Division and Felony Review were all waiting for me on the second floor.

"Lorenberg from Felony Review is looking for you."

Kinsella made a jerking off motion with one hand and took the stairs to the second floor two at a time. I followed, keeping my head down, not surprised but also not heartened by the announcement. Felony Review is the section of the State's Attorneys office that takes the first look at evidence compiled in major criminal cases and makes the decision whether charges should be filed. But the felony review attorney is usually a kid just out of law school and a cop like Kinsella can run them like a lawn mower.

The Area Three offices always remind me of a TV newsroom, minus the sense of humor. A big, squared-off bullpen with desks hunched together as though mating, surrounded by the various boss' offices and interrogation rooms. The grunts of Property Crimes, the Auto Theft Task Force and Homicide all work together with the Youth cops and you'd never know who was who without a couple of ill-placed signs and the various cartoons posted on phones and elsewhere on their desks. After midnight on a Thursday, a handful of the desks were occupied, a kid in gangbanger pants and a net shirt slumped in one of the visitor chairs with one hand cuffed to its leg. The air conditioning tried without much success to keep the humidity at bay. Guys and gals with guns stuck in their belts and in shoulder holsters milled about, some typing, some talking. Two of them hovered over a lively looking Hispanic man who kept refusing to sit down and be questioned. Every time the female officer touched the guy's shoulder he shrugged it off, voice louder than before. The other detective, Buddha-belly straining his white shirt, had one hand unobtrusively behind his back. It rested on the heel end of a leather sap stuck inside his gun belt where he could easily reach it. He and his partner were the only people in the room paying attention to what the guy was doing.

"In here, McCarthy," Kinsella said.

The interrogation room was brick-walled on three sides and painted an institutional green. Large ring bolts were attached to the walls in two places to hold handcuffed suspects. One wall was dark glass and I knew it would be mirrored for observation from the room or office next door. I sat at a gray metal table that was anchored to the floor in the middle of the room. The front legs of my chair must have been cut shorter than the ones in the rear because I kept sliding forward. Great technique.

Kinsella went away, closing the door. When he came back, he towed along a skinny, long-necked guy with dark rimmed glasses whose pointed beard and high forehead gave his face a diamond shape. He might've been all of 25.

"Howard Lorenberg, Assistant State's Attorney," he said. His hand moved as though to shake mine or maybe, because he was a lawyer, slap a business card into it. Then he remembered who I was and where we were and reached for a chair instead. Kinsella leaned against the wall, between the ring bolts. Lorenberg took a piece of paper out of his inside jacket pocket and put it on the table with a pen next to it.

"I'm required to read you your rights and have you sign this waiver indicating you understand them," Lorenberg began. He breezed through Miranda, hoping I wouldn't notice he'd used the word "waiver." If I signed, I would not just be acknowledging I understood my rights but would be giving them up. I ignored his proffered pen.

"Am I under arrest or is this just some friendly questions?" I asked. My nose felt heavy, as though it were dragging my face downward.

"This is formal questioning, pursuant to…" Lorenberg began.

Kinsella over rode him.

"You kill her?"

"No."

"Then for now it's three guys sitting around shooting the shit."

But Lorenberg insisted on jumping in again. "Do you wish to speak to an attorney or have one present while we talk to you?"

There's something scary about having that said to you in a police interrogation room. A tremor ran through my stomach and I felt the shakes start. Almost like switching on a car's ignition. I stared at the little guy from Felony Review. Good thing I was the television news professional used to hiding my nervousness from people.

"I think I'll reserve the right to call a lawyer," I said, pleased my voice didn't crack. "Let's see where you go with your questions."

His mouth turned down and he made a note on the form.

"How long have you known Brooke Talmadge?" Kinsella asked.

I'd made up my mind to give them all of it. There was no reason not to. But something shifted as I sat there and I decided to start a little further into the story than the beginning.

"I didn't know her."

"You just chose her at random?" Lorenberg asked.

Kinsella's dour face showed a moment's irritation. "OK if I do this, counselor?"

Lorenberg turned red but shrugged.

"Let's try the Sesame Street version. What were you doing at her place?"

I told them about the hotel, the fight. I told them I'd followed her home to make sure no one else was waiting. Simple, right?

"She ask you to follow, or you just decide to do that on your own?"

I shrugged. "She looked like a girl in trouble."

"Oh, right. So you're who…Batman?" Kinsella asked dryly. Lorenberg snickered. One of the boys.

"Just trying to help."

"Didn't you used to have a hooker for a girlfriend?"

And where did he come across that nugget?

"What's that have to do with anything?"

"You hang out at there at the Marriott pretty regular? Chasing out of town puss?"

"I stopped in for a drink."

"OK, so you follow her home and she what? Invited you in for a nightcap 'cause she was so grateful?"

"I saw her in and up to her apartment. Watched her go inside…"

"Then you went back and kicked in her door."

"You have a little timing problem there, Detective. I kicked in the door after I heard her scream. After."

"So you say. I think the only reason she screamed is because you were battering her door down, intending to kick her ass. What'd she do, tell you 'no nookie' and slam it in your face?"

"Why don't you act like the pro you're supposed to be? Do a canvass of the neighbors. Every one of them will tell you the scream came before the racket I made trying to get through her door."

He leaned down and smiled at me. His breath was sour. "That's the funny thing. Everyone we've talked to so far says the scream came after."

"Even the guy who was yelling for her to knock it off while I was running down the hall?"

It's amazing what you remember when you need to. I hadn't thought about that until just now.

"What can I tell you, hotshot? Maybe your lawyer can scare him up for the trial." Kinsella went back to his place on the wall. Lorenberg looked toward the glass and rolled his eyes. I wondered who was watching and why.

"What d'you want from me, Charley?" I tried to sound reasonable. "You think I smacked myself with the phone after I did her? You find my prints on it, or hers for that matter, then you got me. I mean, sure, hers may be on the receiver but I'm thinking I got hit with the base of the thing, given the damage and all." I sat back, hands in my lap, legs straining to keep me from sliding off their damned rigged chair. Fury was causing my nose to throb.

"Come to think of it, you've seen her body. Has she got my blood all over her? Is there *any* of my blood on her? Cause, goddamn it, there's sure plenty of it all over me! How about prints on the knife or whatever, huh?"

It occurred to me I had no idea how Brooke Talmadge died but, hey, I was on a roll and probably would have just kept talking myself right into a cell. A knock at the door saved me. It opened and a gray-haired guy with a handkerchief in the breast pocket of his shiny blue suit said, "See you a minute, Charley?" He looked like an actor. Or a boss. Some of them dress to impress.

Kinsella took a deep breath, stared at the mirrored wall and went out. Lorenberg almost turned over his chair getting up to follow him. Prosecutors Handbook probably didn't cover What To Do When Left Alone With A Suspect. I glanced at my reflection, looked away.

I didn't really want to see myself just yet. The quick glimpse I'd had coming in was enough for awhile. I felt the strongest nicotine craving I'd had since my last year at Channel 14 when I gave up cigarettes. Must be all those movies where the guy stuck in the interrogation room lights up. The one thing I didn't dare do, even if I could have, was fall asleep. Even wet behind the ears detectives-in-training know that, when a perp they leave alone for awhile nods off, they probably have their man. Something about how the guilty ones relax when they know they don't have to keep hiding their sins.

They wouldn't arrest me.

I hadn't killed her so they couldn't prove I had. Could they? It's funny how naive we can be under such circumstances.

Who was I kidding? This was Chicago. They could do anything they wanted to do. If they backtracked just a little at the Sports Bar, they'd find out I came in asking about a gal named Brooke. And then where would I be?

I realized I needed a lawyer. Were I still a reporter at Channel 14 and not Frank's private gopher, that would be no problem. The station's attorney would probably be right out there waiting for me. As it was, maybe I could call Frank and lay it all in his lap. *That*, actually, seemed to be a better idea. Let him get a legal beagle down here for me.

The interrogation room door suddenly slammed open with just as much force as the one I'd kicked earlier in the evening. I snapped to my feet, half-expecting Kinsella, from the anger on his face, to start throwing punches. But he just stood in the doorway, glowering at me.

"This interview is concluded." He picked up the consent form I hadn't signed and tore it in half, then into quarters.

"Scram."

I wasn't about to question this gift horse. On noodle legs, I got up and walked toward the door. Kinsella didn't move. The heat of his anger seemed to shimmer in the air around him. I slid past him. Everyone in the squad room was turned to face us, or him, even the Hispanic man who had finally taken a seat. The guy in the blue suit looked like he'd swallowed someone else's spit.

Lorenberg stood near the stairs doing everything but wringing his hands. "See the desk sergeant on your way out. You need to sign..." I passed him and headed down, "...a release form."

No wonder cops don't have enough time to chase the bad guys. They really are drowning in paper. The form was already on the counter when I got there. A uniformed black woman with a cheerful disposition slipped a pen down next to it as I approached.

"Would it sound strange if I asked what the hell is going on around here?"

She laughed. "Just another night at the Fun House." When I had signed, she gathered up the paper with one hand and pointed with the other. "Now if you'll just step outside, I believe your limousine is waiting."

A black Crown Victoria, a bristle with antennae, waited just outside the front door, engine idling. When I saw the driver, I felt like I'd been punched. Then I wanted to run up and kiss the guy.

Vincent Seamans sat behind the wheel with a cigar clamped between his teeth. It was burning away, too, even though his doctor orders him to quit at least four or five times a year. I know this because Vinnie Seamans was my dad's partner for most of the time he worked as a detective.

Vinnie retired a few years ago, but not completely. Now he works for the Cook County State's Attorneys Office. It's not an unusual job for an ex-cop but I doubt there's a written job description anywhere that encompasses all the things Vinnie is and does.

"You look like you've been living in the back seat of your car," he said around the cigar.

"Always better looking than you," I shot back.

"Get in." Normally he's more than ready to keep the banter going but that's all he said until he'd put us up onto Western Avenue, headed north.

"Car still at the girl's place?" he asked.

I nodded. "Unless they towed it."

"Nope. They didn't do that yet."

I sank back into the seat. There were four two-way radios mounted in a console between us, all murmuring. Vinnie always listened to everything. I recognized the common city and county frequencies, knew he kept one radio tuned to the O'Hare Police detail ever since terrorism had become a pre-eminent fear of law enforcement, and I suspected the black box on lowest volume and with no alphanumeric display showing covered a full range of federal government channels.

After a moment I said, "Thanks for the bail out."

"I was in the neighborhood when the word came down they were cutting you loose. Figured I'd save you cab fare."

"Sure. What'd they do, put out a citywide broadcast?"

He grunted. "Something like that."

In his early sixties, Vinnie is six feet three inches tall, a slab of granite with a bowling ball on top. Megan once, giggling after four or five glasses of wine, told me he reminded her of the guy in the movies who hangs people out windows until they agree to pay off the money they owe his boss. I'm not so sure there wasn't a time in his life when he did some of that. Now though, he twists arms a little differently. Another friend in a position to know once told me Vinnie's never been on the county payroll, despite his title. State's Attorney F.T. "Jim" Quinn pays his salary out of his own pocket.

"So what made you slap the collar and leash on Kinsella?"

"The Old Man." Meaning Quinn.

"You want to be a bit more forthcoming about that? Or are you just so pissed you can't talk?"

He wrapped bratwurst-sized fingers around the cigar stump and flipped it into the street.

"I always hoped you'd smarten up some as you got older. Stop getting your ass into jams. You got fired from that TV station, I thought maybe you'd settled into a nice little routine. You sound good on the radio."

I waited. We'd been over this subject before, which is how I could tell his silence signaled anger. He's not any more fond of reporters than Kinsella and most cops I know. He likes me, however, and that's caused him to lean on me a little less when certain stories I've done caused grief for him or his boss.

"You stepped into it now. You have any idea who the girl's father is?"

"She never bothered to introduce herself."

"You're going to wish she had. Stacey DuMount was Brooke Talmadge. The only daughter and youngest child of R. Edwin Talmadge. That put it together for you?"

Click, click went the mental gears. Red Talmadge. An attorney and former state senator. Around since the heyday of Lady Jane Byrne when he was thought to be her most trusted informant in Springfield. Hadn't run for anything in years because he'd been too busy becoming a well-connected lobbyist, both Downstate and in Washington. His name surfaced occasionally, whenever the feds put a corruption case together. I also remembered him stepping up as a character witness for one of the judges nailed during Operation Greylord and hovering in the near background when his former law partner ran for Lieutenant Governor.

"Red Talmadge's daughter was a hooker?" Sometimes I have to state the obvious to myself to believe it.

"You're the one who was following her around town. You tell me."

Smooth would be the best way to describe Red Talmadge. That's why the idea his daughter was a prostitute seemed so unlikely. His firm represented major business interests, the Fortune 500 variety. He personally negotiated the kind of deals that often turned into headline-grabbing legislation. Big Tobacco was rumored to be beholden to him for work done well before the various state attorneys general started scoring hits against cigarettes. I tried to remember other stories I'd heard about the guy. The thing was, he no longer wore a public face. The key to his success lay in the fact he could fade into the trees. Having a hooker for a daughter, especially one with the talents I'd heard about, would have been a monumental liability.

If I'd had a headache before, it was now developing world-class proportions. I closed my eyes.

"Has it leaked?"

"Somebody always manages to drop a dime with you people. Why should this be any different? For sure, morning news shows will have her daddy's name."

"How about the juicy stuff?"

"Right now she's a suburban businessman's daughter killed in a brutal attack." He looked my way. "What *is* the rest, Reno?"

I wasn't about to spin the same story for Vinnie that I'd created for Kinsella. The Mobile Data Terminal which was part of the communications package between his car seats didn't have access to as much information about people and their secrets as he has in his head. Chances were good he already knew as much or more than I did. Even if he didn't, lying to my Uncle Vinnie had never been an option.

By the time I'd finished talking, he'd sucked a second cigar halfway to embers and we were sitting in the shadows across from Brooke's building. Two blue and white squads from the 24th District remained parked in front, along with a Ford Expedition I knew belonged to a skinny snake of a freelance TV cameraman. I watched him leaning in one of the police car windows as he chatted up its female occupant.

Vinnie tapped ash into the street. He'd listened without interruption, no doubt one of the reasons people tell him as much as they do. It's why I've confided in him ever since I was ten and ran away to his house one night when my dad was so blitzed he chased me out the back door, whipping the air inches from my head with his thick leather gun belt. I got away only because he tripped and fell as I vaulted the back fence. Vinnie took me home. He made me wait in his car while he went inside and checked to see Dad passed out on the couch. Then he guided me back inside and up to my room. Whatever passed between Vinnie and Dad after that kept my old man from ever raising a hand to me again. Didn't keep him off the booze, though.

"Why the hell you get with this Hanratty mope again, anyway?" he said after a long silence. "You figure him or that empty suit he works for have changed since they fired you?"

"How about I needed the money?"

He snorted. "Your daddy paid off that house about a month after you and your mama moved in. What's that been now, twenty-five years or so? And you don't work for free at that radio station."

"I don't collect both a fat paycheck and a fat city pension like some people I know."

He waved away my explanation as though it was so much smoke in his face. "You want that TV job back, don't you? That's the whole reason you're willing to do their scut work for them."

"Damn. You beat it out of me."

"You know something? You're a *damn* fine investigator, Reno. I didn't like some of the stuff you did on TV and I still don't. That lost drug evidence story got two friends of mine, friends of your dad, fired and brought up on charges. That was hard to take. Still is because you've never shown an ounce of regret. They were good men and they screwed up but they didn't deserve the public humiliation you caused them."

"Doesn't matter they sold out to a street gang?" I said. But his compliment made my nose throb and, surprisingly, my eyes burn.

"They were old men! One of 'em had a wife with cancer. You think he should've sat back and watched her just die?" He held up a hand again as I opened my mouth. "No. That's why I never brought this up before. We got different ways of doing things. No point going off on that right now. I just wish you hadn't gone over to the Dark Side. That TV stuff. You're good enough, you could have followed your dad. And wouldn't that have been something?"

He sucked the life out of his second stogie, watching it flare, then flung the butt into the street the way he had with the first. Neither of us spoke. The cameraman loaded himself back into his Expedition and drove off. Pretty soon the two police cars left, too.

"This's gonna be a heater case even without the whips and chains." He sighed. "That part of her life gets out, we'll have us a nice cluster fuck. Plus, the old man and Red Talmadge aren't exactly friends but close enough there's already been a phone call."

"Don't I remember your boss calling Talmadge six kinds of sonofabitch when he stood up for Judge Bledsoe in Greylord?"

"Sure he did. And back in Mayor Jane's time, Red handed out a lot of favors. Far as he's concerned, there's no statute of limitations on paybacks." Vinnie shrugged.

"So what you're saying is," I stopped. It was getting so any motion of my head started the knives again. "Talmadge is why you sprung me so fast?"

"He wants it to stay under the radar for as long as possible. That works for us, too. If we'd let Charley Kinsella keep after you, we'd a had not only a pretty little victim with a famous daddy but a half-ass celebrity suspect. Think your media brothers would cut you any slack? Kinsella was yanking your chain 'cause you wouldn't give him the whole story, not because there's any evidence. You were right about the blood. If she'd hit you with the phone first, and then you'd grabbed her, she'd have it all over her. Body's clean, so you're clean. Lucky you didn't fall on top of her."

So Vinnie had been the one watching the interview from behind the glass.

"And the phone?"

"Evidence Techs say no prints except hers, and you scored there too. Hers are only on the receiver. They figure whoever hit you was wearing gloves. He picked the whole thing up as a unit and swung it. Cracked the base, he hit you so hard. I hear the doc at Weiss tweezered some little pieces of it out of your face." He rubbed his face as though in sympathy.

"And yeah, there's a couple of neighbors heard her hollering and then you kicking in the door. Dicks also got a witness who says she saw someone going down the fire escape in back about the same time."

Nifty. I was off the hook. It was funny, though, how the feeling of guilt didn't just disappear at the news.

"How did she die?"

Vinnie must have heard the bad thing in my voice because he looked over at me before answering. "Looks like he suffocated her. ME's going to do the autopsy first thing in the morning but the dicks figure the mope grabbed her from behind, she tried to fight him off. Somewhere in all that, she was gone. Maybe it wasn't even meant to happen that way."

For some reason I chose right then to remember the fierce look she'd had on her face after she kicked Yevvie in the nuts. I thought about that for a moment, then a little longer. I felt sleep reaching out to me. I automatically shook my head to clear the cobwebs and then wished I hadn't.

"How you feeling, Reno?"

Even with my eyes closed I could tell he was still watching me.

"Oh, I'm just peachy. Never better," I said. "Who killed her?"

"Got to figure boyfriend first. But her wallet was gone. Looks like a laptop computer, too. Makes you wonder if it might have been just a random thing."

"A third-floor apartment in the middle of the night? And he hangs around just long enough for her to walk in on him?" I opened my eyes and met his gaze. "My ass it was random."

"Too early to know. District guys say they've had a few smash and grabs from the fire escape in that building. Yeah, mostly daylight stuff while people are at work but you don't know. Back door was standing open."

"She was running from somebody, Vinnie. Somebody connected enough to send a big mean bad guy after her. She called him Michael. If this Michael sent one where she hung out, don't you think he'd be smart enough to cover her apartment, too?"

"Dicks are going to follow up all that stuff. Kinsella's staying with it, even though he lost his star suspect."

He gave me the first grin I'd seen since he picked me up then touched me gently on the shoulder. "He might be an asshole but he clears his cases."

I thought about that, thought about what I wanted to say, realized there was no point in letting my intentions be known and said nothing. I reached for the door handle instead.

"Thanks for the ride. And the information."

The tone of his voice suddenly changed. He was back to being Uncle Vinnie again. "You sure you should be driving? Why don't you let me take you home? You can pick up your car tomorrow."

"If I let you do that, you're going to insist on staying and checking on me every half hour like they would have done in the hospital. I won't get any sleep cause you walk like a rhino, and I'll feel like shit in the morning and I'll be out of coffee and my last Mrs. Fields cookies 'cause you will have finished it all. I'm fine. My nose is broken but when was the last time I tried to drive with my nose? I'm fine."

I got out of the car and closed the door slowly, not out of a desire to be quiet but because I wanted to lean on it for a moment. I said through the open window, "Thanks again, Vinnie. And thank Quinn for me, too."

"Reno? One more thing?"

Oh shit, I thought. This is where he was going to order me to stay away from the investigation and I was going to have to lie to him for the first time and tell him I would.

Instead, he said, "Be sure and get back to the hospital in the morning. Call me tonight if you think you need to go sooner."

I waved and he pulled away. As I unlocked the door of my car, though, a wave of nausea caused me to take a deep breath. My nose burned. I fumbled out my keys and climbed in behind the wheel. I thought about how Lauren had warned me not to drive.

I felt better, though, with the windows down and fresh air blowing in. I tried to call Hanratty from the cell phone and got a machine with a message in his wife's voice. Tried again thinking he was letting it ring through. Gave up. It was 2:30 a.m., still an hour or so before Sunny would be awake. She'd slept though it all and wouldn't she be pissed? I didn't try to call her. I concentrated on my driving for the rest of the way home, checking the rear view mirror for signs that Vinnie was back there somewhere. I saw no black Crown Vics. Meant nothing. He'd been an artful shadow all my life.

Andy Nunez's voice was waiting on my machine when I got home. I'd forgotten about asking him to trace Brooke's pager number. He'd done so and had left the address to the Rogers Park apartment. Wonderful irony in there somewhere. I lay down on top of the covers without getting undressed and realized Vinnie hadn't asked a single question about anything I'd told him. Nothing to clarify who the boyfriend might have been. Nothing about whether I thought Lynn might know more about Brooke than she'd told me. Those would both have been standard Vinnie questions. No matter how much you gave him, he always wanted more. Information was his business. So why hadn't he wanted more from me?

CHAPTER 5

▼

To say I slept would be stretching the truth. A volley of thunder jolted me about four hours after I lay down and the raindrops rattling against the skylight in my bathroom drummed me out of bed. I'd managed a kind of painful stupor filled with frightened awakenings as images of the telephone slamming out of the darkness kept recycling. If I'd been a second or so sooner.... I stumbled for the bathroom like a sleepwalker, hands out to protect my nose.

A sickly raccoon face greeted me in the mirror. Both eyes wore shiners; my nose was misshapen and bulbous from the packing. Dried blood and mucous caked my mustache and beard. Probably matched the design that had drained onto the pillow. I rinsed a washcloth and dabbed carefully at the mess, then gave up and showered. By the time I was finished I was well-scrubbed but felt no cleaner.

While coffee perked, I retrieved the *Sun-Times* from my porch.

It didn't say much about Brooke Talmadge's death and made no reference to her family ties. That meant the night-side cop reporter hadn't tumbled to the connection and would get a nice ass chewing from his editor later this morning. I booted the computer and looked for a story online in the *Trib*. They update their web site edition more often than the *Times*. There, Brooke rated two paragraphs, but was sandwiched between the shotgun slaying of a gas station attendant and two torture murders that appeared gang-related.

TV at the top of the hour was no more informative but showed some nice video of the front of the apartment building. I switched to Channel 14, expecting to see myself being marched to the waiting cruiser but they didn't use the footage and didn't mention my name.

WGN finally broke the family connection at 8:30. Sneaky. No doubt they'd waited so the TV's couldn't lift the information for their own morning shows. I watched again just before nine and all four were hinting they'd have more on the story later. That meant they'd all been listening to WGN and all of them had people working the phones, but none of them had confirmed the information yet. I smiled. The news business is often like the childhood game of Simon Says, with Simon being the first media outlet to snag the facts. If one TV station has a "new" angle, pretty soon all the rest do, too. If it's a front page story in the morning paper, you can bet some version of it will headline the evening news. It may be updated with new facts but in the budget crunch economy, don't count on that.

Sunny chattered away in my place on the radio dial. Murder stories aren't a big priority on my station unless they have talk value for the hosts. Asa might have heard about my connection to the case but, crude as he is, he's not stupid. This one was a little too close to home to banter about on the air. As a rule, radio station general managers are more sensitive to scandal than a preacher in a small town.

I took two sips of coffee, poured the rest down the drain and washed out the cup. My face felt stuffed with rolled newspapers and ached like a bitch. I downed two Tylenols, considered, shook out four more and chugged them, too. I needed to call Frank, had another call I wanted to make, but I'd been through the broken nose routine before. Putting off having it set never made it feel better. I'd make the calls when I got home.

I clocked it as 9:15 when I buttoned up the house and set out for the hospital. It wasn't raining, but a soupy mixture of clouds and fog had drifted in from the lake. By the time I took Dempster to Sheridan Road and turned south, I couldn't see the water even though, in places, it was less than 15 yards from the street. The meteorologists call it Lake Effect. To me, it was like trying to drive inside a damp coat pocket. It was weather that perfectly fitted my mood.

I should have prevented Brooke's murder. I'd stepped in to help her once; I should have stepped in again, insisted she let me not only follow her home but precede her into her apartment.

I'd let her down, let myself down, hell, I'd even let Frank down.

I should have been there.

Why? I didn't know the broad, had never been formally introduced. She was a hooker and a vicious one at that if I could believe the people I'd interviewed. She was what we call in the business a target. Nothing more.

But I couldn't shake the memory of her aloneness in the bar full of people.

The expressions on her face after the jerk attacked her in the parking lot. Surprise, hurt, fear and a harsh joy when she took her shot at good ol' Yevvie.

She hadn't backed down from the fight. Something to be said for that.

I wondered what it had felt like for her. Had she relaxed when she opened the door to her apartment, thinking she was finally safe at home? Or had she seen her attacker the moment she stepped inside? I was betting he'd taken her by surprise and that she'd screamed first when he grabbed her. If she'd found someone there waiting, she would never have turned her back to him.

I reviewed what little I'd seen of the apartment. I'd been woozy and shaken but the images recorded nonetheless. The living room had been in disarray but my impression was that she was just a sloppy housekeeper, not that the place had been ransacked. Clothing spilled from an overnight bag on the floor near the bedroom door and a chair near where she'd fallen had more clothes tossed on and around it. The furniture included a ratty couch and nearly new coffee table. There was a table next to the couch with a broken lamp atop it, and a wastebasket that looked like it had been overturned in a struggle.

Pain, this time of the emotional variety, washed over me.

She'd fought again, for the second time that night. Kicking, trying to gain any advantage that would let her escape from the arms that held her, grappling with her assailant, eyes wide with fear. As wide as they'd been when I saw her after breaking down the door and tripping over her.

Goddamn it, I should have been first into that apartment.

The upstairs windows at Weiss Hospital glared at me through the same glop I'd driven through in getting there, ghostly and accusing. I parked and walked through a fine mist into the Emergency Room. No lovely Doc Goddard this time. A brusque young resident who looked as if he was running on even less sleep than I and who had a mustache so thick he seemed to have trouble speaking through it prepped me, shot me up and realigned the bone with a tool that looked like a small spatula. A tight strip of tape and I was finished. While he worked on me, we were treated to the screams of a kid in the next room.

The sun was trying to burn through the overcast when I got outside again. No mist or rain now and, if my nose was working properly, the air would have that lake smell to it that's one part water, one part fish and one part marine gas. The fog had lifted enough so that I could see multi-colored sails moving just offshore. I couldn't derive the same joy from that simple sight that I'd experienced yesterday but drove back to Evanston with the windows open.

There were two messages on my voice mail, one from Sunny, the other from our erstwhile program director. I listened to Rudy's first. It was a simple "call me as soon as you get in." Didn't take a genius to figure what he wanted to talk about. Sunny's was more explanatory.

"Reno, Rudy's going bonkers. Somebody told him you're a suspect in that murder up in Rogers Park. What the HELL is going on? Call me on the cell as soon as you get this and I'll fill you in."

I have no better friend than Sunny DeAngelis. She spent five years in the Marines, but could pass as a Victoria's Secret model. She's the unlikeliest private detective and bail-skip chaser I've ever seen. We met a couple of years ago while both of us were trying to track down the scumbag owner of a furnace repair company. I'd developed information that Karl Stokes' outfit was a fraud. An elderly couple nearly died after Stokes' "repair crew" charged them three thousand dollars for a junker furnace he called new. Coincidentally, Sunny was after Stokes as a bail jumper out of Colorado. The carbon monoxide leak from a Stokes-installed furnace had killed her grandmother. He'd been arrested, made bond, then skipped. Oh, what a wrong thing to do.

Given Sunny's background, I'd wanted to be the first to find the guy. I imagined rolling up second, only to find Sunny had done some irreparable damage to him that I'd have to report. I liked her even then.

She promised me that wouldn't happen and she'd been absolutely true to her word. She was with my crew when Stokes showed up to clean out his office in the middle of the night and we got great video of her slapping him in cuffs, most professionally.

She answered on the first ring of her cell-phone, knew it was me from her Caller-ID readout.

"I'm not believing what I'm hearing."

She has a slight Texas hill country accent that becomes more pronounced if she's agitated.

"That's good. Who are you hearing it from?"

"Dumb question. Who at your radio station would be the first to spread nasty gossip and innuendo?"

I sighed. "Asa. Did my name make it into the wire story?"

"Nope. The village drums of the sicko and perverse tribe he belongs to probably sounded. He whispered to Rudy and Rudy opened a new case of Pepto and started chugging. Are you okay? You're not in custody?"

"Didn't even have to post bail."

I filled her in on what had happened. When I finished, she didn't say anything for a couple of moments, prompting me to ask if we'd been disconnected.

"No," she said, stretching the word out. "I'm just waiting for you to tell me what comes next."

"Next?"

"Knock, knock. Is anybody home inside your brain? I know you, McCarthy. You aren't going to sit home watching this case on the news, are you?"

"Not exactly."

"So you're going to ask for my help, right?"

"This isn't like when we worked stories together," I began doubtfully. "Even for me to start nosing around Brooke's murder is borderline and I'm not the one who has a detective's license to protect. The cops…"

"Yeah, yeah. The cops hate it when us snoops play Rockford or Magnum on an active homicide case unless we're working for a lawyer. Then again…if you hired me to protect your good name…that sounds like a legitimate job to me."

"Protecting my name qualifies as legitimate?"

"Sure. You're a media celebrity, right? Big-time famous guy?"

I snorted.

"Whatever! You don't want anybody thinking you had any part in this, do you? It's perfectly logical for you to hire a private detective to protect your interests."

"Tell me that argument didn't just pop into your head."

"Buy lunch and we'll plot strategy," she said.

"OK, I'll call you when I finish talking to the senator."

"Whoa" she said quickly. "I was thinking maybe I'd do the running around for awhile. Rudy was sweating bullets this morning, lots of calls back and forth to New York. I think the plan is to suspend you until the rumors cool down. If you get too high profile nosing around and the police complain, you could be looking for another job."

Wouldn't that be a hoot, I thought. Trying to get back the job I lost, I lose another one. I ran a hand over my beard and looked out the window of my study. The lilacs were in full bloom and I wished I could smell them. They'd been my mom's favorite, planted the year we moved in. Two cardinals twitched their wings in the dripping faucet that constantly rippled the water in my backyard birdbath.

"I'm going to talk to Talmadge myself."

"How did I know that was coming? How about the cops? They'll be all over him."

"They probably got to him early this morning. If they're still with him, I'll back off. But I think he might want to talk to the guy who at least tried to help his daughter, don't you? And after all, I'm on the street partly because he leaned on the States Attorney. I want to thank him."

"Sure." She let the sarcasm steep a moment. "Is there anything I can do while I'm waiting for you to finish doing your stupid human tricks?"

"See if you can get Asa talking. He's the one who started me down this road. Maybe he has more connections we can use. If he thinks we're going to drag him into this by name, that may be the fastest way to finding Brooke's boyfriend."

"Oh, I can get him talking. It's getting him to say stuff that doesn't begin with," she raised her voice into a falsetto, "'You're hurting me.'"

When we hung up, I called Rudy. Our conversation was shorter but far less pleasant than talking to Sunny. He said the station's New York brass had decided it would be best if I took a vacation for the next couple of days to avoid besmirching the company's good name. They still had full confidence in me, didn't believe I could have had anything to do with Brooke's murder but, Rudy stressed, mud was already being flung and they wanted to minimize stickage.

"Bullshit. How did my name even get mentioned? Sunny says it wasn't on the wires. I know none of the other stations had it."

"You know I can't get into that with you, buddy. Shall we say, you're not the only one with good sources?" I imagined him sitting on the corner of his desk, puffed up with self-righteousness, winking at his secretary.

"Tell me something, Rudy. After I win my discrimination lawsuit, when I own the station, you think you'll be program director or emptying wastebaskets?"

My next call went to Frank Hanratty. His voice mail picked up and told me, in a voice that sounded like he was fighting a cold, he was taking the day off and if I left a message, he'd get back to me tomorrow. Come to think of it, he hadn't looked at the peak of health at lunch, either. I tried his home number, got voice mail there, too. What I wanted to tell him was best not recorded and anything less probably would leave his wife wondering what was going on. I called back to Channel 14 and left a quick message with my cell phone number.

A little research and two phone calls later I was on my way to put my head in the lion's mouth.

*   *   *   *

R. Edwin Talmadge lived in the Indian Hill area between Winnetka and Wilmette. Trees engulfed the Mustang as I rolled between brick gateposts that announced this was Woodley Road, and under a stone arch proclaiming it "Private—No Trespassing." If there were guard towers or snarling Dobermans they were hidden in the woods. The undergrowth gave way intermittently, however, and I could see large, professionally groomed yards that, often as not, included pools or tennis courts or sometimes both. It was a hideaway neighborhood where the homes were mostly pre-World War Two and the dominant theme ran to variations of Colonial, many of them with wings added that seemed to dwarf the original structures.

Talmadge's was three stories done in white brick with black shutters bordering the windows. A circular gravel drive led up to a white columned portico. Mine was the only car in the driveway, although there was undoubtedly another driveway and garage in back. I stepped out into the sunshine. Somewhere on a lawn nearby a mower purred, but the trees prevented me from seeing it. I wished I could smell the new mown grass. Then again, Talmadge probably wished his daughter could still breathe. I wondered if this was the house where she'd grown up. The property looked like a child's paradise. Plenty of trees with low slung branches for climbing and a brush and tree-filled border between the homes that would have been perfect for hide and seek and fort-making.

I grinned at myself. Next I'd be imagining the families from the TV shows of my childhood all having a picnic together in the grass.

I rang the bell and heard it echo inside. I felt the same flutter of nerves I used to get when approaching "gotcha" interviews. Those are the ones you used to see Mike Wallace do on "Sixty Minutes" where even the most distinguished interviewee invariably looked as though the camera caught him leaving a park washroom with a pre-pubescent boy in tow.

"Yes?" The voice came out of a white speaker I hadn't noticed mounted on the wall above the door. I looked and saw a tiny lens beside it.

"Reno McCarthy," I said. The speaker's tinny audio had disguised the person's gender."For Mr. Talmadge."

"Does he know you?"

I constructed the sentence as I spoke it. "No, but I was with his daughter briefly last night. I'd like to talk to him about that."

No response came back and for a couple of moments I wondered if a call was going out to the cops. Then one of the double front doors swung inward, opened by a large, square-shouldered guy in a short-sleeved polo shirt that hung outside khaki shorts. If he wasn't a body builder then someone had been spiking his breakfast cereal with steroids.

"You're a reporter," he said. "I listen to you do the news."

"I'm just here to offer my condolences."

"I'll pass that along." The man started to close the door.

"I watched her try to beat up a guy about your size. I thought her father might like to hear about it."

"It's OK, Teddy." Another voice came from the speaker over my head. "Bring Mr. McCarthy to the sunroom, please."

The guy named Teddy showed no more expression than he had when he opened the door but, as he moved to allow my entry, the polo shirt pulled tight and I saw the outline of a small automatic against his belly. He watched me notice.

He led me through a formal living room to a sun porch with a view of a lush backyard that seemed to stretch for an acre or two away from the house. Talmadge stepped from a paper-strewn game table where he'd apparently been working on a notebook computer and extended a hand. He was shorter than I remembered from the last time I'd seen him in Springfield, a compact and wiry man with black hair combed back and trimmed as perfectly as the lawn beyond the window screens. In dark slacks, suspenders and white shirt, but with no tie or jacket, he looked like I'd interrupted him getting a few things done before he grabbed Metra to the office, not as though he was mourning his daughter. Or maybe I should give the man a break. Could be he was waiting for friends to stop by to offer their sympathy. Maybe he'd shed all his tears in the middle of the night.

The guy with the gun slipped out of the room.

"Edwin Talmadge, Mr. McCarthy. May I call you Reno?"

He had a sincere handshake and the assured baritone of someone who's trained himself to meet people and make friends. Gesturing me to a rattan couch with comfortable cushions, he took a matching chair across from me. *Brooke wouldn't have liked this room*, I thought. I wasn't sure why.

"Would you like something to drink? Orange juice, perhaps?"

"I'm fine. I'm sorry for your loss. I apologize for intruding like this."

"Nonsense. A colleague briefed me about your efforts on Brooke's behalf and told me how abysmally the police treated you. I planned to reach out to you in the next few days. I appreciate what you tried to do for my daughter."

"I just happened to be where I could do some good. Not enough, I'm afraid."

"Don't denigrate yourself. From what the police tell me, you happened by as she was being mugged?"

If we'd been in court, the judge would have admonished him for leading his witness.

I don't like being led.

"It was a little more than a random mugging. She thought the man who attacked her had been sent by a guy named Michael. Would that be her boy-friend?"

"I'm sure I wouldn't know." His smile was tolerant. "I don't want to bore you with Talmadge family history, Reno, because I'm sure you have better things to do with your day. But I'll tell you this. Brooke was an exceptional child. Excelled in school, sports, social activities all the way through high school. Then some-thing...happened. I'm at a loss to know what it was." He pointed to a decaying tree stump about twenty feet from the house.

"That was a fine, strong oak until August last year. All of a sudden, I looked out one day and noticed the leaves had turned brown. It was a marvelous shade tree so I immediately called an arborist. She told us there was nothing we could do. It had rotted away on the inside. When they took it down, the arborist showed me handfuls of this awful, black fungus. Like string. It's called Armillaria. It's unique in that it can live for years in symbiosis with the tree. Then a little stress, perhaps just over watering of the grass nearby, and the Armillaria becomes an enemy and begins to destroy the roots."

He leaned forward.

"It was that way with Brooke during her senior year of high school. Severe depression, periods of fugue, extreme paranoia. Her doctor thought it might be the 'Graduation Anxiety' many seniors experience. But it persisted. I'm sure we didn't help by suggesting hospitalization after her first year of college. Unfortu-nately, by then she was of age and just chose to leave. Nothing we could do. She became a lost soul."

He appeared to be trying for a sad smile but it came out a grimace. "Perhaps that explains my lack of tears and the fact the neighbors aren't lining up to bring us casseroles. She turned 23 this year, Reno. I haven't seen her since she walked out of a family therapy session when she was 19."

"You've had no contact with your daughter in four years?"

"Oh, there's been contact, if that's what you call telephone calls in the middle of the night when she would scream at me. She accused me of many wrongs. If you believe her therapists, her mother and I were horrible parents. After all, ther-apists know fanning parental guilt is the best way to keep the checks coming. But to answer your question, Brooke hasn't come home or had a rational conversa-tion with me in four years."

"And you have no idea why?"

He spread his hands. "Who knows with young people?"

A lawn sprinkler activated with a muted "chchchch." Within seconds, others followed suit, their arcs of water crossing and recrossing like lives intertwining.

"My son, Alan, tells me Brooke refers to me in her e-mails as The Evil One. Not quite the image you hope your youngest child will have of you. But, her doctors say she's paranoid and delusional. What should I expect?" He stopped, glanced at his watch.

"I told you I wouldn't make you read our family's emotional scrapbook and here I am doing just that. You're a good listener."

If he went to pat my knee I was going to break his wrist.

"How's Mrs. Talmadge holding up?"

"I don't know." He smiled ruefully. "Elaine has also chosen not to live here any longer. I phoned to tell her what had happened, of course. As soon as the police contacted me. She hasn't returned my call. That's horribly dysfunctional, isn't it? Alan, of course, was devastated. Neither of us slept at all last night."

"Was that Alan...?" I glanced toward the door where the bodybuilder had departed.

"Oh no, that's Teddy Case. He does odd jobs for me, driver mostly. No, Alan's probably at the Club. Brooke was the tennis player. Alan's a fine golfer, thinks he has a good chance of turning pro, someday. He plays 18 at Glen Grove every chance he gets."

He glanced toward a line of trophies displayed, strangely enough, among the bottles above a wet bar. I realized I had not seen any family photographs since entering the house.

"Alan is older than Brooke?"

"By five years, yes." Another pointed look at his watch. "So, Reno, what really brings you here? It strikes me you're not the type of man to make a visit like this without something on your mind. Please tell me you're not going to use anything I've said in some kind of news story."

And he'd called his daughter paranoid.

"I wanted to thank you. I was told you interceded with the cops on my behalf," I said.

He looked surprised but only for an instant. "Inasmuch as I thought they were wrong to jump to conclusions, yes."

"I also wanted to you to know that Brooke handled the incident outside the hotel as well as anyone could. You would have been proud of her. For what it's worth, I don't think she was delusional, at least not last night. Someone sent that guy after her."

"You must be remarkably perceptive. Assessing all of that within a few moments and under pressure."

"I didn't have to be real perceptive to see she recognized the guy. He used her name. She knew someone named 'Michael' had sent him. He didn't deny it. In fact, he told her this Michael wanted to see her. It wasn't a random attack, sir."

He nodded, as though my words were the most fascinating thing he'd ever heard.

"Have you shared your impressions with the police?"

"Some of them."

"Then I'd say you've done all you can do. I appreciate it." He stood up. It was time to go.

He walked me back to the front door at the pace of a bouncer getting rid of the riff-raff, doing everything to hurry me along but grab my elbow. He paused in the foyer, under a chandelier that probably drew as much power as half my house.

"You know, I enjoyed your work on Channel 14. I was disappointed when you left."

"I was, too."

"Not your choice as I recall?"

"Not really."

"Have you had any thoughts of trying to get back into that line? You know, perhaps by breaking a big story, the way disenfranchised reporters always seem to do in the movies?"

I was tired of being patronized. "Not a bad idea. Thanks. Any suggestions where I might find a story like that?"

"Not around here," he chuckled, his grin suddenly a little less hearty. "Besides, now's probably not the time. I'm sure a lot of people in your field are out of work and jobs aren't plentiful. Best to stay where you are and ride it out. You won't lose anything that way."

I'm not real bright sometimes but that sounded remarkably like, "keep your nose out of my business or you'll be looking for a job under the Golden Arches."

I said, "Then again, didn't somebody write that you can't steal second while keeping your foot on first?"

This time he acted as though he hadn't heard me. Evidently, in his mind, I was already out the door. "Just some friendly advice from an old politician. Good luck to you, Reno. Thanks again for stopping by."

Out in the driveway, I could almost feel the impact of a shoe against my butt. I'm seldom speechless but Talmadge's threat had come out of nowhere and had been delivered in a manner so benign that most people might have passed it off as idle conversation. Not me. The best politicians don't tell you they're going to steal your socks. They just do it, and then try to sell them back to you before you realize your feet are cold.

First, the thug with a gun guarding his front door. Then, was that the quiet promise of retaliation if I stuck my nose any further into his daughter's murder? So much for my subtle approach at information gathering. But what was all that about?

Lobbyists get paid to make you see their point of view. As I drove out of his driveway, I guessed Talmadge had gotten his message across.

I thought I'd take a ride and see someone who might be able to explain why he felt the need to send such a message in the first place.

*   *   *   *

It was half-past noon and cruising toward 90 degrees when I followed a winding elm and oak-lined driveway past the split rail fences that framed a perfectly manicured golf course and parked near the pro shop of the Glen Grove Country Club. Unfolding into the distance, the grounds looked serene in the bright afternoon. A well-smacked drive would be visible for at least a couple of hundred yards against the dense backdrop of trees. Glen Grove bordered one of the largest forest preserves in the Chicago suburbs. The quiet was substantial. I could see a foursome working the nearest green, another waiting on the fringe. Sunlight glinted off the shank of a club as someone stroked a putt.

I wondered what they talked about out there, those bankers and lawyers and upright businessmen. Stocks and bonds? Limited Partnerships? The tushes on the women they'd let play through?

There were half a dozen golf carts lined up under an awning at the pro-shop's back door. Two teenaged caddies lounged there in folding chairs. No doubt waiting for the late-starters with one o'clock tee-times. Hip hop played as softly as I'd ever heard it from a radio on the table between the kids. Neither rose at my approach. Probably didn't see too many duffers dressed in jeans and a blazer. Or maybe it was the surgical tape across the bridge of my nose that clued them I wasn't a big tipper looking for someone to tote my bag full of Pings or Haig Ultras around the links.

"Alan Talmadge come back in yet?" I asked.

The shorter, pudgier one of the two snickered. "Oh yeah. Probably sinking in the water hazard at the 19th right about now."

"Excuse me?"

"Check the bar," his buddy translated without opening his eyes. He reached out a fist and the pudgy kid met it lightly with a fist of his own.

The clubhouse was a rambling Tudor affair complete with turrets. Instead of a drawbridge and moat, it had a simple awning-covered entrance which opened into a high-ceilinged lobby that should have been filled with serfs and ladies in waiting. Instead, an Asian woman in a black and white maid's uniform used a feather duster on a collection of trophies inside a glass cabinet.

I found the right place by instinct. Heavy wooden beams braced the ceiling and the tongue-in-groove paneling shone as though buffed. Behind the bar, the bottles could have been fine art on display, lighted with a muted spot. Alan Talmadge wasn't the room's sole occupant but he was the only one with a table to himself off in a corner. None of the other men finishing lunch or quietly playing cards paid any attention to him. I'd thought I'd have to ask someone to point him out but that wasn't necessary. I'd seen him about twelve hours ago getting out of a Beemer in the street in front of Brooke's apartment.

He gripped a tumbler in both hands at eye level. It could have been iced tea, but more likely was something from the whiskey family. He stared at it as though waiting for an image of his dead sister to appear. Watched by pictures of Arnie and Jack and Tiger and Payne, I walked across a hardwood floor scarred by a couple of generations of golf spikes and pulled out the chair opposite him.

There was no way to tell how long he'd been knocking back the cocktails. But when he looked beyond the glass to my face, I could see his eyes were red-rimmed, swollen and just beginning to slide out of focus. He had the tan and sun-dusted hair of someone who takes to the links for a couple of hours a day and looked more fit than what I'd guessed seeing him across the street last night.

"'the hell are you?" he asked in a voice that suggested he didn't really care.

"My name's Reno McCarthy," I said.

He processed that, blinked and said, "Wait. The TV guy?"

"Used to be."

He seemed not to hear me. "Sorry, man. I don't have any fucking comment, okay? Talk to my old man. He's the one who likes the cameras. Good for his image. I, on the other hand, have no image or don't care about it, or something. At least that's what he'll tell you. My old man, that is. Ol' Teflon Red."

It wasn't a long speech but it was louder than I would have liked. It also made him thirsty. He gulped from his glass and then lowered it slowly.

Conscious of heads turned our way, I said, "I just came from talking to your dad. He told me you might be able to answer some questions about your sister." More my interpretation than what he'd actually said but who was keeping track?

"You wanna ask *me* stuff?" He pointed at his chest with the hand that still held the drink. Some of the liquid spilled onto his Izod shirt. He reluctantly put the glass back on the table and wiped at himself. "I was just her older brother. What the hell do I know?"

There were probably a dozen more subtle openings I could have used but my patience with drunks doesn't stretch very far under the best circumstances. Seeing him headed toward an alcoholic haze in these rich surroundings while his sister spent her first few hours in oblivion ticked me off.

"You tell me. You can start with what you handed her on the street in front of her building last night."

The sun-pink complexion under his well-barbered features turned to an unhealthy gray.

"What are you talking about?"

"What was in that envelope anyway? The manila one about, oh, yea big?" I held my hands apart. "What'd you do, Alan? Give it to her then change your mind? Drive around to the fire escape, go up and choke her to get it back?"

"Oh Jesus!" He surged to his feet and plunged toward a door that led to the men's locker room. Heads swiveled. I got up wearily and slogged after him through a set of swinging doors, down a short plush-carpeted hallway, then into a large bathroom. He staggered into a stall and dropped to his knees. While he barfed club Scotch, I plucked a hand towel from a stack near one of the sinks and wetted it under an ornate spigot. A mirror ran the length of the room. I met my own gaze and looked away. Nobody joined us.

Pretty soon the john flushed and Alan emerged from the stall. He saw me and blinked. When I didn't disappear like the illusion he hoped I was, he joined me at the sink. I handed him the towel. If the radio station fired me, I could have a fine career as a rest room attendant.

"Christ," he said and swabbed his face. "I don't know why I drink that stuff."

"How long have you been at it?"

"You asking hours or years?" he grunted. "Since they opened the bar. Eleven I guess. Played a round first. Wouldn't want anyone thinking I just came here to drink." He sounded more sober than he had at the table. Shock will do that to you.

"Is there somewhere we can talk?"

"Yeah. Yeah, I suppose. Just let me get a clean shirt." He threw down the towel and we walked into the locker room.

A couple of the guys with deep tans and bellies acquired from too many board of directors' luncheons were lacing up golf shoes and razzing each other about a bet on the Cubs. I heard the figure "one thousand" mentioned prominently, and not as a batting average. Neither of them paid any attention to us and, by the time Alan finished exchanging his shirt for one of several hanging in his locker, they were gone. He led me to a small solarium at the far end of the room, away from the dressing area. A bay window with casements on either side offered a view of the 18th green. We sat at one of several heavy wooden tables, the lacquered tops of which were inlaid with backgammon boards. He leaned forward earnestly.

"First of all," he said. "I didn't kill her. So fuck you very much."

"Who did?"

"You think I haven't been wondering? There's always shit going on in that neighborhood, man. Rapes, robberies. Whatever. Musta been something like that, I guess." He wiped at a tear that leaked from his right eye and then he half turned to look out the window.

"And if it wasn't random?" I prompted.

"Oh come on. Brooke wasn't the easiest person to get along with but nobody she knew would kill her!"

I interrupted before it got any deeper. "She was a prostitute, Alan. She was into stuff that makes some other hookers blush. Whips, dog collars. I think you know what I'm talking about. Why don't you start there."

He turned back to me and rubbed his face roughly, as though trying to erase himself or what he knew about his sister.

"OK, yeah. She was a hooker. So what. It's not like she hurt anybody…anybody who didn't ask for it anyway."

"And?"

"She…she was always sort of that way. Out there sexually. Ever since, I don't know, probably high school."

"How do you mean 'out there?' She was hooking then, too?"

"In high school? No way. But she was always after to me to fix her up with guys I knew at Northwestern. Or she'd tell me she was on campus for some party and met some professor and and ended up making it with him. Older guys really turned her on. She was always getting them to do stuff for her. Buy her drinks. Take her places. She liked the professors because they could teach her things and not just in bed. Not the teachers in high school, just professors or even guys she'd meet in bars. A couple times she just took off for the weekend, nobody would know where she'd gone. Later she'd tell me it was Lake Geneva, sometimes Vegas. Once she said she went to Hilton Head with this guy on his company jet."

"How did your parents react to that?"

He shrugged. "In order to react, you have to care. Mom was always doing her Realtor thing. When I was in high school she was just getting her license so sometimes she'd be around when I'd come home in the afternoon, sometimes not. It was worse for Brooke 'cause Mom's business took off and she'd have showings at night and on the weekends. We'd tell her about something we were doing in school, she'd be like 'have fun, be careful, don't get hurt.' That was her standard response, like a mantra almost. She was there but we could probably have stabbed the maid and left her in the living room and good ol' Mom would have stepped around her until she started to stink. Unless it was on bridge night. Bridge night, shit. House better be spotless and the bar better be full."

He lowered his voice to a whisper. "She drinks, you know. Big surprise, there."

"How did your dad and Brooke get along?"

"They didn't. You're not thinking he did her, are you? That'd be a trip and a half if he did. Think I'd inherit if he went to prison?" He said it with a joking lilt but I heard an edge there, too.

"You think it's possible he had something to do with her death?"

"Nah. Now if *he* was the one dead, I might say they should be talking to her but not the other way around. See, you gotta understand something Mr. McCarthy. Teflon Red pretty much always ignored his family unless he needed us for something. Yeah, he has all these cute and cuddly pictures on the desk in his office and, yeah, he used to send out Christmas cards every year, all of us on vacation or skiing or something. When he'd have campaign donors or clients over to dinner or whatever, there we'd be, playing in the other room, happy as two little kids could be. Then you know what happened? We grew up! We started asking questions and wondering why he was never around. We wanted to hang with our daddy but he never had the time. And when he was around, there was nothing we did that was good enough. I gotta say, he only really yelled at me a couple of times. He was all over Brooke, though. Like it was his special plan to make her feel worthless from about the time she grew tits. Now aren't you glad you asked?"

"He mentioned something happened her senior year."

Alan ducked his forehead and started massaging his temples. His voice rose a bit.

"Man, why are you asking so many questions? I'm tired of reliving this shit. Let's get off the topic of dear old dad, you mind?"

"Then try this. Who's Michael?"

I wasn't sure he was going to answer but he finally lifted his eyes and met mine.

"You know about him?"

"Not enough."

"I don't…I don't really know much, either. Brooke told me she had this boyfriend, he was taking care of her. It was like the first time I can remember her being happy, you know? That's who it was, a guy named Michael. If she ever said his last name, I don't remember."

"How long ago was this?"

"Maybe…a year?" He twisted in his seat, looking longingly back toward the bar. Or maybe just his locker where I'd seen he had a fifth of Cutty Sark stashed.

"I need a drink," he said.

I didn't want him climbing back in the bottle just yet.

"Where's he live?"

"I don' know. Someplace in the city. Fancy."

"He's older than her?"

"I told you. They all were." He gestured toward a wall phone on my side of the table. "You mind punching 12 and asking Henry to bring me a Cutty and soda? Tell him make it a double."

"You can call him yourself in a minute. Everything peachy between Brooke and Michael lately?"

"No. She bitched there was something he had her do that she didn't like. She wouldn't say what it was. It just got her really worked up." He shrugged. "I don't know what it was but she was really upset."

"Was Michael her pimp, too?"

His eyes darkened and he shook his head vehemently. "No. Boyfriend. She was in love. That's why she was so pissed he had her do whatever it was."

I sat back and regarded him. He stank of booze in the way only a serious drinker can, when it leaches from the pores and becomes a vile, yeasty body odor. I lived with that smell for a time. Until my father moved out.

"What was in the envelope you handed her on the street last night?" I asked.

"Man…" He shook his head then bent forward again and rubbed his eyes with the heels of both palms. If I didn't let him go pretty soon he was either going to wet his pants or drop into the D.T.'s or both.

"Focus on this, Alan. I sort of forgot to tell the cops I saw you there. You be up front with me, maybe I keep forgetting. You fuck with me, and my memory improves considerably."

Holding up a hand he said "I know this guy, ok? He's an ID supplier. Mostly he makes fake driver's licenses to get kids into bars, that kind of stuff." He paused, took a breath. "Brooke…she wanted out of her relationship with Michael. I mean she *really* wanted out. Like she wanted to split town, go to Seattle, start over again, get her head straight. I got her some ID's from my friend. That's what was in the envelope. Fake ID's."

"You're saying Michael frightened her enough to make her leave town under a phony name? Who is this guy?"

"I told you, I don't know! That's the truth. But she wasn't really…I wouldn't say she was scared. More pissed off. You didn't know Brooke. Even when she was little, she'd get really angry, really over the top. That's how she was about this. And when she got angry, she was unstoppable, man. She'd get an idea in her head, somebody was fucking with her or whatever and she'd break windows or smash eggs on their car. This time she wanted to leave town."

"Your father know about this?"

"Teflon Red? The guy everything slides off of?" he snorted. "I told him. He acted like he already knew and it was no big deal. 'She chose her path', he told me. That was it."

"How did he find out if you hadn't told him?"

"How does he find out anything about anybody? You're a reporter, right? Don't tell me you don't know about the great Red Talmadge! He uses his influence and pretty soon he gets what he needs or somebody gets screwed."

He was starting to squirm in his seat like a little kid and I knew the draw of the alcohol was strong. He wouldn't last much longer.

"Think her friend Michael had her killed?" I asked.

He looked startled. "Why would he? The way she talked, he wanted her back, not dead. I mean, I didn't know all that much about what was up between them, but, no, I don't think he was trying to kill her. Control her, yeah. Just like good 'ol dad used to. That probably pissed her off big time."

"Can you think of anyone else who might know what she's been up to lately? What might have gotten her killed?"

"It's not like she had a lot of friends besides me." He stopped and looked out the window at a couple of men approaching the green. "But maybe Sela Grauman. They lived together that year she tried college. Brooke would talk about her sometimes and say they were getting together. I think she lives with her parents in Kenilworth."

I rose from the table and could see the relief as he glanced up at me. I expected him to bolt for the bar but he didn't move. I thanked him for his help. I sensed there was more he could tell me but saw no way to push him any further.

"I would have done more for her," he said, his voice growing hoarse. "If I'd known what was going to happen, I could have stayed with her."

He swiveled his chair to look out the window again. I stood there for a moment, following his gaze. One of the men was using a wedge to try and get out of the sloping trap next to the green. The first time he swung, a spray of sand fanned out around him but no ball popped up. The second time, there came the ball but it dropped shy of the trap's lip and rolled a foot back toward him. The duffer looked like he wanted to bend his club around someone's throat. I turned to leave. I knew just as well as he did how it felt to screw up. I didn't want to see if the third time would be his charm.

$$\ast \qquad \ast \qquad \ast \qquad \ast$$

I called Sunny and suggested we meet in Glenview for lunch. I was within a couple of miles of Frank's house and since I was in such a happy mood from interviewing Alan Talmadge, I figured I should seek out my former employer and brief him about my adventures. It wouldn't be the report he'd been hoping to get, but he'd paid for it and deserved to be told my version of the story. I also owed him one for sitting on the video Marisa and her cameraman had of me being escorted out of Brooke's apartment building.

I didn't call in advance. He'd either see me or he wouldn't.

A little more than 24 hours ago, Brooke had been a candidate for a more or less simple background check. Now she was a dead hooker with a boyfriend who'd had muscle chasing after her and a politically-connected daddy who didn't want me looking into her murder. I wished I was back in the business of news-gathering. It's an arm's length process. You may dig up dirt on folks but you don't have to wallow in it. If you're lucky you don't even get too messy. You verify facts and double check them. You arrange them in suitable fashion so as to be understood by someone with…what did a long ago J-school prof tell me about TV's usual audience? A 10th grade education level? Then you add a few grim pictures and let people on the other side of the screen react as they will. After all, you're just telling the story. You aren't a part of it.

That's what I craved here. Distance.

No such luck. I was going to live with this one for awhile. The thought brought back the throb in my nose with a vengeance.

*   *   *   *

i had been to Frank Hanratty's home only once before. The occasion had been a retirement party for a charming old guy who had been Channel 14's weatherman since the end of the Civil War. The three-story Georgian was set at the end of a shaded lane, on a lot that sported two huge willows in the front and a spacious lawn with a pool in the back.

As I walked up the brick path from the driveway to the front door, a woman's shouts reached me through an open window on the second floor. It must have been my day to become a part of other people's family troubles.

"You sanctimonious bastard! Why should I believe anything you say?" Elise Bascomb Hanratty at full volume. Oh, this was just dandy.

There was a pause during which I strained to hear the response. Go for it, Frank, I mentally urged. Elise had taken swipes at him within range of my hearing several times before but he'd always tried to grin it away. It wasn't like him to duck a fight and I'd been mightily embarrassed for him. As a recipient of his bellowed fury in the newsroom on many occasions, I knew how withering his verbal skills could be. I wanted to hear him fire off a round now but that wasn't going to happen. Elise let loose with another volley, instead.

"Yeah, well, you better think about what your priorities are, buster, because I'm tired of explaining to our friends why I'm always alone at their parties. Why you're always in that goddamn newsroom and not with your wife…"

Her voice faded and I assumed she had walked away from the window, if not from the fight. I waited an appropriate few minutes and pressed the doorbell.

Frank wore chino slacks and a long-sleeved white shirt, sweat staining the armpits. The look on his face probably wasn't far from what you'd see on a Kodiak bear interrupted while feeding. He didn't appear to be any more or less sick than he had yesterday.

"It's about fucking time," he growled.

"Well hi, Frank. Thanks for inviting me in out of the heat."

Without another word he turned and went back inside. I followed him into a book and paper-cluttered study I had only glimpsed in passing on my prior visit. I imagined the lady of the house hadn't wanted us to see the only cluttered spot in what, otherwise, was been a Laura Ashley/Martha Stewart pristine home.

He closed the door behind us.

"A simple trace job and you wind up accused of murder."

I liked his smooth transition from domestic argument to berating the employee.

"Questioned in relation to," I corrected. "Not accused of. Which is why you told Marisa not to use the video from last night. So don't start with me."

He sank into a Morgan chair and gestured me to the leather couch on the side wall. A locked gun cabinet featured two Browning shotguns, a Remington and two automatic pistols, one of them a Glock and the other a Beretta. I remembered using the Remington 1100 several times when we shot trap together at a gun club up in Kenosha County. There were pictures and plaques in here, too, although not as many as I remembered from his office at the station. He seemed to study the ones that showed a young Frank Hanratty, the college athlete. In front of me was the older, tired version.

"Would it have been too much to ask for you to call me afterwards? Clue me to what had gone down?"

"I tried. No answer."

"You didn't try hard enough. I was sitting in *that* chair behind *that* desk."

His voice was cold enough I could have chopped it and sold slivers to the golfers I'd been watching in the hot sun. Even so, he had a line of sweat at his brow.

"I got called into Chazz's office this morning. Your name came up. He tells me Red Talmadge is an acquaintance of his. A friend even. He thought it was some coincidence that the cops found you in the dead girl's apartment. He wanted to know if you being there had anything to do with the investigation he'd suggested we might start on the escort services. You and I both know he's a rat bastard, but he's not stupid. He remembers how I stood up for you back when. He knows what I think of you."

"Wait a minute. You're telling me that Brooke called Chazz and dangled her escort service story in front of him, knowing he was her daddy's buddy? Something off about that, don't you think? She must not have been too concerned about daddy finding out."

If possible, Frank's face reddened even more. "Reno? I flat don't give a holy rat fuck about that now. Chazz said he never met her, never talked to her. Hell, he didn't even know Talmadge had a daughter. I don't care. It doesn't matter."

He sounded bitter and scared and furious, all at the same time. The furious I recognized right away. It had been common when I'd worked for him, the fuel that kept him chugging after he got off the booze. The bitterness and fear were something else again. I wondered what had passed between Owner and News Director, father-in-law and son-in-law, in that big sunny office atop the Channel

14 building with its priceless view of the lake. I'd been canned while staring out at that view. Obviously, Frank had been given an up-close look at his own professional mortality in the same spot.

He took a pipe cleaner from his shirt pocket. "I thought he was going to have a coronary. Chazz. I've never seen him that pissed."

He pretzeled the pipe cleaner and threw it at the wastebasket alongside his desk. It missed. He wiped a hand over his mouth.

"So I lied and told him I had no idea what you were doing. Because you know what would have happened if I admitted I brought you aboard without getting his permission? I'd be toast. Out in the street. Fired, blacklisted, probably told I had an hour to get outta Dodge. And that could still happen." Hence the sweat and the shaking hands. He continued.

"Talmadge told Chazz the story you gave the cops. I owe you one for that, buddy boy. Now, for my sake, you gotta stick to it. Chazz, Talmadge, they can't ever know. Whatever's left of my career is in your hands. It's sounds melodramatic but it's just that fucking simple."

"There's no benefit for me in taking back what I told the cops," I said.

"How about the people you talked to? The ones who led you to her?"

"No reason they'd come forward. If anything, they'll burrow a little deeper."

His reaction was like watching a fist unclench, even though he didn't say anything. We sat together like that for probably five minutes. The clock on his desk ticked. He took a few deep breaths that finished as sighs. I imagined I could hear his blood pressure dropping. There were still thicker pouches under his eyes than I remembered, though, and deeper lines indented around his mouth. Pounded on by both his boss/father-in-law and then his wife within hours of each other. I bet he regretted taking the day off.

"So what are you going to do?" he asked. "I guess, more importantly, what's your station going to do?"

I hadn't told anyone but Sunny that I planned to keep nosing around and I saw no reason to trip Frank's apoplexy again by getting into it with him. He'd just warn me off and I'd just ignore him. Like old times.

So I said I was going to keep my head down, sit out my suspension then go back to work. I'm not sure he believed me but when he walked me to the door he shook my hand and told me he was sorry he'd gotten me involved. He must've been. He hadn't even tried to light his pipe in my presence.

Maybe my broken nose had him feeling sorry for me.

CHAPTER 6

▼

McGinley's is a bar that serves burgers and sandwiches along the Metra tracks in downtown Glenview. Mostly it's a family joint, unless you're there late on a Friday or Saturday night. Then it turns into a meat market for hip, upscale singles from the North Shore. It has wooden floors and wooden tables and best of all wooden booths toward the back which afford some privacy. I wasn't too worried that anyone might tune in to my conversation with Sunny. The couple behind us was having an intense discussion about how he might convince his wife he needed to go alone (without wifey anyway) on a business trip to Florida and how his companion might escape her boyfriend and job as a health club trainer for the requisite length of time. In front of us, the hearing-impaired owner was comfortably settled with a beer, a bratwurst and his bills.

I often tell my friend Sunny that she looks like a taller version of the actress Holly Hunter. She tells me I'm nuts. She can be an imposing sight. When she wants to down scale, however, she could blend with a caravan of soccer moms and no one would be any the wiser. She had her hair pulled back and wore a Cubs hat and a light jacket over a short-sleeved shirt and jeans. The jacket concealed the 9mm Sig-Sauer that rode in a high-rise holster on her right hip. It isn't for dramatic effect. Sunny doesn't have to impress anyone. As a bail agent, she chases down serious bad guys and puts them in jail. She has a state license to carry a firearm as a private detective and she is seldom far from either the Sig or an illegally cut-down shotgun with side-by-side barrels. I hope I never see her use either, but the shotgun would be the worst. At nine feet, the shot pattern is the size of both my fists held together.

Jobs, she doesn't have a problem getting. Dates, well, that's not a subject she and I discuss much. I know she won't date cops and a lot of other guys just can't get past the nine millimeter. Wimps.

She smiled as I slid into the booth opposite her.

"Is that your nose or are you wearing a tomato on your lip?" she asked.

"Very funny, Groucho. See how you like sleeping flat on your back."

She looked down at her chest. "We've been doing that since we were 12, haven't we boys?"

"I love it when you talk dirty," I said. "But when you're finished communing with the Grand Tetons, could we do a little business?"

"Only if I get to tell my story first."

"By all means. More onion rings for me that way." I picked one out of the basket she'd ordered and sat back in the booth.

"The guy you nearly neutered in the Marriott parking lot is named Yevgeny Olokoff. Here's a surprise. He's Russian and his driver's license says he lives in Buffalo Grove. He also was carrying a big automatic pistol, a Desert Eagle. He had it in a shoulder holster and landing on it may have broken one of his ribs. He was in pretty bad shape when he drove off."

"I know you want to tell me how you found all that out," I said and took another onion ring.

She cocked her head. "Why?"

"You're a show off."

"Ha. You're right about that, my bulbous-nosed friend. There's no back I'd rather pat than my own. I took a ride out to the hotel and, after a minimum of questioning, I found and bribed the security guard who discovered your Olokov friend trying to get back into his Toyota."

"The security guard didn't try to get him to wait for an ambulance if he looked all that bad?"

"Ohhhh yes. Told him it was hotel policy, even. That's when the Mad Russian put the Desert Eagle to his forehead and told him he was way underpaid. The man says he reads all the gun magazines and he recognized it was an Eagle right away. He decided it best not to push 'hotel policy' on the guy."

".50 caliber, right?"

"Sure enough."

"So the guard still has the guts to ask to see some ID? Or had he done that already?"

"No, he found the guy's wallet on the ground and gave it back. I guess he snooped a little first."

"Enough to get an address."

"Duh! I only use the finest informants. The only problem is that Yevgeny apparently lives in the parking lot between the clubhouse of the Buffalo Grove public golf course and the village police headquarters."

"No! He lied to the Secretary of State?"

"I think the village fathers would have noticed a lean-to, particularly there, don't you?"

"One would hope."

"But," she said, pausing long enough to liberate three onion rings and put them on her plate, "There's an interesting little web site called AutoTrac where all sorts of useful information can be had just for the asking. You enter the name and it shows you what vehicles are registered."

"He couldn't be that dumb," I said.

"Apparently he is. He probably figured the state would just forget the first address he gave when he re-registered for this year."

"Maybe that's how they do it in Russia."

"Could be. But you haven't asked me where he used to live."

"You know, when you're being a tease your lower lip sort of pouts out?"

"Ever since I was a kid. You never noticed before?"

"So where did Yevgeny used to live?"

She grinned. "No place special but just the fact I found a prior address is pretty impressive, don't you think?"

"Are you like this when you find a bail-skip, too? Make the bondsman grow a few more gray hairs while you tell the story?"

"No, they're all a bunch of grumps. You, on the other hand, appreciate the art of suspense. And since you aren't paying me as much as they do, it's only right I get to have my fun."

She finally parted with an address in the Edgewater neighborhood, just off Broadway.

"It's a weird sort of place," she said. "They have a tiny parking lot jammed in right behind and partially under the building. But you know what's parked back there?"

"A fleet of Oscar Meyer Weinermobiles?"

"Cabs! There are regular cars, too, but mostly cabs. Those awful off-green ones from that Old World Transportation Company. And most of the names on the tenant list out front are Russian, or at least Eastern European. It's like a cab driver dorm."

I thought about the guy I'd seen and then tried to envision him driving a cab. Maybe. He sure wouldn't have many fares run out on him.

"Did you go in?"

"I couldn't think of any plausible reason for being there, so no. There's a manager's office on the first floor but what was I going to do, tell them I wanted to rent but I'd forgotten my cab?"

She took two more onion rings and I took two more and then our burgers came. She told me what she'd gotten from Asa and it was essentially useless. He'd been more defensive with her than he had with me about the women he knew and their manner of employment. He'd also been very pissy about the fact I'd told Sunny about his other life.

"As if I didn't already know he'd have to pay his dates! God, what an arrogant ass he is. I got to make the point that anything said about you that was traceable back to him would make me very unhappy. That was fun. To see his mouth open and close like a fish. Me just a bitty girl and him with those big muscles. And I scare him."

"But your heart is pure," I said.

"If not my mind. So tell me about Talmadge."

I gave her a synopsis, emphasizing the threat, then told her what Hanratty had said about Talmadge being good buddies with Chazz Bascomb. And Hanratty's fear that Bascomb would find out he'd hired me.

"And they talk about six degrees of separation. This is more like two. But help me with this." She reached for the last onion ring, swatting at my hand when I moved to intercept. "Why doesn't Talmadge like the boyfriend-as-killer angle? What's worse about that than the random deal?"

"Suggests complicity. She interrupts a burglary in progress, that's a passive thing. Not her fault. Hanging out with a guy who kills her means, somewhere along the line, she made a bad choice."

"Oh come on, Reno! Every third parent out there has kids making bad choices about boyfriends or girlfriends. Politicians may be rancid little people but they aren't naive."

"Exactly. So it's that specific boyfriend Talmadge doesn't want anyone finding out about."

"Because *that* boyfriend has a leg breaker to send after little girls who run away from him. Even better, maybe Talmadge knows why this Michael character has someone like Yevgeny on his payroll."

"You've got to wonder. But here's another thing. Talmadge is a lobbyist. Why does he need a bodyguard?"

"Michael threatened him, too?" she suggested. "I mean if he's such a heavy hitter and all."

"It would be interesting to see if the two have any connections, wouldn't it? Other than through Brooke. Or maybe because of her."

She nodded, making a note on her napkin. "It shouldn't be hard to run a background on friend Talmadge. He's high-priced and well-known. Little tougher on the Michael guy when you don't have a last name."

I told her I was working on that.

*   *   *   *

When I was a kid, my mom was an assistant professor of English at Northwestern and we occasionally went to the Union Church in Kenilworth with some of her faculty friends. Back then, the village had real elms lining its parkways, branches intertwining above the streets and creating leafy corridors through the wealthy landscape. Disease killed them off but I read somewhere that they've been replaced by a Japanese hybrid. It has the same vase-shaped form of its American cousin but it's a tougher variety of tree now and resistant to the vagaries of Dutch Elm. Most of them haven't been around long enough for their branches to embrace but they've gotten a good start.

I came up over the Metra commuter tracks from Green Bay Road, rounded the fountain and continued east on Kenilworth Avenue past the elm sentries. In no hurry, I paced a couple of kids on bikes pedaling toward the beach, towels slung over their handlebars. Kenilworth used to be regarded as the wealthiest suburb in the nation. The dot com folks and others built some stiff competition, however, and while Kenilworth has now fallen from the top ten, it's one that retains a real sense of neighborhood. With only one or two exceptions, the million dollar-plus homes are all visible from the curbs and cluster several to a block, even those with backyards overlooking the lake.

The house where Sela Grauman lived with her parents stood on the lake side of Sheridan Road a couple of blocks south of the Kenilworth beach. Ivied trellises on brick gave it English country-manor dignity. A black Jaguar convertible sat along the circle drive, poised to depart. I parked the Mustang behind it as the front door of the house opened and a young woman hurried out. She had the presence, grooming and easy stride you see a lot of on the North Shore. Khaki shorts showed off long, tanned legs and a pink Lauren shirt did the same for her slender throat. Straight shoulder-length hair was bunched and tied off in back and she wore a pair of aviator sunglasses I could have used to watch myself shave.

"Ms. Grauman?" I said.

"My parents don't allow salesmen on the property." She reached for the Jag's door handle.

"I'm not a salesman. My name's Reno McCarthy. I'd like to talk to you about Brooke Talmadge."

She snapped her head around and brought one hand up to her throat. "I'm sorry. I have a doctor's appointment."

She opened the Jag's door and started to get in but good reporters learn early how to snap questions at a target in motion.

"Her brother called you her best friend. You want to help find who killed her?"

"And who exactly are you? You're some reporter, right?" Snide. I bet she wasn't a journalism major.

"I was the last guy to see her alive."

"How unpleasant for you."

"Did Michael order her killed or did he do it himself?"

She put her key in the ignition. "How on earth would I know that?"

"You were her best friend." I repeated. Sometimes you have to take a leap of faith. I remembered seeing Brooke on the phone as I followed her on the Kennedy. "She called you on the way home from the hotel last night. She told you about being attacked. I'm betting you haven't volunteered that to the cops, have you?"

"I...really don't have anything to tell the police."

"You were one of the last people she talked to. You might have more information than you think."

"I think I would know what she told me. It wasn't anything important."

"Look, Ms. Grauman, I'm not reporting this story. I'm looking into Brooke's death on my own time, for my own reasons. I need your help."

"You said you were the last person to see her alive. Maybe *you* should talk to the police."

"I followed her into her building and then I left. I have to live with that. I left and someone killed her."

She finally looked up at me. "What were you doing following her? Are you some kind of kink or something?"

In some ways, she was as feisty as her friend. I gave her the version I spun for Kinsella then added, "The cops want to believe she surprised a burglar. Her father's going along, or maybe even encouraging that point of view. Why do you figure he's doing that?"

"Because he's a son of a bitch?"

"So you want her killer to get a free pass because Talmadge is playing some political game?"

"What do you want me to do?" she snapped. For the first time I saw a scared college kid instead of a poised, almost-career woman. "Who's going to listen to me? I can't testify against anyone. My parents would disown me if I even got my name in the paper. Excuse me. My parents' *good name*." She used her fingers to make quotation marks in the air.

"Do you see any cops or lawyers here? Is anybody asking you to go to court? It's just me. I listen very well."

Her shoulders slumped and she sat there saying nothing and shaking her head slowly.

"There's nothing…"

"Tell me about Michael." I gentled down my voice. "How did Brooke meet him?"

She took a deep breath and pushed the words out with her exhalation.

"She told me he saw her in one of her videos and arranged to meet her. I…I think she was lying. She wanted people to think those videos were a really big deal but…you know about them, right? Even in high school she thought that would be a sweet way to make money. The year we roomed together in college? She found this guy." She shuddered.

"She said he was this greasy little man but that he helped her make a couple of videos. Then I'm supposed to believe Michael saw her in one and, like, went after her, swept her off her feet. I think he was buying the company or something. The whole thing sounded lame to me but…" She shrugged. "I told her I believed her."

"What do you think really happened?"

"I don't know. Maybe she met him while she was doing her escort thing. He sort of fit the pattern, you know? Older, wealthy. That was what turned her on."

A BMW convertible playing rap with heavy base slid by on Sheridan and the driver honked. Sela waved absently. I leaned on the hood of the Jag, probably a felony in Kenilworth, and watched her through the windshield.

"When did she become an escort?"

"You think I know the exact day or something? We were good friends, yeah, but she never really told me she was into that stuff, okay?"

She pushed her hand into the compartment between the seats and came out with a crumpled pack of Dunhill Menthols. Fumbling the last one out, she shoved it between her lips and jammed a long finger at the dashboard lighter.

"Look, there was a lot she didn't share, the older we got. She was always a secretive person. A control freak really. Like I said. She was my roommate for a year. I thought we'd get closer but she stayed pretty much to herself. Big surprise. Then all of a sudden she was on her cell all the time and meeting with these older guys. After awhile I just, I don't know. I guessed what was up. I'm not stupid."

"Did things change after she met Michael?"

"Well, yeah. She eventually moved in with him."

"When?"

"A year and a half ago, I think? I really wasn't keeping track of her living arrangements." Her face suddenly hardened. "What's the use of this? What are you trying to do anyway?"

"Find out the truth."

"Oh, like that's going to happen," she scoffed.

"Why not?"

Her mouth dropped open and she shook her head slowly.

"You don't get it at all! They're too big. Do you know anything about who Michael is? Really?"

"I'm hoping you'll tell me."

"See? You don't know. You have no idea who these people are. They'll squash you." She slapped the dashboard. "Just like that. That's what they can do."

"Like they squashed your friend Brooke? Because she was Michael's girlfriend and she wanted out?"

"You are such an asshole! I told you I don't know who killed Brooke, okay? But she knew an awful lot about Michael's business because she lived with him."

The way she said it stopped me. My spine suddenly felt suffused with cold water.

"And his business was…what?"

"They're mobsters. They kill for a living. They steal, they beat people up, they kill more people. Now you know. That's all I'm going to say because I don't want them to kill me." She jerked the lighter free but dropped her cigarette on the floor. Rather than looking for it, she shoved the lighter back into its receptacle and snapped the key in the ignition.

"Mobsters. You mean gangbangers?" I shouted over the roar of the engine.

"I'm going to tell you this once," she snapped. "One time. You want to think I'm a little girl who doesn't understand the big bad world, okay, that's your ignorance. Call them what you want. Michael's last name is Fredericks. Except it's not really. It's something Russian. They're all a bunch of Russians and they kill people."

I saw her put the car in gear and took a step away from it. A good thing. She left me, literally, in the dust of her parents' driveway. Not much dust because this was the sanctified North Shore, but still. The Jag roared out into the street and, if there had been a cop watching, he would have filled his ticket book before she got a block. Racing away from me and from her fears.

"They're all a bunch of Russians and they kill people."

Over lunch a couple of years ago, a suburban cop friend of mine alluded to the fact we had Russian thugs in our midst. We'd watched an argument between a little Jewish lady and a blonde-haired, thick-bodied cab driver with a strong Baltic accent. My friend had left his roast beef on rye to mediate what turned out to be a fare dispute. When he returned, he sighed heavily as he sat down.

"When I retire," he said, "I'm going shopping at 25th and California, or maybe even Menard or Pontiac. Maybe I'll try the federal lockup in Marion, too. I'm gonna stand outside the gates and I'm gonna pick maybe thirty or forty of their biggest, dumbest and meanest graduates. Then we're all moving to Moscow and I'm going to start my own taxi company. See how those fuckers over there like it."

*   *   *   *

I called Sunny the moment I was back in the car. I wanted to make sure there wasn't anything she was doing, computer traces, hacking or phone work, that could be linked back to her. She didn't give me the chance to tell her anything.

"Reno, what was the name of that movie guy you went to see? It was Eddie Marn, wasn't it?"

"Yeah, but let me hammer him."

"You lost your chance. He's been murdered. Turn on WLS. Cisco has been live with the story every 15 minutes since right after I left the restaurant. I tried getting you on your cell but you must have turned it off. Cisco's calling it a bloodbath."

*   *   *   *

I drove like hell to get there but, when I finally did, the cops were keeping everyone about a block away and enough mini-cam trucks had beaten me that it looked like a little village with microwave masts sprouting everywhere. I arrived in time to see a group of cameras and reporters circling two harried-looking uniform cops, one of whom showed a chief's gold braid on his shoulders. I hustled to join what is referred to in the trade as a "gang-bang" but managed to get close only for the last question and then couldn't hear the answer over the din of a Metra train pulling into the station behind us. The cops ducked under the yellow tape and didn't linger for any one-on-ones. The driveway I'd walked down yesterday was jammed with both marked and unmarked cars and a van from the Northern Illinois Police Crime Lab.

As the media horde dispersed to their vehicles, I shook hands with a couple of former colleagues and got pats on the back from a few more. They all wanted to know if I had returned to covering murder cases. I told them I just happened to be in the neighborhood and thought I'd check this one out. No need to tell them my station never covered news that had anything to do with real life. The closest I come to reporting murders is when some celebrity's wife or kid gets gunned down in Hollywood. They all knew that to go to an FM radio news reader's job after working on Chicago television feels like going back to selling commercials after you've owned the network.

While I was talking to a friend from Channel 7, I caught a glimpse over his shoulder of a Medical Examiner's investigator I knew. I excused myself and made my way over to him as he unlocked the door to his car.

In my experience, the ME's people usually drove their own vehicles and collected mileage rather than checking out anything provided by the county, given the spotty maintenance county cars usually receive. Liam O'Dell is an exception. He drives the county's cars, uses only county-issued equipment down to the pencils with the county logo on them, and, while on duty, cannot be persuaded to even talk about anything except that which directly relates to his work. From looking at him and his desk in a back room of the Stein Institute, you'd never know if he roots for the Cubs or the Sox, if he fly-fishes, builds World War Two-vintage model airplanes or tends an award-winning rose garden. I've run into him from time to time over more than ten years and I couldn't even tell you if he drinks coffee. If he does, it's probably not during on-duty hours. For all I know, they turn him off at the end of his shift, put him on a charger and stand him in the back of a closet until he's needed the next day.

Liam never spoke to me until we both ended up working a mass murder at a fast-food joint in Palatine a number of years ago, me in front of a camera outside in the snow, him trying to make sense of the seven sprawled corpses inside. Something about the viciousness of the crime and the media circus atmosphere tripped a switch in him and he sought me out while other reporters were interviewing his boss.

He's a friendly enough fellow, tall, sandy haired, with narrow shoulders and blue eyes that have a sadness in them, maybe reflecting all the things he's seen. He looked up from stowing his camera in a worn briefcase in the back seat of the Impala and showed no surprise, even though it had been at least two years since we'd run into each other.

"Hey, Reno. Can't tell you much."

"Anything is more than I know at this point."

He took a box of wet wipes from the briefcase, slid two from their little packages, and began washing his hands, "Three dead," he said. "Two men and a woman. Executed is what it looks like but don't quote me on that."

"Names?"

"Can't say yet. You know how that works."

"Eddie Marn? A kid named Archie something?"

"Off the record, yeah. The cops giving that out already?" He pitched the wipes he'd been using into a trash can on the floor of the car and didn't wait for me to answer. "No ID on the girl but I'm going to guess she's not from around here. 'Here' meaning the United States."

"Why do you say that?"

"Bad teeth, bad diet. Built like a plow horse. Biggest thing would be Mongol features, as opposed to Caucasoid. Jaw and shape of the head basically tell you that. Even the hair is all wrong for an American girl. Styled like someone thought she should look to fit in. I'm also going to disagree if the cops told you she's a teenager. That woman in there last saw 19 about five, six years ago. They're going by the makeup."

"Russian?" I suggested.

"Could be. Not far away. Maybe Polish. Those hands, she sure hasn't been having regular manicures at the beauty shop. At one time she did hard manual labor."

"How do you figure it went down?"

"The cops would probably like you to wait and get that from them," he said.

"I don't mind waiting but we both know you're the only one who's going to get it right. I'd appreciate the accuracy."

He scratched the back of his head while at the same time surreptitiously making sure no one was paying attention to us.

"Well, I've seen a few mob hits and this doesn't look that different, you know? Entirely a guess. That guy, Marn, got it first, I'd say. Two shots the back of his head, close range. Shooter knew him, probably knew he had a .380 under his shirt, too, but you didn't hear me say that.

"Way I figure it, the shooter maybe walks in with him, pops him, then does the kid. Archie Lehman was his name. We found him lying on a chair that had gone ass over end. Kid had a brace on his knee, couldn't go anywhere. He took two right in the middle of the chest."

"Nine?"

"Found one right on the floor. Beretta it was."

How neat. Both guns accounted for. And Archie, the surfer dude who talked like a black man, had the bum knee I'd given him, and it had killed him as certainly as if I'd just finished him off myself.

"You feeling all right, Reno? I'm not getting too graphic for you, am I?"

"No. No, I'm okay. What about the girl?"

"Well." He reached into his car and extracted a water bottle. "You know what they were up to in there?" I nodded. Head tilted, he took a long drink and then wiped his mouth with the back of his hand. "Far as I could tell, she was doing it to herself on the bed. Had one of her toys still vibrating, in fact. Cops were laughing about it. First guy on the scene thought a pager was going off somewhere."

He smiled briefly and, when it faded, he took another drink. "Your man seems to know something about handguns. He double-tapped her, too. I'm not a firearms guy but it sure looks like he was across the room when he did it."

"Given that it was a porn studio, I suppose it's too much to hope there was a tape rolling through the whole thing?"

"There might have been but all the cameras were empty when I got there."

Someone who took his time and knew where to look.

"How about a time?"

"Oh, they're fresh. Not more n' maybe a couple hours? That's what I'm giving the detectives anyway. And, by the way, you know none of this comes from me, right?"

*   *   *   *

I found out the reporters working the story had the gist of what Liam had told me because one of the truckers pulling his rig into the yard next door had thought he'd heard shots. While unloading, he had mentioned that to one of the guys working the freight dock. They'd batted it around, decided they didn't want to look like suckers to the cops, and walked over to have a look for themselves. Either the shooter had left the front door ajar or they had pushed it open. One had apparently puked on the steps after discovering what was inside.

I called Sunny back.

"No coincidence?" she asked.

"I'd say that's pretty damned unlikely. Eddie was a sleaze but he was relatively inoffensive. And low-level."

"Then why kill him?"

"Maybe he had something else to tell me and they knew I'd be back to ask him for it. Or maybe they just didn't like the idea he talked to me at all."

"You're thinking the Russians?"

"I told you about the older guy I took the gun from. I think he was Russian. He wasn't one of the victims. I'm thinking he could have been the shooter. Eddie was afraid of him. Maybe he had reason to be."

"Reno…" she stopped.

"I sound like a lunatic right? 'The Russians are Coming, the Russians are Coming.'"

"I'm hearing just a touch of paranoia, yeah."

"Eddie tells me a probably-Russian money man has suddenly taken an interest in his movies and then a Russian thug tries to grab a hooker to take her back to her Russian boyfriend who may or may not have ordered her killed. Then the girl and Eddie both end up dead within 24 hours of each other."

"Take a breath."

"Yeah." I closed my eyes and did what she suggested. When I opened them, I saw a familiar car ease into a parking space a block and a half down from me and well away from the TV trucks and other reporter-mobiles. Sure, there were probably a dozen or so black Crown Vics that looked like antenna farms wandering Chicago streets. It could have been bringing a relief crew for one of the TV stations. I suspected that was not the case.

"Have your mighty machines turned up anything interesting?" I asked Sunny.

"As a matter of fact," I heard her clicking keys. "There's a Michael Fredericks listed as the owner of two substantial units at Lake Point Tower. Wait, I lied. United Citizens Bank is the property owner but their U-C-C filing with the state shows Fredericks as President and CEO."

"He's a banker?" I said.

"On paper anyway. But get this. It's a privately-owned bank and its FDIC information says it's capitalized by a holding company called Balkan Global Systems with a home office in the Ukraine. I'm still trying to run down the other named officers."

"So it's a Russian bank subsidiary."

"That's the way it looks."

Most of the TV reporters were getting ready to do their 6 p.m. stand-ups as I walked over to visit with Vinnie Seamans. He sat behind the wheel of his idling Crown Vic like a ward boss overseeing a street-side voter registration drive, tapping ash from his cigar out the driver's side window. I joined him inside the cool interior. The police radios burbled on low volume as the familiar voices of the evening anchors on WBBM came out of the dashboard speakers.

"You have some reason to be here?" he asked.

"Yes, I'm feeling better, thanks," I said and handed him the can of Dr. Pepper I'd appropriated from a tub filled with ice near one of the TV trucks. "No double vision, no headaches. But you know? The damn thing throbs like hell."

"When I saw you, my butt started to throb like hell. What's your business here, Reno?"

His voice was tired and scratchier than I remembered. I wondered if he had slept since our last conversation. His wife died a few years back and mutual friends tell me that he stays out all night just cruising the streets, dropping by whatever crime scenes catch his attention. He can go from Cabrini to the Taylor Homes to anywhere on the West Side with impunity. His career included tours in a majority of the city's police districts so even the most gang-ridden neighborhoods give him no reason for concern.

More than a few times as a teenager I rode along with him as we hashed out one problem or other in my young life. If he suspected there might be trouble, he stuck his old Colt .45 automatic under his right thigh and nodded toward the glove compartment where I knew I would find a loaded Chief's Special were I to need it to back him up or defend myself. No matter my age at the time, it always gave me a grown-up feeling to know he trusted me.

"I think somebody killed Marn because he talked to me," I said.

"The locals don't see it that way."

There was a 'phish' sound as he popped the top on the Dr Pepper and drank some of it down. "For your ears only. There's a boy and girl in there with Marn. Chief Sabato tells me they're looking for her old man. He was the foreign guy you ran off yesterday. They think he took exception to the work she was doing and who she was doing it with."

I blinked. That didn't mesh with what I knew or had seen.

"I don't agree."

"Well then. The Chief's right there on the other side of the yellow tape." Vinnie extended a hand in the direction of the crime scene. "You feel that strongly about it, go ahead and offer him your input."

"If this is just a domestic, I'll ask you the same question you asked me. What are you doing here?"

"Last time I checked, the seal on my official ID said "County of Cook." That's where we are, right? They haven't jiggered with the boundaries have they? And, as far as I can tell, this is a major crime. You figure it out."

His sarcasm suggested he didn't want to take the discussion any further. His cryptic explanation would have made complete sense, too, except for one thing. Vinnie refuses to deal with suburban police departments. Hates the boot licking required and flat out won't do it. Leaves it to subordinates.

I knew he wasn't lying to me about his presence. He was just being Vinnie and skirting the truth. He was here because Marn's murder was linked to Brooke's. For the moment, I decided to let that conclusion go untested. For the moment.

"You went to see Talmadge," he said.

"I also took a nice crap this morning. You know about that, too?"

He belched softly and excused himself. Always the gentleman. "What's the bottom line here? Why are you chasing…this?" He motioned toward the murder scene but both of us knew the gesture was meant to be all-encompassing.

"Somebody killed Brooke Talmadge in front of me."

"So you feel responsible."

"I should have scoped it out, Vinnie. If I had caught up to her, walked her to her apartment…"

"What if you had? What would have happened? Think on it. If you'd gone up to her outside the building, how would she have reacted? It's not like you were old friends. Man, get it through your brain! Girl would've thought you were one of the mopes, too."

"She might be alive if I hadn't decided to play Secret Squirrel," I said stubbornly.

"It was your business to follow her inside? Hanratty didn't hire you to body-guard her did he? Besides," he inclined his head, listening to a state police bulletin on one of his radios then, just as quickly, tuned it out. "If she thought people were after her, what's she doing going home anyway?"

I didn't have an answer but that thought led me to another and I changed the subject by asking a question of my own. "Did you see the inventory from her apartment?"

"Why?"

"I told you I saw her brother hand her an envelope. He said it was phony ID's to help her hide when she split out of town."

"Wasn't anything like that on the list."

"I wonder what happened to it."

He looked at me with something like the expression he'd had during the rides of my youth when I'd come up with some particularly insightful observation about life. "You'd think, she's carrying an envelope when she gets grabbed, she drops it right there on the floor."

"You'd think."

"Good point. I'll reach out for your buddy Kinsella and ask if he's checked. In the meantime, you done now? Through poking around?"

"Not necessarily."

"Is there some reason you insist on always making life tough for yourself? Tell me that.

Getting yourself fired from the TV station. That girl you were dating, that hooker..."

"That's low and it's off-limits, Vinnie."

My tone must have convinced him. He sighed.

"Suppose I told you the word from the top is for you to cease and desist 'cause you're in way over your head on this case."

"Which case are we talking about now?"

"Both. Either."

"Ah. Now see? That right there tells me this and Brooke's murder are connected. Could it also explain why Russian names keep popping up?"

Shaking his head, disgusted, he said, "You're intent on getting your butt shot off, aren't you? Just leave it be, Reno."

"I intend to find out why Brooke Talmadge was killed. I also want to know why her daddy, the Chicago P.D. and you are all trying to pin it on some home invader."

"Better a home invader than you. Get intent on that."

*   *   *   *

I put up with Vinnie's grumbling for another ten minutes. It was long enough for me to see a Buick Regal pull to the curb and discharge a well-dressed woman and well-dressed man who wouldn't have been any more obvious if they'd had "Fed" stenciled across their foreheads. They glanced toward us then sauntered across the street and ducked under the crime scene tape. I took the hint and excused myself from Vinnie's car but not before he apologized for his bad mood. I apologized for mine, too.

I circulated among the TV folks, shook a few more hands, listened in to another media briefing. Nobody said anything about a fat Russian. Nobody announced there were Feds poking around, either.

I checked in once more with Sunny, knowing she would be going to bed shortly to pull my shift for me in the morning. She was still working on Michael Fredericks. She told me to be careful. I gave it another fifteen minutes and saw the two federal guys get into Vinnie's car, one in front, and one in back. I took out my phone and dialed.

Lynn Robinette's phone rang three times until call-following clicked in, then rang twice more before she picked up.

"Lynn, it's Reno," I said.

"My! Twice in as many evenings. Aren't I the lucky girl?" She was playful but more subdued than usual.

"Are you alone?"

"Oh no. Not tonight. Sorry, guy. You had your chance."

There was no point sugar-coating it.

"Eddie Marn's dead. You'll see it on the news. It wasn't pretty."

She lowered her voice. "Does this have something to do with…what happened to Brooke?"

"Looks that way."

"Reno, um, can I call you right back? About ten minutes?"

I told her that was fine. When I hung up, I realized I was tired. You get that way when you spend the better part of a day sparring with people, trying to get information. I also had a low-grade headache and my nose felt like someone had taken another swipe at me. I wondered if I had accomplished anything since that morning. I knew a little bit more than when I woke up but not much. Brooke's death had spooked quite a few people. One of them seemed to be her own father. Still didn't know why. Seemed to me the cops were spooked, too. Still didn't know why on that one either.

The phone rang.

Lynn rushed her words. "So why are you telling me this? You don't bother to call about Brooke but, oh, you sure are quick to drop a dime about a scum like Eddie. What's that all about?"

"You led me to believe your relationship with Brooke was essentially a one-night stand. Was there more to it?"

"For god's sake, Reno! If it had lasted five minutes my relationship with her would have been more significant than with that little piece of shit."

I took a deep breath.

"I thought you should know what happened to him in case you want to take some precautions."

"Precautions against what?" she snapped.

"I suppose that depends on what you haven't told me about Brooke."

"There isn't anything else to tell."

"No? How about the last time you saw her?"

"I told you. At the hotel, the Marriott."

"And after that? You saw her again, didn't you?"

"What if I did?" she said petulantly. "She was lonely and we'd had fun before. I didn't see the harm. Apparently she didn't either."

"What did you talk about?"

"Don't you have anything better to do than quiz me about my sex life? Are you really that hard up?"

I wondered if counting to ten would help. I tried again. "Lynn, listen to me, okay? Take the sex out of it. The people who ordered Marn hit are mobbed up, big time. Killing is no big deal for them. They took out a man and woman just because they happened to be in the same room with Marn. If Brooke told you anything about the relationship she was in, anything about her boyfriend, I need to know what it was. And you need to think about maybe getting out of town for awhile."

I heard her suck in a breath.

"We slept together two nights after I saw her at the Marriott. She cried on my shoulder a little."

"What'd she cry about?"

"She...I don't know. Her boyfriend, Michael. He was being a prick. She loved him, she said, but he'd done something really rotten to her. She told me she had to get away from him, away from Chicago entirely. Out of the business. She kept saying someone was going to pay."

"Someone being who...Michael?"

"I don't know, Reno. I really don't. A lot of things about that night are really jumbled for me. She was bummed about leaving him but really angry at the same time."

"What did she tell you about his business?"

"Not very much. From the little she said, it sounded to me as though he was a Russian gangster. She said he had a bunch of Italian guys sucking up to him, too, like he was some kind of new Godfather or something. I guess one of the goombahs came on to her a little bit, pinched her ass or something. I don't know. And this Michael had his fingers cut off or broken or something. It wasn't the kind of thing she would've made up."

I could hear the fear in her voice now. That was a good thing. She told me she had to get back to her client. I told her she should think about taking a trip somewhere for a couple of weeks.

"I live in a secure building. You saw the doorman. And there's a security service."

"You told me who you think these people are. You think it's going to be secure enough if they try for you?"

"Okay, okay. The guy I'm with now?" I heard a lighter strike. After a moment, she said, "He wants me to cruise the lake with him for a couple of days. Maybe go up to Mackinac or something. He's asked a couple of times."

"Good. Do it. Stay a week if you can, maybe two. Watch the papers. Call me if you want."

"What are you going to do?"

"I thought I knew when I got up this morning," I said. "Now I'm not so sure."

*   *   *   *

I was tired enough I wanted to go home and lie on the porch swing until it got dark or I fell asleep, whichever came first. It was 7:30 and still in the upper eighties. The sun burned crimson edges onto the clouds that strayed across it. A 757 lifted from O'Hare and banked over us to head west. I thought of another errand I could run before heading back to Evanston but I decided I could handle it well enough by phone.

I caught a break and made good time getting to the house. Socks, a black and white neighborhood cat with a fondness for my air conditioning system, was asleep in a camp chair on my front porch. He opened one eye as I trudged up the stairs and then followed me with a subtle head movement as I keyed the lock, opened the door and disengaged my security system. He squeaked once and I swept my arm sideways to welcome him as though I were the maitre'd at a five-star restaurant. Then I fed him from my stash of Fancy Feast and left him stretching out on the perch I made for him in front of the windows in my study while I went to make a phone call.

John Gennaro is a former FBI agent. When he's not penning a column for *Chicago* magazine, he writes true-crime books that make him appear to be a cross between Eliot Ness and Spiderman. Before he left the Bureau about five years ago, he was one of their experts on organized crime. He spent most of the Sixties and early Seventies avoiding the undercover assignments and black bag jobs Hoover frequently ordered on the radical groups. Instead, he carved out a special niche for himself by becoming the Bureau's top guy for installing bugs on top mobsters.

Even though his efforts put a number of them away, he won an odd sort of respect and near friendship from a number of the old-timers. Now, in addition to his writing, he does the occasional consultation with Hollywood and even some security consulting but, if you see him at a restaurant, he'll as likely as not be the guest of a guy whose name is on the Chicago Crime Commission's master mob intelligence list. More than a few cops have told me it was those kinds of friendships that caused him to leave the Bureau a few years before mandatory retirement.

Just because the politicians and the federal prosecutors like to say the Outfit is dead in Chicago doesn't make it true. Oh, there's no Al Capone running the show and taking a piece of everything criminal in the city. But anywhere there are casinos or the gaming industry in any fashion, you'll find organized crime. A few suburban mayors and police chiefs are in the mob's pocket. Some the feds have nailed, some they haven't. Some of the unions maintain their ties to organized crime. You hear about a sizeable theft or hijacking from an interstate shipment, or when the cops break up a big-time fencing operation and recover warehouse loads of goods, there's no question an Outfit street crew had at least a hand in it.

Gennaro picked up the phone on the first ring. When I identified myself, he slapped on the brogue he learned from having a very Irish mother.

"Reno me boyo. And it's about time you be calling me, ya homo bastard. Likely as not you're wanting something aren't ya? Jayzus, can't you sometime just ring me up to go for a pint or two?"

"The Irish Repertory lost a fine talent when you decided to go into law enforcement."

"I'll be telling my sainted Mother that the next time I go calling at the home. She gets a wee bit teary eyed and a compliment like that from someone such as yerself will give her a smile."

He paused, quite possibly to take a nip from the flask he always carries, and then in his own voice said, "To what do I owe this honor? You want to sit in on poker night next week with the Cardinal?"

"You can't fool me. The Cardinal's a gin rummy man. I do have a question or two about the Russian mob, though."

He didn't respond right away. When he did, the joviality in his voice seemed strained. "Russians? I have enough trouble keeping track of La Cosa Nostra to worry about some entire other country."

"I'll bet you know if there's any crossover between the two groups. Are the Russians trying to muscle in locally or have they been invited?"

"The one thing I always admired about you, Reno, is your ability to small talk and schmooze around before getting down to business. You realize there are a few things I still can't discuss, even in retirement?"

"Cases and informants that are still active. You've waved that flag before."

"Consider it waved again, my friend. I get too many consulting jobs thrown my way to piss off my former employers by talking to the press about things I shouldn't even be thinking about."

All this was pretty standard Gennaro-ese. John considers every phone to be tapped, every room he hasn't visited with an RF scanner to be wired and everyone he doesn't know a potential federal snitch. Well into a bottle of Makers Mark one night, he confided to me his greatest fear is to have his former colleagues haul him before a grand jury and indict him for transgressions he's never been specific about. I didn't pry. Just saying as much as he had left him looking like he'd seen the ghost of ol' J Edgar staring at him from over my shoulder.

"So you're saying you won't answer a couple of simple questions?" I pressed.

"Not won't. Can't. Someday when we're over at The Spot I'll buy a round or two and explain how many ways I could still get fucked for talking out of turn."

I smiled as I hung up and went to grab my keys. For a moment, I'd thought he was being serious about not talking to me. But his reference to The Spot, a defunct pizza place we'd both liked in downtown Evanston, was a code to meet him in a coffee shop around the corner from where it used to be. You want to play with Gennaro, you have to become as much a secret agent man as he thinks he is.

I spent the thirty minutes or so I had to wait in the back of The Cup, reading in a discarded two-day old *Tribune* about how an enforcer for an un-named street gang had been shot to death in his West Side living room along with his brother and his brother's wife. It rated a half-column on page one under the fold of the Metro section. This was surprising given the Chicago media's cynicism about gang violence. It was continued on page three inside but I'd have to live in suspense because page three was missing. I'd seen a brief clip on one of the TV stations about it the night it happened, though, and the wire copy the next morning, and remembered thinking what a slow news day it must have been. Had the victims been 13 or 14, the story would have qualified as lead material.

Since the youngest of trio was 19 and the others 20 and 21, their advanced ages virtually guaranteed most news editors would use the story only as 'fill' when nothing else caught their attention. The *Tribune* reported, however, that the city's murder rate at the halfway point of the year already approached 400 and if the rat-tat-tat of automatic weapons continued unabated for the next six months, we'd be looking at the largest homicide hike in recent years. Police Commissioner D'Amato, the first female to hold that post in Chicago history, noted that the heat likely was a contributing factor. She also said she was ordering all tactical officers into uniform for higher visibility.

Gennaro slid into the booth across from me and gripped my hand. He looks formally dressed even in a sport shirt and slacks, his perfectly black hair brushed back without a single strand out of place. With his even tan and capped teeth people always give him a second look, wondering if they've seen him before. It's likely they have. John's his own best PR rep and his picture on the back of his books is always as big as the jacket allows.

"Whose husband did *you* piss off?" he asked. It was refreshing to run into someone who was clueless about what happened to me.

"If you know she had a husband you could probably solve her murder, too," I said wearily and compressed my last 24 hours into several long headlines. I was as tired of telling my story as I was of living it.

By the time I finished, Gennaro had a cup of coffee in front of him and was doctoring it from his elegant gold flask. He lifted it in my direction but I passed. I couldn't even taste the iced tea I'd ordered. Typically, he had no comment about anything I'd said. Rather, he segued to a recent phone call received from Bruce Willis asking for his help with a new role as a Mafia Don, and then spoke at some length about the novel his agent had suggested he produce.

After a few minutes he wound down as he always does, not the slightest bit embarrassed that he embodies the old joke about the guy who says to his date, "Enough about me. Let's talk about you. What do *you* think of *me*?"

He said, "So you think this Michael Fredericks ordered the girl hit because she ran out on him, huh?" He ran his finger lightly over the lip of the flask and then capped it. "Interesting. *La storia intera,* the whole story, I mean, not just your assessment. See, I've been trying to create this novel. Well, to give credit where it's due, I've been working with the guy who's going to actually write it. From my notes, of course. Anyway, I haven't paid much attention to the real world for the last couple of weeks."

"I can see how that could happen."

"And you say Michael Fredericks is a Russian banker," he continued. "With a nice place at Lake Point Tower. A big place. Probably a home office, too, from what you're telling me."

Sometimes, this, too, was Gennaro's way. Repeat the facts as offered, sometimes more than once. If he'd used that approach as an FBI agent I could see why the Bureau canned him. His interviews would have stretched for days.

"And you want *my* help because one of your sources suggested the Mothers and Fathers Italian Association might be involved. If not directly, maybe some members of a crew working independently. You see where I'm going? Depending on who was there. If they were even connected. Maybe they just looked Italian? Maybe they were Italian but not Family. Lots of good, solid, reputable folks of Italian descent out there."

"One of them supposedly had some fingers crushed or amputated for grabbing the girl," I said.

He'd been roaming the room with his eyes but now they came back to meet mine and I realized again how scary it was that the federal government had let him carry a gun for some twenty years.

"Now that's interesting," he said.

I waited but he went back to repeating what I'd told him instead of elaborating.

"She went home," he said. "Do you know why?"

"To meet her brother, I think." I told him about the phony ID that Alan had said he obtained for her.

"Right, right," he said. "If she was a hooker, she'd probably know where to get phony ID's." He looked off in the distance again and then, more quickly than I expected, finally jumped to the point of our meeting.

"I never spent any time on the Dark Side when I was with the Bureau. The Dark Side. That's Counterintelligence. They worked the Russians. Still do. Used to call 'em the 'Soviets', remember? There's still some spy versus spy shit but now there're two, three CI squads work what they call the Mafiya. The RED Ma-Fee-ya as opposed to the Italian Mafia." He grinned.

"Lemme tell you the difference. The Italians, when they try to squeeze some store owner for protection, they'll say 'we want this much cash every week and 'cause we're nice reasonable guys, you got a couple days to decide if you're gonna pay or not'. Then in a week they come back and the *sciocco* says 'yeah, of course, how much?' If he says no, they beat on him 'til he's convinced. Now, these Russians, they walk in, tell you how much you're gonna pay, and if you make any bones about it, bang, they shoot you dead. No argument, no appeal, no *discus-sione.*"

He gestured. "You know any of this? Am I boring you?"

"Not in the least."

"They've been all over New York for years, you know. The Russians. Brighton Beach in Brooklyn is Moscow West. I know some guys work in the Manhattan Field Office say they'll never go over there. They'd quit first. The cops…well let's just say the NYPD allows off-duty bodyguard work and some of them are count-ing their take in rubies."

"I always thought Brighton Beach was full of little Neil Simons."

"Yeah, well, this Brighton Beach's fulla Russian Jews now. And they aren't writing plays. They're shooting each other and cutting each other's throats and blowing each other up. You think we got problems with gangs here? This is a candy store to them, my friend."

I smiled. "But you don't know anything about the Russians."

He ducked his head. "Maybe I know a little. I know enough to tell you they're in New York, they're in Miami, Christ it's a toss-up whether there's more Cubans or Russians in Miami, and they're in LA. They own part of Denver. Some people say the own more than a few professional athletes, too."

He stopped and looked at me like a math professor who wants his bright stu-dents to finish a complicated equation.

"Now they're here," I said.

He pointed the flask at me. "Now they *want* to be here. Now they're *trying* to get in here. A candy store, I said." He shrugged. "And, yeah, some of 'em have a foot in the door."

"Michael Fredericks?" I said.

"Michael Fredericks, the Lake Point Tower guy, the Russian banker. Michael Fredericks, the one you think had the girl killed. The one who mashes guys' fin-gers." He finished his coffee in a gulp. "Reno, you got anything doing for the next couple of hours? Anywhere you gotta be?"

I glanced at my watch, thought of my air-conditioning and a shower and the bed.

"What do you have in mind?"

"Got a guy I want you to meet," he said.

CHAPTER 7

▼

Riding in Gennaro's Cadillac was as comfortable as sitting in my living room. The air conditioning kept us at a cool 68 degrees, as noted in a display on the dash, and his XM satellite music receiver played a mix of New Age and real jazz while I reclined in what he pointed out was a Roccaro-designed passenger seat. He yanked out a cell phone as we pulled away from the curb and conducted three lengthy conversations, all in rapid-fire Italian, complete with hand gestures. We didn't speak to each other again until we'd traversed the 'burbs and were headed south on the Tri-State Tollway. I was getting used to this stretch of road. Then again, any investigator knows you often have to cover the same ground several times before you get anywhere.

"Listen up, m'man," he said as we passed the turnoff for O'Hare. "You aren't carrying, are you?"

"Not even a pocket knife."

"That's a good thing. Where we're going, the security setup is tighter than they got on El Al. In fact, I aingt sure it wasn't designed by one of those Israeli guys."

"Where are we going, John?"

"That's the thing. There's a chance, not much of one, but a chance, that you may have your picture taken. I don't think it's going to happen because the Bureau sure don't have the manpower or any reason to be doing a surveillance what with chasing Bin Laden and Sadaam and all. But a picture is something you got to accept going in."

"Going in where, John?"

He grinned and looked over at me. "You ever met Polo Tony?"

If he was hoping to surprise me, he got his wish.

"It's almost nine on a Sunday night and you're taking me to meet the Godfather. Just like that?"

"Hey, it's not like I called and told him we were in the neighborhood and did he want us to pick up the Colonel on the way over to take a dip in his pool. You saw, it took a little to set up."

"It's almost nine on a Sunday night," I repeated stupidly.

"You think he keeps office hours? Besides," he lowered his voice. "He's had a little health problem. He doesn't sleep too well anymore."

The phone rang. He flipped it open and the Italian began again.

I considered what I knew about Polo Tony LaMotta. Protégé to Anthony "Big Tuna" Accardo, he'd risen through the ranks from leg-breaker, to the Tuna's driver and then to a sort of freelance counselor. When the Tuna died in 1992, Polo Tony managed to slide into the top spot of the Chicago Outfit. Initially the Chicago Crime Commission and other mob watchers thought he was merely a straw man representing the other guy who was the more logical choice as leader.

It wasn't until the other man died and Polo Tony thrived, keeping himself free of indictments and even avoiding major publicity, that everyone realized he really was Number One. Nothing happened that he didn't order, or at least give thumbs up to, in juice loans, gambling, prostitution, cartage thefts, union organizing and a dozen other sorts of esoteric crimes. Word on the street was that dope pretty much stayed a no-no, something it had always been for the Chicago Outfit under Accardo. Given the major heat and high profile it brought, he hadn't wanted the trouble and neither did his protégé.

I remembered standing next to a high-ranking Chicago narc at a news conference several years ago. U.S. Customs had seized a $10 million shipment of highly refined black tar heroin coming from Mexico, run by a crew of Mexican nationals. The fed was saying the Outfit had likely been involved. The narc snorted and said to me, "When we start finding a bunch of Mexicans in car trunks, that's when you'll know the Outfit has gotten into dope. Not before." The trunks stayed empty.

Polo Tony didn't pick up his nickname from his devotion to the sport, which he'd once played with Prince Charles, or the fancy digs he has off the polo club grounds in Oak Brook. It came from his unique approach to discipline. He discovered one of his collectors was shaking down taverns in one of the western 'burbs for more than what was turning up in the kitty each week. The way the story went, Tony ordered that the collector be brought to the practice area he had on his own property, one night. He told the guy he didn't like to be cheated and, when the guy protested his innocence instead of confessing honorably right there, Tony had him staked at mid-field. For the next half-hour or so, Tony galloped up and down, using the guy as a target for his mallet while he practiced his swing.

And we were going to drop by for a visit. Apparently, on Gennaro's whim.

Gennaro flipped his phone closed again.

"OK, here's the deal. I'm speaking up for you so my ass is on the line for anything you say from the minute we go in, all the way through afterward. And I like my ass. So this interview will have never happened and nothing that's said, nothing you see, nothing you hear ever gets out. We square on that?"

I nodded, wondering if I hadn't stepped onto a sound stage without knowing it.

"Ask a question?"

"What?"

"Not that I don't like meeting your friends, but what's this little session all about? And why the urgency?"

"I was gonna tell you that, but Tony says to wait."

I scratched my beard and thought for a moment. "John, not to be disrespectful, but what sort of relationship do you have with this guy that you let him tell you what to do?"

He kept his eyes fixed on the road. For the first time, I noticed a line of sweat above the collar of his LaCoste shirt. "Don't ask me that, man. I've answered a lot of questions for you on the QT over the years but that's one I can't touch. Just take it on faith that this is a good idea. You want to know something about the Russian Mob? This is how you find out."

I supposed this was sort of like asking General Motors about Ford, but kept my mouth shut.

It was fully dark by the time we approached Polo Tony's property, a quarter of a mile or so from the Oak Brook Polo Club. Gennaro turned down a winding lane and, after a quarter of a mile, stopped at an electronic gate set into an iron fence that stretched away into the woods on either side of us.

"Nice location," I said.

Gennaro said nothing. He ran the window down and waited, motor idling. In the dark, I couldn't see the security camera that was surely watching us. Neither had I observed any sign of surveillance as we pulled in from the road. That made me edgy as hell. I thought about the mob movies I'd seen. Maybe back a few years, there would have been Lupara shotgun-wielding guards holding back snarling Dobermans. Village boards frown on stuff like that nowadays. They prefer a kinder and gentler approach to burglary detection. The gate and fence might be electrified, but a touch would probably just set off a vibration sensor. Low-light cameras with overlapping fields of view were likely set up to track anyone dumb enough to think they could approach Polo Tony's home through the woods. All the alarms and video would be monitored in a room on the property, not by the local cops or a security company. Basic security for the rich and famous. Or infamous.

A clear voice speaking Italian came from a speaker on a post outside the Caddy's window. Gennaro muttered a response and the gate swung inward. We drove another twenty-five yards down the tree-lined driveway until it broke into a clearing. Two guys waited in a Jeep in a blacktopped turnaround. Beyond it, there was an expanse of lawn lit with floodlights and then the kind of sprawling brick home you'd expect to see behind a gated driveway in Oak Brook.

"We'll go with them," Gennaro pointed at the Jeep.

We got out. Both of the Jeep guys were over six feet tall, broad-shouldered and wore automatics upside-down in shoulder-holsters over short-sleeve shirts. Neither spoke as one ran a metal detector wand over our clothes. It chirped at my pocket. I slowly brought out my ring of keys. It had a small pocket-knife on it which the guy with the metal detector unclipped from the ring and slid into a small brown envelope. He handed back only the keys. I wasn't surprised. They do that in courthouses now, too.

They drove us the rest of the way to the house where a white-haired guy I took to be another factotum, this one wearing a dark jogging suit, waited at the open front door.

"Hey pal," he said with a nod toward Gennaro. "How's the handicap?"

"Seven, eight, somewhere in there. I think I'm stuck for life."

"Stuck, he says." The guy laughed, but when his smile turned professional and he took my hand with the grip of a bricklayer, I realized with a start who he was.

"Reno, I'm Tony LaMotta," he said. "Can you believe this guy complains about having a seven handicap? Stuck is when you're trying to break goddamn ninety for a year and your putting goes to shit. Come in, come in."

Anyone familiar with movie mobsters would have been disappointed. This was no Edward G. Robinson or even Marlon Brando. Polo Tony was in his early sixties but he appeared to be a decade younger. I had seen his picture once or twice but still had trouble matching the physique and tan of an active country squire to his history. His crow's feet could just as easily have come from laughter as from the worries created by planning a million-dollar truck hijacking or figuring how to squeeze more cash from an ailing labor union. Not even his eyes betrayed the truth behind the image of the kindly, horse-country neighbor. Contacts, I thought. Nobody has eyes that blue. There had been no mistaking the strength behind that handshake, however, or the way his gaze checked me out as thoroughly as the bodyguard's metal detector.

He kept up with the golf chat, nodding his head slightly, as we entered a foyer that would have done the Augusta National clubhouse proud. "I played yesterday. You know, I can read a balance sheet, sometimes even read a woman, but greens? I need one of those topographical maps."

"You been using that Ping putter?" Gennaro asked.

"Love that putter. When I bend over, though, I start up with the sciatica. Plays hell with the swing. Getting old, I guess. Come this way. John, I know you'll drink with me. How about you, Reno? I'll bet that broken nose doesn't help your taste buds does it?"

"Sure doesn't. Water's fine."

His study was large, paneled in cherry wood and unique only in its lack of traditional furniture. Aside from the floor to ceiling bookcases and the busts of horses on two pedestals near the windows, there was a large but plain desk and six leather armchairs arrayed in a circle in front of it. No comfortable couch for a quickie nap, no tables for guests to rest their drinks. As the door closed behind us, I felt that change of pressure in my ears that says a room is acoustically tight. I didn't want to think about the kinds of things that had been discussed in here. A lamp on the desk and a track that ran across the paneled ceiling provided muted lighting that could be cranked up or down as needed. A book lay on the desk and even from where I was standing I could see it was an old and well-handled copy of Sun Tzu's *The Art of War*.

Polo Tony went to a wet bar behind his desk and began fixing the drinks. We joined him there. He used stainless steel tongs to lift ice cubes from a leather-wrapped bucket and drop them into glasses he brought out of a small refrigerator. They each had famous golf holes etched on them. Mine was the 18th at Pebble Beach. He glanced at me as he filled it with Perrier and smiled. "Like the room?"

"It's unusual," I said. He handed me the chilled glass.

"I got the idea from a man who was dean of the Harvard Business School. He liked short meetings. He said the best way to keep them short is to make sure people don't carry in a lot of papers. If your lap has to be your desk and you're juggling a drink, too, you won't try to dazzle me with flow charts and all that other high-tech BS. That's something John's come to realize about me over the years," he said. "My low tolerance for BS. Give it to me straight or keep your trap shut. I'll do the same."

He handed Gennaro a glass, took a bottle of Beck's for himself, and led us to the circle of chairs.

"Oh, and feel free to stand your drink on the floor. Spills, fluids of any kind, it's a special surface that dries quickly. Doesn't leave a trace." He grinned. "Great when you have kids."

Or bleeders, I thought. His casual but direct manner put me more on edge than if he'd grabbed me by the throat. I wanted to look at the crossed polo mallets on the wall over the wet bar but I kept my head still.

"We're both looking for information," he said and spread his hands. "Under normal circumstances, I would never speak to a reporter. I'm making an exception because John thinks you and I can help each other. This room is clean. So are you, by the way. You've been swept three times since you came into the house. Speak your mind."

He settled into his chair.

That focused me. Questions, after all, are my business. I always have a few handy.

"I'm looking into Brooke Talmadge's murder. It's a personal thing. Because of her involvement in prostitution, it strikes me that she might have come to your attention."

I thought I heard John make a noise. Nothing like insinuating that the Godfather is a pimp. However, Polo Tony didn't seem to take offense.

"Her father and I have some mutual acquaintances," he said gravely. "I never met Brooke, although I understand she was a lovely young woman. I became aware of her, shall we say tangentially, about a year, year and a half ago. As I understand it, she was romantically involved with the banker you also wish to ask me about."

"Were you aware she was offering to provide information about the outcall business in Chicago to Channel 14? Specifically about her involvement with a high class escort operation?"

"Isn't that what kids all do these days? Live outrageously then titillate everyone with a book or a video or an appearance on television? I'm sorry to hear that she would do something so foolish but, no, I wasn't aware of her plans."

"You didn't have her killed to keep her quiet?"

He winked at Gennaro. "I like this man, John! You tell him to speak up and he cross examines. If Brooke Talmadge was employed as you claim she was, she worked independently and under the radar. As such, any allegations, any finger pointing from her, would have been meaningless. She simply wouldn't have been in a position to gather any incriminating information."

Translation: I've checked, she wasn't involved with us, and we had no reason to kill her. Fine. I'd had to settle the point in my mind. I mentally flipped a page in my notebook.

"You mentioned Michael Fletcher. What can you tell me about him?"

"Mikhail Federov, you mean? You look surprised! You thought he was an American running a Russian bank? The Russians would never allow that. I've known of Mr. Federov for a couple of years. For one relatively young, he's managed to rise amazingly fast in his chosen profession. I believe he was born in Chechniya and brought up in Moscow. In some circles he is considered brilliant, a master strategist."

He held up a hand before I could speak.

"You want to know if he's the one who killed the girl. I can't answer that for you. Was he capable of it? Of course. Now it's my turn to ask *you* a question. I merely want to clear something up that's been bothering me. You told John that Federov hurt someone for fondling the Talmadge girl. I'd like to hear about that."

Perplexed, I spun Lynn's story without mentioning her name. By the time I finished speaking, however, all traces of the genial host had vanished from his face. I wondered what I had just done. He reached behind him for the phone on his desk.

"Danny? Bring TJ in here. I don't care where he is or what he's doing."

He replaced the phone in its cradle and watched the study door. I now exchanged a glance with Gennaro. He leaned back in his chair, ankles crossed, expressionless. He'd known this was coming.

TJ was a kid of eighteen or nineteen who stuck his head into the room then followed it with an insolent, hands-in-pockets, ghetto walk. He threw a look at Gennaro and me, disregarded us as irrelevant, and then focused on Polo Tony. His head was shaved down to bone and gleaming as though he'd just buffed it. Each ear and his nose sported a ring and his outfit was the usual baggy shorts and a t-shirt. Despite the rapper wannabe appearance, I knew who he must be. His stony expression was a younger version of the one Polo Tony wore.

"'Sup?" he muttered.

"Step here," Polo Tony snapped. "Right here."

The boy would probably go six feet if he stood up straight but that wasn't going to happen. He rolled his eyes and slouched to the side of his father's desk.

"Sol says you haven't been to work in a week. Tell these gentlemen why."

"You know."

"Look at *them* when you speak. Show some respect."

The boy turned, aware of his audience and playing it up a bit. He stood there a moment, hands still in his pockets.

"I got hurt on the job."

"My son works in a warehouse," Polo Tony explained. To the boy, he said, "Take your goddamn hands out of your goddamn pockets."

The room's noise-deadening feature couldn't conceal the snap of command.

The hands emerged, first left and then right. I saw immediately what I was supposed to see and suddenly felt the way you would if you were watching someone walk in front of a speeding Mac truck.

The fingers of TJ's right hand were splinted together and wrapped in surgical tape.

"Tell these gentlemen just how you got hurt."

"Hey what is this, anyway? You woke my ass up…"

Polo Tony's hand flashed out to crack against the back of his son's head.

"Tell them."

"Ow, man! Fuck you. I was working on the loading dock and a crate came down too fast off the front loader. I couldn't get my hand outta the way in time."

"No," Polo Tony said. "That's not what happened."

"Whaddya saying? You talked to Sol!"

"Sol told me he didn't see what happened. He believed you. I believed you."

He walked around to face his son.

"This goes beyond the boundaries of our family. If I find you have given your new 'friends' information about any 'business' you've heard discussed in this house, I won't be the one determining your punishment. Nor will I take exception with those who do. Do you understand me?"

The kid paled. One moment he wore a tiny "fuck-you" grin and the next his features crumpled.

"You got it wrong, man. Whatever you think it is I done."

"You have ten seconds to reconsider your answer."

"I told you…"

"Goddamn it!" Polo Tony snapped and, faster than I would have expected, he slapped the boy across the face. It sounded like a tennis ball hitting the sweet spot on a racket. His son rocked back against the desk only to howl when his hand flailed out and collided with the wood. Polo Tony pointed at the door. Tears streamed down the boy's face and he stumbled past his father. Polo Tony followed him and closed the door.

"Man," Gennaro said, audibly breathing out. "Man."

I realized I was half out of my chair, hands gripped tight against the armrests. I settled back. "What the hell, John?"

"Jesus, Mary and Joseph," Gennaro said. He looked a little gray, too. "I wasn't expecting that."

"What *was* that?"

"Discipline. That's what. You don't lie to Polo Tony. He told you that himself. No bullshit. Not from me, from you, or his kid."

"I figured that much out for myself," I said. "What's going to happen to the boy?"

"He'll tell his dad everything. No way he won't. They've almost been to this point before. Nothing this serious, but the kid will fess up on this, too. We just might be here waiting awhile."

"You still didn't answer my question."

"You got that right, buddy. Even I don't want to know the answer to that one."

I sat back in my chair and tried to remember the warning signs of a heart attack.

*   *   *   *

Polo Tony was gone about a half an hour. When he returned, he walked straight to the bar. Ignoring the beer, he poured something from a decanter and swirled in a thimble-full of water. The glass rattled against the bottle and he put it down abruptly, some of the dark liquid sloshing out.

"Anybody else?" he asked. Still the gracious neighbor, but one distracted by the rudeness of his errant child. Gennaro shook his head. Even though my mouth was dry, I declined, too.

Polo Tony sat down behind his desk. Whatever had passed between him and his son now manifested in the rigid posture and careful movements of someone having back spasms. He took a long swallow of his drink and when he put it down on a coaster he'd brought with him from the bar, I noticed two knuckles on his right hand were freshly abraded and one was beginning to swell.

"I'm in your debt, Reno. I must say that doesn't make me comfortable but you've helped me avoid what could have become a substantial problem for my colleagues. For my family as well. It still may become an issue, but at least I am forewarned. For that reason alone, I will discuss some things with you that I otherwise would not."

This was a guy brought up on some very tough streets who had gone genteel and taught himself manners because his position in the community required it. He couldn't have the neighbors and his fellow polo players thinking of him as a thug. He'd edited the "deez and doze" from his speech and taken up polo and golf. He didn't hang out in a "social club" like John Gotti loved to do, but in a two-million dollar home with its own polo field. From what I'd seen, he was as comfortable in his mannered role as he was in the Enrique Signi cashmere sweats he wore. But now, as he sat there behind his desk in the soundproofed den, part of the suburban businessman persona slipped away and I saw the guy who ran the Chicago Outfit.

"Tony Junior, TJ, has told me several things of consequence. The details are unnecessary. Suffice to say, he was welcomed into the Russians' inner circle. We have an understanding with them. They knew he was my son. Without my knowledge, TJ was running errands for some of them. He drove and fetched. They knew he would not be privy to any critical information here and, likewise, they didn't allow him to learn anything of consequence from them. If I had to guess, I'd say your 'Michael Fredericks' saw him as a rather curious pet. One he was apparently not afraid to abuse."

His eyes locked on to something behind and above me.

"TJ admitted to me he touched the young woman in an inappropriate way. He also described his punishment. They broke his fingers. He says he took it without a word and I believe that as well. He's a strong-willed young man. He knew what my reaction would be and he kept his mouth shut. There are men who work for me, those who introduced him to the Russians, who should have reported what happened. That's a separate issue."

He swallowed more of his drink, big hand wrapped around the glass. The room seemed smaller than it had been when we entered and I realized his fury was doing a good job of swelling into the empty spaces.

"You want to know about our relationship with these people, what they call their '*organizatsiya*' if I have the pronunciation correct. For obvious reasons, I will not go into specifics. I give you my word that we had nothing to do with the Talmadge girl's death. So what if she made some films? We didn't know her. I can't tell you if this Michael Fredericks ordered her hit for some reason of his own. I am told they were lovers. From what I know of him, he is a consummate businessman. Mixing the emotional with the professional is bad for business. However. What he did to my son makes me question his judgment. He is no stranger to ordering violence."

"Thank you for your frankness. I have one more question."

Polo Tony inclined his head and ripples of humor touched the corners of his mouth. "Please."

"You don't like working with them do you?"

"*Just* the thing I'd expect a journalist to ask. It is a measure of the confidence I have in your companion's judgement and your discretion that I will answer you."

The threat couldn't have been any clearer.

"This you probably know. In some cities, New York for example, those in the hierarchy made the decision many years ago to deal in narcotics. When the Russians began to arrive in the 1980's however, they told the New York Families, 'we can get it for you cheaper and safer.' They had the resources to go deep into Asia to get product and to bring it straight to the U.S., eliminating the existing supply network. That was fine with New York. The Russians and the New York families were already friendly. No doubt the former suppliers from south of the border were upset but that was a manageable problem. The distribution network remained essentially the same. Here, however, because Chicago has never trafficked in narcotics, because it is a filthy business, there is an entirely different distribution system."

"The gangs sell the dope."

"Exactly. Now, these Russians," he said and his mouth twitched again. "They believe they will manage it more effectively. They see themselves as the Steven Jobs and Bill Gates of the industry."

I sat up a little straighter. His words and their cadence had become more formal.

"You ask if I like working with them. I would say this. In some respects, they make fine allies. They are brutal, just as brutal as Chicago used to be. They are prepared to fight. Sitting right where you are now, this Federov told me that his grandfather was a general who defended Stalingrad."

He touched a corner of *The Art of War*.

"The professors at the business schools recommend reading this. 'It is better to keep a nation intact than to destroy it,' Sun Tzu says. I reminded Federov that his grandfather's Stalingrad was left in ruins. He just smiled at me. I remember others who smiled in that same manner. Joe Batters. Aiuppa. Defronzo. They were men who liked the killing."

"There is a problem, however," he continued. "The street gang leaders are more sophisticated than they were twenty or thirty years ago. Many of them have gone into the military just to prepare themselves to train others. Many of them are your age, my age. Older even. They have grown up at war. That is all they know. These are the people who wanted to get involved with the terrorists some time ago. You should remember. All that reporting about building a 'dirty bomb'." He nodded to himself.

"These are the people the Russians want us to fight! And they presume we will help, even though we've never wanted anything to do with the drugs. I have grandchildren. I don't want to worry every time their mother walks them down the street that they could become targets. If the Russians, this Red Mafiya, make a war..."

Polo Tony stood, wincing as the abrupt move brought pain.

"I'm sorry I couldn't answer the question you came here to ask. I suspect I've enlightened you in other ways. I hope my faith in your good judgement about this conversation is not misplaced."

*   *   *   *

If anything, we were ushered out faster than we had been welcomed in, as though Polo Tony had other things to attend to and he was eager to get to them. Or maybe he was having second thoughts about telling us so much and wanted us gone before he decided to take care of the oversight.

I sat without moving as Gennaro got us back on the highway. The first thing he did when we were rolling along at 75 was reach into the console and take out a second flask identical to the one he'd used in the restaurant and polish off a good third of the contents before stowing it again. He didn't offer me any this time.

"How much of that did you know going in?" I asked.

"Pretty much all," he said. "Pretty much all of it, Reno. I've been at this shit a long time. I know these guys, how they think."

"He always so chatty?"

"Surprised me, too. I've never seen him go off like that. I mean, he knew who he was talking to and he still did it. A reporter and an ex-fed, I mean. All I got to say is he sure took a liking to you. Or he's planning to have you whacked."

I stared at him. "That's comforting."

He glanced over and winked. "Nah, nah. I'm just breaking your balls. But don't get the idea he's in love with you or nothing. He's got an agenda and you're just part of it is all."

"If he thinks I'm in a position to do anything to help him, he's definitely got the wrong guy."

"Beats me, buddy. All I know is he's as cold a motherfucker as you'll ever want to meet and I've never known him to back down from a fight. This Russian deal has him turning inside out. And this thing with his kid…man, Federov best watch his back."

"How long have they been here? How tight is the connection?"

"The Russkies? It's been building gradually over maybe the last five years. OC's got the traditional stuff locked up. The Russians basically came in and started some new action. Money laundering 'cause they own banks. Lots of stuff with computers, hacking in and getting credit card numbers and running frauds. Financial scams. They're easing in real nice to the Board of Trade, pretty much all over LaSalle Street. They've bought a few politicians. Taken over some formerly legit businesses."

"The Outfit just let them in?"

"You gotta understand something, Reno. The Russians have got the kind of set-up in the old country that OC had here in the old days. They pretty much run the cities, the whole fucking government! Hell, they're selling off weapons to anybody that'll pay. You want a warhead? That's a blue light special to them. But what they really got is contacts, a little international network set up by the old KGB. A lot of these Russian mob guys are former KGB or *Spetznatz* Special Forces soldiers or what have you."

"So it's a trade off."

"They scratch each other's backs all the time. Russians want to put up a building, the Outfit arranges the zoning, the building permits and locks in the unions. You can figure how that shit works. The Outfit needs an extra guy to help 'em jack somebody up, they take some ex-KGB mug who knows a hundred different ways to hurt you without leaving a mark."

"Are the Feds on top of this?"

Gennaro snorted. "Got a grand jury taking testimony as fast as the U.S.Attorneys can come up with evidence. They've made some dope busts. A strip club racket where some Cechniyans were bringing broads over and forcing them to work as dancers. The Bureau's running surveillance. The mandate is to keep them from getting a foothold like they have in New York but I'll tell you right now, it's not working."

"That's comforting, too."

"They couldn't shitcan the Russians in New York, they sure as hell aren't gonna be able to do it here," he said. "Not without the Outfit's help."

I let that thought rattle around in my brain as I leaned back in the seat and closed my eyes. As a kid I loved sleeping in the car when my dad was driving. It always felt like a moving cocoon, the darkness outside and me inside sliding right on through it, invisible, not stopping for anything. That was then and this was…not then. The seats in the cars my dad drove weren't half as comfortable as this one but I couldn't drift off. The realization of what I'd walked into kept me right on the edge of sleep. Keep pushing against an immovable object, I remember an old cop once telling me, and suddenly you may find the resistance disappears and you have nothing left to push against, just air. That's what I felt like right now. I'd shoved myself through a barrier into an empty shaft of some kind and needed to get to the other side without falling.

"What's your plan, man?" Gennaro asked.

I opened my eyes. We were back in Evanston, parked behind my car. It was nearly midnight and the coffee shop where we'd met earlier was dark. I felt like I'd been teleported, not driven, and that I'd left some molecules behind. I rubbed my face, carefully avoiding my nose. There was a vile taste in my mouth and my eyes felt like sparks had flown into them.

"My plan. Funny you should ask. That's not something I've quite worked out yet."

"You going to keep after it, trying to find who killed the girl?" He had the flask open again in his hand. I was tempted to snatch the sucker away and drain it.

"You know, John, much as I loved palling around with you and your friend tonight, I can't get enthusiastic about developing a deep, abiding relationship with a guy who kills people for a living AND beats up on his kid after the kid's had his fingers broken by some other scumbag. You know what I'm saying?"

"He was trying to help you."

"For what, exactly, in return? You said he's got an agenda. How does that involve me?"

He took a drink, seemed to hold it in his mouth for a moment, and then swallowed it. His lips moved as though tasting it for the first time. "You're an ungrateful bastard, you know that?"

He wasn't drunk but, as Dean Martin would have said, he was leaning that way. I got out of his car and started for mine. Gennaro gunned the engine of the Caddy once and then laid on the horn. I looked back toward him. He got out with the flask dangling in his left hand.

"You know, Reno, I just thought of this. You wanted to know why Polo Tony invited you to come see him? You're like the priest in that old joke. The priest who sneaks out of saying Mass to go play golf and gets a hole in one? He knows it must be Divine Punishment because who can he tell? Who can *you* tell, Reno?"

"Hey John?" I called out. "What's your connection to Polo Tony, anyway? Are you still with the Bureau?"

He laughed, flipped me the finger.

"And the horse you rode in on, young man."

*   *   *   *

I parked my horse in my driveway ten minutes later. I'd left the lawn mower in the way of the garage door and the floodlight mounted along the side of the house had burned out. I didn't feel like stumbling around in the shadows so I could put the Mustang away for the night. Instead, I made sure the convertible top was latched and the windows rolled up and then I slid out.

I stopped moving the moment I heard the cat's tentative squeak from the shrubs along the driveway.

"Socks?" I said, puzzled. He emerged from under an arbor vitae and trotted toward me, squeaking again with pleasure at having a friendly leg to rub against. I picked him up and nuzzled the side of his face with my beard. I'm sure the movement would have looked 100 percent natural to anyone watching and that's exactly what I intended. I smiled, talking to him in low voice, keeping it calm even though I felt a sliver of ice touch the back of my neck. When I'd left I locked the door behind me with him inside, sleeping on his perch in front of the windows in my study.

"You learn how to unlock a door while I was gone, little man?"

I stroked his back with my right hand. There are three people who have keys to my house: Vinnie, Sunny and my neighbor who I knew was at Disney World with his family as of the day before. If Sunny was inside, her car would be parked in front. If Vinnie had come visiting, he would have left upon realizing I wasn't home. Given all the things he learns about people in his work, he is scrupulously careful not to invade the privacy of his friends.

Of course, Sunny could have come over for some reason and then departed. She wouldn't have let Socks escape, however. She doesn't believe any cat should be allowed out to roam. And, had she entered my home for any reason, she would have left a message on my cellular. The same applied if an intruder had broken in and activated the burglar alarm system. The central monitoring station would have tried to alert me. But there was no message symbol blinking on my phone.

The icy feeling traveled the length of my spine and I shivered in the mild evening. Socks squeaked softly and looked up at me, as if to say, "What's up?"

"You tell me. You were here," I said.

He blinked his eyes but remained silent.

There was no doubt my visit with the boss of the Chicago crime syndicate and all the talk of a Russian mob power-play had me spooked. Combined with a lack of sleep and the return of the dull throb in my nose, that could have skewed my thinking. Sunny might have dropped by and Socks could have scampered past her to freedom. Such things happen when animals choose to display they are far brighter than the dumb humans they encounter daily. But if that were the case, where was the cell phone message? And what would have been so urgent that it caused her to forsake her normal eight hours of sleep?

Suddenly, the loss of the light that normally illuminated the driveway and front of the garage struck me as ominous. It was controlled by a timer on a wall switch inside the back porch door. All someone would have needed to do was flip the switch to off.

I let Socks down and walked across the front yard toward the front door. If an intruder were waiting, he'd have been anticipating my arrival. He might even know I'd been alerted to his presence by seeing Socks outside. Hidden inside, though, he would think he still had an element of surprise. Except that I knew the house and its entrances far better than he did.

An open front porch runs the width of the house and its railing is far enough off the ground that it had often, in the Spiderman days of my teenage years, allowed me a nice perch from which to climb to the roof and, from there, gain access to a second floor window. My mom had allowed me to perform this gymnastics feat for the simple reason that she knew I was agile enough not to break my neck. What she hadn't known was that I'd had another, surreptitious and riskier, route to the second floor. My dad created it by accident during one of his attempts to be useful around the house, even though he'd never lived there and had been ordered by a judge to stay away from us.

I started up the front steps and called for Socks. He'd dodged under the porch, however, which is part of his nighttime routine. When I find him in the yard after dark, there's no way I can cajole him to come inside. That's only accomplished after I go in myself, open the sliding glass door to the patio, and then crack the top of a can of tuna.

I called his name again, louder and exasperated, and then trotted around to the side of the house as though in search of him. I had no idea if my act had been believable but it allowed me to dodge out of sight and to get next to the only part of my home that has no windows on the first floor.

My dad's idea had been simple. A large, spreading maple tree sits in the side yard, just a few feet from the house. It's a quiet area, bordered by a small copse of shrubbery and trees and then the side yard of the house next door.

Dad wanted to hang a hammock between the maple and the house. Without telling us or asking for my help, he came over one day during the first summer of their separation while I was working and mom was teaching a class. As usual, he'd been drunk. He'd sunk the hammock's rope bolt into the trunk of the maple with no problem. But he had obviously downed a couple more beers while doing so. I counted no less than five bolts in the brick wall of the house, an indication he was trying to get the hammock to sit at the right height to hang evenly with the tree.

I saw the possibilities the moment I realized what he'd done. The heavy ring bolts, all deeply imbedded at varying levels, formed crude steps I could use to scale the side of the house and get far enough up so that the sill of the window to my room was within chin-up distance.

This was no staircase but it was similar to the footholds on rock-climbing walls you see in some of the high-end mountaineering and sporting goods stores. I'd used it often, sometimes for fun, sometimes to keep Mom from knowing I'd spent the night elsewhere.

I crouched in the now overgrown shrubbery and thought about the many times I'd reminded myself to do some brush trimming in this part of my yard. I was glad now that I'd held off. I was invisible from the street, from the backyard and from the house. This was the point at which I needed to make a choice.

I had the cell phone in my pocket. I could call Evanston P.D., report my suspicions, and let them take over. I knew how they'd handle it. I'd been on enough ride-alongs to appreciate the precision a well-trained squad of cops brings to entering and searching a house after a burglary in progress call. A small glitch there, though. They'd be assuming the offender was armed; they always do. But how could I tip them who they might really be up against? What was I going to say? "Watch your asses; it could be an ex-KGB man or Russian Special Forces trooper."

I almost laughed out loud at myself for that thought and the paranoia it suggested. What if the cat had, somehow, wormed his way through a partially open window? Maybe I had let him out myself before leaving and, in a senior moment of the type that seem to occur more often with each day I travel past forty, I'd forgotten.

No, I wouldn't be dialing 9-1-1.

I stood and stretched, reaching up along the wall for the handholds I remembered from some twenty-years past. Small outcroppings of brick slightly misplaced, just enough for the fingers to curl around. My weight hasn't changed much since I was in college and I work out whenever possible. I stepped up to the first grommet and balanced there, then quickly brought my other foot up and over to the next one. I hoped I wasn't being optimistic about my climbing ability or how deeply imbedded the bolts were.

After first finding this unusual entrance, I had set the screen into the window opening in such a way that a simple finger tap from outside would pop it free. Fortunately, I'd never seen a good reason to make it more secure. I pushed in the right spots, the screen came loose and, from my precarious perch, I let it slide down the wall to the nice cushiony pile carpet inside the room.

I was up and over the sill a moment later, careful to protect my still-throbbing nose. I was in my old room which I had converted for guest use. The door to the hall was closed. No surprise. I usually left it that way.

Now was the moment of most concern. I slipped off my shoes and sat on my haunches just inside the window, waiting. Shadows crept around me as clouds scurried and broke in the night sky.

My house has its idiosyncrasies as most do. For one thing, no central air. Large window AC units in the living room and study cool the downstairs quite well and I have another in my room. I use them in extremely hot weather but mostly prefer to sleep with open windows and beneath a slowly turning ceiling fan. I'd left all of my refrigerated air machines cranking through our unusual June heat wave, however, and, as I waited by the window of the guest room, I could just barely hear the low hum from the one in my room down the hall.

My house is also thickly carpeted. As a professor at Northwestern, my mom spent long hours on her feet in wooden-floored classrooms. When we moved into the house after her divorce, we found my dad had made sure she wouldn't have to worry about hardwood here. It was one of the thoughtful things he'd done for her from time to time that often made her cry with regret that he couldn't get his act together and come back to live with us. When I'd gotten rid of the original deep shag years ago, I laid new carpet in every room. The result was not only comfortable but a soundproofing that pleased me as much as the soft feel had pleased my mother.

I rose to my feet after a moment and eased open the door to the hall, slipped through, and closed it gently behind me. I stood there a full two minutes. Dim light came from the lamp on the front-hall table downstairs. While the noise of the air conditioners would mask most of the sound I made, it also kept me from hearing anyone else who might be in the house. If you're used to living alone, though, there's a subtle difference to the feel of your home when someone else enters. I was depending on that sense. I moved down the hall a slow step at a time and kept my eyes on the top of the stairs.

The master bedroom door was closed and that would be the next challenge. I needed to get in there. For one thing, that's where the alarm control panel was and I needed to know the status of the system. For another, I kept my dad's old Walther PPK-S backup piece clipped to the underside of a shelf right below it.

The knob turned easily under my hand. I pushed the door into the cool darkness beyond. Just that simple movement reminded me of bursting into Brooke's apartment and rushing forward, only to be tripped by her tangled legs. The memory of her face haunted me. I crossed to my closet and glanced inside.

A green light glowed on the alarm panel and sent the ice slithering down my back again. It had been turned off in my absence and not reactivated. No doubt lingered now. Those with keys to my home know how anal I am about engaging the alarm on departure. Since I leave windows open, I engineered the system to take that into account. No one can move between floors when the alarm is in its "away" mode. No one can enter my study downstairs. And no one can open any of the exterior doors. I've made it clear to everyone with a key to my house that they need to set the system before exiting, damn it. Whoever had deactivated it was either still inside or had left, intending for me to know he'd visited.

I reached beneath the shelf for the gun.

I felt better when my hand closed around the PPK-S. I withdrew it to check the clip. Full. That's something you never assume. I worked the slide and silently jacked a round into the chamber. It was the original German model, not the American knock-off, and the action was smooth and noiseless. My heart rate slowed, slightly. Things would be a bit more even now. I moved back through the bedroom door and stopped at the head of the stairs to stand motionless again. From there the sounds of the AC units in the living room and study were slightly louder, but that was the only thing I could hear. I started down the stairs with the Walther up in front at eye-level. It was weighted nicely and felt snug and deadly in my hand.

No one jumped out at me and there were no gunshots or explosions as I walked slowly down the stairs, taking care to ease my weight onto each step. As I moved, the house seemed to close in around me and my focus became sharp enough to make me forget the needles of pain lancing my face. In that state of heightened awareness, I couldn't sense the presence of an intruder. By the time I came off the last step, I was convinced I was alone.

I crossed the front hall quickly and slid the double doors to my study aside, leading with the gun. My desk lamp was on. I hadn't left it that way. Papers that hadn't been there earlier rattled from underneath a paperweight in the center of my desktop. I itched to go look at them but paranoia made me complete my sweep of the house first. I didn't totally trust my instincts and didn't want any surprises at my back when I approached the desk.

I checked the living room, kitchen and small pantry. The door to the basement was locked and the door slightly warped, besides. If anyone was hiding down there, thinking they'd come crashing out to blow me away, it would take them so long I could go buy a .50 caliber machine gun, mount it on a tripod and have them in my sights before they emerged.

Slipping the Walther into my waistband in cross-draw position, I went back to the study.

What my visitor had laid out across the center of my desk was the operating manual for my alarm system, or one like mine. Circled in red on the open page were the instructions for remote-accessing the control and entering commands via telephone. I'd forgotten that feature even existed. But how had they known what code to enter? Answer: they have the resources of every electronics whiz in the federal government at their disposal. Next to the manual was a government business card. It read, "Jesse Dark, Special Agent. Underneath that it said: Joint Terrorism Task Force. Under that: Chicago Region and a Dirksen Federal Building address. I picked it up and turned it over. What appeared to be an 800 pager or cell phone number had been stamped there in red ink with the notation "24-Hrs" in parenthesis after it. There was no note.

I felt anger at the violation of my home rising in my chest. I thought for a moment my nose was about to burst. I took a deep slow, breath, then another, then turned and walked out to the kitchen. After I'd gotten a can of tuna for Socks, I inspected the back door and the jam. No signs of forced entry. I looked at the switch for the driveway light. It was turned off. I flicked it up. The light illuminated the lawn mower and part of the open garage. I let out a breath. I'd been sort of hoping to see Special Agent Jesse Dark standing there smirking at me. I wouldn't have shot him but I might have whizzed a 9mm round past his ear just for fun.

I followed the usual routine to encourage Socks to come in and spend the night. He trotted across the patio but stood just outside the door looking hopefully at the can of tuna. I scooped some out and put it in his bowl. He didn't seem to want to come in. I had a sudden fear that Agent Dark, or whichever of his minions had been in the house, might have hurt him and I squatted down and ran my hands over his soft, glossy fur again. He was fine. Being a cat, he wanted to sleep outside. The temperature had dropped about ten degrees. Under other circumstances, I might've wanted to sleep outside, too. Nevertheless, I carried him in and deposited him in front of his food. He accepted the

tuna-for-freedom trade-off. I closed the patio door while he chowed down and I fumed.

The government had learned the one flaw in my alarm system and had used that to breach it and break into my home. For what? So some terror task force agent with a flair for the dramatic could leave me his business card? Didn't they know what happened to federal agents who messed with reporters without a legal basis to do so? What they'd done was called harassment and burglary. Or would be if I could prove it. Hadn't they learned from the FBI's black bag jobs of the 60's?

Sonofa BITCH, I was pissed. If I had still been a television reporter, it wouldn't have happened. No matter what provocation I provided by nosing around, they wouldn't have dared try something so stupid. An on-leave and nearly discredited radio reporter was another story altogether. Were I still in TV I could have caused them big-time trouble, even with mere allegations, if I put the story together the right way. As it stood now, I could do nothing. The radio station would never risk the legal repercussions of an assault on the government, and evidently this Jesse Dark knew it.

The Joint Terrorism Task Force draws agents from all the federal bureaucracies that have jurisdiction in the subject matter. I wondered what three-letter agency signed Dark's paychecks. FBI? CIA? NSA? Some group with a name the public would never know?

I considered calling Gennaro. He'd still be in his car. I even reached for my Palm Pilot to look up that number before another thought stayed my hand. Wiretaps. If they'd had the balls to break in, and the know-how to come up with my alarm code to boot, what would have prevented them from bugging my phone? Now that could be something to work with. Were I to find their gear attached, and then bring in one of the camera guys from Channel 14, even a freelancer…?

How would I prove it had been the JTTF that pulled the stunt? Somehow I doubted their equipment was stamped, "Property of US Government." Then again, given what I'd read about the current state of intelligence-gathering, it wouldn't surprise me. The tags would probably read "Do Not Remove This Tag," too.

Waves of exhaustion pounded me. Standing there, watching Socks eating, I massaged my head with both hands. I'd call Gennaro in the morning from a phone away from the house and see if he had the equipment to sweep my lines. I'd do a lot of things in the morning, maybe even call Agent Dark. I might even take a ride down to the Dirksen Federal Building and confront him in person.

For now, I turned out the lights, locked up and walked my sorry butt upstairs to bed. I was glad no one had been waiting in the house. I could feel the adrenaline leaching out of me with each step.

I thought I was safe.

CHAPTER 8

▼

I awoke on my right side. I'd fallen asleep with an arm under my head, apparently to keep my nose from brushing against anything. My hand rested lightly on the butt of the Walther under the pillow.

Notwithstanding the gun's proximity, I awakened with the gnawing sensation that I was in serious trouble. I had no idea of the time or how long I'd been asleep. A door opened and closed. My bedroom door? No way....

Someone else was in the room with me.

Terror froze me to the bed. I could feel the handle of the Walther and clutched it firmly but I didn't have the strength I needed to roll over and bring it to bear. I wanted to. Jesus, I wanted to dive for the far corner of the room and come up shooting. But I couldn't move. What the hell was going on?

My heart faltered, then began to pound. I could feel the hairs on the back of my neck prickling at the sensation of a large mass displacing the air nearby. Then my bed shifted, the way a bed does when a second person sits on it.

I tried to turn. My body wouldn't obey. My eyes stayed closed. I pretended I was asleep even knowing that the thudding in my chest would give me away. I had a sudden, startling vision from outside myself. A man lowered his face until it was inches away from my left ear. His whisper came, sibilant and mocking:

"Having a nice sleep, asshole?" he asked. And then he repeated himself, the breathy sound fading into the white noise of the air conditioner.

I screamed pitifully, whirled and sat bolt upright. The Walther came up with me and I hid behind a wobbly two-handed grip. Luckily, I didn't fire. Lucky because I faced only my bedroom, devoid of any threat. There was only furniture and morning shadows and a smell I recognized as my own fear.

A dream. A fucking nightmare.

*   *   *   *

I needed to get out of the house for awhile. I put on running shorts and a t-shirt, let Socks out to prowl, and headed for the lake. I didn't even check to see if it was raining. Made no difference. Outside, at least, any bogeyman who came after me would have to be real, not spectral. Unless I was farther around the bend than I thought.

Sunshine and ninety humid degrees greeted me like an overbearing relative. I looked at my watch for the first time since waking up. Only a little before 8 a.m. I wondered if the poles had shifted to bring the humidity of the rain forest to Illinois.

I took it easy for the first half mile, gradually easing up to speed as I headed uptown a couple of blocks to Davis Street. Once in the mix of commuters headed to either the "L" or the Metra, and students stumbling out of Starbucks on their way to early classes, I had to watch myself, but I kept a pretty good pace.

Evanston has left its portion of the lakefront au-naturale. A good chunk of it is owned by Northwestern University and a few million dollar-plus homes but the public areas are parks and a cinder track meanders through them. I followed the track south aways, enjoying how the lake cracked the sun's reflection into bobbing slivers and pitched them in my direction. For the first time in days, I thought of Megan and wished she was with me and that the memory of Brooke lying dead on the floor was not. Given the time difference in California, Meg might well be running on a beach right now, too, and trying to put her demons behind her. I wondered if she considered me one of them.

Then an amazing thing happened. I'm sloppy, as is much of the population, when it comes to physical fitness. Talking on the radio each day doesn't call for catlike agility worthy of Steven Seagal. Like a guy whose doctor spots a shadow on his x-ray, though, I was beginning to get motivated. They tell me turning any age above forty will do that. I'd recently spent a bit more time at the gym than usual, punching the bag, working the balance beam and adding some distance to my runs. I'd taken to swimming a few laps, too. Mostly I'd ended my workouts with a tightened chest and my breath coming more in wheezes than measured gasps. Now though, I started to feel really good.

They call it a Runner's High, when all the endorphins click right and the kinks leave your muscles and thoughts of bad things disappear from your head. I was clunking along when suddenly the tension was gone, the pain and itch in my bandaged nose was on hold and I could kick it up a notch and not feel any strain. I held onto that great feeling all the way home, turning in a total run of about eight miles. Even winding down to a light jog for the last half mile or so didn't spoil the sensation. Neither did seeing an unmarked Chevrolet squad parked at the curb in front of my house and Charley Kinsella perched on my front steps, gnawing at something.

I stopped at the end of my drive and ignored him for the moment. My legs trembled a bit so I bent over to let my body absorb the fact it was finished moving at more than a walk. Had I taken a swim, my sweats wouldn't have been any more soaked and I was breathing heavier than usual, but I wasn't panting or wheezing. In fact, I still felt good. Energized, even.

"'Morning, Detective," I called.

He shoved the remainder of what looked like a Danish into his mouth, grunted a greeting, then stuck his hand into the white paper bag at his feet, withdrew a family-sized muffin, and looked at it the way Socks eyes a mouse after he's just finished two cans of food. Never too full for a favorite snack. I walked up to him.

"Want a muffin?" he rattled the bag. "Got one left."

"No, thanks."

"Don't tell me. You're one of those wheat germ and sprouts guys."

"Not hardly."

He wore the same sports jacket from two nights ago and the blue shirt underneath looked as though he'd rescued it from being plunged into a washing machine. If he'd slept recently, it didn't show. A Motorola walkie-talkie sat next to him on the stairs looking and sounding as worn as he did. The calls came in ragged sequence, violence taking its toll even in daylight.

Units in Twelve and on Citywide, youths with guns and gunshots heard…Units in Fifteen and on Citywide, use caution, civilian dress officers are responding to the fight in the gangway…Units on Citywide and in the Seventh District there's a man shot, a man shot, he's laying in the road and the offender is still on the scene, use caution….

"What can I do for you, detective?" I asked.

He dropped the muffin into the bag with obvious reluctance and withdrew a napkin to blot his lips.

"First off," he said around the napkin, "you can drop the 'detective.' You sound like an asshole. 'Kinsella' works just fine for me."

"Worked for me up to the other night. When somebody tries to slam me for murder, I tend to get more formal."

"That was two nights ago. I've moved beyond it, like that Dr. Phil says. You ever watch him? He gets going, he kicks pretty good ass. For a shrink."

He had to be playing some angle. Either that or a clone was sitting in front of me and the real Charley Kinsella was back at the station beating a suspect into submission.

"See, I've already surprised you, haven't I? Well, here's another flash. I don't think you killed that girl. I'm not saying you weren't trying to run a program by me but you didn't do her."

"How very perceptive."

"And it wasn't a home invader, either. That's the company line, y'know. Random burglar, got caught, grabbed her the wrong way and oops!"

"You don't go for that?"

"I might buy that the guy didn't show up planning to do her. But random? That would be one of the Great Coincidences of All Time."

"I hear there have been a few burglaries in that area. Even in that building."

He peered up at me. "Funny thing. I hadda drink with the guy from Property Crimes who looked in on those. Every hit was during the day. Like three in the afternoon or after, up to about five or so. And they always took little shit, always the stuff easy to carry. What's that tell you?"

"Kids."

"You're not as dumb as you look. I don't see a kid who just pulls a few kick-ins on his way home from school suddenly graduating up to a middle of the night home invasion. But it's a funny thing. My boss? He's just pissing all over himself telling me that's what happened and when we get the little fucker he'll cop to it all. Oh and, by the way, I don't have to worry about it 'cause I've got enough on my plate."

"You're off the case?" I said, surprised at my disappointment.

"So they say." He took a handkerchief out of his pocket and mopped his face. "You have any problem taking this inside?"

"I have a problem with not knowing why we're having this conversation."

He pushed himself to his feet like it pained him to do so, and then glowered at me.

"I've had City Hall yank cases before. Political shit. Right before we snatch somebody up, they give it to one of the guys likes to be on TV. I got no problem with that. The mope still goes away. My evidence, somebody more photogenic gets the credit. I don't give a rat's ass. I put enough bad guys away, one or two more don't get me a monthly bonus. But this don't have that kind of feel to it."

"Meaning what?"

"Federal people are hanging around. Some kind of special federal-state task force is doing the work, not our guys. Nobody in Area Three got assigned anyway, which is strange all by itself." He lifted his chin at the front door. "There some reason you don't want me inside?"

I looked at him and tried to assess whether I was being suckered. From what I knew of Charley Kinsella, I didn't think so. He was the sort of guy who'd come at you slow, lumbering, but always straight on. No sneak attacks.

"The 'G' has been here, too," I said. "And I'm not so sure they didn't leave a microphone or two behind."

I told him what I'd found, including the card. He looked more closely at the house, as though using x-ray vision to find the bugs.

"That's the fucking Feebs for you. Always with the drama." His eyes came back to my face. "That means they either think you got something, or they're afraid you're gonna turn up something by snooping around and they want to be on top of you when that happens."

He sounded like it wasn't a half-bad idea and he wished he'd thought of it.

"You're saying this is something they pull on reporters all the time?" I asked with a little heat.

His lip curled. "That's what's wrong with you people. You figure that press pass you carry is like a gold card membership to the human race. Lets you go anywhere, fuck with anybody you please, then hold it up and hide behind it when the heat comes on. Lemme tell you buddy, the G don't look at it that way. It's just cardboard."

"So what are you here for, Charley?" I snapped.

"Most of the Feds I deal with are OK. For being little J Edgars, that is. But I don't like the way these particular buttholes been looking at us, like we're pigeon poop they picked up on their shoes. I figure they don't much care about this case except how it plays into something else they're working on. You get that feeling, too?"

"Go on."

"I could see this being one of those situations where they give the do-er a pass if he agrees to help them climb a ladder, know what I'm saying?"

A furious light came into his eyes, only at partial wattage from what I'd seen the other night but enough to tell he was pissed at the thought.

"That's not happening. They can take the credit, lock the fucker up with all his Outfit buddies for all I care. But he's not walking."

He shook himself suddenly and reached into the bag for his muffin, bit into it. "I figure you been out sniffing, I'll stop by and see what you got. Guy like you, big shot newsman, you probably have the whole case wrapped in a nice, neat package."

"Is this where I'm supposed to start a monologue and keep it going until you tell me to shut up? Or can I expect some back and forth?"

I got a fishy eye for that. "We might be able to arrange something. What've you got?"

"'Lie down and do everything the nice policeman tells you?' No, Charley. You drove all the way out here. You get to start."

A cell phone rang. He fished it out of his pocket, grunted hello and listened.

"No, no, you did the right thing," he said after a moment. He patted another pocket and came up with a notebook. He scribbled something. "Who else is there with you? Okay, that's fine, but none of the assholes, right? Yeah, I'm on my way. Go ahead and make notifications but keep it real neutral. Gangbangers, that's all you have to say. Don't get into any of the rest of the shit. If the Street Deputy shows, call me back. Yeah. Thanks, Sheila."

He snapped the phone closed and regarded me for a moment.

"Tell me right now. Not details, just how far into this are you? You know what the Feds are doing, that kind of thing?"

"Yeah, more or less. A basic idea, I think. Why?"

"You got a strong stomach?"

"Reasonably. Why? What's…?"

"We got a double murder in Uptown I wanna look at. Take a ride with me."

*   *   *   *

Compared to Gennaro's Cadillac, Kinsella's Caprice rode like a farmer's truck taking hogs to market. I'd forgotten about the waxy paste on the windshield, exhaust from his hand rolled cigarettes, and the way a spring in the passenger seat was trying to work its way through what was left of the cloth upholstery. He chose not to smoke, fortunately for me. But he had a question.

"What d'you think you're gonna get out of this? When it's all said and done?"

I had to give that a few moments thought.

"Maybe my job back if I can put together what happened to her. Satisfaction at least."

"That's important to you?"

"Absolutely."

"Even though she was a hooker?"

"Even so."

He nodded as though I had confirmed something for him.

"Way I look at it, one victim's as important as another. Some of these guys nowadays, they call the killings of 'bangers, hookers, street people misdemeanor murders."

"I've heard the term."

"Yeah, well it's crap. Call me 'Reverend' or whatever else you want, but everyone counts in life, everyone counts in death. I don't let 'em slide to the bottom of the drawer just 'cause they didn't make the best choices. Or because some numbnuts from the G tells me to back off. You hear what I'm saying?"

He had the wigwag headlights flashing and now hit the siren to clear Clark and Howard and get out of Evanston. Late morning traffic moved sluggishly and he alternated one foot on the brake, the other on the gas. I hoped I didn't get car sick but, with all the crap on the windshield already, who would notice?

"So she was a hooker." he continued. "Vice didn't know her, not a big surprise if she was independent and kept herself low key. From what we found in a closet of that apartment she was into the S and M shit. Had a little briefcase with some of the tools of the trade. Also bandages and what not. Nice of her, whip you, cut you up, then fix it all and send you on your way with a kiss. You sure you never got any of that?"

I had my eyes fixed on the Honda in front of us, willing him to tap the brakes before we slammed into its trunk.

"No, Charley."

"Well, from the autopsy it looks like she was the giving sort, not the receiving. No sign any of the equipment had been used on her and the docs can usually tell. Marks on the nipples, ligature around the wrists or the neck. Not with her. Healthy gal, other than that she was dead. Your turn."

"She had a boyfriend."

"Surprise, surprise. Who?"

I told him the two names and what Federov/Fletcher did for a living. He turned his head toward me.

"Federov. No shit."

"You know him?"

"Nope. But it fits. Damn if it doesn't."

He didn't elaborate right away and raised his hand when I asked him what he meant. We had gone eight more blocks, him blatting the siren whenever we approached a corner, when he spoke again continuing his narrative.

"Looks to me like she walked into the apartment and he was right there behind the door. Probably heard her coming down the hall. Grabbed her," he held his left arm out in front of him, elbow bent, demonstrating how the killer would have maneuvered. "Tried to get her to keep from screaming is my guess. You get somebody in the crook of your elbow like that, you can torque the head and break the neck or go with pressure on the carotid artery. M.E. says he just kept squeezing and shut off the carotid. She was struggling and, when he got a solid grip on her, that was it."

"I would think grabbing someone like that you'd have control right away. He had to have been a big, strong guy, right?"

"Probably. But she bit him. That's something we held back from the news. Don't you go saying anything about it, either. Bit him enough there was blood on her teeth and in her mouth."

Though my sense of smell was blunted, I suddenly tasted something coppery and vile and nearly gagged. Tugging on the crank for the passenger side window, I moved the glass just enough that I could feel a slight breeze. Even the super-heated air was better than the stagnancy inside the car.

After a moment, I said, "No threatening notes from her boyfriend lying around?"

"The only mail we found was her brother's. None to her. It was his place after all."

He glanced across at me and must have seen my surprise. "Yeah. She was apparently just hanging out there. Looked like she hadn't really even moved in. She had suitcases laying around and her stuff was all over."

Packing, I thought. Getting ready to run.

"You talk to the brother?" I asked.

"Tried, yesterday morning. Him n' the old man together. Didn't get much from either of 'em. Talmadge is slicker n' goose shit. 'Course, by then, I had a little FBI shadow at my elbow. Showed up right in the middle of my interview. Why? You talk to him?"

"Yeah, for a couple of minutes. He didn't lay claim to the apartment. Basically he said she was fed up with the boyfriend and wanted to get out of town."

He swerved to avoid a produce truck that appeared, suddenly, from the mouth of an alley.

"Hammerhead!" he snapped and cranked the siren into wail mode. The sound bounced off the buildings as we picked up a little speed.

"He also told me he'd picked up some phoney identification for her," I said.

I expected him to snort at that but all I got was a nod. "Like she wasn't just fed up with the boyfriend but that she figured he'd try to come after her."

"You didn't find any false ID's?"

"Nah. You see paper like that, you remember it, especially if it's any good. What'd he say he got? Driver's license or something?"

"He didn't say."

"Nothing there. Now, what's giving the bosses a hard-on about the home invader angle is her computer. Plug-ins are all there, printer, no machine. That says 'kids' to the bosses. Tells me somebody was worried their name mighta been in some kinda John-book file."

We rounded a corner and then immediately jounced into a short street that ran parallel to the El tracks.

Uptown's not a neighborhood on any tour routes, even though you can get terrific ethnic food at some of its joints. That is, if you don't mind sharing counter space with a gangbanger or two, maybe a guy whose appetizer came out of a Dumpster or a bottle of MadDog. Uptown's salad bowl mixture of populations means you'll find a Vietnamese grocery on one side of the street, a Greek greasy spoon on the other and still be able to smell curry coming from the Indian place around the corner. While you're making the rounds, maybe you'll get mugged by a cowboy teamed up with a dreadlocked Jamaican Rasta. Equal Opportunity Crime.

Uptown's full of kids, too. And kids who have children of their own. Little fourteen- and fifteen-year-olds raising families. You can see them in doorways or sometimes playing in alleys, always cat-alert to what's going on around them and ready to disappear at the first whisper of danger. You notice them duck inside unexpectedly, you'd better look for cover yourself because Mr. Drive-By may be in the neighborhood. A psychologist I interviewed years ago suggested they're the same urchins you'd see on the streets of Belfast, Beirut or Baghdad. Just offspring of a different war.

The address where Kinsella delivered us was north of Clark and Lawrence, not far from St. Boniface cemetery. It's an area where rusted hulks of cars fought with man-sized weeds for dominance of empty lots and where I once covered the story of a teenager who'd been blown into the street by the force of a broken fire hydrant and then swept under the wheels of a passing CTA bus.

The action this time, though, centered around a sagging two-and-a-half-story clapboard house with boarded up windows that stood alone on a street corner. Behind it, the El jogged past on top of its stilted platform heading south toward Wrigley Field. In front, the uniforms had closed off the sidewalk with bright yellow barrier tape. Two TV camera guys focused on cops standing around the building's front stoop. Near the cameras, a dozen or so gawkers pressed at the tape like Cubs fans waiting for the ticket office to open. A woman from WBBM radio was trying to interview a shirtless guy who was using a lot of hand gestures.

I counted four marked squads with Mars lights spinning, a crime-scene-unit station wagon that had probably been in the same roll over crash Kinsella's had, and a couple of unmarked Caprices and Crown Vics that would belong to the detectives and the District tactical guys brought in to help with the neighborhood canvass. There were also two mini-cam trucks salted in amongst the official vehicles, one from Channel 14 and the other from Channel 7.

Kinsella saw the TV people, grunted, and cruised past, turning into the alley entrance as far from them as he could get. I wondered what had brought them out. This was the wrong neighborhood to attract much TV news attention save the occasional mayoral photo op or CTA bus shack opening. Budgets being what they are these days, gang-related homicides seldom even win passing mention in an anchor's "reader" copy, much less rate pictures to go along.

As I eased out the passenger door to follow Kinsella down the alley, I saw Marisa Langdon hop from the Channel 14 truck and hustle toward her cameraman. I turned my face away, conscious of the fact I would stand out as obviously as a Packers cheese head hat at a Bears game if any of my former colleagues looked in my direction. Trendy as I had been along Evanston's lakefront in my warm-up jacket and running togs, it was hardly the usual wardrobe seen at the site of an Uptown shoot out. Or whatever this was.

A chest-high, wire fence encircled the yard behind the building. Steps climbed to a broken wooden porch where a clothesline sagged under the weight of a chewed up blanket and several pairs of blue jeans that a roomful of Tide would never scrub clean. I'd noticed the front door was a wooden board nailed to the frame, and that all the front windows were similarly filled, giving the impression the building was abandoned. The hanging clothes suggested differently. On the porch, an attractive woman in pants and a short-sleeved blouse had a cell phone to her ear. When she saw Kinsella, she snapped it closed and came down the steps.

Up close, the blonde had some miles on her but they looked highway, not city. She also had a star in a leather clip on her belt next to a holstered 9mm

Glock and the flat cop-stare they develop after, maybe, a week on the street. I guessed her at 35, tops.

"What it is," Kinsella said with a deadpan nod.

She smiled with real affection. "Hey, The K Man."

Her voice rasped and I suspected a nasty bruise along the side of her throat might be the cause.

"Good to see you walking around," Kinsella said.

"Thanks to you." She shifted her gaze and took in my outfit. "This your trainer or have you been trolling for joggers again?"

The byplay and the slight but detectable red flush that appeared on Kinsella's neck intrigued me, given his reputation for being a loner and nearly friendless. I said nothing and quashed a grin.

"Sheila Yount, Reno McCarthy," he said gruffly.

Her hand was as cold and dry as the look she slid into place.

"Yeah, he's the asshole who helped the State's Attorney indict Bruner and Kellog from Gang Crimes. Hard to forget that face."

"A pleasure meeting you as well, Detective," I said.

"He's going in with me for a quick look see," Kinsella said, slipping on a pair of disposable gloves. Then quickly added, "I'll take the heat if any comes down."

"Charley, for chrissakes. You know we're gonna get bosses up the ass on this. And it's my case…"

"Five minutes. You see any white shirts, you click me on the radio." His hand came up, fingers splayed and we edged past her. "Five."

"Kitchen and basement," she said, shaking her head. "Watch it on the stairs."

She was right, however. Cops learn up front in detective school that the crime scene is sacrosanct. A couple of times in twenty-some years I've had dicks bend that rule for me but they were extraordinary circumstances. I was curious about what was getting played out here so I kept my objections to myself, jammed hands in my pockets and followed my host.

The porch entrance was a plywood door with a broken padlock and a "Condemned" sign stapled to it. We pushed past and entered a kitchen where the centerpiece was a worn table that lay upside down with its legs in the air like road kill. Two green trash bags sat in lumpy heaps off to our left. The wall behind them and the linoleum underneath were dolloped in red and a blackish-red trail extended toward a hallway that led to the front of the house.

The heat, which had been trapped inside the boarded up house, felt gooey and a fetid stink made it past even my broken nose. I couldn't quite identify it. I wasn't sure I wanted to, either, seeing that the room had more than what I would consider its fair share of flies. An evidence technician wearing a black jumpsuit and shoulder holster patiently took photographs, pausing to scribble in a small notebook each time he changed his point of view. Kinsella asked permission, then stepped in front of the tech, parted the plastic and peered into one of the bags. A second later he grunted and backed away.

"Just the two bags? All the parts there?" he asked. Something undigested from my last meal began to sizzle in my stomach.

"You've seen more than I have. I just take the pics. ME's people'll count the pieces and take the inventory."

Kinsella glanced at me. "You wanna look?"

"Thanks. Never was big on jigsaw puzzles."

The problem with the basement steps was that many were missing or rotted, with holes that suggested feet had broken through them. Kinsella swore but balanced his hands on the banisters on both sides before moving forward. The staircase creaked but held his weight. He continued slowly down. His shadow on the wall, caught in the back splash of a floodlight set up below, made him appear to be a hulking creature from Hell, descending back into the depths. Never one to be seen as a wuss, I followed him.

Compared to the basement, the kitchen had been a suite at the Drake. There was less trash but that was because someone had carefully swept it out of the way so it wouldn't catch fire while they used the blowtorch. The blowtorch, that is, which sat in the middle of the room next to the body that hung, suspended by chains around the wrists, from two hooks drilled into the ceiling studs.

The corpse was that of a muscular black guy who hadn't passed on gently. I stared at it, aware of three other people in the confined space sending curious looks my way. The facial flesh had gone pink and bubbled under the searing heat and the rest of him was charred in places where the pain would have been indescribable. Few smells attack the senses the way burned skin does. Once again even my packed nose didn't quite spare me and I even felt my eyes water. I was racking up quite a score of visuals the past couple of days. First Brooke, then the garbage bags full of parts, now this poor schmuck. I've gotta get out more, catch up on the latest things people are doing to people. I heard the sound of gagging and realized it was me. Very uncool. I swallowed twice. Even worse than being a wuss is to barf at the crime scene.

I heard my name and realized Kinsella was talking about me in low tones to an evidence tech and a short black guy in shirt and tie, both of whom wore white surgical masks and gloves.

The other detective looked at me and nodded toward the victim. "Get down and party, huh??"

"Whaddya got, Jack?" Kinsella said.

"Well, that there was Deon Sims. Twenny-six if you believe his driver's license. Beaten first, then a touch of flambe' in all the popular spots. Nips, under the arms, under the nuts, feet.

Deon's been quite a busy fella the last few years. Running for office you might say. Started out as a dealer, graduated to doing drive-bys. Primo shooter. I'd guess he got all the way up to, what you might call operations manager of the BGL." That would be the Black Gangster Lords, the largest of Chicago's street gangs.

"This his crib?" Kinsella asked.

"You kidding? This boy liked to style. Joint here got to've been just a hole-up. Found some clothes, a couple guns in the bedroom upstairs. MAC-10's and a nice Benelli shotgun some asshole chopped the barrel on. That's probably where they snatched him. Looks like they caught him sleeping."

"Quiet little fuckers weren't they? It's not like all that plush carpet upstairs was gonna muffle their footsteps."

"Ghosts," Jack agreed. "What I'm trying to figure is what he was doing *here*. I remember Deon from when I worked Area One. He's a South Side boy. He hangs in Pocketown, around 78th and Stony Island."

"Got an ID on the one upstairs?"

The detective named Jack shrugged. "That's the other thing playing with my head. Deon had a couple of bodyguards, Mookie something-or-other and a 'nother one, I forget his name. I'm guessing the one upstairs was one. Thing is, he always traveled with both those boys *and* he had a stylish ride."

"The missing one could have given him up."

"True. That'd explain why Deon's SUV's not around. Nice Caddie Escalade, all decked out. Still don't seem right. I gotta make a couple calls, see what this boy been up to lately. If I got Deon placed right, he's had those boys with him since he started slinging on the corners. I don't see either one 'jacking him. One of 'em mighta even been like his brother or something."

He looked thoughtful for a moment, trying to remember.

"You figure it out, gimme a call on my cell." Kinsella said.

"I thought you weren't..."

Kinsella interrupted him. "They do the cutting in the bedroom?"

"Oh yeah. Even left the chain saw. Take a look as you go out. These folks came prepared. Real Boy Scouts."

Kinsella looked at the blowtorch and its victim for another moment then motioned to me and we risked the stairs again. Now that my eyes were adjusted, I noticed that a lot of the damage looked recent. Likely from the weight of a body being dragged, or even thrown, down to the basement.

The evidence tech was gone when we got back to the kitchen but the flies around the bags appeared to have multiplied. I passed on taking a look at the bedroom where Sims had "holed up." I listened, though, as Kinsella stepped over the bags and clomped down the hall. He was a big guy, and not making an effort to be quiet, but I couldn't imagine anyone managing to sneak anywhere on that wooden floor.

I nearly ran into Yount in my desire to get into the fresh air. I took a couple of deep breaths through my mouth, bent over and took a few more. She came off the porch and suggested I wait for Kinsella in the alley rather than in the yard. For appearances sake. I didn't care. I would have climbed the El trestle if it meant I didn't have to go back in that house.

When Kinsella emerged a couple of minutes later he paused briefly to talk to Yount then trudged across the trash-strewn yard and back to his Caprice without looking at me. I couldn't read his expression but something in the way he moved signaled complete disgust at what he'd just seen. Just as he reached the car, a shiny Buick made the corner and slid in behind him.

If the woman who got out on the passenger side had sported a blonde brush cut instead of brown hair in a bob, she would have been a perfect clone of the guy who emerged from behind the wheel. Both were suited, groomed and polished as perfectly as only two employees of Uncle Sam can be. I reached the Caprice as they joined up and moved in on Kinsella like they intended to throw him on the hood of his own car.

"Detective, do you have some purpose for being here?" the woman snapped. She had a sorority-girl-makes-good voice that still carried a trace of privilege and the cheekbones and posture to back it up. Ivy League college, then law school, then right into government service without a moment spent as a street cop.

Kinsella squinted at her. "Sure do. How about you?"

"Your commander tells me you were not assigned to this case."

"No, that's not quite right. You told my commander not to assign me to this case. Or any case that your task force might be interested in. Isn't that the way it happened, Agent Dark?"

It hadn't occurred to me that Jesse Dark could be a woman. Wasn't this going to be fun? She chose to notice me at just that moment.

"You brought this man with you?"

I realized where I'd heard that imperious tone before. Bebe Neuworth on the old TV show *Cheers*. Except Bebe was acting in a sit-com and I was pretty sure Special Agent Dark was taking herself most seriously.

"Lady, if you were a guy, I'd tell you to piss off. Seeing how you ain't, piss off, anyway."

Kinsella slid into the car and slammed the door. I leaned across the roof.

"You know, this is an interesting coincidence. I had some pilferage while a maid service was cleaning my house recently? So I had an engineer buddy install a pinhole video camera in the ceiling of my office, looking right at my desk. Flips on when the alarm system is deactivated."

A complete lie but with just enough ring of could-be-truth that it socked her right between the eyes. I smiled broadly, winked like we were old buds sharing the best and latest joke off the Internet.

"Tape at ten," I said.

*   *   *   *

I was barely back in the car before Kinsella mashed down the accelerator and we smoked through the alley like Starsky and Hutch on speed. I saw the startled look on Yount's face as we flashed by and then we were out into the street.

"Federal buttholes," he snapped.

We managed to get through the next intersection without running over two nuns just stepping off the curb, but the way one of them crossed herself made Kinsella slow down considerably.

"You know what you were looking at in there, right?" he said. I opened my mouth to answer but it hadn't been a real question. "Exhibitions. Not retribution. Not someone getting offed cause they shorted somebody else some weight in a dope deal. Fucking messages to someone. With decoration to show how bad the bad guys think they are."

"Decoration as in blowtorching the one guy's face off and reducing the other one to parts?"

I was beginning to feel like a huge hand was pressing against my stomach. If I belched, I wouldn't be able to hold back from vomiting. The memory of what I'd seen, now being tugged this way and that, kept expanding across the fertile ground of my imagination. Had those bulging eyes blinked?

"Yeah. They been doing 'bangers all over the city the last couple months. And that's not for publication."

"Who's 'they?'" I asked, but I knew the answer.

"I'm dead serious, McCarthy. It's bad enough I'm talking to you at all. This comes out on TV tonight, you best move outta town."

"Russian mob?"

I could feel the heat as he glanced my way. "'The fuck you know that?"

"The boyfriend was Russian. You flashed on the name. Everybody's trying to point me away from him for some reason, but I keep running into Russians. And there's rumors floating that the Russian mob wants in on the dope trade."

"Rumors?" he snorted. "Yeah, well, you just saw two of those 'rumors', pal." He worked his mouth as though he was about to spit.

"I been calling the other Areas the last few days. Buddy a'mine down on the South Side told me he had this weasel who'd been dumped in a car trunk and then burned couple weeks ago. Case got yanked away from him. He figured it went to some murder task force outta Headquarters and didn't think much about it. But then he asks around coupla days ago. Just curious, seeing if it mighta played off anything else he was working. All of a sudden, bang! He says the Feebs are putting the lid on. He's got twenty-three years on the Job. They flat out told him, he mentions his case to anybody else, he kisses his pension g'bye."

"They think they can hide a gang war like this indefinitely?"

"You're not getting it. This has been going on for three months and they're even hiding it from coppers on the street. Gang crimes guys get wind of it, they sit 'em down and talk to 'em, tell 'em the facts of life, like they did my friend in Two. Tac guys working gangs, got snitches telling 'em shit? They buck the information up the ladder like they're supposed to and it just disappears. They ask about it later and *they* get sat down and talked to."

I leaned on the window crank to see if I could get the passenger side glass to drop any further. It screeched about an inch and stopped. We had just crossed back into Evanston and probably had about five more minutes driving time to my house. I could run it in about twenty. Anything was better than this.

"Pull over," I commanded.

"Huh?"

"You want me to puke all over these Big Mac boxes? Pull over."

The Caprice bumped up over the curb and we came to rest on a grassy strip in front of Calvary Cemetery. I hit the door with my shoulder and stumbled out onto my knees, sucking deep lungs full of humid morning air. After a couple of minutes, feeling stupid, I got my feet under me and leaned into the car's open doorway. To his credit, Kinsella looked worried. Probably thinking of all the paper he'd have to do if I stroked out or grabbed my chest and had the Big One in his squad.

"I'll make it home from here," I said.

"I ain't done with my questions."

"I don't have any more answers for you, Charley. I need some time to think this through."

He regarded me as sourly as my stomach felt. "I want to hear from you, McCarthy. This is a two-way deal." He found a business card, scribbled his pager number on it and handed it across the seat. I took it and slammed the door. He hit the siren, jounced off the grass and executed one of the worst u-turns I've ever seen to head back into the city.

I took it slow, my second run of the day. The squeezing pain in my stomach and the cotton-on-fire feeling inside my nose subsided gradually, the more fresh air I breathed. I pushed the thoughts of the scorched corpse aside. I was into something maniacal here. It was the type of investigation that when, done right, gave hard-ons to the members of the Pulitzer committee. We had murder. We had organized crime. We had street gangs. We had the Red *Mafiya*. We had the start of a gang war that, so far, seemed pretty one-sided but that could turn into a bloodbath. And to top it all off, we had an enormous federal/city cover-up. Well, that wasn't quite accurate. A city coverup. For the federal government, it was silent, sneaky, business as usual.

But what a story! And there was not a damned thing I could do with it unless I was able to lay the whole thing out for Hanratty in such a way he'd have to bring me back aboard to sort it out. The only way to do that was to find sources willing to go on camera and I was a little short of those. I'd started out in the minus column in that regard, in fact. Brooke surely could have put much of this in perspective.

Brooke. Three blocks from my house I suddenly halted as though I had run smack into an immovable object. An idea scratched at the back of my head like Socks does when I'm reading on the couch and he wants my attention. What's wrong with this picture, I thought?

Here's a chick fed up with her gangster boyfriend. She's got the same problem with leaving him that most women face when trying to dump the abusive man in their lives. He doesn't want to let her go. And in this case, it's a guy who has the capacity to make sure she stays. He's got a long reach, with muscle.

Question: If she'd been that terrified of him, why hadn't she just split out of town immediately? Why would she hang around playing footsie with a television station, for example? Why would she take the time to dangle an expose in front of a reporter if she wanted to get out of town as quickly as possible?

Question: Why would she go hang out in a bar if she thought the head of the Russian Mob in Chicago was after her?

Question: Why would she move into her brother's apartment? At the very least, a hotel would have provided far more anonymity and, with her background, surely she had some contacts in that industry.

She was trying to hide, but she wasn't trying very hard.

What was that about?

I walked the rest of the way home puzzling with those thoughts, anything to keep from replaying the scene in that house.

This time no police car waited for me in front of my place. I scanned the yard and then the neighborhood. No unusual cars, in fact, all along the street. No vans or utility trucks with Acme Electrical on the sides like in the Roadrunner cartoons or the telltales that always give away a surveillance vehicle when you see them in the movies. I smiled at my little bit of self-cheering humor. If the government had me wiretapped, their listening post was sure to be somewhere I'd never see. For that matter, if any thugs, federal or otherwise, were about and waiting to have a word with me, they, too, would be well-hidden.

I mounted the steps to the porch, scooped up Socks who was dozing on one of the chairs, went inside and plunked him down on my desk in the study while I grabbed the phone and speed dialed Sunny's cellular. Looked around while it rang. Sun spilled in through the sliding glass door. I crossed the room and closed the blinds. When she answered, strained of breath, I realized I'd caught her at her normal workout time. I wouldn't have to ask where she was. Always good if someone else was listening.

"Hey, lots to tell you," she said. "Where have you been? I tried a little while ago."

"Went out for a run. Ran a little farther than I thought I could."

"Good. Nose is better?"

"Nose is painful," I said.

I opened the desk drawer as I said it and fished around until I found a bottle of Excedrin.

"I found out a couple of things…" she began.

"Why don't you wait? I'll come to you. That place next door to where you are, in about thirty minutes."

She hesitated, then told me that would be fine. I could tell she'd figured out why I'd been so abrupt. We know each other pretty well.

I hustled through a shower, slipped into khaki shorts and a polo shirt and was out the door in fifteen minutes.

Sunny waited in the Jamba Juice next to her health club and she'd started without me. There was an extra large container in front of her at the little round table next to the window and she had a tiny trace of strawberry smoothie on her upper lip. Today, she wore fitted blue shorts that came to about mid thigh and a half tee that had already attracted the attention of every male in the place. That would have been me and the guy behind the counter who was reading a health-food magazine and trying hard to show he wasn't interested. I distracted him long enough to get my favorite peach concoction with a spritz of protein and ginseng. I had a feeling the little energy boost would come in handy if today provided surprises like yesterday.

"Asa didn't come in this morning," Sunny greeted me as I sat down opposite. "It was Goofy and me making silly through all of drive."

"A new morning duo. The wet brain and the karate expert," I said.

She made a face. "He's not very bright all by himself, is he?"

"Asa must have called in late. Normally when he's out, Rudy brings in Patrick or Dell from afternoons to baby-sit Goofy. I sure wouldn't want to try it alone."

"It wasn't too bad. But that's not what I was going to tell you. Asa is in the hospital. He fell down a flight of stairs, he says. He has a concussion and a broken arm. Barb went to see him right after the show. She called a few minutes before you did. She says he's got two shiners and his face is all bruised. She thinks somebody beat him, Reno." Barb was the morning show's producer, a veteran of a longtime abusive marriage.

I took a sip of my juice. "She say who did the pounding? And why?"

"He's a total asshole for one thing," Sunny said. "And of course I mean that in the nicest possible way."

"Timing is a mite suspicious, though. Along with everything else that's happening."

"Your paranoia must be infecting me because that's what I thought, too. I called Russ to go babysit him."

Russ Traynor is another "bail agent" like Sunny. Except he looks the part. Six-foot-five, bald, with a mustache and goatee and weighing in at 250, his forearms are easily the size of my thighs. He's a young guy, in his late-twenties, but also an ex-Marine who works as a bouncer on weekends "just for fun" at one of the toughest biker bars in the city.

"You know, it could be totally unrelated," I mused. "But if it's not, what do we have here?"

"He denied knowing anything about Brooke. He says the lead he gave you came totally from the rumor mill. Then again, like my daddy used to say, he'd run outside to tell a lie when he could shout the truth from a window."

"I talk to him, he gives me Marn. I go to see Marn and a day later he gets whacked and Asa gets put in the hospital. Not to mention I follow Brooke home and she gets killed. I'm beginning to feel like a leper. Is your insurance paid up?"

She smiled. "I'm not exactly worried. You know?"

I knew. She's fearless. I have no doubt she could keep a resting heart rate while throwing someone through a plate glass window. Yet, I've never seen her angry. I've never seen her unhappy. Hence, her nickname. I have often wondered if she'd be able to keep her usual merry disposition if she had to kill someone. I've also wondered if she hasn't already done so. Not someplace I want to go with her.

"I did some computer work before I went to bed last night," she said. "I have some pieces of information but I'm not sure how they fit together. Or if they do. They're interesting, though."

A couple in workout gear pushed through the door and nodded at Sunny. They crossed to the counter and began ordering. Sunny fished in her backpack and came out with several sheets of paper.

"Michael Fletcher is actually one Mikhail Federov born in Chechnya. Records I could access on-line list him as President and CEO of United Citizens Labor Bank, a subsidiary of Balkan Global Systems, a banking corporation headquartered in Geneva. He emigrated here five years ago. He has a legal name change on file with the state."

"Really?"

"Yes. His public records are immaculate. I've done a lot of document searches, Reno. He and his lawyers have been exceptional about making sure everything that should be filed is done so perfectly. Of course the Federal Reserve is a little picky about things like that, too."

"So it's a real bank."

"Absolutely. The parent, Balkan Global, is well known according to *Forbes*. They're the bank of record for a couple of large Eastern European oil companies and textile manufacturers. They do business with two of the largest shipping firms in that part of the world. One of their other specialties is trading in banknotes and gold."

"How about Federov's bank?"

"United Citizens Labor Bank is just establishing itself. Lists starting assets of fifty million. That's peanuts in the banking world. It takes substantial work for a foreign bank to get U.S. authorization. Four years worth of hearings and bureaucracy for United Citizens, in fact. What's strange is, I couldn't find a lot of news coverage. A couple mentions of Federov and others appearing in front of different congressional committees. Hearings by the Comptroller of the Currency and the Federal Reserve."

She shrugged as she paged through the papers from her bag.

"There were objections raised along the way, it looks like. References to a history of massive money laundering by Russian banks. Some testimony that the majority of banks in Russia are mob-controlled. A bigass gasoline bootlegging scandal in New York run by the Russian mob using a couple of banks to get the profits out of the country. No one could relate any of that to either Balkan Global or United Citizens, though. They seem to be squeaky."

"Anything on Federov, specifically, since he hit town? I can't believe the opening of a Russian bank would go unnoticed. Somebody had to have done at least a story for the business section."

"Charity work," Sunny said. "Those reading centers in all the projects? That was United Citizens idea. They also opened a couple of community resource centers on the South and West sides, sort of Boys Clubs for families. And they spearheaded the financing for a low-income housing complex."

She dug back into her bag and came out with a copy of a banking trade magazine. Folding back the pages she pointed to an article entitled, "Russian Bank Helps Chicago Neighborhoods, Kids," and a picture of a guy with a Groucho-thick mustache and salt and pepper hair standing in front of a building on Wacker Drive at the Chicago River. The photo caption told me, "A child of the old Soviet Union, Michael Fletcher now leads bank effort to encourage community growth."

The Saville Row suit and sixty dollars worth of barbering gave him that just-stepped-from-the-boardroom appearance that, I supposed, the photographer had been trying to create. But there was something in his posture and folded arms that made me think of pictures I'd seen of Roman soldiers with one foot on the bloody chest of a vanquished opponent.

"Nice looking guy."

Sunny wiggled her hand, "Ehh. I tend to go for the ones who don't send the hired help to drag you back after you leave them."

"I don't recall a bank in this building."

"It's not the usual kind of bank. No give aways of fuzzy stuffed animals or toasters. They only deal with businesses, administer wealthy kids' trust funds, make loans. No tellers. No fat security guys."

"Oh, I'll bet they've got fat security guys all right. Probably named Ivan and Boris." I tapped my fingers on the glossy magazine page. "But this has to be all smoke and mirrors. What I want to know is how an outfit run by a foreign mob manages to meet the Fed's qualifications. That can't be an easy process."

"You're thinking they paid off most of Congress?"

"They have money. It's a bank, remember? Gold? Oil reserves? Gotta love those campaign contributions."

"Come on. That's so obvious! The Washington press corps isn't stupid. Someone would have at least looked…"

"They probably did. Or tried to." I thumbed through the clippings and noted the dates. "When did the bulk of the approval process take place? Did you notice the front pages of the papers you took these from? What was in the headlines?"

"The murders of those child-abuser priests and the Hawaiian Cult standoff." She winced. "Okay, okay. Duh. Nobody's going to pay for a big investigation when the whole country is watching a kinky trial and Waco Two: The Tropics."

"Exactly. Plus you said the paperwork you saw was pristine, right? Every document they had to file was probably just as pretty as the one before it. You know how bureaucrats love their paper. Fill out everything just as it calls for in subsection 23 of rule number two part a, b, c and d and you give all the little bean counters massive chubbies. What do they care about a criminal conspiracy if all the blanks are filled in and there are attachments attached to the attachments?"

"So where do you want me to go?"

"I want to know if Federov is in the movie business for one thing. Brooke's friend says that's how she hooked up with him."

"Maybe a little closer look at Talmadge, too? See why he's so jittery he has to have a bodyguard?"

"Good thinking. Maybe I'll…" I stopped. Sunny had chosen a table in front of the window and, through most of our conversation, I'd been glancing outside. People sometimes tell me the way I let my eyes roam when I'm talking to them can be annoying and rude. This time it allowed me to spot a familiar face in a car a half block down on the other side of the street.

I would have missed seeing him if a kid on a bike hadn't misjudged his position in traffic. He'd been riding in the same direction the car was facing when he evidently thought he'd edged too close to a passing delivery truck. His hand, and then his right handlebar, dipped down to graze the shiny hood of a Lexus ES 430 and the driver popped his head the window out to snarl at him as he tottered and almost fell. The kid shot the guy the finger and the guy yanked his head back, but not before I glimpsed an unruly shock of white hair.

"Sergei," I said. "Son of a bitch."

Sunny didn't move her head. "The Russian from Marn's studio?"

"Himself. Driver's side of a black Lexus across the street and four spaces west."

"No doubt whatsoever?"

"It's him." I didn't have to look again to be sure. "He's even wearing the same kind of ugly shirt."

She sipped her juice. "But not the *same* ugly shirt? Totally grosses me when guys wear the same shirt two days in a row."

"No, this one appears to have orange vertical stripes. Like a traffic vest."

"Guy like that, he probably has a whole closetful of ugly shirts. Or maybe it is a traffic vest."

"Part-time thug and dirty movie financier, but by day he's a full-time highway flagman? Could be. Maybe he's waiting for road construction to start."

"I suppose we have to consider that he could be waiting for you," she said. "Should we go ask him?"

I nodded. I could feel the adrenaline buzz straight up through my chest. Sunny's eyes, focused on mine, were dancing with excitement even though her tone of voice betrayed none of it.

"You ready?" She asked.

"You don't want foreplay?"

"Here's your foreplay," she said, winked, and toppled her drink. We both jumped backward as it splattered us. She yanked her backpack away and then kept moving toward the counter. "Give me a minute of mopping then go straight out the front door."

"Holy target, Batgirl," I murmured.

I saw a flash of metal as her hand came out of her backpack, then she passed the startled attendant and headed for the back door.

I grabbed a handful of paper napkins and began blotting at the table while doing a fast backward count from sixty. I'd make a lousy Robin, though. At thirty I gave it up and charged into the street.

Sergei was a big fat guy but not a stupid big fat guy. He had locked eyes with someone he was watching and that's a no-no from Chapter One of every surveillance manual ever written. Our act hadn't fooled him, either. When Sunny disappeared, he'd cranked the engine and hard-turned the wheel to vamoose from his parking spot. Problem was, he discovered the Lexus was wedged a shade too tightly for a smooth escape. He was still trying to maneuver loose when I burst through Jamba's front door. He saw me and gave up trying to finesse the extrication. He jammed the accelerator to the floor. The big Lexus tore from the space with an ungodly screech that suggested somebody parked either fore or aft would soon be calling their insurance agent.

I saw Sunny emerge from the mouth of the alley onto the sidewalk. She had her automatic pistol pointed in Sergei's direction, hollering at him to halt. He ignored her. His head swiveled toward me and he bared his teeth in a vicious grin. As I slipped between two parked cars into the street, I realized there was no way either of us could reach him before he straightened the wheel and took off.

Sergei had something else in mind, however. Still grinning, he just kept the wheel hard over and pointed the Lexus right at me. Caught totally by surprise, I had zero time to reverse direction and get behind the cars on my side of the street. I heard the Lexus engine roar. Tires squealed.

My bullheadedness should have gotten me pasted up against the side of the old Marshall Fields building or, at the very least, across the hood of a very nice new Cadillac, splattering blood and other precious bodily fluids. Didn't happen. Instead, a tow truck driver, lead footing one of those diesel flatbed rigs, came barreling down the street at just the right moment and eliminated the Sergei problem as quickly as it appeared.

The high prow front of the tow truck smashed into the Lexus at the driver's side pillar and kept going, sweeping both vehicles past me in the blink of an eye. While I stumbled backward and fell on my ass, the Lexus was lifted and, in a cacophony of shrieking metal and explosive force, flipped onto its top. The truck's forward momentum carried its front wheels up and over the ruined sedan and all that weight compressed the roof as though a giant foot had come down to stomp it into the pavement.

The silence following the impact lasted about ten seconds. It was broken first by the screams of two co-eds who had missed being mashed into hamburger by a couple of feet. I saw the door of the tow truck move and then blow open. The driver climbed out carefully. He was a small man in dirty overalls with a red handkerchief stuck in his pocket. He clambered to the ground and then suddenly appeared to realize what he'd done. He looked around helplessly then bent to peer into what was left of the Lexus.

"Oh God," I heard him say. "There's…someone still in there!"

He backed away from the wreckage, hands against his face as though it had been burned by unseen flames. His next exclamation was a hoarse bellow for help that joined those coming from the women.

I found myself leaning on a parked car with no memory of getting to my feet. Sunny jogged up and put her hand on my shoulder. It tightened when she saw my expression.

"Stay here," she commanded. She had her 9mm held down along her leg. "I have to put this away and then I'll be back. Just stay here."

We should leave, I thought. We should motivate out of here with great haste and be long gone by the time officialdom arrives and begins spreading its tentacles.

Sunny hustled into the juice bar and I saw her dip to slide the automatic into her backpack. The counter guy was at the window but he craned around, probably to see down the front of her shirt. Sunny straightened and his head swiveled back to the window. She went over to him and it looked as though she put her hand on the back of his neck. His blush was evident. She handed him something. He looked at it and then up at her. She leaned close and brushed his ear with her lips, still talking. His eyes closed and then opened, almost as though in ecstasy. She suddenly patted the top of his head and spun away, striding out of the place and up to me with the guy watching her every step.

"I take it we just disappeared off his radar?"

"The hundred bucks will keep him quiet for the first round of questions. My promise to come back and see him should keep his lips glued for everything after that. If I'm his type, that is. Whattya think?" Her grin made me smile, albeit weakly.

"If he gets any weaker in the knees they're going to think he fainted from seeing the crash," I said. "Let's get out of here."

She'd parked her Explorer with the tinted windows in the high-rise parking garage Evanston built a couple of years ago. My Mustang was two spaces down. We listened to sirens converging on the crash scene while we walked. The concrete walls of the garage seemed to pick up the sound and bounce it around. I waited until it quieted before I spoke. I was pleased to hear my voice sounded normal.

"They're following one of us," I said.

"Don't look at me, bucko. I graduated top of the class from counter-surveillance school."

"Which means they either picked me up at the house or put a transmitter on my car."

We both looked at the Mustang. She opened the door to the Explorer and reached into a Halliburton case behind the driver's seat, coming out with a device that looked like a cross between a Palm Pilot and a walkie-talkie. Extending a flat antenna, she prowled the perimeter of my car, dipping low as she circled the front and rear.

Returning to my side, she shook her head and put the device away. "Good old fashioned tail job would be my guess. Did you ever look behind you?"

Point of fact, I hadn't. "You just carry one of those wherever you go?"

"Borrowed it just for you, sweetie."

"I'm going to go see Asa," I said.

"Why don't you just park your butt somewhere for awhile?"

I shook my head. "I'm okay. I want to talk to Asa before anything else happens to him."

"Barb told me he's in pretty awful shape. You may not get much"

"If Sergei is any indication, they'd like to do the same or worse to me. I'm motivated."

Sunny's expression was banker-lawyer serious, the one she usually reserves for when she's wearing a suit and ready for a power lunch with a high dollar client.

"You know I have a lot of contacts. We compete for business but we help each other out in a pinch. Now's not a bad time to back off, Reno. I can think of three or four really good guys I could bring in to nose around. Not bounty hunters. Real investigators. A couple are even ex-feds."

"You know what's funny? I could make somewhat the same speech to you."

"I figured you were going to try. Beat you to it. We're friends, you goof. I'm not going to bail on you."

She took my hand and squeezed it. A little jolt went through me just as it had when we decided to go after Sergei. What had brought it on this time?

"Thanks, kiddo," I said.

We stared at each other and I wondered if she was waiting for me to do something. I didn't. Eventually looked away. I couldn't tell what was in her eyes. She let go of my hand, then, and went around and opened the Explorer's rear door.

"C'mere," she said gruffly.

I stepped to where I could see an open footlocker that could have been a police supply catalog come to life. I spied several pairs of handcuffs and leg chains, plastic ties, two large canisters of Mace, a Kevlar vest and a short-barreled shotgun. In a drawer along the side were two Glock 9mm automatics and six clips, all fitted into foam cutouts. She reached into another drawer and came out with a small 9mm Kahr automatic in an ankle holster. She offered it to me.

"I have my dad's Walther if I need a gun. I don't have a carry permit like you do."

"So? Do you think any of these people have the legal right to carry a piece? I really doubt they care. And spouting the statutes to them isn't going to keep you alive."

Chicago likes the Illinois law against carrying a concealed weapon and has even come up with one of its own. If I got caught carrying, I'd take a fast trip to Gun Court, have a misdemeanor conviction stuck on my record and likely get hit with a hefty fine.

"I don't want it."

"I'm not offering it to you. I'm ordering you to take it. When somebody hires me to protect them I have one rule. You do what I tell you to do or I quit."

"That's when you're bodyguarding…"

"What do you think I'm doing now? Don't give me that look. You're gonna say who says you need a bodyguard? And then I'm gonna say do you think the guy underneath that car out there was keeping an eye on you 'cause he liked staring at your butt? If you'd let me hang around with you twenty-four/seven until this is all over, I would. I know you won't. This is the best I can do."

"What if it falls off while I'm dancing?"

She gave me the scornful look I deserved. I took the holster from her.

"Go on," she said.

I dropped to one knee and lifted my right pants leg. Strapping the Velcro around it, I positioned the gun, popped the snap that secured it, and lifted the little automatic out. It was nicely balanced. From its weight, I could tell it was loaded. I dropped the clip out of the butt and looked anyway, testing the spring with my thumb before snapping the clip back home. I slipped the gun into the holster and covered it.

"You get killed and that's not in your hand I'm going to kick your ass," she said.

"You know that's the second time in the last minute you've referred to my buttocks?"

Her face had taken on a flush as she tried to convince me to accept the gun. Now, the flush deepened. Or maybe that was just the lighting in the garage and I was imagining things.

"I don't know about that, but you can kiss mine."

She slammed the Explorer's rear door.

CHAPTER 9

▼

On the way to the hospital, I punched up WGN in time to hear Lyle Dean get to the Asa story.

"Chicago morning radio host A.M Driver is known for the odd practical jokes he often plays on celebrities and politicians. Police say it was no joke when they found Driver injured and wandering near Belmont and Halstead last night. Police say Driver reported being carjacked. Investigators, however, found a parking stub in his coat from a nearby garage where his Dodge Viper was parked. Doctors say Driver suffered a broken arm and possible internal injuries. He's listed in serious condition at Roosevelt Lakeshore Hospital. Officials at his radio station have no comment."

It wasn't much, but with the rumors about me already flying I knew Rudy at the station would be rippingly pissed. It's funny how those of us in the media are so quick to slam the door when our colleagues turn the cameras and microphones in our direction. You'd think he would have had the grace to wish Asa a speedy recovery. Asa was, after all, the joint's major cash machine, FCC censure, fines and all. It made me wonder if Rudy knew something that caused him to back off from making the usual bland statement of support.

I shook my head and realized I was smirking. More than likely Asa had passed on the info to our bosses about me getting picked up in connection with Brooke's murder and now he was the target of the same kind of paranoid ass-covering. If New York ordered a suspension for him too, pretty soon our morning program would be showcasing the talent in the janitorial pool.

Hospital security guards ran a mirror under my car to check for explosives before allowing me into the parking lot. Another guard reminded me on my way

through the lobby that I needed to turn off my cell phone. Once on the right floor, though, I was next to invisible in the movement of doctors, nurses, med students, candy stripers and other visitors. I found Russ Traynor leaning against the wall just inside the door to Asa's room, his back to the bed. He wore sweats and a warm-up jacket. I thought I could see the outline of a shoulder holster under the jacket.

"Hey Reno," he greeted me in a low voice. "Your buddy's been pretty much out of it. He nodded off again a couple of minutes ago."

"He say anything about what happened?" I looked across the room. Asa's face on the pillow looked misshapen and his right eye was swollen. We're twins now, I thought.

Russ glanced at Asa and then back at me as though he'd had the same thought. "Not really. I guess a couple guys jumped him as he was getting into his car. Beat the crap out of him and pitched him over the wall of the parking garage. His girlfriend, or whoever she is, told me he was on the second floor and he bounced off a Dumpster instead of hitting the ground. He should buy a Lotto ticket, huh?"

"Girlfriend?" I asked. "Was she there when it happened?"

"Says she was. She's all shook up." He motioned for me to step out into the hall and pulled the door partway shut after us.

"I get here and he's awake. He says no, he doesn't want me hanging around. I give him what Sunny told me to say, that the station sent me over. He's bitching up a storm until the girlfriend, Cindy, tells him *she* wants me to stick and if he makes a stink she's gonna take off and not come back. That was about an hour ago and he hasn't said a word since."

"Where's this Cindy?"

"Lounge maybe? She said she wasn't going far. Sort of big butt, fairly nice knockers though. Looks like a housewife."

I asked a passing nurse for directions to the visitor's lounge.

Only one woman was in there and she sat sideways on the couch, talking on the phone. I went over to a cooler in the corner, poured a paper cup's worth of water and downed it. I pitched the cup into the trash as I heard her hang up.

"You must be Reno McCarthy. I recognize you from the publicity shots in Asa's office."

I turned. "That's me."

"Cindy Royer." She extended a small hand. I'd seen Asa shadowed by a number of women at the few station functions I'd attended, but they'd all been model-types, possibly even professional escorts. They enjoyed being noticed.

Cindy was not one of them. Everything about her was unremarkable except a grudging smile which made her look a little like the actress Sally Field. She wore her straight brown hair to just above her shoulders and was dressed the way someone might be if they were out for a very casual night on the town. The weariness in her eyes and the wrinkles in her cotton shirt suggested the night had stretched well into the next day.

When I gestured to the couch she sagged back onto it as though she'd been waiting for permission and used both hands to push her hair back behind her ears. "This is all pretty unbelievable," she said.

"What happened?"

"I'm an attorney, Mr. McCarthy." She held up a hand. "No, I don't work for Asa. We're just friends. I practice school law, actually. But I have to respect his wishes and he's made it pretty clear he doesn't want me discussing this."

"I just need some blanks filled in. TV and radio already have the basics from the cops. You briefed Russ, didn't you?"

"The bodyguard told you what I said to him?"

"Yes. Sunny Dee and I sent him here."

Bewilderment came into her eyes. "I thought the station...Why would you do that?"

"You saw what happened and you have to ask?"

"We just got robbed. Do muggers come back for second helpings?"

"You tell me," I said quietly.

"You know, Asa said if you showed up I'm supposed to have security make you to leave." She glanced toward the hall.

"Why do you suppose he'd want that?"

When I didn't get an answer, I squatted down in front of her. "You said you were robbed. Did these guys actually take any money?"

"Asa said something to them and they started to punch him. Afterward they just, I don't know. They left. Maybe they were scared off."

"Did they look scared? Or did they just sort of stroll, like it was no big deal?"

She hesitated and then nodded."Well, yes. It was sort of like that."

"You had money on you, right? Did they take it? Asa had his wallet. Did they try to go in his pockets?"

"Okay. I don't like this." She stood up. Her eyes looked frightened more than angry. "You're cross-examining me. I'd like you to leave."

"Asa gave me some information a couple of days ago. He probably had no idea where it would lead, but now it involves a murder. He didn't tell you that, did he?"

"No, but…"

"Asa's involved with the Russian mob, Cindy. The beating was to shut him up. He doesn't want me around because they told him there's more waiting for him if they find out he talked to me again."

"That's absurd!" But she stared at my nose as though its damage was confirmation.

I came out of my squat, knees creaking in a forty-something kind of way, and slid into a chair enough distance from her it wouldn't make her any more jumpy than she already seemed to be. It took her a few moments. I watched her walk a tight circle on the carpet, occasionally glancing out into the hall. She had her arms crossed in front of her but made small gestures with her right hand as she spoke.

"We were getting into the car. The hospital parking lot, on Sheffield? These three men just appeared. I suppose they followed us from the bar. They…"

She paused. I waited.

"They shoved me against the car and then two of them led him away, over to the wall. I tried to go to him but the third man held me back. He said it was none of my business."

"Did he have an accent?"

"Yes." She gnawed on a knuckle. "Asa said something to the two men and they just started pounding on him. He fell down. They…they started to kick him. There wasn't anything I could do. I screamed but the guy, the man with the accent, grabbed my arm and twisted it. Then they just…they just picked Asa up and rolled him over the wall."

Her voice had the distracted, hollow sound of someone detailing what they see inside themselves.

"And afterward?"

"You're right. They just walked over to their car like nothing had happened. Strolled." She blinked. "They looked at me like they didn't really see me. Or, as if I didn't matter. The one who had grabbed my arm made a shushing sound and put his finger to his lips. 'No police or we come back,' he said."

"The story I heard said the cops found Asa wandering the streets."

"Yes. He…got up and ran. I went to see if he was okay and he was gone."

Her hair had fallen in front of her face. She pushed it back. Tears ran down her cheeks. "He ran," she repeated. "He must have been very scared."

I nodded but kept my mouth shut. Yeah, scared. Good ol' Asa. Always looking out for his friends. Cindy stood in the middle of the room, head bowed, arms gripping herself, crying without a sound.

I walked back to Asa's room. He was awake. When I stepped into his field of view, he pointed at the door.

"You. Out. And take your guard dog with you. I don't want to talk to you."

I guess he figured I wasn't there just to wish him a speedy recovery.

I motioned for Russ to leave and then I sat in a chair next to Asa's bed. He sank bank against the pillows and his undamaged eye stared balefully at me.

"I'm not saying a word."

"Uh huh," I said. He wasn't exactly pale but his face had a waxy look, almost as though he'd been prepped by a mortician instead of treated by doctors. A cast immobilized his right arm and one finger of his left hand wore a splint.

"Cindy seems nice," I asked in a conversational way. "I haven't met her before, have I?"

"She's a fuck buddy. She's also my lawyer, so back off."

I nodded. "I see. That's why it was okay to run off and leave her to play with the goons who beat you up? Because she's just a fuck buddy?"

"Hey man, fuck you. I didn't run off! I was three kinds of out of it. I didn't know where I was or what I was doing."

I wondered if he'd been lying there working out his story, polishing it just in case someone tripped over the truth.

"And it was just a random mugging. That's your story and you're sticking to it?"

"That's what it was. Shit. Leave me alone." Petulant. Like a little kid.

"Asa, what do you know that Federov doesn't want you telling me?"

"Who?"

"Michael Fletcher," I said. "Mikhail Federov. Take your pick. The guy who sent the goons."

He closed his eyes. Because he wasn't wearing his shades and he didn't want me to see the fear?

"Never heard of him."

He'd bailed on Cindy and now he was trying to do the same to me. It was the tone of his voice that set me off more than anything else. Like he couldn't be bothered. Typical Asa. I felt a flash of anger at him. Almost instantly, however, an explosion of guilt left me lightheaded. I wasn't exactly the poster boy for being available when others needed me, was I?

I'd ignored my old man's cry for help the night he shot himself because I couldn't be bothered to leave my girlfriend's apartment to hang out with a drunk. Even if it was my father. *Especially* if it was my father. Later that night, I'd watched them zip him into a body bag.

A year later, learning nothing from that experience, I'd ignored Vinnie Sea-mans when he called me at school at the University of Kansas to tell me Mom had been acting a little strangely, forgetting things, sometimes slurring her words.

I couldn't be bothered. After all, I had parties to attend. Drinks of my own yet to slug down. I'd see her at Christmas.

A week after that, Mom collapsed at the kitchen sink, no one around to watch her have the stroke that killed her. Where was I at that moment? I never knew the precise time she went down, of course, but I had no doubt it happened while I was headed to a football bonfire with the Chick of the Week. Had my mother suffered? In her last moments, had she wished I was there?

And then there was Brooke.

I hadn't been there for her, either, but by God, I would make up for that. Grief and guilt, fury and revenge, all came together for me at that moment.

I leaned forward so that my hands rested on the edge of Asa's bed and lowered my voice to just above a whisper. It wasn't a gentle sound. I felt like prying his good eye open and sticking my thumb in it.

"You ran out on your friend. Fuck-buddy or not, you left her behind."

"That's not…"

"You know what you did, pal. So do I. I've been there. I don't get a free pass on the responsibility. Neither do you."

His eyes opened and his head snapped around. He winced at the pain his effort had caused. "You bastard."

"Noticed that, huh? What was Eddie Marn's part in this?"

"You just don't get it. I don't have a death wish like you do."

He fumbled for the nurse call device Velcroed to the side of his bed.

"You really want to push that button, Asa? You do, and when I walk out of here, my next stop is going to be the upstairs bar at Sensation. Your moaning friend's name is Julia, if I remember right. She shouldn't be too hard to find. In fact, if she's not there I'll just ask around. I bet one of your dirt-bag buddies will know what your silly ass has been up to."

From his expression, you'd think I'd pointed a shotgun at him. He snatched his hand back into his lap.

"Jesus. Don't even…we're talking about my life, here. If you go asking about me, and they find out, I'm dead."

"Who's 'they?'"

"Don't. Don't fucking do this to me."

I glared at him. "Talk, and you keep Sunny's 24/7 protection. Stay clammed up, that goes away. And I'll make you so hot on the street, your nurses will be coming in here in radiation suits."

Asa's eyes closed again and he shook his head.

I stood up. "So be it."

"They need sponsors," he blurted. "They want people, connected people, to sponsor visitors. If you're a Russian, you have to have a sponsor for your visa. Someone to vouch for you. The sponsor has to be somebody well known or have bucks for it to work."

"Federov asked you to be a sponsor?"

"Not him, personally. Another guy, one of his people."

"So why did they need to blackmail you? What's the big deal about being a sponsor?"

"You have to promise the government you know the person you're sponsoring. Sign an affidavit. Stand up later, if there's heat."

"Nifty. They blackmail you into perjuring yourself. Don't tell me. The person you sponsored wasn't somebody's sweet old granny."

His mouth twisted. "Not quite."

"Who was it?"

"Like I'd even know? He was just a piece of paper to me. They told me to forget the name so I forgot it. He licked his lips. "What are you asking about all this for, anyway?"

"Your Russian *Mafiya* buddies, Federov specifically, may have killed Brooke Talmadge."

He looked at me for a moment, mouth open, eyes dazed, then blinked and shook his head.

"I don't know anything about that, Reno. I swear I don't. I never even met this Federov. Shit, I didn't even know the bitch. What happened was, I fucked up. The Russians told me they'd…make sure people found out what I did. That…that would have been unacceptable. Then they told me if I helped them, they'd make it all go away. Everything."

"*Who* told you?"

"This douche who came into the bar. He had a couple other guys with him. We were partying and he says 'come out to the car, score some good blow.' They looked the type, right? Black suits, blond hair, big shoulders. So we go out to his SUV and, suddenly, showtime! He plugs in this video of me and…you don't need to know who. Just leave it that I got suckered. There wasn't any question. He had me and it wasn't something cash was going to get me out of."

He shrugged, put his hands out palm up. "Then he says if I co-operate, he'll make the video disappear."

"Who was this guy? I need a name."

"Olokoff."

"Was sponsoring all they wanted?"

"No. I had to introduce some of their people around. You know I...party. I got a lot of friends. I just...made some introductions."

"I need their names, too." My notebook was in my hand. "The people you sponsored. Who you introduced."

"Yeah, that's good. Our connection, you don't think those fuckers'll know you got that shit from me? They broke my damn arm, Reno. Next time they said they'll push my head into a tree shredder."

"Sensation," I reminded him.

"You motherfucker. You'd let them do me, wouldn't you?"

My shirt was sticking to my back. I yanked it free. "Begin with Marn. How does he fit?"

"He shot the video of me that started all of this. We'd seen each around. I...I heard he was good with hidden cameras. I needed a guy like that. I paid him to..."

He stopped and used the edge of a sheet to wipe his forehead.

"You don't need to know the situation, OK? Just know that he fucked me up hard. The little prick. I found out later he was peddling pictures of a lot of people in a lot of situations. Once he turned the vids over to the Russians, they had their hands wrapped around our collective nuts. They owned us."

"When did this happen?"

"A year ago, somewhere in there."

"Who else did they tap when they nailed you?"

"I...Jesus, Reno."

He gave me a beseeching look. With each answer more of his bravado, his cockiness leeched away.

"Keep talking," I said.

"You'll stay away from Sensation if I tell you this, right?"

"Focus on this, Asa. If I find out you're feeding me horse pucky, Sensation will be just the first place I go."

"Ok, just calm down. Jesus. After they showed me the video, they had this list of names. 'Do you know him? Do you know her?' They were shopping for certain people. We narrowed the list down to four. I agreed to set up casual meetings. They wanted…weaknesses. I told them what I'd seen and heard. Most of it was drugs. With one it was sex."

"And the Russians boxed these people the same way they did you?"

A sigh. He nodded.

"From what I hear, yeah. Basically. I mean what could I do?"

"Who are they?"

He told me three names. One was in the recording industry, a guy he'd met through his work at the station. Another was a honcho at the Mercantile Exchange. A third was a radio jock from a competing station. He hesitated before giving me the fourth and last name. "The chick, she's big into Ecstasy. A raver."

I waited. Both sympathy and disgust lobbied for my support. I didn't like Asa and never had. I didn't know what he'd been caught doing on tape but the fact it had been used as blackmail against him meant it was a career buster. And he was right about the Russians. If they found out he'd snitched them off to me, they'd turn him into mulch.

"I got to know her pretty well. From the times she came into the station when we'd have her boss on the air. She and I partied some. Nothing heavy. I got to know…some of her nasty habits."

He stopped again. This time his eyes were wet. Feeling sorry for himself or what he'd done to the woman he had yet to name?

"Who is she, Asa?"

He mumbled the punch line. I heard it nonetheless.

"Alicia Witting. She's the administrative assistant to Senator Brian Ferguson."

CHAPTER 10

▼

Being closed up with Asa and his demons left me feeling claustrophobic. I had to walk afterward. I needed the sunshine, the people and the energy.

The hospital is just off the lakefront and about eight long city blocks from the venerable Tribune Tower where the 'Worlds Greatest Newspaper" gets written. My buddy, Paul Calandra, had been one of their top political correspondents in Washington for the past five years but, as Fate would have it, was in his final week of service to Mother Tribune before taking a job as chairman of the journalism department at one of the top universities on the West Coast. I knew he was back in town to receive a Sigma Delta Chi Award and to attend one of several retirement parties his many friends insisted on throwing.

I wanted his help but I didn't want to call and lay this out for him. I don't trust newsroom telephones, whether they're in newspaper newsrooms, TV stations or radio stations. Reporters play the one-up game as well as anyone else in business and I could think of three stories I'd lost early in my career because a nosy colleague had listened in to my phone chats as I tried to put pieces together.

I trudged toward the Trib, playing back Asa's wretched little tale in my head. Whatever sordid game he'd been playing had left him an easy and exploitable target. When the Russians nailed him, he had not hesitated a moment before giving up others to be similarly squeezed.

This bunch knew exactly what they were doing, not surprising if Gennaro was correct and many of them had been recruited from the old KGB. Spies are adept at blackmail; they're trained until manipulation becomes second nature. Their goal is not to have one good source in place to feed them information but an entire network. It was pretty obvious that's what they were trying to build, one hapless, caught-in-the-act sucker at a time. They might be loudly moving in to swipe the drug business away from the gangs, waving one big hand where everyone would focus on it but, like a magician, they were sneaking the penny up their sleeve with the other hand. Frankly, that sneaky, hidden part of their scam scared me a hell of a lot more.

The coachmen and women were at their posts next to the Water Tower, smoking and talking to each other and hoping to land some midday business while knowing it was unlikely. Rush-hour traffic doesn't make for the most romantic of carriage rides. Their horses seemed as bored as they were. I moved with the crowds of power shoppers and tourists along Michigan Avenue, starting slightly as a black guy about twenty slid into my path and opened one side of his lightweight jacket. But there was no gun, just fake jewelry and knock off watches hanging almost as neatly as they would on a rack in a store.

"Got a Rolex for you man," he said in a voice designed, as was his furtive manner, to suggest he was nervous about getting caught. He wasn't. It was all part of the routine. For all I knew he'd bought a license to do this. He probably did a better business than the carriage drivers.

I've always liked the look of Tribune Tower. With its Gothic arch entrance and the awesome exterior that includes chips of famous buildings from all over the world in its facade, it always makes me question just what good 'ol Colonel McCormick asked for when he held the international competition to find an architect to design the building. Cathedral? Castle? I passed the statue of Nathan Hale in the courtyard of the Annex and stepped inside the lobby. Security procedures put in place after the World Trade Center attack make it impossible to move past that point without an escort. I used a pay phone to call up to Paul's office.

"Reno! You dog! What's up? How have you been?"

"You busy?"

"Yeah, I'm sitting here trying to decide whether to wear a blue shirt or a white shirt to the awards ceremony tonight. You gonna be there?"

"Wish I could be. You have a couple minutes to talk?"

"Where are you?"

"In the lobby."

"Buy me a late lunch. I'll meet you in Nordstrom's food court."

I went back out on Michigan and, like a typical Chicagoan, didn't think twice about crossing against the light. And then an odd thing happened. Foot almost into the street, I froze, remembering the look of the grill of that Lexus as it roared toward me, saw once again the grimace of the guy behind the wheel who wanted to mash my body against the side of the building, no matter what happened to him.

A cab blatted its horn and I stepped back from the street, bumping into a woman with a briefcase who looked at me oddly when I apologized. I stood there a moment, pedestrian traffic swirling around me, as I waited for my adrenaline to quit pumping and for my heart to drop back into normal rhythm. It had been like watching an instant replay of the experience that came within several feet of ending my life. I breathed out slowly a couple of times then walked to the corner. I waited for the light to change before attempting to cross again.

I felt on edge for the time it took to get inside the Nordstrom's mall and ride two escalators to the food court. I knew where and what Paul would want to eat and, by the time he got there, I was sitting at a table at Salsa and had a cold Corona and two fajita rolls waiting for him. I'd swallowed my Corona in three long gulps, belched, and felt better. By the time I saw him, the slight tremor was gone from my hands, too.

Paul has never been shy about letting people know he's a reporter. When I was just starting out in Chicago, fresh from a similar job in Kansas City, we met on the crime beat. He wore his media credentials, both those issued by the city and his Tribune ID, everywhere I saw him. Made no difference whether it was dinner or a 3-11 alarm fire, they dangled around his neck on an old leather lanyard that he always maintained one of his many female friends had made for him. He confessed over too much beer one night that it actually was something he'd constructed at camp one summer when he was eleven.

That odd necklace was the first thing I noticed about him as he came off the escalator, spotted me and waved. Think of a red-haired Hugh Grant look-alike who peers down on my six-two by a couple of inches. He wore a blue blazer and blue shirt with collar open, tie askew, and rumpled khaki slacks. That was something we had in common. Neither of us ever wanted to take the time to iron. Most of our clothes looked like they came from a pile thrown on the floor the night before.

He climbed over the small railing next to the table instead of going around it and sat, grabbing the Corona right off. "You must want information."

I saw his collection of credentials had gained a new one. I reached across and fingered the White House press pass. "You figure this'll get you laid out there in the land of sprouts and granola?"

"Is there ever a reason not to try?" He winked. "Hey, I walked into the newsroom this morning and the first thing I hear is that you're hung up in a murder investigation. What's that all about?" He took a gulp of the Corona then set it down and hefted the fajita roll. I noticed for the first time a slight thickening of his neck and belly.

"How long have you got to talk?"

He shrugged. "The awards thing starts at six. I spent the morning trying to hide from a twenty-something editor who's got the hots for my Rolodex. I told him to send in some nice looking blonde gal with big knockers and he might have a shot. Instead, he goes to *his* boss who goes to the twenty-fourth floor with the idea that it's my ethical duty to pass along my sources before I leave. So, if you want to talk the afternoon away, be my guest."

I summarized the events of the past two days, ending with what Hanratty had told me about his boss's aspirations and then laying the bomb on him about Ferguson's AA. He'd gotten halfway through the second fajita roll and was on his third Corona when I said that and he dropped the tortilla wrapped meat and lettuce on his plate looking like I'd just told him it was full of fire ants.

"You're telling me the Russian mob owns 'Licia Witting? Not that I don't believe you," he hastened to say, "but Jesus Christ. Not to mention that Ferguson's sleeping with *another* Russian asset? That's seriously fucked up."

I hadn't warned him that my tale was for his ears only. Hadn't even considered it, in fact. Didn't need to. He's one of the most diligent journalists I know. One of the reasons he can score exclusives the way he does has to do with his relationship to his sources. He understands how they think and when they're giving him a story or just speaking on background.

"As Ferguson's A.A. she has that much influence on policy?"

"Trust me, Reno. Yeah. Jesus. Look. I've known 'Licia since she started in the office. She runs his life! You know politicians, especially the major players. They could single-handedly be negotiating peace in the Middle East, duck out for a break and get lost for the rest of the day trying to find the potty. She keeps him on track. She prepares all his briefing papers and pretty much has the final say on who has access to him."

"Doesn't he have a Chief of Staff?"

"In name, yeah. Older guy, good schmoozing on the Hill. He gets the dregs, everything 'Licia doesn't do. That's not much. Word is she even beats him in salary. Let me put it this way. If Ferguson ever makes it to the White House, and I think that's where he wants to go, Alicia Witting will get Chief of Staff."

"You know her well?"

"Fairly well. All business, zero sense of humor. I don't see her much, though. What the hell do the Russians have?"

"My source says she's a raver. Maybe something sexual, too?"

"Well, shit, she's gay, but so what? Unless she's screwing ten-year-olds or goats, that lifestyle is fairly common in D.C. Not really blackmail fodder any more. She doing the drugs associated with the raves, too?

"That's what I hear."

"Yeah, that's not so unusual either but, at her level, if someone snitched her off, the FBI might get a little snarky about it. Damn. Almost makes me want to stay on the beat just to track this down."

"Not to interrupt your reconsideration of career choices but I need to know. She sees everything? All the top secret stuff, intelligence memos…"

"Everything that relates to foreign relations, she gets. She holds a top level security clearance, same as Ferguson. Sits in on private meetings at CIA and State. She may not sit next to him in the Oval Office when he chats with The Man but I'll bet she ain't any farther than outside the door."

"Oh."

"Exactly." He made pistols out of both hands and pointed them at me. "You nail this, buddy, and it's Pulitzer time."

We both sat for a moment, not moving or speaking, considering what it meant that the right-hand woman of the most powerful man in Congress might be working for the Russian mob.

"You know, though," he said, thoughtfully. "What you're telling me could fit with something else I heard. Depending how long 'Licia's been corrupted. 'Scuse me. 'Allegedly' corrupted.'"

"How's that?"

"There was a move, oh, about two months ago for a Congressional investigation of U.S. banks doing business with interests in Russia. Money laundering was the key issue but there were a few others. Industrial espionage, stuff like that. Word was that the FBI and CIA came up with some major information. It was all over the Capitol that it was a done deal, committee appointed, ready to break some balls. Then zip. Couldn't even get anyone to even admit it had been on the docket."

"That's not real subtle. If you're thinking Ferguson shut it down."

"He doesn't have to be subtle, Reno. Just careful. You think Rostenkowski, when he was The Chairman, pussyfooted around? You always knew where he stood. If Ferguson wanted to be slick, he could claim…oh hell, I don't know. He could say he had some deal in the making, maybe on nuclear security. That's heavy now, trying to get the Russians to help account for all their WMD's. Especially post 9-11. He could claim a Congressional investigation would jeopardize some agreement he was trying to get them to sign to count and verify all their nukes. Point is, Ferguson carries the big hammer."

"Sounds like Alicia Witting is the one swinging it. She's got so much influence with him she could get him to block an investigation on her say so alone?"

"Probably. Sure. He depends on her to sort through the BS and she's no dummy. Masters in Business from Kellogg and in International Relations from U of C. If she came up with what sounded like a reasonable objection, he'd buy it. Ferguson is smart but, for somebody with all his background and clout on the Hill, he's a little naive. Wants to believe the best of everybody, I think."

He took another bite of his lunch and chewed. When he'd washed that down with a final taste of the Corona, he stared over my shoulder for a moment, lost in thought.

"You know, the rumor mill is a 24/7 operation in DC," he said. "It's funny. It's like a big engine that runs the town. Everybody's connected to it somehow. Like the Internet. Even I plugged into it once awhile. Mostly it's for comedic relief. Sometimes, though, you get a nugget of a story. So what I'm about to say may never have happened but I'll tell you anyway 'cause it might fit with what you're telling me."

I waited. The lunchtime worker-bee crowd had come and gone. Only the tourists remained, swirling through the food court and taking pictures of each other, even here. The kids lined up at the hot dog joint and their parents either chose Mexican or Italian or just sipped latte's and looked in the store windows.

"About a month ago, some lower echelon folks, read that staffers, claimed they'd seen Ferguson out once or twice with Witting and another girl. By 'out' they were talking the clubs. Out on the town."

"So?"

"Ferguson was supposedly drunk. Mean drunk. That's way not something you'd ever expect to hear about him. I'm not saying he's the straightest Baptist who ever lived, but you know what kind of image the guy has and it doesn't include schnappsing in a back alley jazz joint at two in the morning and getting obnoxious with the waitresses." He wiggled a hand.

"'Licia, of course, denied it. I couldn't confirm it anywhere else. Apparently nobody could because nothing ever was said, print or broadcast. Even Matt Drudge and the gossip rags kept quiet. The rumors just stayed rumors. But, be that as it may, it *does* make one wonder."

I thought about what Hanratty had told me on Navy Pier. And how he ordered me to stay away from Ferguson right afterward.

"Was there ever any description of the other girl?"

"Not that I remember. But hang with me a sec. I got a call around that same time from a guy who's a District cop. He has an off-duty gig working security for one of the upscale markets in Georgetown. Sometimes he hears things and he passes them along. Basically, he says Ferguson was with this other chick one afternoon and they ran into the little woman. Mrs. F. Or maybe she followed them and chose the market for the confrontation. Whatever. It wasn't pretty. Now this was information I could reach out and touch, so I did a little checking. The next day Mrs. Ferguson left town and came back here. The next day. She may still be here. No explanation. Their religion and all, they aren't into the DC party circuit but she's normally full of good works, as they say, so her absence has been noted."

"You know what I'm thinking," I said.

"Sure. You think Red Talmadge's kid was the 'other woman' and maybe 'Licia was the beard? If that's true and it gets out that Ferguson was putting the wood to a hooker who later got murdered you might as well give your old buddy Chazz Bascomb the keys to the official Senate bathroom. And award the Senate to the Democrats. Forget that Ferguson's surrounded by the Russian mob. The sex angle alone will bring him down."

He stood up. "I'm going to get another fajita. You want anything?"

"No."

When he came back, he sat back in the chair and stretched his legs into the aisle between the tables and grinned ruefully at me. "If everything you're laying out here is true, it's one hell of a story. You couldn't have come up with all this six months ago?"

"You don't have to leave. You could hang around. Work the Washington angle. Work Witting. Maybe go out with a Pulitzer under your belt."

"Lemme tell you, Reno," he said and his smile disappeared, replaced by an expression of such burned-out weariness that it startled me. "I filed my last piece three days ago. That's all they're sucking out of me. Not my Rolodex, not any last minute tips, no friendly words of advice to the up and comers. I even scraped my list of favorite pizza joints off the side of my computer monitor in the Washington bureau. I hope you win that Pulitzer, buddy, and God bless ya if you do. This business..."

He looked as though he was poised to make another point then smiled a small smile and shook his head.

"Ah fuck it. You know better than most how it chews you up. Get back to what you were saying. You're making more sense than I am at the moment."

"Federov uses Witting to get Brooke close to Ferguson," I began, then stopped and thought about what I'd just said.

"But why not just use Witting?" I wondered. "Why stick Brooke into the mix?"

"For a guy who's in the news business you're sadly out of touch, m'man. She's big time out of the closet. One of Limbaugh's Femi-Nazi's. Pisses off Ferguson's far-right-wing constituency to have her working for him at all, but it dulls some of his straightedge image, too. That's good with the gays here in his district. Point being, I doubt she'd be able to carry off a seduction very believably. Plus, she's what you might call 'looks-impaired.' On the tall, skinny, side. More bumps from the shoulder blades than the chest."

"Okay. So. He meets Brooke. Through Alicia maybe? There's chemistry. But...Ferguson's wife tumbles to what's going on. Who knows what kind of fall-out that caused or what she threatened to do? Federov suddenly sees Brooke as a liability and has her whacked."

"Could happen."

"What if Brooke realized she was suddenly disposable? She was a fighter. Going to a TV station with her story would be a hell of a way to kick Federov in the balls on the way out, wouldn't it? She might even have figured it would give her enough distraction to disappear."

Paul raised the Corona and winked. "You just might make it in this business some day."

Time to replace some of my guesses with facts. "Now I need to talk to that DC cop buddy of yours..."

CHAPTER 11

▼

Paul caught the DC cop at home. He agreed to look at a picture of Brooke Talmadge that would be sent from the Tribune photo department files. Paul ate two more fajitas while we waited for a callback. I just sat and fretted, occasionally tapping my fingers on the table. Paul's phone rang as he was headed to the rest room for the third time in two hours. He handed it to me.

"Danny Posini," said the guy. He had a strong Brooklyn accent. "I got the broad's picture. I gotta tell ya, it's a pretty damn good likeness. It's hard to forget a fine looking piece like that."

"Was she the girl you saw with Ferguson when his wife braced them?"

For the first time in three days I felt the rush I always get when facts match up.

"No doubt what-so-evah. 'Course I'd never say that to anybody official."

"You won't have to. How did the confrontation happen exactly?"

"Not much to it. The wife marches in like she owns the place, not like she plans to do any shopping. That's what caught my eye. She takes a turn down one aisle, sees the Senator and the broad with him. They're in the meat department, you follow? Wifey there lights up like the Fourth a' July. Specifically, I got to say it made me think I was gonna have to throw her out. Until I realized who all the players were, you unnerstand. You don't just go putting your hands on the wife of a U.S. Senator. Even if every other word she's using starts with 'fokkin.' 'Fokkin' hoor,' 'fokkin bastard.' Like that. Real colorful lady that one was."

"She called Brooke a whore? How would Mrs. Talmadge have known she wasn't just one of her husband's aides? Maybe an intern…"

"Beats me. She called her by name first, though. Now that you say it, I remember. Brooke, right? Second, the way this chica was dressed, I mean, come on. Short-ass skirt and one of them half-t's showing off her belly button. Tight, too. Nice tatas on that broad."

"She's dead."

"Yeah? Fokkin' waste." He said it like someone who'd left the egg salad out too long and now had to throw it away.

"What did Mrs. Ferguson say, exactly?"

"Lemme think a minute." I heard a cigarette lighter snap. "Something like, 'I always knew you were trash,' or 'knew you'd turn out to be nothing but trash.' Something like that. There was alotta shit flying both ways and the Senator was trying to quiet 'em both down but that's the gist of it."

"How many people saw what was happening?"

"Oh, maybe a half-dozen. I got 'em away from the crowd pretty quick. Nobody seemed to make any connection as to who they were. I guess if they woulda, there'd a been something in the papers."

I ended the call just as Paul came back from the rest room. I said, "Do I need to make a cash contribution on this or…"

"To Danny? No way, man. His on-duty job is in Metro P.D.'s Internal Affairs. He'd never take it. Straight as can be. Anyway," he winked. "Mother Tribune would never let me pay a source. You know that."

He sat down and I said, "Posini says Karine Ferguson recognized Brooke."

"Yeah? So?"

"You suppose Ferguson and Red Talmadge know each other?"

"Know *of*, sure. I doubt their families do backyard barbecues or movie nights together. Talmadge made his nut with Big Tobacco when they still figured Congress might do them some good. He and Ferguson probably had some face time back then."

"Both from the North Shore. Same constituency."

"Same neighborhood, too, if I remember. But the cigarette companies pretty well wiped Talmadge off their shoes when the lawsuits started flying. And remember, Ferguson's got his squeaky clean, Baptist thing going on. He bucked the party and came down with the state AG's against the cancer-stick makers on that one. So it's not like he and Red would have been tight. And by the way, since tobacco, I don't see Talmadge in DC at all. He's back hanging with the homies in Springfield. That's always been his real base anyway."

"Let's assume their families have at least a nodding acquaintance. You serious when you said Talmadge'll pick up a few points when Ferguson's affair comes to light? Even if it's Talmadge's daughter who played the other woman?"

Paul picked at the label of his empty Corona bottle and grinned.

"*If* it comes out, you mean. Weirder shit than that never sees its way into the press. I think they're teaching Cover Up Theory in college these days. But IF it comes out, the Democrats'll have their very own Monica and Bill to snipe at."

"I'm not talking about the party. What happens to Talmadge?"

"I may have overstated a bit saying he'll get brownie points. But it won't hurt him. Unless somebody makes a case he *aimed* Brooke at Ferguson and that's not what you're saying happened. You have any idea 'zactly how wired Red Talmadge is?"

I shrugged. "He's always been a mover and shaker."

"He's the Gov's favorite fundraiser. They call him Golden Touch. He taps his clients for donations and for some reason they keep reaching deep. Funny thing, most of them are the ones who get the lucrative state contracts. The few that boot him as their lobbyist all of a sudden see their business drop off or maybe the state doesn't write their checks as quickly any more."

He signaled the bartender and pointed at his empty bottle.

"Then there's the story that one of the companies he owns is the disbursement operation for some nice kickbacks coming in from a couple of the state's major vendors. Absolutely no confirmation of course."

"The Republicans have to be sniffing around on that."

"Think again. The Democrats may be Talmadge's party, Reno, but you best believe they aren't his only clients."

I let that percolate for a moment. "OK. He's insulated. What's to say he didn't drop a dime to Karine Ferguson? Who would ever know?"

"Now that's a 'Daddy Dearest' if I've ever heard one."

"Talmadge admits he and Brooke didn't get along. What's the downside for him if he snitches off her affair? From what you're saying, the party's not going to ostracize him. And with Ferguson having to quit, the Governor chooses a replacement and Talmadge is right there at the table."

"And he pitches your old buddy Chazz Bascomb for the job. Exactly. Ever think about becoming a political reporter? The way your mind works you'd be a sure thing for the Sunday morning talk shows, ol' buddy. They'd love you."

I stayed with the thread.

"Brooke has to tell Federov the Senator's wife knows about her. Federov sees the affair is going to be revealed, doesn't want Brooke available for anyone to question, so he has her killed." Just saying the words laid a chill on my neck.

"You probably know this already," Paul said as he reached out to the approaching bartender and took the Corona from his hands, "But you're going to play hell getting your old job back if you blast Chazz's chance at becoming a U.S. Senator *and* link him to a murder plot."

"I'm a long way from doing that."

"Long on supposition, a little short on facts? You know I was going to mention that a couple of minutes ago but you had this sappy smile on your face." He tasted his beer. "Don't worry. When you crack the case, I'll never tell that you floundered a little trying to put it all together. After all, I'll be too busy being retired and filling the minds of youth with all sorts of ideas how they can help humanity by writing about the imperfections of government."

*   *   *   *

By the time I got back out on Michigan Avenue and headed for my car, I felt like I'd been the one filling up on fajitas and beer instead of Paul. Every sound along the street seemed magnified a hundred-fold and the heat coupled with exhaust fumes to make me feel I was fighting my way through a shimmering wall of humidity.

At least now I had a working theory. That's the backwards way of working an investigation, of course. Normally, you find facts and assemble your theory from them but I was happy to take logical guesses at this point. It wasn't as though I was going to be standing in front of a TV camera and postulating anytime soon. If at all. In fact, the prospects of getting my job back, or any job in television news ever again, seemed as dim as my mood.

A triple beep from the cell phone in my pocket startled me. Voice mail waiting. I dialed in as I walked, smiling to myself when I noticed a handful of others walking near me also had phones to their ears.

Three messages. I'd been unreachable inside the metal maze that made up the Nordstrom's mall. Cellular signals bounce crazily along the Magnificent Mile.

Message One: Gennaro. "Reno, you damn fool. Call me as soon as you get this and *not* from your fucking cellular." He muttered more invective as he hung up but I couldn't tell if it was directed at me or to someone in the room with him.

Message Two: Sunny. "Your efficient Girl Friday, Kato, here. Are you still wearing the nice jewelry I gave you? I just got a phone call you'll want to know about. I'm at home."

Message Three: I didn't recognize the number on the Caller ID readout and whoever it was hadn't left any more of a message than what sounded like an exasperated sigh.

The mystery caller won out. I punched in the number on the screen, waited through three rings and got a "We're sorry, the customer you're calling is not available right now..." I clicked off, irritated as I always am by people who don't leave messages or even their name.

When I was working in TV, I used to wonder if hang-up calls were from people with tips to great stories. Now I figure all those calls come from News Directors with once-in-a-lifetime job opportunities that could have been mine if only the call had not gone to voice mail.

Yeah, I hold a pity party for myself about once a week.

I ducked off the street and rode an elevator up to the lobby of the Four Seasons. I used to meet the occasional confidential source in the hotel bar and I like their public phones. They're in cubicles almost like tiny guest rooms, soundproofed and away from prying ears. I walked around the elegant lobby for a few minutes, pretending I could smell the fresh-cut flowers, before slipping into one of the booths and making the call. I figured Gennaro would be proud of my evasion tactics. He didn't sound so proud when he answered.

"Y'know for somebody who's been working the street as long as you, you sure have your head up your ass."

"You're absolutely right. I sure do. What's doing, John?"

"I got a little friend who works on the Dark Side, that's what." The Dark Side was how he referred to the Bureau's Intelligence section. "You know what the Joint Terrorism Task Force is?"

"Old news. They black-bagged my house, right?"

"I don't know specifics. I do know they're on you right now. Have been all day. You nearly got to be the hood ornament on a Lexus this morning, am I right?"

Jesus. I looked over my shoulder through the pane of glass in the booth door. I half-expected to see a couple of lurking guys wearing trench coats and talking into microphones in their sleeves.

"Why? What's the point?"

"I don't have all the particulars. Far as I know, nothing was said about your new friend. All the watching started today."

He sounded relieved. By "your new friend", he undoubtedly meant Polo Tony. I wondered about that. Gennaro wasn't an agent any longer. Why would he care if the Feds saw us paying a visit the Godfather?

"How are they doing it? I had the car swept."

"Fuck the car. Don't you keep up with the news? His Holiness, our Attorney General, opened his wallet to all the Terrorism Task Forces. Who knows how they're tagging ya? Satellites. Maybe they hit you with one of those new GPS darts, sticks in your clothes. I'm a little limited in the information department here. Not like I can just call the Chicago office SAC and ask him."

"What's with the task force, anyway? Don't the Bureau's Organized Crime squads handle a Russian mob case?"

"Yeah, normally OC-3 has the Russians and the Asians. Maybe one of the Criminal Enterprise Squads. This…this is all different." He paused. "What the hell are you up to, anyway?"

I told him what had happened in Evanston that morning but edited the part about visiting Asa down to the basics, mentioning only that I'd been to see him and he didn't look so hot. I didn't mention his confession. Gennaro wasn't buying.

"And," he prodded when I finished.

"He says he got mugged. His girlfriend backs him up."

"What aren't you telling me, Reno? Now's not the time to play pocket pool. How'm I supposed to help if I don't know what you're doing?"

I changed tack on him.

"I'm more curious about why the terrorism task force is so interested in me. Maybe your little friend can find a way to tell you about that."

"Does it take a fucking university class to help you figure it out? You never were this dim a bulb when you were working for the TV. Think on it. You're stepping all around in the middle of a domestic terrorism investigation, for chrissakes."

"Oh it's domestic terrorism, now? They figure I'm smarter than they are and want to be right behind me when I find the clue that breaks the case?"

"Yeah, laugh now buddy. See how funny it is when you're sitting up in the MCC looking out one of those little slits in the wall they call windows."

The MCC is the Metropolitan Correctional Center where federal prisoners are housed awaiting trial. It's an angular, brick building just a little east of LaSalle Street and the financial district and what windows it has look like gun ports.

"So, what is it they expect I'm going to find?"

"It's not anything specific. I told you. This Russian crap is a potential major embarrassment to the bosses, especially in Washington. They want it kept quiet until they bag somebody and can hold a press conference and show 'em off. How's it gonna look, you come up with some kind of major story before they have their ducks in a row?"

"That's why they're threatening cops, too?"

I heard the clinking of ice cubes in a glass and realized it was almost the cock-tail hour.

"You think it's just the Bureau that wants this quiet? Gimme a break, Reno. You of all people don't need a primer in Chicago politics."

He grunted in surprise as a doorbell sounded in the background. "Gotta go. But think about this. What's going to happen to the convention business in this town if there's a gang war that makes the Capone days look like a bunch of snow-ball fights?"

I listened to the buzz of a dead phone line until the automatic disconnect gave me silence. Even then, I hung up slowly. If I got any more ancillary pieces of information I was going to have to find a computer to store them on. I rubbed my forehead with the heel of my hand. The idea that Dark's people might be nearby, watching, caused a thrumming of dread in my chest. I took a couple of deep breaths with my eyes closed. It helped. I sat back in the phone booth's com-fortable chair and tried to distract myself by sorting through what I had learned so far, formulating basic questions.

What if Talmadge found out about his daughter's affair with Ferguson and decided to use it to further his own agenda? He could have done so without much difficulty. Tipped off the Senator's missus for example. It would take a cold man to do such a thing, wouldn't it? Did having a stone for a heart mean I should make him a suspect in his daughter's murder? If so, what was his motive?

Asa pointed the Russians at Ferguson's chief aide. OK. Had the Russians then used Alicia to fix the Senator up with Brooke Talmadge? They could have chosen any number of beautiful women for that role. Why pick Brooke? What would have made them think Brooke would catch his eye? I'd never read or heard any-thing to indicate Ferguson was a womanizer, much less that he preferred a certain type. Why her?

Of course, at this point, the affair was only an assumption. Could have been a total setup. An elaborate blackmail scheme. Put the hooker next to the straight-edge U.S. Senator in enough different circumstances, create some phony intimacy, get a few pictures, do a little doctoring of those images, start a few rumors and pretty soon you have a scandal. Or even better, I thought with a chill, when you're done stage managing, take it one step further and kill the hooker. Sprinkle enough clues around that, eventually, the cops start to look at the Sena-tor as a suspect in her murder.

Now there's mud that won't easily dry.

Someone moved through the light just outside the phone booth, snapping me out of the trance-like state my thoughts had created. Two well-dressed women stood about twenty-five feet away, talking to a bellman. If they were the "G," Uncle Sam had been more than generous with a clothing allowance. Their Armani duds would have set him back an easy grand.

I opened the door and stepped back into the lobby. A man in business casual, strong of jaw and hair tousled like he'd just parked his convertible, walked through the arch leading into the bar and disappeared. Two other men, more formally attired, sat on a couch looking through documents from the briefcase open on a coffee table in front of them.

In truth, any of them could have been federal agents. The people working the front desk might have been CIA or KGB, for that matter. That elusive mastermind Osama Bin Laden could be lurking behind the potted ferns. Thanks, Gennaro, I thought.

I left the hotel expecting a dark sedan full of G-persons to be waiting curbside in front of the charming statue of a man hailing a cab, but there was only a kid in a yellow Corvette and a priest getting out of the back of a stretch limo. Neither braced me with a badge. No snipers opened fire from a nearby rooftop and Elliot Ness didn't step from a Model A and confront me with his .38 and a pair of handcuffs. Halfway back to the garage where I'd parked my car, the cell rang with Sunny's number displayed on the Caller ID. I had forgotten to call her and check in.

"I was beginning to wonder if I should send a couple of guys looking for you." She tried to hide her annoyance with a lighthearted tone.

"Went to see Paul at the *Trib*," I said.

"I thought he retired."

"Just about. What's going on?"

"Russ just called. Right after you left the hospital, a mess of federal agents showed up. Russ says they sealed off the floor, questioned him and then ordered him out of there. Asa has federal protection now."

I was stunned.

"How the hell did they get to him so fast? And how the hell did they know he had anything to tell them?"

"It sounds like someone has some pretty good informants."

Gennaro had been right, I thought. They were following me, dogging my tracks, and eager to question anyone I talked to. This could get cumbersome and annoying very quickly.

I started to tell her about my watchers but stopped before saying anything. Gennaro's message had been very specific that I not call him on the cell phone. That niggled at me. I told Sunny to stay put and that I'd get back to her in a few minutes. I disconnected the call and turned the phone off. Then I went back into the hotel and up to my phone booth again.

I'd been watching for surveillance all day. I'm not a professional at that sort of thing but have heard from the experts how difficult it is to maintain an eyeball on someone in the city unless you're right up on your target or use a variety of vehicles, and people, and leapfrog frequently so the person being followed doesn't get suspicious. That's all fine and well but it requires heavy resources if you're going to do it right. Sure, the feds could have assigned enough manpower to handle the job, but just having someone behind me when I drove into the hospital parking lot wouldn't have told them why I was there. No one had been on the elevator with me when I went up to Asa's room and even if agents had been among the other hospital visitors, they wouldn't have overheard our conversation.

Even if the feds found out I was going to see Asa, why would they think he was a relevant figure in the case? From news reports, they'd know only that he'd been mugged and was in the hospital. I worked with the guy every day. I could have just been visiting as a concerned colleague. If they'd wanted to know what we'd talked about, sending in one agent to do an interview would certainly have been more reasonable than deploying a squad and kicking out Asa's bodyguard.

I didn't like the direction my thoughts were jogging.

To know for certain that Asa was involved with the Russians and worth throwing a net over, the Feds would have had to have previous information or…my addled brain squeaked and whirred…have listened in to our conversation. If they'd known how valuable he might be before I went to see him, more than likely they would have wanted to keep me out. Ergo….

I looked down at the Motorola phone in my hand. It was the only electronic device I had carried in the last couple of days, but it had been with me everywhere. Because I have a number of friends who are electronics geeks, I knew some things about cellular phones. One was that federal legislation had recently gone into effect requiring all cell companies to adopt technology allowing emergency calls to be automatically traced, in the same manner as landline calls to 9-1-1. Which meant the cellular systems now all had tracking software in place. Could it be used to trace non-emergency calls? That was a no brainer. Of course it could. That's why the civil libertarians had howled when the bill was first proposed. Arguments about the tracing of errant spouses and checking up on teenage children came to mind.

I also knew, from covering federal drug cases, that eavesdropping law allowed agencies that obtained an "overhear" warrant to tap cellular phones. The Feds, my geek friends told me, commonly used a device called a Celltracker which recorded a phone's unique electronic serial number and automatically locked on whenever that phone was in use. Could a cell phone be made to transmit without the user being aware of it? I didn't have to dig far into my personal data bank for that answer either. Motorola invented the technology originally so dispatchers could work magic with stolen police radios. The bad guy thinks he's listening to the good guys' radio traffic but has no idea the good guys are also listening to him. Why not cell phones? I looked at mine again. I remembered turning it off at the request of the security guard in the lobby of the hospital. I'd forgotten to turn it on when I went to meet Paul. Yet, when I'd left the Food Court, it had rung to signal I had messages waiting.

Had to be, I thought. Son of a bitch. The feds hadn't bugged my car and probably hadn't bugged my house, either. They'd eavesdropped on me from a distance through my own damn phone. I felt the special kind of anger that being manipulated generates in me. I couldn't be certain but I didn't need to be. It seemed like just the kind of emotional sucker punch that my new nemesis, Agent Dark, would use and that's what I had to act on.

I left the booth and crossed the lobby to the rest rooms, the cell phone feeling hot in my hand. When I came out, I had left the phone behind, turned on and ready for use, wedged into the back of the paper towel dispenser.

Agent Dark could now listen to the sounds of flatulence and flushing while I went about my business.

*   *   *   *

Some people go off on tangents when they're pissed. My anger focuses me. I suppose a dollop of fear should have gone along with being a target of the Joint Terrorism Task Force, arguably one of the most powerful law-enforcement units in the country since 9/11. When you break stories about public corruption and private frauds as I had been doing for years, however, you get used to threats, attacks and attempts to intimidate. I'm not saying I was taking the government's intrusion into my life in stride. Not at all. The key to handling power when it's aimed at you is the same as it is in so many other endeavors, beginning with the first bully in the schoolyard. You don't back down. You don't show fear. And, as I'd learned in my martial arts classes, you make every effort to turn your opponents' strength against them.

Closeted again in my favorite phone booth, I called Sunny back. Sunny is a very careful person and has her office and home phones swept regularly. She's very proud of the fact that the guy who does the work is retired from the Israeli Mossad. He's very damn good at what he does.

"Your buddy Shavitz know anything about turning a cell phone into a bug?" I asked.

"Excuse me?"

"I think the feds have been listening to me through my cellular. Run it by Shavitz. In the meantime, though, do you have a phone you aren't using? Maybe one you've never used?"

"I have a drawer full of them. I also have some of the encrypted two-ways we use on surveillance. Want one of those?"

"What's the range?"

"With a repeater on Sears, what do you think? Parts of three states. Nobody listens without the code key, and the encryption logarithm is changed daily."

"I'll take one of each if you'll drop them at the house."

"That would be a smooth move. Right in front of a bunch of government cameras?"

"I don't think the feds are watching the house. I think they wanted me to think that and did the trick with the cell phone instead."

"And you're willing to gamble on that?"

"I'm willing to work around it. We've been spinning our wheels on this thing and if I could break Asa down I'm sure the Feds won't have any trouble, either. If I'm going to stay ahead of them, I need to move fast. Did you find a way to get Talmadge's client list?"

"As a matter of fact, that was the other thing I wanted to talk to you about. Wait a sec while I call up the file."

I took the moment that she was clicking keys to glance over my shoulder and eye the lobby again. Staying in the area where I had parked the cell phone probably didn't make for good trade craft, as they call it in the spy business, but I wasn't particularly worried. I didn't plan to remain long, nor did I intend to leave the way I came in.

"OK," Sunny said. "God bless elections laws. This is a pretty comprehensive list. He and his clients try to get sneaky every once in awhile with corporate misigosh but they obviously didn't think anyone would try to unravel it all."

"Misigosh?" I said.

"Shut up. You know my grandmother was Jewish. First of all, Talmadge had to register both with the Federal elections people and the state's because he lobbies in both arenas. He's got several of the large cigarette companies listed, but that goes back a couple of years. He also works for a dozen or so electronics firms.

Hi-tech stuff. He's got the City of Chicago listed and I have a feeling he was in on the airport expansion plan in some capacity, maybe getting a site authorization or new runways or something because it's the Department of Aviation. Then there's the Metropolitan Pier and Exposition Authority and the CTA and the CHA."

"All those initials don't impress me. You're just teasing."

"You think?"

"Who else is on there?"

"There are two parts to that answer." I could tell she was smiling, proud of her work. "The laws say lobbyists only have to list the clients they're representing in Congress or with the state legislature, but there's mention here of a Judicial Retention Fund. I think somebody who didn't know the rules put it in the file by mistake. Talmadge's firm does full-service public relations along with political consulting. Didn't you mention Charles Bridges to me at one point?"

"Damn," I said. "Hanratty said Brooke brought up Bridges' name when she was trying to prove she had good information about the escort services. He was her father's client, too?"

"It looks that way. I did some newspaper research. Bridges was probably right in thinking he needs some PR help if he wants to stay on as a judge. He doesn't really hide his opinions very well, does he?"

"Never has."

Charles Bridges was a Black Circuit Court judge who had fallen off a fast track to the Appellate Bench when his tactics and a lack of tact landed him in front of television cameras one too many times. During an assignment to the Criminal Court at 26th and California he often ranted that police officers who testified in his court were "liars," much to the glee of the defense bar. Transferred to Family Court, he repeatedly ruled in favor of husbands over wives in matters of custody and distribution of assets. Once, while a columnist for the *Sun-Times* sat in the gallery, he had ordered a well-to-do Barrington accountant to remove her jewelry and hand over her purse as she and her attorney showed up to protest an order that she provide support for her unemployed and abusive husband.

What had caught the columnist's eye, though the judge apparently missed it, was the large bruise along the woman's right temple. It was a bruise, witnesses testified later, that resulted from the husband slamming her face into a wall when she refused to pay off his gambling debts. The crowning touch had come, however, when Bridges removed a container of birth control pills from the woman's purse, displayed it to onlookers, and remarked that, "If she'd kept her legs closed as tightly as she hung onto the family purse strings, maybe we wouldn't all be here today."

"Charles Bridges appears to be a recent client. He's on this year's updated list. He's not the only surprise, though."

"I'm sitting down."

"Remember Balkan Global Systems?"

That one caused me to hunch forward in my chair and hold the phone a little tighter to my ear.

"Federov was Talmadge's client?" I said. I felt like something was stuck in my throat.

"His bank's holding company was. We were talking about how the whole background investigation into Federov's bank application was kept sort of low key and out of the news? On deeper search, I found a number of references to a Congressional investigation that never materialized. Apparently Mr. Talmadge did a good job for the Balkan people. There was even a suspicion of money laundering. Never went anywhere. The subcommittee that was supposed to look into it was never formed. I'm still trying to figure out how a lobbyist managed that."

"He didn't. Correction. If he did, he didn't do it alone."

"Come again?"

"It looks like our friends have a lock on Senator Brian Ferguson." I heard her intake of breath.

"No shit. No *shit*. Wait. Did Paul tell you that or…"

"They targeted Asa for some peccadillo, probably a sex thing. Had video. When they leaned on him, he started giving up his friends, one of whom turned out to be Ferguson's AA, a woman by the name of Alicia Witting. The timing works out so that she's probably the one who pushed Ferguson to shut down the hearings. Who knows, maybe Talmadge performed some magic, too. The point is, Federov stage managed the whole thing."

"This is getting scary, Reno. You might note that 'scary' is not a word I use very often."

"Wasn't it you, yesterday, saying something about my paranoia?"

"I eat my words, ok? What the hell have we walked into?"

"Talmadge worked for Federov," I mused, swept away momentarily by the implications of that more than the idea of the Russian mob with its tentacles wrapped around one of the Senate's key members. "And his daughter *lived* with Federov. That raises a whole bunch of questions for me."

"I guess we know how Brooke and Federov met."

"Daddy fixing daughter up with his client? Not in this family. Talmadge didn't have a kind word to say about Brooke. If he was acting, he deserves an Oscar. Alan says Federov saw Brooke in some movie and reached out that way."

"Wait," Sunny said. "Another tap of the keys and a pause. "Actually there's a connection between Federov and movies. I called a couple of friends in Vice and at the Federal Building. You're going to have to follow me for a minute, here. Two years ago, the three biggies in the porn business around Chicago, you don't need the names, merged into one. It called itself Erato Productions. Last year, a company out of Denmark bought Erato Productions. I can show you a nice paper trail of ownership for that company right back into the Ukraine. Once it gets there, though, forget it. The records basically disappear. From what I can tell, the company name is Donetsk Data Communications but there's no statement of ownership, no names of officers, not even an address or town. A federal bank examiner, for example, wouldn't be able to make a case that Balkan Global Systems is into fuck videos. I note, however, that Balkan Global lists their headquarters in the city of Donetsk. A city that, I happen to know, is just full of corruption and *Mafiya* types."

That made me grin.

"You just happen to know that, huh? Checked your personal data bank on that one?"

"Yes. Of course, it's mentioned in the on-line encyclopedia too, but that's just coincidence."

"Of course it is." My smile ran its course and turned into a yawn. I wanted a nap. I closed my eyes and reopened them, looking over my shoulder to see if there was any activity in the lobby suggesting the feds had arrived. I couldn't spot any likely candidates.

"I need to nail down a reason for Brooke's murder," I said. "All we've been doing is speculating. Federov still has my vote as the most likely suspect. Brooke could have given the Feds some pretty good insight to his operations. But what's to say the motive wasn't just simple blackmail? I want to talk to Bridges. If he's kinky, she could have threatened to go public with it."

"Here's another thought, Reno. You don't suppose Ferguson could have found out he'd been set up, do you? That Brooke wasn't boffing him out of love and respect but because she was told to? Talk about humiliation…"

"The Senator discovers Brooke jumped from Federov's bed to his and has her offed to cover it up? Why don't you see if the Senator's wife is still staying here in town? She goes on my list, too."

"On the other thing, I'll run the phone and radio over to your house before I crash for the night. You headed home now?"

"No. While the evening is still young I want to see if I can catch Bridges."

*   *   *   *

Before leaving the phone booth, I dialed up a contact in the hotel's PR department and outlined my situation. A couple of minutes later she sauntered by, winked and moved on. I followed her through a security-card access door, down a short flight of stairs and then to a card-access elevator that took me to a door into the first level of the parking garage. I circled around the block to avoid the front part of the hotel and jogged back to where I'd left my car. I was on my way down the Outer Drive to Bridges' home in Hyde Park a couple of minutes later.

By the time I took the 53rd Street exit off South Lake Shore Drive and drove under the Illinois Central railroad tracks into downtown Hyde Park, it was nearly seven-thirty. With the University of Chicago's main campus just a few blocks away, and summer session just started, the streets were plenty active in a small-town-old-college-neighborhood sort of way. Even so, that didn't mean Bridges was going to welcome company, if he was even home. I shy away from calling to announce my visits when I know there's a good chance that advance notification will just allow the person to leave or not answer their door. Surprise in such cases is seldom a bad thing. In fact, taking people off guard is one of my favorite tactics.

Hyde Park has changed a bit since Mayor Harold Washington lived there while in office. Back then the police patrols were obvious, both by city and U of C coppers, the streets were kept immaculate and the homeless almost invisible. As I searched for a place to park, I noted a re-emergence of gang symbols on Dumpsters and alley walls, a number of storefronts that were empty and a different look to the crowds on the sidewalks. More students kept to groups and those who walked alone moved quickly, focusing their attention straight ahead.

I nosed into a parking place near a Pier One Imports and locked up as two young Asian men standing on the corner eyeballed me. Both wore low slung baggy pants and t-shirts big enough to conceal small howitzers. I was very aware of Sunny's 9mm automatic hanging off my ankle. I was rehearsing in my head just how I would react if they approached me when one of them smirked at the other and they both turned and walked away.

Bridges' place was a two-story stonemason's dream set back off Dorchester and surrounded by an eight-foot-tall, black, iron fence. Ivy covered the entire front of the house that wasn't glass, giving the appearance that nature was attempting to reclaim the lot, structure and all. I mounted the steps to the porch and resisted the urge to sit in a padded wingback chair that faced the street, while I waited for someone to respond to my pressing of the doorbell. Wouldn't do to be discovered sleeping. A minute later a heavyset black man in gray slacks and bright red polo shirt peered out through the glass and then opened the door.

Charles Bridges had the wrinkled and benign features of a gentle grandfather. His eyes were something else again. Enrico Fermi, who spent a little time working beneath a certain football field just a few blocks south of where we stood, might have described them as being in the first stages of fusion.

"Judge Bridges?" I said.

"I'm Charles Bridges."

No attempt at a handshake, no neighborly smile, no expression whatsoever. Was this guy really a politician?

"My name's Reno McCarthy. Sorry to bother you this late in the evening..."

He chopped off my apology with an irritated wave.

"Goddamn right, you're sorry. You don't look the type to be selling anything. What's so important you can't wait and see me in the office tomorrow?"

"Suppose I told you I was a wealthy but disillusioned Republican looking for a jurist whose ideals for good government closely match my own?"

"You're full of shit," he said and slammed the door. Or tried to. It rebounded off the shoe I had placed in its path and nearly smacked him in the face. He sucked in a breath.

"As abysmal as the police are in this city, they certainly will respond if a Circuit Court judge calls them. Take your bullshit off my property."

A woman, younger but nearly as big as he was, materialized from the shadows behind him. She blitzed me with her own version of the look he wore. I felt sorry for any Jehovah's Witnesses who wandered within range of that glare. The voltage would probably wither them into agnostics.

"Is everything okay, dad?" she asked.

"Go call 9-1-1. This kook doesn't want to leave."

He shoved the door at me again but this time I caught the edge of the frame with my hand and held it steady.

"Brooke Talmadge," I said, hoping to take him off balance.

He stopped pushing the door and swung it back so abruptly I almost took a header into their foyer. His face still gave away nothing but the pitch of his growl changed.

"You're a damn reporter aren't you?"

"Dad, you don't have to talk to anyone…" his daughter began.

He patted her on the shoulder and his eyes lost some of their flint as he glanced her way.

"You go back inside. I'll listen to the man. Don't mean I have anything to say to him."

"Dad…" she persisted.

"If he gets annoying, I'll just send him on his way. Never met a snoop I couldn't handle." He stepped outside and, as if to illustrate his point, grasped my arm. "We'll take a stroll, I think."

We walked out to the sidewalk that way, his grip tight on my upper arm. He was in his early sixties but had ping-pong-paddle sized hands. I'd have a bruise in the morning.

"What do you mean coming to my home and bringing up that shit for?" he asked. "You're working for somebody aren't you? Mossbacher and his citizens' watchdog group put you up to this?"

I snatched my arm free and turned to look at him. We were the same height but years of rubber-chicken dinners and bar association lunches left him out-weighing me by forty pounds. Over his shoulder, I could see his daughter still standing on the porch and lasering me with her look. She held a portable phone in one hand.

"You have an alibi for the night before last? Say about 11 or so?"

"Alibi!" he sputtered. "What the fuck are you talking about, alibi?"

"Brooke Talmadge is dead. She was murdered."

His head twitched and he took one involuntary step backward.

"What? The hell you say."

I had expected to see the feral expression a politician often gets when he's headed for cover. Instead, his features twisted and I thought for the barest moment he might cry. He brought a hand up to pass across his forehead.

"My God. I didn't know," he said simply. He glanced back at his daughter and motioned for her to go inside. This time she moved back into the shadows and I saw the door close.

"My daughter and I…we've been at our summer home in Michigan. Neither of us reads the papers or watches TV much anyway and we had the phones turned off. Just drove in tonight. I didn't know." He repeated. He looked at me. The fury that had been in his eyes when he found me at his door was gone or, at least, in abeyance.

"What happened?"

I saw no hint of guile or deceit. If anything, he sounded like the news had sucker-punched him. I told him the story, without mentioning my role in it. When I finished, he turned abruptly and began walking. He had the brisk stride of a man who's been told daily walks could keep him alive a few more years. We traveled two blocks in silence before he slowed. He spoke without looking in my direction.

"You get some kind of tip about me or what?"

"Something like that."

"You took me off guard," he said. "Hard to do, all the bullshit I see. I heard you say 'alibi,' I almost felt like I did sixty years ago, my older brother pushed me so hard on a swing I fell over backward, hit the ground and couldn't get my breath. Seemed like forever. I remember looking up at his face, thinking I wasn't ever going to breathe again.

"Alibi," he said and grunted softly. "Saw you at the door, thought you were some political guy, maybe from the ward. Then you brought up Brooke and next thing I was expecting to see was pictures or some such. Blackmail. Never 'spected to hear you say she was dead."

We walked another block in silence. A mixed bag of teenagers shouting playful obscenities at each other passed us going the opposite direction. Somewhere to the west a siren began to warble and a white U of C campus police car with its lights jitterbugging roared down the street, headed in that direction. I thought of the sudden rise in the homicide rate I'd read about. To the west of Hyde Park is the 2nd District or what the cops call "the Deuce," one of the most gang-infested neighborhoods in the city. I wondered if 'the Deuce" had just added another name or two to the roll of the dead.

I let him lead me across the street to Harper Court. When Chicago urban-renewed Carl Sandburg and Vachel Lindsay and others of their literary ilk out of their bohemian digs down around 57th Street in the 1950's, Harper Court was where the planners hoped they would settle. However, the masters of city design failed to consider the higher rents Harper Court charged over the ram-shackle leftovers from the Colombian Exposition. Sandburg, Lindsay and the others took their creative genius elsewhere.

Bridges stopped at a cement bench with a checkerboard painted on its top and eased himself down onto it. Digging in a pocket, he produced a clean white handkerchief and wiped his face. He carefully refolded the material when he was finished, concentrating on the task the way someone does when they're working through a problem. I watched his fingers move. They seemed stiff. I realized his hands shook slightly, too. Suddenly, he looked up and met my gaze.

"Did she suffer?" he asked.

"I don't think so."

"What was she to you? Were you a...client?"

I thought about how to answer. His gut-level reaction to her death had changed my game plan.

"She offered Channel 14 some information about her business. I was in the process of checking out what she'd told them when she was killed."

"You getting your nose broken a part of that 'checking out?'"

"A part," I admitted.

He was clearly ready to snatch the role of inquisitor away from me. "Exactly what information about her business did she offer? Is that how my name came up?"

"From what I was told, Brooke identified you as one of her johns."

"Just to your station," he pressed, "Or to the police, too?"

"I don't know who she told, Judge. I don't really care. What I'm curious about is what you did to piss her off so badly she'd give up your name to anyone, much less a TV station."

"Are we on the record?"

"Not necessarily."

He snorted. "You think this old lawyer's accepting an answer like that?"

"If you tell me you killed her or had her killed, it's on the record. Anything short of that falls into a sort of gray area for me right now. I'm more interested in finding the person who murdered her than I am in getting a story."

"Then sit. I'm getting a stiff neck looking up at you." He slid over to make room.

I took a seat. Cajun music played softly from outside speakers on the verandah of a Louisiana Crab Shack across the small plaza. There were a few people out walking, mostly couples, but none of them paid any attention to us.

"You were fond of her," I said.

"You think that's strange? Old black man taking a liking to some college-age white girl?"

"Who was a hooker," I added.

He looked at me stone-faced for a moment and I waited for him to snap a reply. Instead, his features softened.

"Why don't I just tell you the story before you go getting all high and mighty?" I nodded but a strange tension had formed in my chest as I thought about him and Brooke together and it wasn't going away.

"You may find it strange, given how politically incorrect your friends in the media think I am and all, but I used to teach a class over there," he gestured toward the U of C campus. "*Legislatures and Judiciaries.* I got elected to four terms in Springfield before our previous governor appointed me to the bench. I always liked politics. Teaching gave me a chance to say things I couldn't say otherwise."

"Brooke took your class," I interjected. I didn't need any more of his resume.

"She was the brightest student I had. Strong opinions, that girl. Good arguments to back 'em up, too. Spirited is what my wife would have called her. We got along well.

"Let it never be said that Charles Bridges ignored a beautiful woman. I may be sixty-three but my wife's been dead almost five years. Hell, I'd be lying if I said I was faithful to her for any more than a couple months at a time. I've always had an eye for the ladies. Brooke seemed to…know that. While I was her instructor, well, I did a passable job of keeping my feelings to myself. Had to with all of 'em. The school environment these days. I know sexual harassment law pretty well. Read up on it before I took the job." He took a breath and let it out painfully.

"I knew what she was the first time we got together. Knew it, didn't give a rat's ass neither."

"I take it she didn't seduce you to improve her grade."

"Didn't need to. Like I said, she was smart. But I sure didn't have to talk her out of her panties, either. She was what they call goal-oriented. Money first, revenge second. The way I see it anyway."

"Revenge?"

"That girl wasn't shy about saying in class she was daughter of a former state senator. Pretty easy to figure out she was Red Talmadge's girl. So laying up in bed that first night I told her I knew her old man, asked if that could get to be a problem. Nope. Said she'd fucked a number of his colleagues and liked it more every time. Said she was sorta making a game out of it."

"Why?"

"She didn't tell me no life story. That wasn't what it was about. This may surprise you, Mr. TV Man but we had fun together. That was what we did. In the bed and out. We went to shows. Traveled a little bit. I took her over to the place in Michigan a couple times when my daughter was out of town on business. Vegas once. You ask me to describe what it was like, I can't quite put my finger on it. I was paying her but we *enjoyed* each other! Argued about politics. She wanted to learn about things, how the system worked, how people get around the law, but she had good opinions, too. Tasted good wine. Had good conversation.

Much as I'd cheated on my wife, I missed her when she was gone, missed her company. Brooke, she…she mighta been out to mess with her daddy by being what she was but…she made me forget the pain for awhile."

He was silent a moment. When he spoke again his voice sounded broken at the edges.

"Ain't the first time I paid for it by a long shot. Most of 'em, hookers, they can't keep from looking at their watches. Most of them *I'd* be looking at *mine*, tell the truth. Brooke just was a good time. That's the best way I can put it. And she was kind. I don't see that much in people."

I watched his big hands clench around the edges of the bench.

"When did you start seeing her?"

"Two years ago come August. She took a summer class. The day it finished, she came straight out with it, 'you want to meet me up at the Fairmont?'" Head down, he nodded. "She knew what I wanted. Knew from the first day of class."

"You're telling me that, in all that time, she never once talked about her father except to say she liked screwing his friends?"

"She didn't. I didn't. Hell, would you bring that shit up, some twenty-one year old let *you* in her pants? It wasn't like I needed to know her family history! She just said something, maybe once or twice dropped it into conversation, about someday she wanted him to find out his little girl had probably led more of his friends around by their dicks than he ever could with any money he passed out. Something to that effect."

"You didn't take offense at that? At the very least didn't you want to know why?"

He snorted again and looked up. "Didn't care, no. Whatever else was going on between us, however much money changed hands, it boiled down to we was having us some rec-re-*ation* time, you understand? *I* talked. Prob'ly more than I needed to, truth be known. But when it was serious chatter, it was *me* talking and her listening, not me playing daddy and asking to hear all her problems."

Wanting him leaning, instead of balanced, I said, "You don't seem like the sort of client she usually chose."

"What's that supposed to mean?"

"Whips, leather, that sort of thing. People say that was her specialty."

He passed a hand over his eyes. "May have been. As a black man I don't need to pay to be degraded. That's about all I ever got from white folks that was free."

He stared at me. "You ever have a conversation with the girl, McCarthy?"

"Not really."

"Can't say beans about her, then, can you? She was good at her work. Period. Way she told me, clients sometimes wanted to be abused so she abused them."

"Oh, and with you she was *Pretty Woman* come to life?"

"You just can't get over a nigger getting some prime white meat can you?"

"I don't care who gets what, Judge," I said wearily. "But it wasn't just good customer service for her and we both know it. She got off on abusing men, apparently men who had worked with her father. When she was tired of that routine, she dated women. I know of at least one. I'm sure there were more."

"All right. I won't argue with you." He waved a hand in dismissal but something in his tone caught my ear.

"Personal experience?"

"We don't need to get into that."

"You just did."

"Hell, McCarthy. She brought a friend to join us once, a year or so ago. I didn't object. Can't say I'm proud of it. The other girl didn't seem too happy afterward, either. I told Brooke that wasn't the kind of thing I wanted to repeat. She never suggested it again."

"What was the other girl's name?"

"I don't remember."

"Older than Brooke? Blonde? Say thirty-five or so?"

He shook his head. "Dark hair and probably Brooke's age. 'Another rich white college girl,' Brooke said. Figured I'd get off on that. She wasn't no pro, though. Nervous as hell."

"You paid her, too?"

"What do you think? She took a liking to me the minute she met me? Had to have some Black meat? This was always a straight-up business transaction for Brooke and yeah, the other one, too. Pay before play. Five hundred apiece."

Sela Grauman. Had to be, I thought. No wonder she'd been scared to talk to me.

"Did you keep seeing Brooke regularly after that?"

"I thought everything was fine," he shrugged. "Then, 'bout two weeks later, I called and her cellular phone was turned off. Didn't think much of it. Figured she hadn't paid her damn bill. That went on for maybe six, eight months, me trying her every couple of weeks. Finally decided she wasn't in the business anymore and just hadn't bothered to say goodbye."

"Or, she was upset you didn't like her idea of a threesome."

"You sure can be a dumbass, can't you? She told me why she up and disappeared and that wasn't it at all."

"When did you finally talk to her?"

"'Bout three weeks ago. She called me at home one night. Clear out of the blue. She never did that before. She insisted we get together right away. I went ahead, got a room, went over to meet her." He lifted his head as though it was heavy with despair.

"OK, McCarthy, this is where we got to have us an understanding. What I'm about to say, it's going to start you thinking I had a damn fine motive to have that girl killed. I'm telling you right now that isn't what happened. No matter what passed between us the last time, no matter I was paying her for sex, none of that's important. I *cared* for Brooke. You want to think otherwise, then god damn your soul you'll be wrong. You hear me, son?"

It could have been just sweat in his eyes that he wiped away with the heel of one hand.

"I hear you."

"She wanted money. She wanted twenty-five G in cash." His jaw tightened. "She walked in the room, stripped, got into bed and we did the deed. Just like that. No pleasantries, none of the…friendliness from before. I'm gonna say it was mechanical. Something she had to do to prime the pump." He didn't mean it jokingly and I didn't smile.

"Then she wants to talk. She tells me one of the reasons she didn't call back after that night was, a couple of days later, she broke her ankle in a car crash. That was one reason. Not the real one, of course. She took her time getting around to that one. She'd taken up with a man, she said. A Russian fella. She said that she went to live with him.

"I said that's fine, you don't need to explain nothing to me. She says she needs me to know how it was. She says it was like nothing she'd ever had before. But it was over and she needed to get away, far enough he couldn't find her. So I tell her, if it's a threat, if he's trying to hurt her, I can put a stop to that damn quick. That's the first time she softens. No, she says. She doesn't want me to do nothing of the sort. She won't even tell me his name. For my own good. She says he buys and sells people, lawyers, judges, politicians. I tell her he's not buying me. She says that's not what she meant, that he's bought other people, higher up. She says she doesn't want me involved, just give her the money and she'll disappear."

"So she was on the run then? He was threatening her?"

"Hell, McCarthy. She didn't act scared so much as just lost. That girl was a mess. She surely was. Couldn't stand still. Paced, back and forth, no clothes on, all agitated. Got me to where I wanted to pull her back down in the bed. That wasn't on her agenda, though, and you'd best believe it was *her* agenda she was working from. She needed twenty-five G and she was gonna get it one way or the other."

"You told her no?"

"Yeah, I told her no." He watched a young couple leaving the restaurant nearby for a moment, sighed, and then returned his attention to me. "I'll tell you this. I was tempted to go the other way. Surely was. That girl…if I'd had the money available, yeah I think I woulda given it to her. That's the effect she had on me. Strong as she was, as sure of herself as she was…" He paused.

"Twisted as it sounds, I felt sometimes like she needed protecting."

"How did she take the turn down?"

"The way my daughter would when she was Brooke's age and I'd tell her no." He smiled sadly. "Then she started in with the pressure. If I didn't give it up she was gonna tell this one and that one. Newspaper. Television. Didn't give me a chance to explain myself, tell her why I said no. Just launched right into her spiel, just like she'd expected me to refuse and had rehearsed what she was gonna say. I stopped her in her tracks, though. I surely did."

A couple who looked to be a few years older than Bridges strolled by, the man inclining his head slightly. "Charles," he said, his manner suggesting he wouldn't have spoken at all if he hadn't been urged to do so by his wife. Bridges nodded distractedly, continuing his story.

"I told her my daughter had been diagnosed with Lupus. Sure, there's insurance but that never covers everything. I don't have 25G to spare. Don't have 2 G's. And me facing a disciplinary hearing. Brooke got this sick look on her face when I told her about my daughter. Started to get dressed right away. Didn't say another word. I tried to tell her I'd give her a couple of hundred if she was that bad off but it was like she wasn't even listening."

"She left?"

He snapped his fingers. "Just like that. I guess I figured she'd keep her mouth shut, me telling her about Daphne and all. Then again, if she told anybody but you people I s'pose I'd have heard about it before now."

"No contact since then?"

"Not a word. Two years and it all comes down to some sloppy blackmail. That's the last thing I would have expected from that girl. Almost anything else but not…" his voice clotted and he stopped. He coughed and rubbed his head.

"What else did she say about the Russian?"

"Nothing. Or, if she did say anything, I blocked it out. I was jealous, can you believe that? She was telling me how happy she'd been and here I am acting like a fucking teenager, not listening to a word of it."

He suddenly thrust himself to his feet. I stayed where I was and he looked down at me, expression stern.

"That's all I'm saying about her, McCarthy. I'm tired. I'm a tired old man. I'm going home. I don't want you following me and trying to ask any more questions and I don't want any phone calls. You feel you have to do some kind of story about me 'n her, that's your business. You leave any impression I had something to do with her death and, by God, I'll sue your ass. We clear on that?"

I started to respond but before I spoke the words, he was halfway across the plaza, an old man walking with his head down, pain evident with each step he took.

CHAPTER 12

▼

Irritated by the lack of a cellular, I stopped at a row of pay phones on the way back to my car and called Directory Assistance to find a number for Sela Grauman's parents' house in Kenilworth. It was listed but answered by a man with a James Earl Jones voice who told me Miss Grauman was driving her parents to the airport and then would be out for the evening. Though that pissed me off, too, I realized as I slid into the Mustang that I was not in any kind of shape to confront Sela about her and Brooke's sexual escapades. I wasn't sure whether it was seeing the flambe'd body of a gangbanger or a Russian mobster crushed beneath the weight of the dump truck or even my confrontation with Bridges that had sucked the energy out of me but I was bone tired.

I also realized I was angry. No, maybe the word was *furious* at Brooke for the life-decisions she'd made that led someone to the point of killing her. Bridges wasn't the only person who told me she was a smart girl with a lot of promise. Even Hanratty said she seemed bright. What a goddamn stupid waste of a life.

One of the city's many summer festivals was underway in Grant Park as I cruised up Lake Shore Drive and I got caught, once again, by the resulting traffic snarl. There are worse places to be stuck on a summer night, however. To my left I could see the festival crowd and hear what sounded like a Celtic reel coming from the Petrillo band shell. To my right, in the harbor, a party was underway on several of the boats while several more moved like wraiths toward open water.

There are few sights more inspiring than Chicago's downtown skyline at night and from the water it's even more appealing. Several times during my years at Channel 14 I debated buying a boat and living aboard through the warm weather months. The proximity of Monroe Harbor to the studios would have made my commute to work an easy jog, even on rainy days. Megan and I even attended several open-water boat shows, trying to decide between sail and motor craft. My firing made the question moot.

It was nearing ten-thirty when I turned onto my street but I slowed abruptly when I saw an obviously government-issue car parked in front of my house. My first instinct was to wonder how they knew I'd been headed home. I slowed the Mustang to a crawl. Unless they had been watching my car in the parking lot, or had found it and installed a tracking device, there was no way they could have caught up with me except by accident. Ergo, they must've been just sitting there, waiting. I grinned. For an overachiever like my friend Special Agent Dark, the forced inactivity would have been hell.

Much as I would have welcomed a confrontation earlier, the anger I'd felt at the Four Seasons, and again when I'd left Bridges, had abated during my drive home. I was feeling pretty mellow now. Then again, maybe that was the right frame of mind to be in for a face to face with the Feds.

So, I ran the Mustang up the drive as though it was nothing unusual to find the federal government on my doorstep. When my headlights swung across the unmarked car, I saw a man and woman in the front seat, presumably Agent Dark and her preppie partner. I was getting out in the garage when I heard their doors close and saw them cross the lawn. I leaned on the trunk, arms folded, and watched their approach. It made me smile when they moved slightly apart from each other as they saw me waiting. Their suit coats were unbuttoned and they walked in the manner of someone who is armed and wants to keep the appropriate hand near their weapon as they approach a subject with questionable pedigree.

When they were close enough to speak conversationally, Agent Dark held up a badge case I hadn't seen her carrying.

"We haven't been formally introduced. I'm Special Agent Dark and this is Special Agent Mohler, Terrorist Task Force."

"That's pretty neat. You keep your creds on a little string up your sleeve?" I asked.

"You might be surprised at what I have up my sleeve, Mr. McCarthy," Dark said. Neither their expressions nor their postures gave anything away except that they were totally alert. At some point, however, Dark had used some cosmetics and a mirror. Even in the residual humidity of evening she looked crisp, her makeup perfect. Except for a dark shadow of beard along his jaw, her colleague could have stepped out of a US government recruiting poster, too. If there were such things.

"I'm surprised you're not somewhere watching the news," I said.

She gave me a look that said I wouldn't be able to hook her twice with the same bait. Somehow she'd decided that video of her shaking down my house didn't exist. "Oh, you're far more interesting to watch than your bubble headed colleagues. They work off a script. Kind of boring, actually. You, on the other hand, just seem to flail about, sticking your nose into things that are none of your business."

"I guess it's all a matter of perspective."

"We look at it from the perspective of the United States government, pal," Mohler said. "From where we stand, you're interfering in a federal investigation. That means prison time."

I held out my hands, wrists together. "Go for it."

He reached behind him, as though to grab a pair of handcuffs, but Dark shook her head. "I think we can reach an accommodation with Mr. McCarthy that doesn't include locking him up."

"You'd do that for me? Aww, Jesse, I'm beginning to like you."

I saw a tiny flicker of anger pass across her face before she remembered she was supposed to be playing good girl to Mohler's bad guy. She inclined her head toward the house. "Are you going to invite us inside?"

"Why? You leave something behind last time?"

Socks appeared from under the porch with a quizzical look on his face. Mohler glanced at him. Socks disappeared. Good judge of character, that cat.

"As Agent Mohler correctly mentioned, interference in a federal investigation carries a significant penalty. However. My superiors have given me permission to tell you that they're willing to overlook what you've done to this point if you agree to step back and let us continue our work unimpeded. I think that's a fair offer, don't you?"

"Nope," I said again. "I think it's a lightweight threat and I don't think it comes from anybody but you."

Her smile was full of a cop's condescension.

"Oh, I must have forgotten to mention something," she said. "You're no longer a reporter. The City has withdrawn your press credentials. I think you'll find a message to that effect on your voice mail."

I laughed. "Withdrawn, huh? All credentials do is identify. They don't license. Ever read the First Amendment in the Constitution you swore to protect and defend?"

Mohler took a step forward and put a finger two inches from my face. He had the mean little mouth of a frat boy who likes hazing the pledges.

"Lemme make it a little clearer, then. Your radio station wants nothing to do with you, OK? Far as they're concerned, you aren't even welcome past the front door. Ask me why."

"Let me guess. You flashed a badge, went 'booga, booga, booga National Security is at stake' and got them to fire me. Which they were probably planning to do anyway." I kept my voice easy, jocular. I was pissed but I wasn't going to let them see it.

Dark touched Mohler's shoulder. He lowered his arm. I didn't move. He looked angry enough to put me on the ground if I so much as uncrossed my arms. I'd faced that kind of hostility from cops before. They're used to asking tough questions, not having to answer them.

"What Agent Mohler is telling you is that you no longer have anyone to report for. So there's really no purpose in continuing to insinuate yourself into what is a very touchy, very confidential matter."

"Now that you mention it, why are you guys trying so hard to keep this Russian mob stuff hush-hush, anyway? Why don't you call a news conference? Try for a little good P.R.?"

"If you persist," she said, ignoring me, "if you go it alone, freelance, whatever, we'll have no choice but to arrest you. Think about what that will mean. With no job, you'll be paying for your own attorney. Bail will have to come out of your own pocket. That's *if* a federal magistrate agrees to release you at all, given what we'll tell him about you."

"Booga, booga, booga," I smiled.

Dark continued. "There's also the matter of your lady friend's private detective license. I'm sure you don't want to be responsible for her losing it."

"She's a big girl. With good lawyers."

Dark shrugged again, more elaborately than before, then looked at Mohler. "At least they can't say we didn't try the friendly approach first."

"No. *First* you tried shoving the murder of a young girl under the rug so the public wouldn't find out that Russian mobsters are in their backyard. Then you tried illegal eavesdropping. You used federal clout to get me fired. You came here and made threats which even your favorite federal magistrate would call prior restraint, if not a violation of my civil rights. So tell me this, folks. Why do I scare you so much?"

"We're not scared of you, Mr. McCarthy. To the contrary. We're concerned for your welfare. Let me read you something." Dark reached into her coat pocket and came out with a sheet of paper which she unfolded and looked at for a moment. I wondered how the dim light of the driveway allowed her to see what was written on it.

"This is part of a transcript from a judicially authorized telephone overhear. You don't need to know who's speaking. The conversation took place late this afternoon." She cleared her throat.

"'And how about that reporter. What's his name?'"

"'McCarthy. I told you he could be…how shall I say it…disruptive.'"

Dark looked up at me and recited the first speaker's words without referring to the paper.

"'If he asks the wrong questions, deal with him.'"

She refolded the paper. "What do you think of that?"

I laughed. "You have to be kidding. You expect me to believe that's Federov?"

"Draw your own conclusions. I'm not authorized to give you names."

"Pretty lame, Jesse. There's no way these guys would say something like that on a telephone. Basic bad-guy tradecraft. Any bad guys. Don't say anything on a phone you don't want to hear later in court."

"What was said that was overtly criminal? Perhaps they wanted to be over-heard." Dark made a show of putting the paper away. "Again. We've tried to be helpful. You've been warned." She turned and started down the drive. Mohler cut across the grass.

"I have a warning for you, too." I called after them, watching Mohler specifi-cally. His head came around. He smiled. In the dim light, it looked menacing.

"You're not about to threaten two federal officers, are you?" he asked.

"Nope just a friendly warning. Like you gave me."

He took a step back toward where I stood. Perfect. I was off the car now, hands at my sides. Even Dark turned slightly, so she faced me full on. Her voice was neutral, the way cops everywhere are taught to speak to deranged subjects. "What's your warning, Mr. McCarthy?"

"The neighbor lets his dog crap on my lawn. Mohler just stepped in it. Twice."

*   *   *   *

The preppie Fed, cursing, spent some time wiping his shoes on the grass before getting into the Bureau car. I wasn't sure, but I could have sworn Dark sti-fled a smile or at least a small grin. Socks reemerged from under the porch and we watched the little drama together until the pair pulled away. Then I picked him up, carried him into the kitchen and fed him. While he was chowing down, I went looking for the package Sunny had said she'd leave for me. As I expected, it was in the floor safe in the office closet. I turned on the phone, saw it was charged, then hefted the radio and flipped it on as well. It was a Motorola XTS, one of the new black ones, and looked right out of the box. The number 12 was stenciled across the front and just beneath it was a folded note. I opened it up.

"Key up with your number. If I've found anything else out you need to know tonight, the guy who's on the other end will pass it along. Love, Sunny."

I keyed up the radio and said, "Twelve."

"*Hey Reno,*" a voice came back, "*It's Russ. Sunny told me to tell you Mrs. F has gone up to their family's place in Northern Wisconsin for a couple of weeks. The Senator is supposed to join her but it's not clear when.*"

"OK, thanks Russ. How was Asa doing when you left him?"

"*Couldn't tell. The Feds closed everything down. They looked like they wanted to hold on to me, too, until I convinced them I didn't know shit about anything.*"

"10-4."

"*And, hey, Reno? I'm on station down the street from your house tonight. Sunny's orders. So why don't you leave the radio on and if I see anything that doesn't look kosher I'll call you here instead of using the phone.*"

"Oh c'mon, you don't need to hang around."

"*Yep. If I want to keep getting business from Sunny I do. I'm here if you need me.*"

I signed off, sighed, and carried the radio up to the bedroom.

✳   ✳   ✳   ✳

I caught a chunk of Channel 7's news, still not able to bring myself to watch 14. It was painful to think I maybe had been close to getting my job back, or at least *a* job, before Brooke's death. Now...who knew? If Marisa broke a story about the Russian mob moving into Chicago, Chazz would write her a lifetime contract. Then again, if she nailed the senator-and-the-hooker angle and Ferguson got defrocked, the networks would pony up the big bucks and she'd be gone.

My nose was starting up a nice counterpoint rhythm with the rest of my head and when I took a look at it in the bathroom mirror I didn't like what I saw. Blood crusted at the nostrils and my eyes had that looking-into-the-abyss thing going. I washed up as best I could. When I came out into the bedroom, Socks was curled up on the chair near my bed. He squeaked softly. He doesn't really meow much. Just a little squeak now and then to let me know he's content. I climbed into bed and shut the light off as he began his bathing ritual.

The lapping of his tongue must have helped put me to sleep. It felt like I'd just closed my eyes when the phone rang. My hand on it in the dark, I looked at the clock next to it. Nearly two. Bad news. What kind of good news do people call and give you at 2 a.m?

"Reno, it's Paul. Buddy, get your ass out of the sack and meet me, man. You awake?" He made a tapping noise that sounded like mini-sonic booms through the earpiece.

"Who's dead now?" I asked, groggy.

"Not who's dead. You should be asking who's *in town.*"

"Say what?" I propped myself up on one elbow, aware of the cat sprawled next to my right leg. I couldn't see him except as a vague shadow but sensed he had his head up, watching me. My brain felt like oatmeal.

"I look up at this ceremony tonight and who do I see walking in the room but Alicia Witting? Man, this is your lucky morning, my friend. She is right here, in this hotel, just down the hall from me."

"Explain this one to me. Small words, talk slowly."

"'Licia Witting? Who we spent a good part of a couple hours talking about…?"

He was making more sense than I was. I tried to catch up.

"What's she doing in town?" I expected this to turn into the kind of joke you expect from a guy who's just attended his own retirement party.

"Would you just come to the fucking hotel? You caught a break here. I'll tell you about it when I see you."

*   *   *   *

The Greentree gave itself a facelift a few years ago, to try and stand out from all the new construction going on in that block just off Michigan Avenue. It strains for character, a fedora amidst the top hats. On the inside, though, lurks that universally plastic feel of a chain hotel.

I give them all the Reno Test. If I see anything in my first glance that could tell me whether I'm in Chicago or Chattanooga, Tulsa or Tiburon, I buy the house manager a drink. The test works best if I run it in my room in the middle of the night. I haven't had to buy a lot of drinks.

The lobby bar still had some hangers on, even though it was way past the witching hour and the servers had all gone home. I would have hummed Sinatra's "In the Wee Small Hours of the Morning," but with the chandeliers ablaze and all that brass gleaming it didn't look anything like the joint Francis Albert describes in the song. More like a place expecting a convention of dentists to blow in through the doors at any moment.

I wooshed up in the elevator, yawning when I stepped out on the floor where Paul had told me to meet him. *What am I doing roaming a hotel hallway at nearly 3 a.m.?* I wondered. *Chasing*, a voice told me. That's what I was doing, even after all these years, now even on my own. Chasing leads, chasing stories. Chasing a witness who might just as easily slam a door in my face and call the cops. *Would that be a problem?* the 3 a.m. voice asked. I thought about that for a moment. Whatever I did now came back on me, not the station. No boss, no corporate lawyer to lay out all the legal pitfalls. My responsibility. Hmmm. Realizations like that could wake a guy up.

Paul must have had his eye to the peephole. He opened the door before I could knock and motioned me inside. He'd changed out of the blazer and slacks to jeans and a just out-of-the-wrapper t-shirt advertising the college where he'd be teaching. I had to smile at his mile-wide 'gotcha' grin. I'd seen it often enough when we were breaking exclusives together.

"Can you believe this shit? She fucking walked into my damn arms almost! I step off the stage and she's standing there with a couple of people from the Senate staff."

His eyes looked clear and the wet bar showed no signs of activity. He was in work mode.

"Why's she here?"

"She says she sat-in for her boss on a couple meetings. Going back tomorrow."

"You ever think maybe she came out just 'cause she likes and respects you as the top-flight journalist you are?"

Paul put the back of his hand up to his mouth and made a raspberry. "I hear Ferguson's on the way to Northern Wisconsin with the missus. He probably had stuff scheduled here that he had to beg off from at the last minute so 'Licia's handling the appointments instead. I'm betting Mrs. F gave Senator F an ultimatum to join her if he wants to save his marriage. Works out well for you, huh?"

"It could," I said. "Is she by herself?"

Paul grinned. "Doubt it. Word is, she's got an off again, on again thing with a research assistant from the Conservative Forum. Who also showed up at the ceremony. The Conservative Forum chickie isn't 'out' the way 'Licia is. For obvious reasons."

"That complicates things a little." I was still working out an approach in my head.

"What's complicated? We knock, she comes to the door and we tell her we have to have a little chat."

"First off, there isn't any 'we'. I'm going to handle this alone."

"Hey, pal…"

"How much talking do you think she's going to do with you there? You're still a reporter. I'm not. You know her friends and colleagues. I don't."

He thought about that, nodded as though he got it, but then he smiled and held up a finger. "But," he said. "How much you want to bet she won't even open her door for you? Middle of the night, hotel like this? She *might* be curious enough to open up if she sees me."

"You intentionally let me walk into that one, didn't you?"

"Yup."

"Think it's enough to convince me?"

He moved toward the door, picking up his key. "Easy guy like you? Yup."

*   *   *   *

We stood on either side of her door like a couple of cops. A small wire of electricity ran down my spine. If Asa had spilled what he knew, the federales could come thundering off the elevator at any moment. Maybe they'd already been here. I rolled my shoulders. Paul knocked twice. I closed my eyes and listened.

The icemaker down the hall hummed softly. I caught what sounded like a querulous murmur from inside the room but it could have been almost anything else. This wasn't a hot-pillow joint. It had been recently remodeled with thick hallway carpeting and acoustic ceiling so not a lot of sounds would be escaping from the rooms into the public areas. I sensed movement on the other side of the door.

"Paul?" A woman's voice, with a slight southern accent.

"Yeah," he said softly. "We need to talk."

"It's almost 3:30 in the morning! Are you drunk?"

"It's important, Alicia. Come on. Get the door."

There was a pause and then the sound of the security chain snapping back and a lock turning. Alicia Witting wore cotton shorts and a Washington Bullets t-shirt with Michael Jordan's picture on the front. Michael was smiling. She wasn't. I couldn't recall if I'd seen her around the station. I must have. Asa had said she was with the Senator when he'd come in to do the show.

A lanky, tall woman with short brown hair and a farm wife's face, she radiated competence. That's not a quality you see very often in someone just awakened after a night that had included maybe one drink too many and then a little sexual indulgence. She wasn't pretty, or even really cute, but there was a bright quickness to her features even as she blinked back sleep. She glanced at me but focused hard on Paul.

"What's so important? Is Brian...has something happened?"

"The Senator's fine," he said.

"My name's Reno McCarthy," I said before Paul took it any further. "I'm the one who wants to talk."

That, she really didn't like. "Oh, you think so." She peered closer. "Don't I know you?"

"I'm investigating Brooke Talmadge's murder. I can ask the questions here or I can show up with a "Sixty Minutes" crew somewhere a lot more public."

"Is that a threat?" Her sudden switch to normal voice sounded like a shout in the quiet hall.

"Sounded like one to me."

"'Licia?" came a worried inquiry from behind her in the darkness. Alicia's face reddened at hearing the young woman's voice and she turned, letting the door close slightly. I had my foot ready in case she tried to slam it. Instead, I heard whispering and then another door opened. Light spilled onto the carpet for a moment and then disappeared as, presumably, the Conservative Forum lady slipped into the adjoining room. Alica reappeared. She lowered her voice again.

"I know who you are now. "Sixty Minutes?" You're from that radio station, aren't you?" She pointed at Paul. "And you call yourself a professional. Shame on you."

"Did Brooke coming on board take the pressure off you?" I asked quickly as the door nudged my shoe. I didn't move it.

"Take your foot out of my door, please."

"With her listening to the Senator's pillow talk, what did the Russians have for you to do? Wash dishes?"

"What on God's green earth are you talking about?"

She met my eyes. Hers were full of fury, but something else moved there too.

"I'm talking about a Senator's Administrative Assistant who's owned by the Russian *Mafiya*. The Feds have your friend, Asa, in protective custody. How long before he starts telling them what he told me? Give us your side, Alicia. Throw the spotlight on Federov instead of on you."

"Paul, I suggest you take your friend with the Tom Clancy imagination and get him out of here. As it is, I plan to call the *Tribune* in the morning and let your managing editor know that Senator Ferguson and I don't appreciate being set upon by drunks in the middle of the night."

She was very, very good. I almost didn't hear the slight change of timbre in her voice. In radio, however, you learn to listen closely to voices. My ear told me she was frightened.

"If Federov capped Brooke because she knew too much, what happens now? You still have chips to play or are you headed for the deep end of the Potomac?"

If I'm ever forced to suddenly, and without warning, confront the fact that my life is a train on fire headed for a collapsed bridge over a gorge full of dynamite, I hope I can do so with the same disdain Alicia Witting displayed at that moment.

"Are you speaking English?" she asked and, damn, if a small smile didn't appear. "Because what I'm hearing is making no sense whatsoever."

"Reno," Paul began.

I ignored him. "You know how Federov's going to react when you tell him I was here? He's already made a try for me. I hope you can swim, lady. I'm your life preserver."

I wrote my new cell number on the back of a business card and pushed it toward her. Alicia Witting let it drop without taking her eyes off mine. The door closed with a ka-chunk. No louder than a sound-suppressed pistol fired into the skull from close range.

I walked Paul back down the hall to his room. He was smiling. "'I'm your life preserver'?" he said.

"I thought it went with the whole 'swimming in the Potomac' theme."

"Sure it did. Now wasn't all that worth waking up for? She looked like you hit her with a two-by four when you mentioned Federov's name."

"Uh-huh," I said. All I could do now was wait. I hate waiting.

He shook his head in mock disgust. "You expected her to fall to her knees and confess? Maybe grab your leg and beg? Ungrateful son of a bitch, aren't you? Go the fuck home."

*   *   *   *

But, because I'd tugged on her cloak, I couldn't do that right away. I had to give her a chance to react.

I went back to my car, aware for the first time of a slight chill in the air. Michigan Avenue had the feel of a small town in the hours immediately before dawn. There was little traffic. A Streets and Sanitation sweeper moved slowly away from me a couple of blocks south and a Transit Police squad car headed the other direction, behind a *Sun-Times* delivery truck. One man stood reading a paper at a bus stop across the street, his paper folded in half commuter-style in one hand, while he drank from a Styrofoam cup with the other.

When I slipped behind the wheel of the Mustang a block south of the hotel, I reached under the front seat to where I'd stowed the Motorola radio.

"Twelve," I said.

"*Fourteen. I'm here,*" Russ said. "*You're clean. No activity. And Sunny's on the net.*"

She cut in before I could speak, voice made harsh by the digital transmission and the tiny speaker. "*You're up past your bedtime.*"

"We're encrypted, right?"

"*You think this radio would sound as crappy if we weren't? You pay for privacy around here. What's up?*"

"Alicia Witting is in town. She came in to handle some of the Senator's local meetings but she showed up at Paul's retirement party."

"*Get out!*"

"I just talked to her."

Even with the lousy transmission quality, I heard her groan. "*Reno. Jesus. What exactly was the point of doing that? She didn't tell you anything, did she?*"

"To see how she'd react. You have somebody you can put on her? I'm wondering what kind of meetings she's planning to take today."

The repeater timed out and the system quieted. Slouched down with my head on the back of the seat, I watched the front door of the Greentree. My eyes had that grainy feel they always get when I've ignored sleep for too long.

"*Ten, Twelve?*" Sunny said. "*Listen up. Mark Cibulski is going to come up on the air in about five. He'll be starting from the South Side. He'll take over as watcher. You don't have a picture of this woman handy, do you?*"

I mentally kicked myself. Dumb. At this point, I was the only one who would recognize Alicia Witting. "That's a big negatory, unit ten."

"*You're lucky. He's more of a computer geek than me. He can Web surf from his van. Just tell him he needs to look her up. Tell him to try Google, first. That's where I found her yesterday. Then you get home to bed.*"

"Yes, Mother."

She talked briefly to Russ, making sure he was alert enough to continue as my minder for another hour or so. He assured her he was. Their conversation made me feel odd, as though I were some kind of delicate package that needed careful handling. I thought of telling her to have Russ back off. Then I thought about the flat look in the Russian's eyes when he aimed the Lexus at me and the charred remains in the basement in Uptown and kept my mouth shut.

I got home at four, shut off all the phones, made sure Socks was inside and sleeping in his chair, and sacked out myself.

*   *   *   *

I awoke eight hours later, shaking and sweaty from another dream that was just a tad too close to reality. I'd felt like someone was smothering me with a pillow. There was blood seeping from the packing in my nose and some of it had run into my mouth and trailed across my right cheek. This time the vision in the mirror reminded me of some of those old black and white newspaper shots of gangland killings, where the victim is lying all bloody on the floor of a barber shop or the lobby of a building. I called my doctor's office, explained the problem, and was told to come right in; he had an opening for fifteen minutes at one o'clock.

He carefully unpacked the gauze then used a cautery tool to stop the bleeding. Satisfied, he pushed his glasses up on his forehead and said, "I can repack it or not. It's really up to you, from a comfort standpoint."

"What's my other option?"

"I'll stretch another piece of tape across the bridge. That keeps the bone stable. Then we just hope you don't get punched again until the break heals."

"That's a plan."

I was feeling better when I walked out of the doctor's office and got back into my car. It was cooler and cloudier than it had been in days. The forecast called for rain but this time it actually looked like it would make good on the prediction and a little spatter even hit the windshield before I got out of the parking lot. Just enough drops to make bullet hole-looking marks in the dust on the hood.

I dialed through A.M. radio looking for a quick news update and was immediately glad I wasn't trying to get anywhere on the outbound Kennedy. Someone had apparently goosed their car up to "estimated speeds of 100 miles per hour" around Cumberland, kept the pedal down for a half-mile or so, and then sliced across two lanes of traffic and mashed themselves against the base of the Tri-State tollway overpass by O'Hare. The only fatality was the driver of the car and that was only presumed, not confirmed, because the fire department was still cutting the vehicle apart. It had been near misses, though, for several others cut off by the lunatic.

When the news guy butted in with speculation the crash had been the result of a police chase, I flipped it off. Liability headaches have caused most departments to shut down pursuits before they ever start. Even so, it always juices things up on a slow news day to suggest somebody might have been pulling a Jake and Elwood from that famous Chicago movie "Blues Brothers."

If I'd had the patience to listen through the less than snappy banter between the know-it-all anchor and the traffic person, I would have heard the local lead story of the morning rather than getting that news first from a phone that was ringing as I walked into the house.

"I drove all the way to your house to deliver a cellular and the damn two-way, and you aren't carrying either one?" Sunny upbraided me.

I tried to lighten her up. "I had to run to the doctor's office. You know how answering a cell anywhere around a hospital could kill twelve heart patients."

"Yeah, well, sometimes you need to stay in touch and this is one of them. CPD arrested Asa late last night."

"For what!" I sank into my desk chair.

"You have to ask?"

"Son of a bitch. Some kind of sex thing…"

"It's just breaking on City News. Channel Seven had it first, right before one. Nobody even mentioned it to us this morning at the station. Not even a squeak." She paused and I guessed she was reading the copy from her home computer. "Story here says he had an orgy with three underage girls and, yuck, an underage boy, at a hotel after the Blues in the Park concert two years ago."

I remembered that concert. The station had been its primary sponsor and Asa and Goofy the on-stage hosts.

"And there was a hidden camera in the room, courtesy of Eddie Marn."

"Where are you getting that? I don't see anything…"

"Asa told me as much. That has to be what the Russians had on him. Marn gave them the tape. Goddamn it! They found out he's surrounded by Feds, they assume he's spilling everything he knows, so they turn the tape over to the cops. To burn his credibility."

"I almost feel sorry for him. But underage kids?"

My nose itched where the doctor had used the cautery. I resisted the urge to touch it. "Have you talked to Rudy?"

"Better. I talked to Angela." Angela is Rudy's secretary. She was a busty, chubby newlywed when she went to work at the joint fifteen years ago but lost the weight, actually buffed up, and for the past two years or so has been doing horizontal work outs with Rudy at the Holiday Inn near the station every chance she gets. She still drags her husband to parties and other station functions but, by all accounts around the water cooler, he doesn't have a clue. Meanwhile, she's picked up the attitude a lot of women get when they're having an affair with the boss. She barks orders as though they were hers to give and speaks up for Rudy in staff meetings even when he's right there in the room. She can't stand me, but she and Sunny have bonded.

"She's already written the news release announcing Asa's resignation. She tells me all he's got to do is sign the letter they sent over to the hospital by courier and his career is finito. Goofy is bouncing off the walls. And then there's the stuff about you. Angela loved that part."

"I'm fired, right?"

"Yeah. It's up on the board in the coffee room. You're not even allowed on the premises. Nobody told you?"

"Actually, I heard last night. Funny how I sort of put that little slice of news aside, huh?"

"Rudy's afraid we're going to get sued by the kids' families…"

"Ya think?"

"You wouldn't believe what a madhouse that place is today. I had to leave by the back door. All the TV stations were lined up out front. Even *Entertainment Tonight* is probably there by now. All Asa's notoriety is coming back to bite him on the butt."

"You're OK, though? With management?"

"Who else is going to cover morning drive news? Hey, even if I'm not OK, do you realize how little I need that job? I haven't lost any money yet, but if I have to pass on chasing a good skip because my butt is plunked in that newsroom, that's going to hurt. If I even stay through the end of next week, it's just because I have a heart of pure gold."

"Just the same," I said. "I'm sorry if it slops over on you."

"No problem. You know I mean that. And if you think you're going to break this case without my help, you're on crack, bubba."

Which brought me back to the other issues that had kept me from thinking about being fired. "What happened with Alicia? Did Cibulski pick her up?"

"I'm sorry, Reno. He just checked in about an hour ago. He saw her leave the hotel and then lost her about thirty minutes later. Not his fault. She rented a car and boogied on him in Loop traffic."

"Crap." I thought for a moment. "She left the hotel to rent a car? They have a Hertz desk in the lobby."

"She grabbed a cab to the Petey's Gym in the Loop. Mark says she stayed in there forty minutes, then zipped into the Hertz place down the street and was out and gone before he could get through the construction on Jackson. She was headed west. Probably toward the expressway."

I frowned. Something odd there. "I slap her with the fact that the Feds are about to find out she's a gopher for the Russian mob and her first reaction is a nice workout?"

"You stressed the poor girl. Maybe she went for the hot tub?"

"Yeah. OK, forget about that for a minute. What time did she leave the hotel?"

Clicking keys. "10:30, by Cibulski's log."

"So she had plenty of time to make some calls. Can you work your computer magic on the hotel's phone records?"

Her voice changed so rapidly and so notably I thought someone else had clicked in on the line. "This is Tamara Hudson in Senator Brian Ferguson's office in Washington. We're doing a congressionally mandated accountability audit on employee travel expenditures." She paused. "Oh you can't help? I'll have two investigators there with a Congressional subpoena before the end of the day."

"You never cease to amaze me, Miss Sunshine."

"Where are you going to be if I find out something interesting?"

I'd forgotten to brief her on what the Judge had told me about his menage a trois with Brooke and her friend. As I was describing it, I realized I also hadn't filled her in on my visit from Dark and Mohler and the 'transcript' they'd read me. I decided that could wait. Smut first, threat later. Or maybe I'd just keep that part of my evening to myself.

CHAPTER 13

▼

The heaviest and darkest of the clouds had rolled to the east, out over the lake, as I headed for Kenilworth. There were rumbles of thunder that seemed to echo from the dark water and lightning flashed in the far distance. The storm looked like it was halfway to Michigan already. Even so, I drove through a brief shower before I reached the Grauman's home and had to dash through the rain to their front door. The Jag I'd seen Sela depart in the last time I'd been there was parked in the driveway. A blue P/T Cruiser sat next to it and the showers left a light haze of steam over the engine compartment.

I rang the bell and wondered if I'd be allowed admittance or if Sela would slam the door in my face. If she did, I'd have to regroup and think about how to proceed. Right now, she was my best source for learning more about Brooke and her relationship with Federov.

She came to the door, in sweats, slightly breathless and with a sheen of perspiration on her forehead, as though she had been working out. Seeing it was me, she frowned and made no move to open the screen.

"Thanks for sticking the cops on me. That made my parents really happy right before they had to leave on their trip."

"C'mon, Sela. You've watched enough TV to know how that works. Brooke was your best friend. Anyone the cops talked to could have mentioned that. It's pretty standard for them to interview most everyone a victim knew well."

"Whatever."

I glanced skyward. "Mind if I come in out of the rain?"

For a moment, I thought she was going to say no. Instead, she unlatched the screen and stood aside. The marble-floored front hall opened up into an immaculate living room of blues and grays. An Asian gnome of about sixty sat on the bench of a Steinway grand. Celia passed him without acknowledgment as he struck a single chord, then tapped a tuning fork beneath the keyboard and hit the chord again.

"Your parents wait too long to have me tune this beautiful instrument, Miss Grauman," he said, his accent noticeable. "You tell them. Call sooner next time."

"Sure," Sela answered. She hesitated, then threw open a set of double doors to a sun porch as though she expected to find someone on the other side of them. They drifted shut as we entered the room and the sound of the repetitive A faded.

The enclosed porch was done in pastels and whites, the lake made a centerpiece by virtue of its proximity through a wall-length window. It offered so much water view, in fact, that there was a sense of the room itself being in lazy motion. It was not an unpleasant feeling. A large white reflector telescope on a heavy tripod sat in front of the window. Sela went directly to it and peered down into the eyepiece. What she saw clearly didn't hold her attention because she dipped her head only for a moment, then turned to face me, back to the storm on the lake, her arms folded in front of her.

"So?"

I eased down into an armchair covered in yellow flowers. I could still see an occasional flare of lightning over the water. When I looked at Sela, there was a tempest in her eyes as well.

"What is it you want, Mr. McCarthy?"

A table with framed photographs sat on my right. They showed Sela with her parents in virtually every shot. In each, she was formally dressed, expertly made-up.

"Did Brooke spend any time here when you were in high school?"

"Some. Not much. My parents didn't like her. My mother always used to say 'she has a reputation.' She had a boyfriend from El Salvador. Big deal, right? But they thought that was inappropriate, like maybe I'd get ideas and bring a Hispanic boy home myself, someday. 'She's not your kind,' they'd say." She looked at me as though expecting a rebuke for talking about her parents with less than total respect.

"Why did Brooke get into the sex business?" I asked.

She shrugged elaborately and then rubbed her upper arms. "I don't know. I guess she just wanted to."

"What happened to her during senior year?"

The rain chose that moment to come roaring down, startling us both. Sela's face jumped with fright and she turned, watching the water sluicing from clouds suddenly much darker than they had seemed during my drive.

I didn't think she was going to answer my question but, after a moment, she said slowly, "You know, my therapist thinks I should…share with you. I asked her, right after you were here the other day. She told me it would be cathartic for me to help you, and that it might make me feel better about Brooke. I didn't want to. I wanted to forget I ever knew her. I can't though, can I? Will talking to you make it better?"

"It helps sometimes." McCarthy, New Age philosopher. Maybe I'd leave broadcasting behind and set up a 900 number.

"What I said the other day? About her boyfriend being a Russian and being in the mob or whatever? Is he going to come after me if I talk to you?"

"Nobody has to find out we talked, Miss Grauman. It's just you and me."

She fell quiet, watching the rain. It took about two or three minutes before she went to sit on a couch to the other side of the table that held the pictures of her family. Her head stayed down the whole time. The palms of her hands were flat on her thighs and she moved them back and forth and stared at the floor as she spoke.

"Brooke was always pretty quiet in school. I mean, she liked guys, a lot actually, and she got it on with a lot of them, but she wasn't obvious about it the way some girls are. Everybody thought she was hot. She had that killer shape, you know? Little, but with big boobs. I even put her on a pedestal because she was just so laid back cool, you know? We worked at Glen Grove Country Club for two summers. Even some of the men there would…you could tell they wanted to do it with her. Their wives would notice them watching her and get really pissed off at them. It was funny sometimes.

"But she had one serious boyfriend. His name was David Tobarro. His family was from El Salvador. They moved here junior year. David was way cool. He really got Brooke to sort of redirect herself. David's father was a doctor. They came up from El Salvador in the middle of all the killing. Brooke said that Dr. Tobarro was a target, because he had worked for the rebels or something. Dr. Tobarro used his connections to get a job at Northwestern Medical School just so his family could be safe out of the country. He got visas for all of them."

She looked down at her hands. They stopped moving.

"You have to understand. Brooke's father hated David. He never said anything directly, though. Brooke told me he would just make comments he knew would set her off. Raunchy things. 'Did you have tacos for dinner tonight?' And when he'd be talking to others in her presence he'd say, "Brooke's going to get married and have nice little brown babies, aren't you dear?' More than anything, I think he hated the fact Brooke was being seen with David everywhere they went. Even Alan, who is pretty clueless most of the time, could tell how he felt."

"Go on," I said, not sure where this was heading.

"Senior year, right before finals in the fall, Immigration lifted Dr. Tobarro's visa for no reason. This was, like, major terror for David's family. Dr. Tobarro was number one on somebody's hit list. He tried to fight it, went through a hearing, all that. Brooke's dad even made a big deal out of stepping in and trying to help. They sent him back anyway."

Sela's hands began moving on her thighs again. Outside, the storm had abated but it was so dark I could see our reflections in the widow.

"Like, the next day, David went to work. He was a busboy at the Club, that's where we both met him? He got accused of stealing tips from behind the bar. They took his visa away, too."

"Just like that?"

"Oh, they had a hearing for him, too, but Brooke said the decision had already been made. He had to leave a month later. Two weeks after that, Brooke got a call from his mother. David and his father were attacked in their car. The bodyguards, everyone…killed." Tears began streaming down Sela's face. She tore a tissue from a box on the table next to her and wiped her eyes.

"David was a really nice guy. And he made Brooke so happy. She was a totally different person around him."

I looked out at the lake. The swells were up to probably four feet. The mid-day darkness gave the room a claustrophobic feel.

"A couple of weeks after that, Brooke told me her father had arranged the whole thing with some friend of his who worked for the Immigration Service."

"Arranged to have the Tobarros deported?"

"Yes. She confronted him. He claimed he was pressuring his friend to help Dr. Tobarro. No way did Brooke believe him. She said he was too calm about the whole thing. She said if he'd really tried to manipulate the people at Immigration and failed, he would have been furious. He hated it when his little games didn't work."

She wadded up the tissue and then began to smooth it out in her lap. "That was sort of when she started to sleep around again."

"For money?" I asked. Once again the image came to me of the lonely figure in the hotel bar.

"No. Well, sort of. Not really for money but, like, power over her dad. The first one was a member of Glen Grove. The man who told her about her father's friend at Immigration."

"I see."

"She really liked that. He was an influential man. Even more influential than Mr. Talmadge. She said she could learn a lot from him." She giggled. "He must not have liked Mr. Talmadge much, either. If he slept with his daughter."

"What was his name?"

"You won't tell anyone I told you?" I shook my head. "Senator Brian Ferguson."

I blinked. Sometimes you get a pop-fly that's aimed right into the old glove and all you have to do is stand there with your mouth hanging open and watch it land.

"How long did that last?"

"Not very long. A couple of months, I guess. He was in the middle of a campaign so he was around a lot for awhile. Then he got re-elected and went back to Washington. Brooke said he wanted her to move there and that he would set her up in an apartment and everything, even put her through school. But she was like 'no way.'"

"This was five years ago?"

"Yes." She started tearing the tissue into strips and dropping each one into the wastebasket next to where she sat. "Except…" She paused.

"You really promise this all is just between us? Reporters don't have to reveal their sources, right?"

I smiled. "The law in Illinois is pretty vague about that. That just means I can be pretty vague with the law, too."

"The thing is, Brooke said if I told anyone I could get in big trouble for even knowing about it." She stopped tearing the tissue, wadded up the rest and let it roll off her fingers. I nodded encouragingly.

"Brooke started going out with Brian again in March, okay? This totally came out of nowhere! I mean, she was living with Michael and everything seemed fine. She was happier than I ever could remember seeing her. She really loved him. And then, just like that, one day she tells me she's going to be out of town, for a month or so probably, and she's going to Washington. When I asked her why, she just said it was really complicated but she had talked to Brian and he wanted her back. I asked her if she and Michael had, you know, split. She just gave me this incredibly sad smile and said no, this was something she was doing for Michael and I was never to let anyone know she had told me."

"Did she tell you what brought on her decision?"

Sela considered the question. "Not really. I was freaked because she seemed to be so down. She just said that it was a business thing and she wasn't going to tell anyone and then she thought she better tell me, because she was going away and all and she knew I'd worry. She told me she didn't agree to do it at first. She couldn't believe Michael had even asked her. She said it made her feel like a whore for the first time in her life."

"Why did she agree?"

"I guess, bottom line, because she really loved Michael and would do anything he asked," Sela said simply. "I said I thought it was sick. I had a boyfriend who wanted me to sleep with one of his friends once, just because he thought it would be, you know, kinky. I wasn't going there. But Brooke said Michael wasn't like that. 'This is just good for business,' he told her."

She locked eyes with me just as a light knock sounded at the door and made her jump. After the barest hesitation, she said, "Yes?"

The Asian man who had been tuning the piano looked in. "I am finished, Miss. You pay now?"

"Sure." Sela got to her feet. "Excuse me for a moment?"

As she swept by, I got up from my chair and went to the windows. The storm was pushing out over the lake, returning the afternoon light. I could now see that erosion had worried away a goodly portion of the Grauman's landscape. The edge of their lawn looked ragged, chunks of it ripped loose by the constant motion of the water. Below the bluff, waves spawned by the storm still churned.

It wasn't tough to understand Federov's tactics. Alicia Witting, as Ferguson's most trusted aide, could report back on, and perhaps influence, official matters and policy decisions. That was the meat. But how to get the gravy, too?

All that sensitive information the Senator might not share across a desk about the back room deals, the gossip about fellow senators and personal observations of the President? If Federov believed in God, then he might well have considered Brooke heaven-sent to accomplish that special task. After all, spies have used courtesans for centuries.

While it would have been difficult, if not impossible, to get Ferguson into a compromising position with just any woman, Brooke was a known quantity. I doubted the good Senator, even with his FBI background, would ever have suspected the girl he'd seduced as a high schooler was now working for the Russian mob. Even if U.S. counterintelligence ran a routine sweep on her, the worst they'd come up with was that she'd been an escort for a few years.

Sela returned several minutes later with her face freshly scrubbed, though her eyes were still red and puffy. "I've been a terrible hostess," she said. "Can I get you something to drink? Beer, water?"

I told her water would be fine. She went to a little refrigerator built into one corner of the room and withdrew a Dasani for me and a Molson ale for herself. When she'd popped both caps she returned to stand at my side and hand me the bottle.

"I tried to kill myself once. Out there." She gestured toward the lake. "I got undressed for bed one night, but I couldn't sleep. I thought a nice walk would help. I walked down on the beach and then just kept going, right into the water. I couldn't do it, though. It was too cold. I just got sick. I was in bed for three days." She took a pull of the Molson.

"Brooke talked me into doing something shameful. With her and one of her clients. She said it would be a kick. She had a way of getting people to do things for her. Not that she had that many friends but...she could be very persuasive when she turned on the charm. Not so much in high school, but after she had gotten into that business. It was like manipulation just became a part of what she was. An evil part. I can see how someone might have wanted to kill her."

"Even you?" I said, gently.

She laughed without mirth. "Yes, but I didn't. I could never hurt Brooke. I think just living her life hurt more than anything anyone could have done to her."

"Why's that?"

"After David? She was angry all the time. I don't mean she'd snap and swear and be nasty. It was just there in her words and how she acted and this...thing she had about sleeping with people who knew her dad. She never got over what he did. It consumed her. She always had to be in control. She told me about some arguments she had with Michael because he was a control freak, too. I guess they got pretty carried away sometimes."

"Do you think Michael killed her? Or had her killed?"

"I don't...I mean I know he was a gangster. I told you that before. I'm not naive. I know what people like him do. Even still, I can't imagine he would..." She stopped and didn't start speaking again for almost half a minute.

"I saw them together, once. I never told Brooke this. It was at the Gold Coast Art Fair last year. This kid I was seeing brought me. It's not somewhere I'd normally go. All of a sudden, we're walking and I look up and there's Brooke, across this little park, holding hands with this really hot, older, dark-haired guy. I mean, duh, I saw Dr. Zhivago. I knew it was Michael right away, even before I saw this group of big bodyguards all around them. Brooke was feeding him ice cream, Mr. McCarthy. Every couple of steps she'd jump around in front of him and hold a spoon up to his mouth and he'd eat it and she'd give him a kiss. I was, like, trans-fixed! This was *not* the Brooke Talmadge I'd grown up with. She was smiling and happy and radiant, I guess you could say."

She leaned her head against the window for a moment. "Brooke told me about Senator Ferguson's wife running into them in Washington. She called me up, really horrified, right afterward. She was worried about how Michael would react. But then, later, she called me again and said she'd talked to him and he was like 'no big deal, come on back, we'll work it out.' Like he didn't think it was that important."

"Was she still frightened?"

"No. No way. *She* was the one who was pissed at *him*, not the other way around. He had sent her off to sleep with another man and now he wanted her to just come back and climb into his bed without a second thought. No apology or anything. She was hurt and angry and…lost. She had been so happy for awhile and…she did it out of loyalty but afterwards, that was when she decided she wanted out. All the way. Out of his life and out of *the* life."

"So if she gave a friend of mine the impression she was leaving town because she was afraid, who was she scared of?"

"Nobody. Nobody she mentioned to me anyway. I told you the first time we talked that Brooke was a very secretive person. I wasn't making that up. She didn't like talking about her clients and I didn't want to hear about them. I knew about some of the more bizarre things she would do but I never knew names or specifics. If she was scared of anyone, she didn't say that to me. She seemed fine. She just wanted to move and get on with her life. She asked if I would go with her. I said no. She didn't even seem upset about that. There were a couple of things she had to do before she left but, next week, she planned to start driving to Cali."

"So she'd obviously picked up enough cash from somewhere."

She shrugged. "She'd said she couldn't leave without money so I guess so."

"Could she have been afraid of Ferguson?"

"No. He was afraid of her, I think. Afraid people would find out."

"How about her father?"

A quick shake of the head. "Maybe at first, when she moved out of the house, she might have been afraid. Not in the last few years. No. No way. It was like, the longer she spent away from him, the stronger she got. I mean, she still despised him. That never changed. Two or three weeks ago even, she told me she still had nightmares about what happened to David, but I don't think she felt threatened by her dad. After all, he never really seemed to care one way or the other about her."

"Why did she prefer seeing clients who knew her father? Just to piss him off?"

"I always figured it was something Freudian."

"Did Brooke ever say, or give any indication, that her dad was molesting her?"

"It never came up, even. Which is kind of strange when you think about it because we were always talking about sex and men and all that. I guess I don't really know the answer. He could have been. She always seemed to be so knowledgeable and experimental, even in junior high. Like I said, if he was interested in her in that way, he sure hid it well. Like, um, showing just the opposite?"

I drank a little of the Dasani and tried to regroup. I felt the cellular phone vibrate in my pocket, thought about answering, and then ignored it. If there was anything else I could ask Sela Grauman I wanted to get it asked and get out of there. Despite her remark that talking about all this was therapeutic, I didn't want to keep putting her to the test.

"One of her clients said Brooke tried to blackmail him," I said, glancing sideways at her. "Does that surprise you?"

"When she came back from D.C. I knew she was hurting for money. She said she planned to tap a few sources. I assumed she meant she would be going back to…doing what she did best." She lifted the Molson to her lips again but stopped. "She asked me if I wanted to help. I assumed she meant like the other time. I told her no. I think the way I answered hurt her. She said she would get her brother or this guy Patrick. I just remembered about him. He's probably someone you could talk to."

"Who is he?"

"When Brooke did those movies? He was her partner. She hadn't mentioned him in a long time but I know they were awfully close for awhile."

"Boyfriend?"

She smiled at the question. "Just in the videos. Patrick is mostly gay. The three of us hung out together a few times but he was strange. He's very outspoken. Sort of, I guess you'd say, outrageous. He teased Brooke all the time that she should sell her story to the tabloids or take it on *Jenny Jones* You know, 'I was the mistress of a Russian crime lord.' it really pissed her off. If she was blackmailing someone I could see him helping. For sure. He'd think it was a wild adventure."

"Did he ever have any contact with Federov?"

"Yes. I guess it didn't go well. Brooke told me she invited him to dinner with them once. Blue Mesa I think. I guess Patrick was a little too flamboyant for

Michael. A little too out of the closet. Michael called him a faggot, told her he never wanted to see him again."

Those Russians. So politically correct. "Any idea where I can find him?"

She cocked her head. "I remember we dropped him off at a hotel or apartment building somewhere on the North Side once. That was right after Brooke got into a crash and broke her ankle. He stayed with her for awhile after that. I think I wrote the address in my Palm. Let me go see."

While she was gone, I wandered over to the music wall. Her parents liked good jazz, the old stuff especially. A lot of Stan Kenton, Tommy Dorsey. Some Basie and Coltrane. Bobbie Short and Julie London. They had every CD by Sinatra, it looked like, even some albums that I didn't know had been digitally re-mastered. Tony Bennett, including what looked like bootleg copies of concerts he'd done at Ravinia. Good grief, even Harry Connick, Jr. snugged away in a corner with Mel Torme, The Velvet Fog.

Sela came back and handed me a piece of sticky-back paper with the name Patrick Vega and an address written on it. She wore a wan smile, like talking to me had taken an enormous effort and now she was finished and surprised she'd been able to do it at all. The phone started vibrating again so I took it out and looked at the Caller ID display. Blocked name, and the number looked like another cellular. I put the phone away. Celia watched me intently.

"I hope I've helped. I hope I can trust you."

When I assured her she could, she said, "No, I mean about Patrick. Now that I've given you his name, I feel kind of funny about it. Like it's going to get him into trouble."

"I'll be honest with you, Sela. If he knew Brooke well, and if Federov knew the extent of his relationship with her, they may be looking for him already. I'm going to try and find him pretty quickly. You never met Federov, did you?"

"Oh no. Brooke never brought it up and I never asked. No way." She crossed her arms in front of her and held her elbows. "I just want all of this to be over."

"Is there somewhere you can go for a few days?"

"Why? Do you think…if Patrick is in danger then I am, too?"

"I think you and Alan Talmadge and this guy Patrick all should be a little extra careful right now. You maybe a little less because you never met Federov. Even so, I'd feel better if you weren't staying here alone."

"Well, I was planning to go join my parents for a week in Michigan. I was just home because of the piano tuner."

"Go. Leave me your cell phone number though, will you?"

The sun was poking tentatively from between a couple of thick wads of cumulus when I stepped from the Grauman's front door and hustled to the Mustang. A rainbow without a lot of oomph hooked over the back of the trees across Sheridan Road and disappeared behind the stone facades of two homes that easily would go for a million or more. That figured, I thought. The pot of gold at the end of the rainbow had wound up in some Kenilworth zillionare's backyard. Or maybe that's where it had always been.

From the address Celia had given me for Patrick Vega, he lived in or near Uptown. Mental coin toss. He was a solid lead, but Alan Talmadge would be closer. If he was home.

I headed north and dialed the Talmadge house. No answer. Alan might still be at Glen Grove, so that's where I would go first. On the way, I flipped on WGN just to have a voice other than Sela Grauman's rattling around in my head for a little while.

> *"...calling it a gang-related drive-by but some witnesses we're hearing from dispute the claim that the men just happened to be in the wrong place at the wrong time. Those witnesses say the three men were gunned down minutes after they left the Grobiesky Resource Center on West Washington. They say the shooters specifically targeted the trio as they got into their car. Police say the men were volunteer tutors at the Resource Center. No one from the Resource Center has been available for comment..."*

Good story, I thought. Three victims always beats one or two in the coverage sweepstakes. Plus, a mid-day shooting meant all the stations would get crews there and probably have just enough time to have their reporters doing live stand-ups by the time the evening news shows began at four. Even better was the fact that the three victims had been volunteers, giving their time to help kids at a community center. A community center. A West Side community center with a Russian name.

It took just that long for the thought to push through to the forefront of my walnut-sized brain. I took the card Kinsella had given me and punched in his desk number at the Area. It rang, was picked up by somebody, not Kinsella. He was off-duty, due in tonight. I tried the cell phone. It rang four times.

"Talk," he snapped. I heard a siren wailing in the background.

"Tell me the three guys who got burned out west weren't Russians."

"What do you know about this, Reno?"

"I know Federov's bank built a Resource Center on the West Side. I know somebody shot three guys who were leaving a resource center with a Russian name. I'm *guessing* those three fellas are Russian, or at least work for the bank."

"Shit!" Kinsella said and the phone went dead.

That was fine because I needed to return the calls that had come in while I was talking to Sela. I was surprised the phone had rung at all, seeing as how only Sunny, Paul and a couple of other contacts had the new number. As I thought about it, though, I remembered I'd written the number on the back of the business card I'd given Alicia Witting. Smart, I thought. She had probably been one of the callers and I'd missed her. Great.

As it turned out, the first caller had been Rudy from the station, funneled to me by Sunny when he had insisted he needed to talk to me directly and immediately.

"Reno, I'm sorry to give you bad news over the phone," he began. His false sympathy irritated me, so I interrupted him.

"Sunny will pick up my stuff," I said. "She has my keys."

He sputtered for a moment. "But. Reno. I can't really allow that. She's not authorized to..."

"She's authorized by me, as of now." I was enjoying this more than I should be, given the circumstances. "If you want, I'll put it in writing."

I wasn't about to go back to the station in person, knowing I'd have to be escorted everywhere I went. Rudy and the other bosses would get too much pleasure from that.

"Wait...wait!" he called. I suspect he's gotten pretty good over the years at knowing when people are about to hang up on him. "You know this doesn't have to be acrimonious. We're just protecting..."

"Just come out and say it, Rudy. Those federal weenies made you wet your pants. You're covering New York's ass. I think that's acrimonious as hell."

"It says specifically in your contract..."

"My contract has a clause that allows you to fire me if I've been arrested. I haven't been and I'm not going to be. Tell New York to get the settlement offer ready. My attorney's really expensive and he'll be including his fees in the lawsuit."

I clicked off, irritated with myself for even talking to him. I was still gritting my teeth as I dialed the next number in the Caller ID queue. It had barely rung once when it was picked up by a guy who sounded like he was standing on the flight line at O'Hare.

"Master Sergeant Craig," was what I thought he said.

"This is Reno McCarthy. You called me?"

"Oh. Yes, sir. Caller ID, huh? This is Master Sergeant Craig. I'm with the State Police, District Chicago. Can you hold for a moment?"

What the hell was this all about? I heard him bark an order that included something about wanting to "see the medical examiner as soon as he gets here" and then, as my stomach did flip flops, a car door slammed and the background noise diminished.

"Sir, we have a situation here. Can you hear me OK?"

"I sure can. What's going on?" I could hear the nervousness in my voice and tried to ratchet it down a notch by taking a couple of deep breaths. Sunny, I thought. No, can't be. I just talked to her an hour ago. Then I realized how many times I'd heard that while interviewing the friends or relatives of people who'd become suddenly and violently dead.

Craig said, "Sir, do you know a lady by the name of Alicia Witting?"

*   *   *   *

The State Police had a unit meet me at a gas station just off the Kennedy. The tall young trooper hit his lights and siren before we even bounced back on the street and by the time he slid us down the expressway ramp and took the shoulder westbound, we were snapping along at probably a good ten miles per hour faster than I would have gambled was safe. We rolled up on the accident scene within a minute.

I stepped out of the state squad to a cacophony of noise and visual stimuli as familiar to me after years in the news business as the sights and sounds of a practice session at Orchestra Hall would be to a symphony conductor. I counted six marked and two unmarked state units as we pulled up, along with two city squads, a fire truck and squad and two CFD ambulances. There were also four or five civilian vehicles, two of which had some front-end damage, and two-large bed-tow rigs, similar to the one that had squashed Sergei.

Despite a reappearance of the sun, troopers moved about in their rain gear with practiced ease, taking measurements that would triangulate the final resting place of Alicia Witting's rental car with the exactitude of a GPS readout. Along the edges of the action, but right down there on the expressway with everyone else, were video camera shooters I recognized from channels 2, 5 and 14 and two still photographers I didn't know. None of them noticed me. I saw Channel 7's helicopter orbiting about a mile out, probably unable to get closer because of the proximity of the accident scene to O'Hare.

The focus of all the attention was the wrinkled and broken remains of what, I learned later, had been a brand new Ford Crown Victoria, the same basic model as most of the police vehicles scattered about. It looked like a child's accordion, thrown away in a fit of rage.

"Sir?" The young trooper appeared again at my elbow. "Master Sergeant Craig is the one over there by the second hook. Ah, sorry. By that tow truck."

Craig was as tall as my escort, with the ramrod posture usually found in Marine Corps lifers. He even wore his hat canted at the slight angle I'd seen favored by DI's. He nodded as I introduced myself. A man with a lot on his mind and a hard, quick handshake.

"'Preciate you coming to the scene, sir. Makes it a little easier for our accident investigators if they don't have to chase all over to find witnesses."

"I'm not sure if I can be much help, Sergeant. I barely knew your victim."

"I see." He gestured toward his car and I followed him past one of the ambulances idling in the middle of things. I hadn't seen a sheet draped over any part of the ruined Crown Vic so Alicia's body had likely already been removed and placed in the back of that ambulance. It's unusual for the Chicago Fire Department to transport the dead. By long city tradition, the fire medics usually get the living and the cops carry away the deceased. I wondered about that.

"It took us more than an hour to extricate her," Craig said, once he was behind the wheel of his own Crown Victoria and half-turned to face me in the passenger seat. "Force of the impact shoved the engine compartment through the fire wall and almost into the back seat. Her body was wrapped up in all that mess."

"That's a tough one."

"You bet. I used to watch you on TV. I know you've probably been to a few of these. That's why I feel I can be candid. If you have a problem with that, say so."

"Not at all."

"Reason I called you out here is this."

He reached into the flap pocket of his uniform shirt and withdrew a small plastic bag with my business card inside. There was some red on one corner of it that looked gooey. I didn't ask.

"When the fire guys got to where she was trapped, they found this in her hand. Clutched in her hand, they said. Did you give it to her?"

"Yup," I said. Strangely, the sight of my card didn't produce the sickened reaction I would have expected. I looked at my watch. "About twelve hours ago."

"You can understand, her holding it like that, at the last minute and all, makes us wonder about its significance. Did she call you this morning?"

"No."

"Because, one scenario we're thinking about is that she might have been using the phone at the time of the accident. We get a lot of that."

"If she was, she wasn't talking to me."

"Could she have been passing your name and number along to someone else?"

"I don't know who or why." I spread my hands. "Really, Sergeant. I don't have a lot to contribute. Last night was the first time I met the woman."

Hell, I had the Chicago cops and feds climbing into my shorts. I'd come out here for one reason only and it wasn't to spend a lot of time answering questions. I wanted to get few of my own in.

I exaggerated a bit. "WGN radio's story has this maybe a police chase that went sour."

"No offense to your profession, but that's wrong." He looked at me, maybe expecting me to react. I didn't.

He gestured with the business card. "You met Ms. Witting last night, you say? Under what circumstances?"

"At the Greentree Hotel. We know some of the same people."

"Her driver's license and ID say she was from Washington."

"That's right."

"Social meeting was it?"

He was looking at his clipboard as he asked and there was no more emphasis on that question than he'd given to any of the others. Even so, I picked up an undercurrent.

"I ran into her as I was on my way out the door. We probably didn't talk for any longer than five minutes or so."

The best lies are those folded in with the truth. It would work, too, as long as Alicia's companion didn't come forward.

"Was she with anyone?"

"Not that I saw, no."

"Intoxicated?"

"She didn't appear to be."

"Was she staying at the Greentree?"

"As far as I could tell."

"Did she give you any indication of her schedule today? Talk about any meetings, maybe she was flying somewhere?"

I bit back the impulse to speculate she was on her way to see Ferguson. If that's where she was going, his people would find that out.

"Not at all. Basically just had time for hello and goodbye."

"You'd never had prior contact with her? As a reporter?"

"I've never covered Washington. I knew of her, recognized her. I introduced myself, gave her a card." I paused. "So what happened exactly? She drive straight into the bridge?"

He lifted his head, peeled off the campaign hat and used a bracket mounted on the ceiling to store it so it hung upside down above his radio console. "I've got our best traffic crash reconstructionist out here. Barring any mechanical problems with the car, he says that's what she did. No skid marks, nothing to indicate she hit the guardrail and bounced off. The witnesses say she seemed to just aim, drive and POW."

"Have many like this? Suicides?"

"Some. This is off the record, right?" He looked up at me, intently. I nodded.

"Could be. Likely is. I've never seen one come in at an angle from the farthest away lane, though. That's new. Almost like the thought just hit her and she couldn't wait another second. It had to be *that* bridge at *that* moment. Damndest thing. The fact she was holding your card at the time, that's odd, too. When you get home, I'd appreciate it if you'd check your voice mail. Just to clear up that loose end."

"She wouldn't have had the number. The station phone and my cell were all that was on the card."

"Can you call the station?"

I had done so on my way over. The receptionist had acted like she was talking to Richard Kimble with Marshal Sam Gerard hovering over her. Any calls for me she was supposed to funnel to Rudy and there hadn't been a one. Let's hear it for all those loyal fans upset over my dismissal.

"How fast was she going when she hit?" I asked.

"Off the record again?"

I didn't tell him that in twenty years in the news business I had never figured out exactly what that phrase meant. Did it mean I could never use what he was telling me? Or that I could use it, but not quote him as the source? Or did I have to forget I'd been told at all? Different strokes for different reporters. I just nodded.

"We're estimating about ninety. Even the stock Crown Vics will do that and she had to move faster than the traffic around her. We'll know better when we finish talking to all the witnesses."

"No sign she could have been forced off the road? A road rage thing, I mean," I added hastily.

"So far everyone has said she was in lane three. That's the far left. Unless somebody came up on the median side of her and there's no indication of that."

The guys from the towing service were using a winch to drag the ruined carcass of the rented Ford onto the long, angled bed of the truck. At just about the same moment, one of the paramedics hopped out of the rear of the ambulance and came over to the side of Craig's squad. He squatted next to the driver's side window and asked if it was okay to remove the body to the Medical Examiner's facility. Craig got out to talk to him.

I thought about the quickness in Alicia Witting's features as she came to the door of her room, and the feral thing I had seen move behind her eyes when I'd brought up her connection to the Russians. All the way out from Kenilworth I had clamped down hard on my emotions. It's something I learned to do years ago.

It's not unusual in the news business to produce a story which has the potential to ruin someone's career and, perhaps, their life. You make sure your facts are correct, you do the little weighing of good versus evil, the "what happens if I *don't* do this story," and then you back off or go after it with every bit of zeal you can muster. I never backed off. As a result, I unseated politicians, put cops in jail, got people fired from their jobs and assured they would never work in their chosen professions again.

I remembered a former real estate mogul, a man who had been at the zenith of his career, who now flipped burgers for a living. I had documented his dalliances with the underage girls he'd seduced while a soccer coach, and then how he'd tried to throw some low-end political weight around to cover it up.

Vinnie Seamans had been right. I was a damned good reporter. I was still a damned good investigator. Or perhaps just damned.

"I did this to her."

The words burned like a hot wire slicing through my brain. My hands shook. First Brooke and now Alicia. "My fault."

I leaned up against the hood, arms crossed, and took in two lungs-full of gasoline-scented air. And saw Agent Dark and an older guy in a dark suit climbing down the embankment from the bridge, trying to keep their footing on the rain-slick grass.

It's funny what fear will do to you, especially when it emerges in the midst of a spectacular guilt trip. My first thought was to run away. Then I considered charging right at both of them, punching, kicking, flailing with every ounce of energy I had. Just as suddenly, though, both urges passed. The hot wire still sizzled but I felt my heart rate returning to normal and the desire to vomit disappeared. I'd been led into a trap but I wasn't about to start wailing and rattling the bars.

Dark's colleague looked more like a boss than a new partner. Mid-to late fifties, he had thinning red hair combed back and sprayed into place and the slight paunch and pale skin of a guy who probably spent more time behind a desk than a steering wheel. His suit was also better quality than what a street agent would wear or could afford. Custom-tailored pinstripes with oxfords that were now a little muddy, but no doubt had been freshly shined that morning. That he managed not to fall in his trek down the embankment suggested good co-ordination or maybe just the fact he'd had to do it a time or two. What he hadn't been able to do was duck a few punches at some point in his life. His face had the battered look of an old suitcase.

He didn't show credentials or offer to shake hands, just said, "Stinson, Terrorist Task Force."

"Howdy."

"Agent Dark tells me she warned you off, last night. You got your head so far up your ass your ears are plugged?"

No anger, no raised voice. Just a glare he'd probably used to win the J. Edgar Hoover Intimidation Award.

"The federal government investigating traffic accidents now?" I asked mildly as I withdrew the reporters' notebook I had slipped into my pocket before leaving my car. I opened it and took out a pen.

He frowned. "What the hell is this? Playacting?"

"What's your first name by the way, Agent Stinson? The *Sun-Times* editors can be a bitch about little details like that. Or should I just say you refused to provide the information? That'll give the readers a nice chuckle."

"You're working for the *Sun-Times?*"

"I figure I'll probably be the only one with this angle, the fact that the federal government showed up in the person of a senior supervisor and a special agent assigned to the Joint Terrorist Task Force. Although, those TV camera guys over there are pretty sharp. They see me doing an interview like this, they'll probably want in on it. Sort of the herd instinct. So what did you say you were here for?"

I put it all out there nice and quick, in the manner of an old-timey traveling medicine man, trying to con all of the folks all of the time. I smiled when I finished and watched him glance toward where the TV guys, especially Leon, the Channel 14 photographer, were taking an interest. They all knew me, Leon better than the rest. He caught me looking and started our way.

"Why don't I just quote you as saying Alicia Witting was being investigated by the feds at the time of her death?" I said to Stinson. "That'll make it seem like you guys are right on top of things."

To his credit, the Fed smiled and there was real humor in his words. "You're a piece of work, McCarthy. How'd you like it if I plunked your ass down in front of a Grand Jury for a couple of days?"

"I appreciate the compliment, sir, but quotes like that don't sell many papers. Linking Alicia Witting to an active investigation, wow. Now that would make an editor really spit out his coffee."

"You better believe I'll check with the *Sun-Times*."

"Did I tell you I worked there?" It was my turn to smile. "I don't think I said anything of the sort."

Leon came up beside me as Stinson and I locked stares. "What's up, Reno? Can anyone else get in on this?"

Stinson snapped, "No comment," and walked away. Leon looked at me.

I was still smiling. "I guess he doesn't have anything to say after all."

CHAPTER 14

▼

With the scene being cleaned up and Alicia Witting's body on its way to wherever the federal forensics people would be doing the autopsy, I persuaded the trooper who had brought me to take me back to my car. Craig was huddled with Stinson and Dark. When the young trooper asked him if I was free to leave, I saw him incline his head to Stinson, then nod and, after leaning forward to hear something Dark said, wave the trooper off.

I said nothing during the brief drive. I felt like I was in a box somebody kept shaking. Every once in awhile I would hit the sides and rebound and before I had a chance to recover I was bouncing off the opposite side just as hard. When I got into the Mustang, I put my head on the steering wheel and closed my eyes. I must have stayed that way a couple of minutes too long because the clerk came out of the gas station and asked me if I was okay. I told him I was letting a brief bout of nausea pass and that I was just peachy.

"Ok, den. You have a good day, den, bud-dee." He backed away uncertainly. I realized I was smiling again, or maybe still. Maybe I'd smiled throughout the whole ride with the trooper. Pleasant thought. Except, when I looked in the rear view, I saw that it was not a happy expression. I looked like someone who wasn't in total control of his emotions.

I tugged the cellular out of my pocket and dialed Paul. It rang long enough, I figured he was either out of range or had turned it off. He answered right before it would have gone to voice mail.

"Sorry, I left the damn thing across the room while I was on the treadmill. Figure I'll use every bennie the paper has to offer until I leave. What's up?"

"Alicia Witting drove herself into a bridge abutment at ninety miles an hour this morning," I said.

"Jesus F. Christ," he said. "Are you...*she* was the crash on the Kennedy?"

"The very same."

"Who else knows?"

"A bunch of state troopers. Me. And a couple of Feds, one of them by the name of Stinson who looked like he's probably out of D.C."

"Oh, man. Fuck me to tears. You didn't tell them we interviewed her did you?"

"I told them I said about six words to her in the hotel last night. I can't tell how much they know. My guess is Asa gave them everything he gave me, but they were a little late off the mark getting to her."

"Late? Yeah, I guess. Jesus." He was quiet for a moment and I could hear his breathing. "Did we push her into it?"

"If anybody did, it was me. I was the one asking the questions."

"Yeah, but Jesus, Reno. How were you supposed to know she was standing that close to the edge of the cliff? She's flat out the *last* person I would have figured to off herself. I didn't know. You couldn't have known. Wait. It was suicide wasn't it? They're sure?"

I clutched the phone a little tighter. "Yeah."

Silence again. He sucked in a long breath. "I better let the desk know. I'm sure we had a photographer out there. They'll want to start connecting the dots."

*   *   *   *

Sometimes you push too hard.

She'd been driving along the Kennedy, I thought. Maybe she had the window open, the radio cranked. I wondered what she would have been listening to. Inching that accelerator down and watching the speedometer needle climb. There probably hadn't been a great deal of outbound traffic at that hour. She could feel the wind against her face. The rain, too. Had it been raining, then?

Was she debating whether to call me? Was that why my card was in her hand when she died?

Or, did she just want me to know? Was the card a message sent by someone very well versed, expert even, in political subtlety? I am doing this because you found me out, you son of a bitch. You backed me into a corner. You gave me no options except to do what I did. You ruined my life so here's what you get.

I wondered if they would find any drugs in her system. Whatever she'd been abusing to catch the Russians' attention. She was a raver, Asa had said. Ecstasy?

Had she been an honest person before they co-opted her? If she had sworn an oath to uphold and defend the Constitution to work where she did, had she meant it? Was the threat of exposure for her illicit lifestyle so great that…well, strike that. Pretty obvious answer, Reno.

Sometimes you push too hard and somebody dies.

*   *   *   *

Sunny's office is in a small office park in the shadow of a Hawthorne Suites three blocks east of the Cook County Courthouse in Skokie. Most of the units are occupied by therapists, a few dentists, some manufacturers' reps who just need a desk and a secretary. She doesn't advertise. The logo on the door just says DeAngelis and Associates. The subtle differences between her quarters and those around her are a small Yaagi two-way radio antenna on the roof, pointed toward downtown, and an electronic lock on the door with a camera mounted discreetly above.

I buzzed, heard the lock click and stepped through into a plain waiting room featuring only some plastic chairs, a floor-sized potted plant and a wall full of current wanted posters and mug-shots of bail-skips. A short corridor to my left led to the cubicles where the handful of operatives who sublet space from her can write their reports, click through research on their computers or use what she calls the second-best investigator's tool after laptops: the telephone.

Sunny came out of the office directly in front of me, brushing back a strand of hair and looking concerned. She wore business casual, khaki slacks and a light blue polo shirt. The only difference between her attire and what you'd see on the thousands of working women getting off trains and busses during rush hour was the 9mm automatic in a Bianchi holster on her right hip.

"Reno. Jesus, you look horrible. What happened?"

"Got a Dr. Pepper hiding in that refrigerator of yours?" Unlike her movie counterparts, who always manage to have a fifth of Scotch in a bottom drawer of their desk, she prefers Dr. Pepper. She can knock back a dozen of them a day without the slightest effect. The whole reason for the bar-sized icebox behind her desk is to store two-six packs of the sweet soda at a time, along with bowls of crushed ice.

I slumped onto the couch across from her and watched as she retrieved two cans, filled two glasses with ice, poured, and handed one across. I rubbed it against my forehead for a moment before taking a sip. The cool liquid felt good going down. I didn't gag as I feared I might. I looked at her awards on the wall. Several from the Illinois News Broadcasters Association for her work at the station. A couple from some association of Bail Agents. No pictures.

"You hear about the crash on the Kennedy?" I asked.

"It was just on Channel 7. Why?"

"Alicia Witting." I said. "And it doesn't look like the Russians did it."

Her mouth opened and she blinked. "Who then? What happened?"

I told her about my morning. I lingered over my interview with Sela Grauman simply because it was easier to talk about than what I had seen on the Kennedy. By the time I finished, she had her game face back on, though I could read the sympathy in her eyes.

"You can't take responsibility for this, any more than you can say it's your fault that someone killed Brooke Talmadge. You aren't to blame! Witting made a choice. Of all the avenues open to her, *she* decided. You didn't yank that wheel out of her hands."

"What do you think she'd be doing right now if I hadn't gone to the hotel last night?"

"Duh. The same thing she's been doing for months. Selling everything her boss does to the Russian mob."

After a moment, I said, "Yeah, there is that."

"God *damn* it, Reno! Okay, you put her in a bad spot. You don't think the task force was about to do the same thing? You're right in thinking they probably got everything you did from Asa. What's to say that the minute they left after they interviewed her, she wouldn't have reacted in just the same way?"

"Except they would have cuffed her and…"

"Oh yeah. Sure they would have." She said. "On what authority? The word of an accused child molester? They might have put a couple of watchers on her. But we did that and look where it got us."

"And she wouldn't have talked to them any more than she talked to me."

"Exactly. From what you've told me about her she probably would have lawyered up, don't you think? This was *her* choice. You didn't make her rent that car."

"What about my business card in her hand?"

"She was thinking of calling you. She decided to kill herself instead."

"Sounds like some of the women I've dated," I said. I felt a little better.

She snorted and drank some of her Dr. Pepper. "If your pity party is over for the moment," She lifted an eyebrow, "...I may be able to tell you where she was going."

"To see Ferguson?"

"She made three calls this morning to an unlisted number in the 715 area code with a 385 prefix. That's Wisconsin, the whole area up there from Woodruff to Boulder Junction. I checked around. Ferguson has a place near Woodruff, on Trout Lake. It's listed in his wife's family name. Witting was at least thinking of driving up there because she picked up a Wisconsin map and asked the girl at the Hertz counter if she could drop the car at the Lakeland airport."

"Question is, was it where she was planning to go all along or did she just decide to go after I talked to her? Did you check Hertz to see if she made a reservation?"

"No reservation. She just dropped by and got one of the last three cars available."

"When she left the hotel, did she check out?"

"Yes. But a day early, according to their records."

I got up to pace. "Going up to confess before Ferguson heard it somewhere else?"

"I can do a lot of things with this computer, my friend, but reading minds isn't one of them."

"Well, work with me on this. Say she freaks out, spends the night thinking about it, makes her decision. Then she gets on the road and something changes her mind. Any other calls?"

"One to her office in Washington and one to the Senator's office here. Three to the health club. That's it for this morning. When she arrived yesterday, she made two calls. One to a law firm. One to the local office of the Conservative Forum."

I sighed and thought for a moment. "Okay, let's go back to yesterday, then. Is there some way to see if anyone at the law firm is connected to Federov? It's probably a stretch, but if we link Witting directly to one of Federov's people, maybe there's a way to lean on whoever it is."

"I'm ahead of you. I was getting ready to compare a couple of lists when I heard you buzz the door." She motioned me to come around her desk and then turned to face the computer on the credenza behind her. As she touched her mouse, the screen which had showed a hunk of beefcake posed on a beach dissolved into spreadsheet. I sat where I could look over her shoulder, distracted for a moment by her perfume. I remembered her saying she often created her own fragrances. This one made me think of incense burning, black lights, anti-war posters hanging on the walls and "Born to Be Wild" cranking out of the stereo. She glanced up and caught me looking at her.

"What?" she asked.

"You smell like a hippie."

There seemed to be more blue in her eyes today. Contacts?

"I smell like a…hippo?"

"You know what I mean. With the incense and all that stuff mixed in."

"It's sort of patchouli you goof. Now, come on." She inclined her head toward the screen, but she was grinning as she pointed to some of the names.

"OK, I criss-crossed the phone numbers the hotel gave me and came up with the firm, Covington, Carroll. Then I went into Martindale-Hubbell and broke the firm down. On the left, here, are the individual names of partners and associates. Over here, Balkan Global, surprisingly, has a Web site that shows their officers and directors, so that was pretty easy. The bank itself was a little tougher. It's a subsidiary but the whole outfit is privately held and they don't have to be as forthcoming with information. Well…except to the Feds." She flashed to another screen.

"A little form called the FFIEC-003 took care of that very nicely. So we now know all the major officers and significant shareholders. Not that they'd want us to, of course."

"This stuff is public and online now? We used to have to file Freedom of Information requests and get lawyers involved if the Feds didn't cough it up."

She kept facing the computer but her grin grew evil. "Right. It's public. In a manner of speaking. Gotta know where to look and how to make it public."

"Oh," I said. "Public. Right. Wink, wink."

We scanned the names in silence, pointing when we saw one possible match or another. Similar names popped up but none came close enough. After a few minutes, I rubbed my eyes and looked away in frustration.

"Fucking Russians probably hired Russian lawyers. Kept it all in-house. Friends from their days in the Gulag or something."

"Nice mouth. Maybe. Or maybe…maybe the name is on a different set of lists." She spun halfway around to paw at a pile of legal pads on the side of her desk. When she found the one she wanted she hauled it into her lap and began snapping back pages. After a moment, she stopped and looked up.

"Son of a bitch."

"Nice mouth."

"Oh, but I can get away with it because I'm clean otherwise. In fact, I am so clean I shine."

She turned the pad and, with her free hand, used a pen to underline the name Jerome Belzer in the middle of a jumble of undecipherable notes. Then she pointed back at the list she'd gotten from the Martindale-Hubbell directory. Jerome Belzer's name was the fourth one down.

"Jerome Belzer is a partner in the firm of Covington, Carroll? Says so right there. And here," she tapped the legal pad. "Is where I wrote down everything I learned about that building in Edgewater I told you about the other day. Where that asshole who attacked Brooke in the parking lot used to live before he supposedly moved?"

"Yevgeny something. The one who used the phony address on his driver's license."

"The very same. Jerome Belzer is listed in Housing Department files as corporate counsel for the owners of that building."

"Son of a bitch," I said and met her high-five.

"He was the cut-out," she nodded. "He gave her orders from Federov and carried her information back to him. Outfit lawyers pass messages all the time. Usually they're criminal attorneys but this is better. The connection to Federov is so ambiguous, you'd never see it. Unless you're a genius investigator."

"Can you background him? Maybe spare some people for surveillance?" I asked.

"Sure. I have just the team in mind."

"With Witting suddenly dead, he's going to be jumpy…"

"Why would he be? Witting is a suicide. Even if the Feds find him, so what? He's not obligated to tell them anything. You and I, on the other hand, can sneak up on his blind side. We know there's some hanky panky going on. We can use that against him."

"How? Supposing you're right and he's not afraid of Uncle Sam."

Her eyes went speculative. "We could tell Mr. Belzer that if he doesn't share what he knows, we'll put the information about his disreputable character on the street." She gave me a bland smile. One that probably would have made the lions cringe back in Daniel's day.

"Gee, Sunshine, why not just pull his nuts off with a rusty pliers?"

"Oh, believe me. If they think he had any part in offing their two friends in Uptown, the homeys will do that and more. Given the choice, I suspect Mr. Belzer would rather talk to us, wouldn't you think?" She batted her eyes and smiled at me.

"The problem I'm having," I began and then stopped, grinning. Sunny was still smiling across her desk at me.

"You love this, don't you?" she said.

"Noodling it out? Figuring the moves? Yeah. It's something we used to do in the newsroom. I miss that the most, I think. The team effort."

I paused, thought about what I was going to say.

"How do we know Belzer was the one Witting called? It's not a small firm. You have, what, thirty names here?"

"Yeah, but look at the number from the hotel's phone records. It's the same number that's listed for him on the management company papers. It's his direct line."

"Okay. What if he has legitimate business with Ferguson's office? Maybe it's on the up and up. She was handling a constituent problem."

"We play the odds. You figure he's not going to just pick up the phone when he wants a chat with Mr. Big. We'll watch him, background him and see where he goes and who he meets. It's not like you need proof to show a judge. And it's not like you're going on TV with it."

"Ouch."

She held up her hand. "Yeah, I know. Sorry. That was low. I didn't mean it the way it sounded."

"The thing is, you're right. I've got to stop thinking like I have to find someone to point a camera at." I stood up, stretched.

"While you see what you can get on Belzer, I want to track down Alan Talmadge. I'm thinking there are a few things he didn't tell me the last time we chatted."

*   *   *   *

I tried calling Talmadge's house and the Glen Grove Club when I got back in the car. I struck out in both places. I got voice mail at the house and a guy in the pro shop told me that Alan's second round had been rained out. I'd missed him by two hours.

That left his apartment, the scene of Brooke's murder. I could think of a couple of reasons he might be there, if the cops had released it to him. It was the one place I really didn't want to see again but I headed toward it anyway. I heard my old man's voice. *Deal with it, son.*

I ran down the Edens and took Touhy across to Rogers Park. I kept thinking about the old adage that there are only two seasons in Chicago: winter and construction. Streets and Sanitation guys were putting down patches in several blocks but city driving habits ruled. Cars swerved around the flaggers and the crews as if the workers were no more susceptible to injury than the traffic cones set out all around them. I slowed to a crawl as I passed one long section under repair and, for my patience, felt the Mustang get nailed with a healthy spit of black goo from the asphalt machine. I thought of the late, legendary WGN morning man, Bob Collins, and his frequent reminder, "Good deeds never go unpunished."

The sun was scratching at the clouds to get out and warming the late afternoon as I drove past the building where Brooke died. I looked for Alan Talmadge's Beemer. I had blocked the images from three nights ago, but proximity to the apartment was encouraging my brain to slap them in front of me like flash cards. Kicking the door. Stumbling over Brooke's body and then, in a flash of lightning…her sprawled there on the floor and…what? I'd seen something else in that moment but I couldn't remember what it was. Then I'd been smacked with the phone and knocked out of it. But what else had caught my eye? It suddenly seemed important to know, but I couldn't drag the memory out where it would do me any good.

I turned around and bumped up into the alley that ran between the building and the embankment that carried the El tracks through the neighborhood. Another alley broke off to my left separating Brooke's building and the houses behind it. Wooden fences bordered the alley on both sides and four large Dumpsters hunkered along the fences.

I got out of the Mustang and stood where the two alleys joined. A broken door through the fence hung on its hinges and a small path led to the wooden back stairs of Brooke's building. Each floor had a small landing and porch where I could see barbecue grills and some cheap lawn furniture. At night, in the rain, and given the layout, it was unlikely a tenant would have any reason to come back here. You could stick a car up next to the fence, pointing out for a quick escape. The only problem was, if another car were to enter the alley, your route would be blocked. A professional planning a hit wouldn't jam himself up that way. I scratched my head.

He could have come from between the houses and crossed the alley but the fence on that side looked sturdy and, as I walked along it and checked, the access doors from the yards were all closed and locked. He could have ambled down the alley after parking on the street. I suppose he could have rappelled from a helicopter, too.

I was puzzled. The rear of Brooke's building certainly lacked reasonable expectation of a quick escape. Yet, Kinsella had said the neighbors reported seeing someone going down the back stairs after they'd heard the disturbance in Brooke's apartment. Weird. Maybe Brooke's killer hadn't been a professional after all. Or, he'd been a very cocky one.

I passed through the fence and trotted up the stairs, hearing music as I climbed past the second floor. Got to be quick about it, I thought. A peek through the window was all I wanted, not a confrontation with a local beat cop called out by jumpy neighbors. Shades were down over the windows and someone had covered the glass in the door with pieces of what looked like construction paper. I couldn't see anything. I knocked anyway.

"Alan? Hey Alan, it's me," I said. Secret Squirrel pretends to be a friend.

Heard nothing. Felt stupid.

Knocked again, a little louder. Still no hint of movement from within. I gave it another minute and then went back down and through the tiny backyard.

The music on the second floor had stopped, as though the person playing it had heard my knocks upstairs, but no one stepped out on their porch to gape at me. I was halfway to the Mustang when my cell rang and startled me. I fumbled it out of my jacket.

"We gotta meet," Kinsella growled. "Where are you?"

*   *   *   *

He named a hot dog stand near Wilson and Kedzie in Albany Park.

Listening to WGN on the way there gave me no hint of what he wanted to talk about. The afternoon drive anchor seemed to be reading the same copy they'd had earlier about the West Side shootings, only now they had the number correct: three dead from multiple gunshot wounds.

Pretty much what I expected to hear. The names were noticeably Russian. The cops were noticeably silent. Sometimes a reporter will luck out and snare the district commander or a deputy superintendent at a scene like that, but most of the time the top cops prefer to avoid the cameras. Unless, of course, they really want the public's help finding someone. More often, they wait until they can crow about an arrest.

I thumped over the Brown Line tracks on Kedzie and found the place Kinsella had told me about, across the street from a falafel joint and snugged between a Middle Eastern grocery and a second-hand store. Given that it was late afternoon, but not yet dinnertime, there were only two customers, both teenagers, sitting at a plastic covered booth along the wall. A middle-aged black guy with slicked back salt and pepper hair and wearing a starched white apron over flared jeans leaned on the counter into the kitchen reading a *Sun-Times*. He looked up and smiled when I came in, then held out both hands to indicate I could plant myself wherever I wanted. I chose a booth on the opposite wall from the kids and all the way back toward the kitchen. He poured water and left the pitcher, then returned with a bowl of what looked like barbecued potato chips.

"Homemade," he explained with a smile.

Kinsella slouched in a few minutes later, his handheld Motorola loud enough that both kids glanced up. He snapped it off and stuffed it into an inside pocket. The kids went back to their conversation and the guy in the apron came out from the kitchen, smiling again. He and Kinsella shook hands and exchanged greetings like old friends who don't see enough of one another. Kinsella actually grinned. I don't think I'd ever seen him use that expression before.

"Hector, this is Reno McCarthy. He used to be a TV star."

"You think retirement automatically means I got Alzheimer's? I knowd his dad." Hector said as he shook my hand. His smile showed a gold incisor on his upper left. "How you doing Reno? Always a pleasure to meet one of Charley's friends. He don't have many."

Kinsella muttered something under his breath about "health inspectors."

"Nothing healthy in here for 'em to inspect," Hector shot back cheerfully. "Cholesterol in the chips alone'll kill you. You want the King, I assume?"

"For three," Kinsella nodded as he grabbed a handful of chips and sat down.

"Three?" I said.

Hector pointed twice at Kinsella and once at me. "One, two, three." Chuckling, he headed back to the kitchen.

"Try the chips," Kinsella said.

I snagged a couple and was suddenly glad there was a pitcher of water on the table. The smoky flavor came through clearly, though. It was the first time I'd tasted anything since having my nose broken. "Wow."

"Hector's an old partner of mine. This's his place. All his recipes, too. Weirdest hot dog joint you'll ever find. Not a roach in sight." He stuffed a few more chips in his mouth. "You make any progress today?

"Maybe. Chalked one in the negative column, too." I told him about Witting. I expected him to gripe about me confronting her but he just grunted noncommittally.

"They come up with anything out west?" I asked.

"You kidding? When the fibbies showed up with the Street Deputy, I took off. No point getting busted again, maybe put on a desk."

He riffled the pages of a notebook and then closed it. Finished chewing.

"Whoever took these Russians out wasn't real concerned about the cost of bullets. Counted eight in one victim and maybe ten or eleven in the others. Close range as they were stepping off a curb. Really chopped 'em up. Maybe three dozen rounds total."

"One shooter or more?"

"Witness saw one firing from the front, one from the back. That's Hispanic gang territory but the shooters were bruthas. Go figure. Silenced weapons, probably Mac10's. They got thirty-round clips, eleven hundred rounds a minute. Shooters fired groups, too. About hollowed out the chests of two of the victims and pulverized the other one's head. Looked like a pumpkin beat on with a hammer."

"Angry."

"No shit. But the most accurate shooting I've ever seen in a drive-by. Usually they just lean out and spray. These assholes paid attention. Crime lab guys accounted for just about every slug, either in the victims or their car. Pretty tight. Makes me think they were being careful to avoid extra casualties. What's that tell ya?"

"In a rival gang's neighborhood but careful who they shoot? They had permission to do the hits."

"You get the cigar."

"Message being, you do two of ours, we do three of yours?"

"Tab's up a bit higher than that." He hunched over the table. "This ain't made the news stations yet. County cops on the north side got a tip, pulled one of those styrofoam coolers out of the river by Skokie Lagoons. Had a Russian guy's head inside. Supposedly the boss of a crew that's been taking off jewelry salesmen in the 'burbs and a guy with huge clout in the organization. Then I'm hearing the Russians whacked a guy named Julio Ruiz last night out in Aurora. One of the top level Latin Deuces."

"Oh, man," I said. A war. Just what PoloTony LaMotta predicted.

"Back and forth it goes, where it stops, nobody knows. You think this's bad? It's gonna get worse. You watch," Kinsella said. "I got to nail this Federov, Fletcher, whatever he goes by. Cut the head off this thing before they start blowing real people away along Michigan Avenue. You got anything to tell me?"

"Nothing. Maybe less. Everybody I'm talking to points me away from Federov for Brooke."

"Maybe you're talking to the wrong people."

I opened my mouth to press him on that but Hector came back bearing a tray of food and spread it out for us. Barbecued chicken, pork, and the thickest hot dogs I'd ever seen, split open with chunks of cheese melting inside. Beer in a plastic stein for Kinsella and a Coke for me.

"The lo-*cal* menu for Chicago's Finest," Hector said and grunted. "Shit. Chicago's Ugliest more like it."

After he was gone, Kinsella reached down and took a chicken breast out of the basket. He made me wait while he gnawed through half of it then tapped his mouth with a napkin before he spoke again.

"Word on the street is the guys who did Deon and his bodyguard were driving a new Jag. Mookie, the other bodyguard, supposedly came back from getting food, saw what was happening inside the place and split."

"Did you pick him up?"

"Only a matter of time."

I looked at him in amazement. "You think they used their own car to drive over and torture and kill two guys?"

Kinsella held back his answer as the front door opened. The guy who stepped inside gave the place the sort of once over, dismissive glance you'd expect from someone wearing a hand made suit, and then headed for our booth. I saw the kids in the other corner stare at him and then duck back to their meals. Kinsella's expression went from slightly bored to amused. He slid toward the wall on his side of the booth, making room.

"Reno McCarthy, meet one of your countrymen. Tommy O'Meara. He doesn't like it if we lesser fools call him by his given name, though. So humor his tight ass and refer to him as Captain."

O'Meara inspected the bench seat to see if it posed any threat to his slacks and chose to slide a chair over from a nearby table instead. He had a wide face and a potato nose and suspicious eyes which he turned on me.

"You guaranteeing this man's silence?" he asked Kinsella. A wee bit of brogue was evident in his speech.

"You want me to say I'll shoot him if he betrays the sacred oath? The fellowship of the ring? Sit yourself down and have a beer."

"I see my name in print…"

"You won't," I said. He didn't look convinced but he sat down.

"Tommy's in Organized Crime Intelligence," Kinsella said. "We went through the Academy together. Of course, that was before people started referring to him as 'The Suit.' Only because of his good taste in clothing, of course."

He put the chicken breast aside, wiped his fingers, and looked with lust at the shredded pork that was slathered in sauce. "You gonna have any of this?" he asked me.

"Go ahead."

"Jesus, I knew you were a food faggot." He forked a pile of pork onto his plate. "Anyway, Tommy here had a nice new corner office down at the new head-quarters building until his friends the Fibbies came in and took it over as the command center for their Russian Organized Crime Task Force. Booted you right out, too, didn't they?"

"You think this is necessary, Detective?" O'Meara snapped.

Kinsella winked at me.

"Quite a slap in the face for a guy who used to Windex his autographed pic-ture of J. Edgar every morning. So I hear all of this and I reach out for him." He took a moment to chew some pork, tapped his mouth with the napkin again, and put his fork down.

"Tommy's been working these Russians for a couple of years. Not on the street. That might scuff his Bruno Magli's…"

O'Meara, red-faced, moved to stand.

"Not finished, Captain." Kinsella said, in the voice a teacher might use on a student reluctant to stay after school. Not quite the way you'd normally hear a detective addressing a Captain, but O'Meara settled back. What was up with that, I wondered.

"As I was saying, he worked the Russians. Went to New York. Even went to Moscow and a few other places inside the old Soviet Union. He wrote all the briefing papers for the Superintendent and the Mayor. He's like a desk-top expert on the *mafiya*. But now that the Bureau's treating him just like it does the rest of us mortals, he's not too happy."

Kinsella was though, obviously. Pork and chicken sat on his plate and he wasn't even looking at it.

"So. The question on the table for the expert is, would a Russian hit team have the balls to drive their own ride on a job? Your turn, Tommy."

O'Meara could have been grinding rocks with his back teeth. "The answer would be 'yes.' The Russians have no fear. It's that simple."

He leaned forward slightly. "You have to understand one thing. You aren't dealing with ordinary thugs. Most of these individuals are ex-intelligence agents, military special forces. At the very least, they are professional criminals. Some were in prison until the Soviet Union fell and the *organizatsiya* bought off the right officials and got them out.

"Anywhere we would lock them up in this country would be the Ritz by comparison. Do you follow me?" His eyes burned into me.

"Smarter than the wops, got the balls of the spics and more money than all the bruthas. Isn't that what you said?" Kinsella asked.

O'Meara kept looking my way. "They make deals with everybody, even people they've fucked with. On the one hand, they're selling military helicopters to the Colombians, missiles, a submarine, even. With the other hand, they're yanking away the dope business wherever they can. What do they need with Colombian dope when they have the Afghan poppy fields?"

"Whoa. Back up," I said. "A submarine?"

O'Meara brushed a speck of lint off his jacket sleeve.

"Drug Enforcement caught the Colombians after they took delivery. Of course, they impounded it. The Colombians claimed they wanted to offer sightseeing cruises off Miami. A search revealed what it had been outfitted to do. Carry forty tons of cocaine right under the noses of the Coast Guard."

"Makes you wonder who tipped off the DEA."

"The Russians get to keep the money and make a friend with the G at the same time," Kinsella offered.

"If I were the Colombians, I'd be taking a second look at the fusing and guidance systems on those missiles," I said.

Unwilling to talk in the beginning, O'Meara looked miffed at our interruption. "Consider this *mafiya* a multi-national company. Fortune 100. To them, putting the gangs out of the drug business represents nothing more than a hostile takeover. The Italians, the Vietnamese, the Hispanics, the Asian triads all recruit at street-level. The Russians, they look higher on the food chain. They want an advantage. They go for the MBA's right out of business school. Most college graduates feel they're owed a nice office and a magnificent salary. The Russians are right there to make the offer."

"What, they set up booths at job fairs?"

He nodded. "Don't you think the top companies have eyes on campus to watch for the best and brightest? No different with the Russians. They can hire headhunters as easily as anyone."

"So the graduates don't know who they're working for until it's too late?"

He squinted at me. "You're thinking these kids are naive, are you? Not very damned likely. Those at the head of the class are often the most rebellious. As I said, they don't want to start their career in the fucking mailroom like daddy did. Offer the right student the right amount of cash and the chance to challenge authority and they'd go to work for the devil himself. Terrorist groups have known that for years. Do you follow?"

"Unfortunately, I do."

"If they don't know up front, they figure it out. By then, they're caught in the middle. They're responsible for targeting new areas of business, estimating market share. They've redefined credit card fraud and identity theft. Not to mention money laundering, and dope distribution."

"What about Federov? Did he start out as a spy or one of these whiz kids?"

"Federov," O'Meara nodded. "Interpol says he got his MBA at twenty. Moscow University. His father was *mafiya* for years. Might even have been KGB or GRU. There's no mention of Federov doing any of that. Strictly a money man. Which is not to say he's ever been shy about ordering people killed. There are some tough boys in the IRA who'd look like virgins if you matched up their body count with his."

"I'd think the bosses would want to keep a rising star like that close to home."

"To the contrary, son. He came to the U.S. about eight years ago. Feds say he ran a smooth little gasoline scam that brought the mob maybe 100 million. Smooth because his name never officially surfaced in connection with it. The Italians took the fall. He's a ghost. Which is why the bosses supposedly wanted him in Chicago. Nice, low-key approach."

"Yeah, that kid hanging from the crossbeams in Uptown was subtle as hell," I said.

O'Meara shook his head. His accent became more pronounced. "For them t'was! No cars have been blown up in the Loop have they? No storefronts torched on Michigan Avenue? Anything less is subtle to these people. In New York, they've been known to walk into a restaurant, shoot a man nine times in the face, then get down on the floor and pick up their brass. That's in front of witnesses, now. What's that tell ya?"

Kinsella who had been chewing his way through two monster servings of barbecue paused and looked up. "Kinda answers the question about what car they'd drive to a job, huh?"

"They have no fear," O'Meara repeated.

"Okay, getting back to the car, then. If you don't have Mookie, where does this description of a Jaguar come from?" I asked.

"Can't tell you. But it's Grade A solid," Kinsella said. Which meant someone had a snitch or an undercover in the Black Gangsta Lords. He held up a finger, finished chewing.

"Got something else, though."

"Federov broke tradition and did the hit himself?"

He snorted. "Two witnesses in Aurora say the car used out there was a Jag, too."

"A drive-by in a Jag?" I could tell he wanted me to be as excited as he was, but I couldn't see how this was going to help me find Brooke's killer.

"Wasn't a drive-by. They set Ruiz's car up with a nail in the tire. He pulls over to fix his flat, they pull over too, make like they're going to help. Get up nice and close and put a .22," he leaned across the table and prodded a thick finger up against my left temple. "Right here. People a couple houses down say they saw two people talking to the guy, then they saw the Jag driving away."

"They didn't see the hit?"

"Didn't see it or hear it. These shooters are pros. What can I say? Aurora cops get enough killings, though. I guess they know how to interpret evidence. Found the guy stretched out next to the tire with his brains leaking into the gutter."

"Thanks for the colorful image."

"You ain't heard the best part. You got people telling you Federov is clear on the girl?"

He reached inside his jacket and brought out his police radio. He stood it upright next to his water glass. Then, he produced a wrinkled piece of paper and shoved it across the table at me. It was a copy of an Officer's Supplemental Report, what a detective or beat cop uses to add information to a case file. I saw the name TALMADGE, BROOKE and the address of her brother's apartment building, 1082 Gatewood Terrace. Following the page down I saw it had been submitted by an Officer E. M. Graff, Beat 2424, yada yada yada…

Reporting Officer was assigned to assist Area Three detectives in their canvass and speak to tenants in neighboring building at 1087 Gatewood Terrace. At 2347 hours this date, R/O spoke with a subject LAZZAR, ELDON, in apartment 4K. MR. LAZZAR stated he came home approximately 2000 hours this date and attempted to find parking. In process of circling the block at that time, MR. LAZZAR states he observed a vehicle exit the alley behind 1082 Gatewood Terrace. MR LAZZAR states said vehicle appeared to be operated in an erratic manner and nearly struck the rear of his vehicle. MR. LAZZAR states Vehicle two then continued eastbound into the alley across the street. MR. LAZZAR states when he found parking and exited his vehicle, he observed the aforementioned Vehicle Two pass in front of 1082 Gatewood Terrace and proceed eastbound on Gatewood. MR. LAZZAR states he believes Vehicle Two to be a late model if not new Jaguar, model unknown, but which he referred to as,"the cheap one." MR.

LAZZAR *further states he was unable to see a license plate number due to distance and darkness.*

I felt a hand compress my chest. "Holy Maude," I breathed. It was my favorite aunt's favorite saying and an expression I couldn't recall ever speaking aloud before.

"I thought the car description sounded familiar so I went back through the canvass reports," he said. "Bunch of people claimed they'd seen cars. I breezed right past it the first time around."

I nodded slowly. "OK," I said. I read through the report again just to keep my eyes occupied while I got my head straight. "So…you've got these guys using a .22 in Aurora, and using a fucking band saw or whatever in Uptown. But they crush Brooke's throat? Make it look like they were just clumsy and she was an accident?"

"Why not?" He flicked the edge of the page with a finger. "Maybe it was just one of 'em. He wants to get on top of her right now, take her down and out so he can finish the job some other way. Who knows? Maybe this Federov said do it quick but up close and personal. Maybe the fucker's a kink. What if they get bored and try new things?"

He stared at me. "Who-the-fuck-knows? We get Mookie and he gives up the plate on that Jag, we may have ourselves a couple of shooters. Maybe one of them did the girl."

"How do you plan to go after him if you're supposed to keep hands off?"

"Tommy O and me ain't the only ones ticked at the Feds, are we Tommy?" O'Meara hadn't moved so much as an eyelash as he listened to our exchange and he said nothing now. Kinsella grinned.

"He's got some guys, I got some guys."

He sounded like the sheriff in an old Western but I couldn't quite read what I saw in his eyes so I refrained from pointing that out. Instead, I said, "The Feds got a lot more guys."

"Hey, fuck 'em. It's our town. And the fucking Russians killed our crooks."

He had inhaled all the chicken and curly-q fries. I finished telling him about Alicia Witting and Sunny's lead to the lawyer.

"Jerome Belzer," I said to O'Meara. "Sound familiar?"

O'Meara shook his head. Then he looked at Kinsella. "Need me for anything else?"

Kinsella was stone faced. "Nah, Tommy. Thanks, anyway. You want some take out? Hector'd be glad to put a plate together for you."

"I think not." He left, back straight, head up looking neither left nor right and without even a friendly wave.

As the door closed behind him, I said, "OK, what's the deal with you and Mr. Happy Face?"

"Liked him, didya? At work he's known as Captain Thomas O'Meara. But at home and to his close friends…well, they know him as Captain Thomas O'Meara."

His cigarette was down to the nub. He stubbed it out in the remains of shredded pork. He scooped up the last hot dog in the waxed paper lining from the tray the food had come on, rolled it in a couple of napkins, and stuffed it in his pocket, congealing cheese and all. A nod to Hector and he was out the front door. I followed him to his car. He leaned on the hood.

"You were saying about O'Meara?" I persisted.

Kinsella held up his right hand and turned it into a fist. "Let's just say I got Tommy's balls right here."

"And?"

"And, shit. He's married to my ex-old-lady's cousin. Second marriage for 'em both. She has a teenage son. Tommy's never been fond of the kid, who knows why. About a year ago, Peggy, the wife, gives me a call. The kid's run off. I go looking. I find this 14-year-old at a friend's house. He's got a shiner and some nice bruises around the kidneys. We go back and forth a little bit, him telling me he got into a fight with some neighborhood kid. The real story I finally get from him is that Tommy found him smoking a little weed and started smacking 'im around. The kid was pissing blood, had a cracked rib, generally pretty fucked up.

"This isn't the kind of thing the department wants to hear about its men of rank, y'know? So I get affidavits from everybody from the kid's friends to the E.R. docs who treated him. I grab Tommy when he gets home from work one night and I give him the facts of life. No O.P.S. investigation. No department sanctions. And I don't throw him down a flight of stairs. In return, I might need his weight inside the department from time to time."

Kinsella fixed his eyes on me. "This's the first time I tried him. The prick. But he's helpful. Give him that. Between the two of us, we can create a little breathing room, maybe time enough to find this Mookie character."

"And the kid's okay?"

"Mama and the boy moved out on ol' Tommy after I told her what was up. Tommy don't like me much. Never has, though." He let his fist fall open. "You want to ride along tonight on Mookie patrol?"

I shook my head. "If you find him, I'd appreciate knowing where it leads. Brooke's girlfriend gave me a guy who might know what kind of games she was playing. Who she was blackmailing. And I still want to find her brother."

"C'mon, Reno. I saw your face when I told you about the car. How much more evidence you need that Federov is the guy?"

"He may be. But I want to run down these leads." An idea occurred to me. "Can you get me the list of evidence recovered from Brooke's apartment?

"I told you, we never recovered those phony ID's you were yakking about..."

"I remember. But there's something nagging at me about that night, maybe something I saw there. I can't dredge up what it is. I'm thinking the evidence list might help jog my memory."

Kinsella fiddled with the controls atop his portable radio as he considered the up and down side of that for him. "I can get it but I'm not feeling warm and fuzzy about making you a copy."

"I don't need a copy. Call me when you have it and I'll meet up with you."

"Jesus Christ, McCarthy. You want a blowjob, too?"

CHAPTER 15

▼

After he left, I sat in my car and watched two vans drop off about a dozen mostly Hispanic day-workers in front of a day-labor agency. Instead of going inside the storefront office, however, they shuffled like drones toward a tavern down the street. I glanced at my watch. 5:30 p.m. Of course. Silly me. It was cocktail hour. The place looked like it could have been one of the joints where I used to find my old man. A different language might be spoken, some of the drinks might have ethnic names and a strange flavor, but I bet I'd recognize the smell of beer and vomit and lives gone stale.

Sometimes, he'd come home with me willingly. It depended on a simple formula. Rate of consumption times length of stay times his case load minus guilt about leaving Mom and me alone. What he was drinking figured into the computation, too. Boilermakers invariably got me cracked upside the head for embarrassing him in front of his friends. The ones still sober enough to realize his son was trying to drag him off his stool, that is.

I checked in again with Sunny to avoid traveling too far down memory lane.

"The bad news is that you probably won't get an opportunity to talk to Mrs. Talmadge any time soon," she said. "Her condo seems to be running itself. Bills are all being paid by a trust officer at Bank of America. The lady is elsewhere."

"Where would that be?"

"That depends on who you talk to. One neighbor has her at Betty Ford. Another put her at Hazelden."

"How long has she been gone?"

"People's Gas and Com Ed bills show her utility usage goes flat starting in March. No water's been turned on, either. There's been zero activity on any of her charge cards for the same time frame. Sort of rules out an extended vacation. Fits with someone who's been institutionalized, though."

"Places like that don't let you camp out there forever, do they?"

"Mmmh, four or five months wouldn't be unusual for a hard-core abuser."

"I take it the neighbors say that's what she is?"

"I didn't talk to them myself. Angela used the criss-cross and called around the building. She says more talked than not. They told her Mrs. Talmadge likes the sauce. They mentioned her son, too. Apparently he'd stay there on nights when he'd been out partying on Rush Street and didn't find a date willing to go home with him."

"Anything about Brooke?"

"That's the good news. According to Angela, the neighbors called Mrs. Talmadge's daughter a regular visitor. Several times she brought along a big Russian fellow."

"How do they know he was Russian?"

"One of the neighbors grew up in Moscow. She told Angela they used to have nice chats."

"Heartwarming. So she brought him home to meet Mom, huh? How long ago was this?"

"Possibly around Christmas. Angela says the Russian woman couldn't remember exactly."

"Lends some credence to the idea they were still lovey dovey," I said. "At least at that point."

"He still could've killed her to keep her from leaving, Reno. And isn't March about the time Brooke moved to Washington? I find that pretty interesting timing."

"You're thinking maybe Mom knew the game plan and drank herself into Never Never Land over it?"

"How about Mom knew the game plan and Brooke wanted her stashed somewhere safe if it all went to pooty?"

"Any chance of…"

She read my mind. "Both clinics have the best firewalls made. Their patient files aren't on an internet-connected system."

Hearing that annoyed me so I changed the subject. "You guys are spending a lot of time on this. Russ, Mark. Now Angela and whoever you're planning to put on Belzer."

"They're between jobs, McCarthy. Just leave it be. None of them is objecting."

"You know I can't pay…"

"Oh, will you leave it?" She snapped. "Mention us from the podium when you pick up your Pulitzer, okay? 'I owe it all to my brave colleagues, who helped me when I was down…'"

I grunted and snapped the cell closed. I was suddenly in a piss-poor mood. I eased my head onto the back of the seat and closed my eyes. I should have been elated that information was starting to come together to link Federov to Brooke's murder. Why couldn't I feel satisfied?

According to Kinsella's cop colleague, the guy routinely ordered people killed and had been doing so for years. Setting up a hit on Brooke would have taken as much effort as downing a shot of *Stolichnaya*. If he even drank. Maybe he didn't. Maybe he'd had an alcoholic father, too, and that was what had driven him to become a murderous mob boss.

Why didn't I like him for doing Brooke? I had Sela Grauman saying they'd been in love. I had good 'ol Judge Bridges saying she seemed more hurt by him than scared.

Wow. Now *there's* some clear and convincing evidence.

Wait. That wasn't everything. No.

I had my memory of Brooke Talmadge standing her ground in the Marriott parking lot as the Russian goon approached her, and then doing her best to cripple him in any way she could after he made his play.

I had the fact she'd stuck around town for several days after her return from Washington, taking time to try a blackmail scheme to raise money for her departure.

If Federov had wanted to kill her, she would have known. The Brooke Talmadge I was learning about was street smart. No question she would have put the obvious pieces together. And, had she known, she would have disappeared.

I had some other stuff too, but as I'd told Kinsella it just wasn't ready to make an appearance. Something had tried to wiggle loose when I'd been at the apartment earlier and now a tidbit from my conversation with Kinsella bugged me.

He had talked about a witness. A car. A Jaguar; the "cheap one." The evidence log.

I had seen something when I kicked my way into that apartment. Something in the flash of lightning. It had imprinted, but not clearly. So make it real, I thought.

I squeezed my eyes closed, as though fighting a headache. The thought stood silent in the periphery of my brain. Animal, vegetable or mineral? I felt, suddenly, if I could just turn my head fast enough, it would reveal itself. It even had a shape. Vague, amorphous, but in the form of a...

A car roared past, distracting me. My eyes snapped open. Damn. I sensed I'd almost finessed it free but picking the brain when it's in lockdown is about as easy as randomly twirling open the tumblers on a bank vault.

I took out my notebook and found the stick-it sheet Sela had given me with Patrick Vega's address. It was on the southeastern edge of Uptown, geographically not really very far from Lake Shore Drive but miles lower in economic altitude. I knew the area. Not as rough as where the two gangbangers' bodies had been found, but it's never a neighborhood to underestimate. I thought about calling Sunny back to see if any of her people wanted to take a ride with me but discarded the idea without acting on it. This I could manage on my own.

I put the Mustang into a lot near Thorek Hospital where I wouldn't have to worry about it. The rag top sometimes invites a knife slash even if there's nothing but a cheap AM/FM radio in the dash. I took the precaution of slipping the little Kahr automatic off my ankle and into the pocket of my sport coat. Then, I walked three blocks back north and east a bit to the Garden Oaks.

One of the few rooming houses that haven't gone the way of the wrecking ball, it had a tired gray stone facade and worn steps leading up to an entrance remarkable only in that the glass panels in the double doors were missing, replaced by two sheets of plywood that announced the name of a board-up service. The doors themselves were propped open to catch the evening's faint breeze. I wondered if the owners had gotten tired of replacing the glass every time someone put a bullet or a body through it.

Two men, one about 70, the other a little more than half that, were sitting on the steps and playing checkers on a board laid out across one of the concrete banisters. Neither looked up as I approached.

Given the tension in the younger guy's shoulders, and the way the older one kept letting his eyes drift toward the shadowed interior of the entryway, I suspected there might be a game of another sort going on inside. Drugs? If so, this set of lookouts made sense. A passing cop wouldn't give the two men a second glance. On a hot night, the front stoop is the neighborhood's living room.

After thinking about it for a couple of seconds, I realized I might have stumbled upon a meth lab. They've drifted into the city from out in the western states in the past few years and I've heard some landed in Uptown. If that's what was inside, even the front stoop wasn't somewhere I wanted to linger. The volatile chemicals involved in the production of methamphetamine, and the occasional ineptitude of the cookers, make explosions an occasional byproduct.

Then again, it could just be two guys playing checkers.

"Evening," I said from the bottom of the steps. I kept both hands in the clear.

"That it be," the older man said. He had a small island of gray hair surrounded by liver spots and more gray in eyebrows as thick as my mustache. His profile sagged a bit on the left side as he bent over the checkerboard, but he used his left hand to move the pieces.

"You the desk man?"

"Desk man!" He hooted. "Nah. Can'tcha tell? I'm the con-see-urge. We gots a full house."

"I don't want a room."

"Didn't figure you did."

When he stared up I saw a wandering left eye, the right one apparently normal. Bell's palsy?

"Ain't got any information, neither." The younger man spoke as he made a jump and crowned his piece. "*Empty* house on that subject you might say."

He was an American Indian, his black hair combed straight back without a part, his face heavily pockmarked. He wore a coffee stained t-shirt under a tan jacket and kept scratching his belly about waist-level as though he liked having his hand near there.

I leaned down and put two tens on the lowest step.

"Patrick Vega. No beef. I'm just a working stiff who wants to ask him a couple of questions."

The old man slid one of his crowns out of harm's way and paid no more attention to the money than he had to me.

"Patty-cake Vega, huh?" The Indian snorted. "Well, buddy, you're saying two of the words he most likes hearing joined together. 'Stiff' and 'beef'."

"He around?"

"Fuck no," the Indian said. Without seeming to move he made both tens disappear. "Nice night, he's on the stroll. Got to keep that rent money coming in, high-class place like this. Gotta make the rent or my man here throw his faggy ass out."

A bit of drool appeared on the older man's sagging lip and then fell. It made a dark splotch on the edge of the checkerboard. "No need for you to bad mouth the kid now. He ain't done nothing to you, has he?"

The Indian made a fist. "He ever tries he'll find him some beef right here."

"Real man, ain't you? Leastways he's friendly. Cleans up after himself. Helps out around the place. Not like some people I could mention."

This had the flavor of a favorite argument and, given what might be just inside those doors, I didn't want to stick around as tonight's referee.

"Does he work somewhere nearby?"

"You got wax in those ears, man? I said he's on the stroll. He's a cock-sucking boy hooker. How much you think he could make in this neighborhood?"

"Any ideas where I should look?"

Perseverance. Always worked for me before. Why not here? So what if he had a nine millimeter a couple of inches from his hand and a brain that appeared to have been dunked in a deep fat fryer?

The old man snickered toward the checkerboard. Whether he was reacting to my question or to the game I didn't know. He had left one of his pieces as bait and now held a king ready for a double jump. The Indian didn't seem to notice.

"That twenty of yours got you where he's *not*. Cost you another ten to find out where he *is*."

I had a five already palmed and let him see a corner of it. He reached for the bill. I didn't let it go. He snickered at me.

The old man spoke up. "You know Hubbard Street, down by the river? That yuppie neighborhood or whatever it is? He likes it down there."

Then, as the Indian sputtered, the old man made his double jump.

*   *   *   *

Vice, assorted tactical units and every uniform who's ever worked a beat car in the area, has tried to shoo away the male prostitutes and he-shes who seem to favor the south end of River North. They don't shoo. Like loons fishing on a northern lake they'll disappear under the surface for awhile and then bob right back up again, mostly around Clark and Hubbard or the few blocks in that immediate vicinity.

Starting in the shadow of a couple of Chicago's most notable landmarks, Marina Towers and the Merchandise Mart, River North is a neighborhood of warehouses gentrified into art galleries, upscale shops, eclectic bars and trendy restaurants, some of which have dinner reservation waiting lists of six months or more. Up to about midnight, especially on a summer evening, you can figure on seeing any number of people walking the streets. There's enough pedestrian movement, in fact, that you might fail to notice the boys in their leather pants and t-shirts or tight jeans and halter tops circulating, eyeing the crowds and checking out each car that slows near them with a scrutiny that would put a Secret Service agent to shame. Most of the boy hookers are Black, but a spattering of Hispanics and even young white males strut their stuff there once in awhile, as well.

I knew Patrick Vega to be a light-skinned Mexican fellow. Sela had described him as just past six feet tall, with thick brown hair and the broad shoulders and narrow waist of a swimmer. She called his looks "boyish, not pretty, but you might think he's a teenager instead of in his late twenties." As to what might make him stand out in a crowd, she told me he loved a brown-fringed leather jacket Brooke had given him. He wore it through all seasons, merely shedding his shirt to stay cooler in warm weather.

It was getting on toward eight o'clock when I did my first, quick circuit of each of the streets in a six-block radius of Clark and Hubbard. I saw a lot of couples walking hand in hand and some families with older, roughhousing kids in tow, but it appeared to be too early for the professionals to hit the sidewalks. Killing time, I cruised up to the Rock 'n Roll MacDonald's on Ohio and waited fifteen minutes in the drive through to get a Diet Coke. Afterward, I parked in their lot for a few minutes to people watch.

I sipped my Coke and gazed at the tourists passing by on their way back to their hotels, burdened with packages from Nordstrom and Orvis and Bloomingdale's and Nike. Two television-station trucks rushed past, one from Channel Five and the other from Channel Two. I could hear sirens in the distance and wondered if the news crews might be headed to a fire.

Much as I miss the I-team work, I miss the adrenaline buzz of breaking news even more. I suspect it's not much different than the sensation some cops and firefighters experience when they're first to arrive at a big scene. You never know what you're going to find. That's the essence of the thing. The unexpected. A huge fire burning out of control along an entire city block. A garish murder.

At the same time, the idea of watching someone's house go up in flames, or talking to a parent who has just lost a child, is gut-wrenching. Interviewing any kind of victim or their survivors is enough to make even the toughest reporter wince and question their level of dedication. Or it used to be, anyway.

More and more I see young reporters and producers floating through the tragedy in other people's lives with a total lack of interest or sensitivity, all the while chanting the mantra, "Get them crying! It'll make awesome video, man."

I'll always remember one of the first fatal fires I covered. Hoping to appear seasoned and cynical, I swaggered into the apartment building and up to the fire marshal. He stood outside the unit where an elderly man had burned to death. A couple of portable lights had been set up but the smoke that hung in the air diffused their illumination and gave everyone gathered in the hall the look of ghosts fearful to leave their mortal remains.

"Where's the crispy critter?" I asked. I carried a video camera on my shoulder and was chewing gum like a tough guy. All I lacked to announce my occupation was a hat with a "Press" card in the brim.

"The victim died in that apartment," the marshal replied quietly, "But his wife and son are standing right behind you."

*   *   *   *

Full of happy thoughts, I pulled out of the MacDonald's just as it was getting dark and took another tour of the area. The boy toys had started to appear. Most of the hookers I saw in my quick check, though, were Black. The others appeared in drag and could have been white, Black, Hispanic or Laotian water buffaloes. I wasn't going to be able to pick Patrick out of the pack without a program. I'd have to wander and ask some questions.

I left my car behind a restaurant, waving off several eager valets who probably would have jammed it between a Mack truck and a garbage Dumpster, or double parked it somewhere sure to win a ticket to the city impoundment lot. Then I went to meet and greet.

Of the first five people I spoke to, four were pros. The fifth was a straight woman who appeared puzzled by my questions and a little frightened that I was asking them of her. The sixth was a guy with glossed lips wearing leather pants, a half-tee and a single handcuff fastened around his right wrist. He leaned against the wall of what had been an office furniture warehouse but now seemed to be a shop selling large, paper-mache horses and dogs. He watched me with the same opaque gaze as the animals in the window display. When I got close enough, my proximity tripped a tirade.

"Oh, man! What is it with you cops, anyway? You get your jollies rousting queers? Is this your idea of fun?"

I had reviewed my options walking up to him. There was only one approach I could think of that might work quickly.

"You know Tommy at the Beau and Arrow?" I asked. The Beau is a gay bar on North Broadway in Boy Town and Tommy Nichols, the owner, is as well known in the gay community as John Ashcroft. Tommy's singlehandedly done more for people suffering from AIDS than most fund raisers. He finds them jobs, places to stay and, for those who are dying, caring, helpful folks to remain with them until they take their last breath. We'd exchanged favors during my years at Channel 14 and I had no doubt he would remember me.

He regarded me uneasily. "So what if I do, Sweetmeat?"

I held up my cell. "Call him. Ask him if you should talk straight, pardon the expression, to a guy named Reno McCarthy."

He didn't respond right away, just stared at me as though I'd asked him to set himself on fire. While he was working out a nasty retort, a Lincoln town car swerved around the corner. A lean black guy in a nylon jumpsuit climbed from the front seat. The guy's feet barely hit the sidewalk before the driver accelerated away from the curb as if a cop, or his conscience, had just appeared in his rear-view mirror.

"Hi, honey," Jumpsuit called to me. "I just love a man with a beard, and such a pretty one. Josie, why do all the hotties show up when I'm otherwise occupied?"

"Tend to your own corner, bitch," Josie snapped. He snatched the phone from me and I stood where I could watch both of them. The newcomer laughed his way down the block and into a wooden shack of a building that advertised "Live Girls Live!" and "Hard Core" in neon over its front door.

Josie's conversation lasted less than a minute but he kept his voice so low I couldn't hear what he said. When he finished, he handed the phone back wordlessly and pulled a pack of cigarettes from a back pocket of his jeans. He lit one up and blew a thoughtful smoke ring before saying anything.

"Tommy says you're OK. What do you want from me?"

"A guy named Patrick." I described him, not bothering to use his last name. That's part of the code of the street. Everybody's on a first-name-only basis with everyone else. No one wants to know too much.

"Patrick the Mouth. We calls him that, and not because he's so talented with it, neither. 'Cause he's jabbering all the time."

"Seen him around tonight?"

He sucked in his cheeks. "Yeah. I seen him tonight. So what? What's he done? I need the info, man."

"Josie, I've known you for five minutes and already you want to know more of my business than my mother ever did. Just chill, ok? I'm not going to rip his fingernails out with pliers. I just want to talk to him."

"Any cash in it?"

"For him, probably. If he can tell me what I need to know."

"Well then you tell him he owes me a referral fee if he talks to you. I could have sent you on a wild goose chase you know. Lied and said he was up north tonight."

"I take it he's around somewhere?"

The tip of his cigarette glowed red. "He's working. He'll probably be back in a few minutes. Dumb bitch."

"Why do you say that?"

"One of his friends got killed this week, a girl he used to work with, and he's acting like life doesn't matter any more. Patrick has had so many breaks, because he's so beautiful? And now he's just being so stupid. Going back to the rough trade and everything."

"What rough trade?" I said.

"Like those Russian boys he went off with just now? I know they're all blond and hung nice, but they barely speak English and they're always so mean…"

I felt as if I'd just swung open the door of one of the Medical Examiner's freezers.

Josie saw my expression change. "What? What did I say?"

"How do you know they were Russians?"

"My auntie lives in a neighborhood where there are a lot of those kind. Russians. Polish, Hungarians, some Germans. A regular United Nations."

"Did Patrick know these guys?" I snapped.

"I…I have no idea."

"What did they look like?"

"Just big blond boys. The one I saw anyway had on a jumpsuit, a plain old thing, nothing fancy like Louis' over there."

"What kind of car?" Please, not a Jag.

"It was a brown panel van. He only left a couple of minutes ago. What's the matter? He'd never let them take him out of the neighborhood."

"Let" wouldn't be the operative word if he had a shotgun shoved up his nose. I pushed a business card with my cell number at his face. "If he comes back, have him call me. Don't let him out of your sight. In fact, take him somewhere there's a crowd."

Now Josie was panicked. He grabbed my arm in one strong hand. "He's in trouble isn't he? I always told him not to go with rough trade. I *told* that bitch…"

I wrenched free and ran for my car.

Logic told me that, in five minutes, a brown panel van could have gone anywhere and that I stood no chance of finding it. That they would come for him now, just before I reached him, infuriated me. Was I being watched again, this time by Federov's people?

OK, maybe the two guys were just johns who happened to be Russian.

The panel van and the jumpsuits made me think not. Panel vans are nondescript, easily hidden. Jumpsuits, also known as "splatter suits," are the preferred kill-wear of pros who want to keep their own clothing free of their victim's blood.

By the time I reached the Mustang, I was out of breath and trying hard to focus on what I should do. Calling the cops, explaining everything to them, would take too long.

I ripped out of the parking lot and headed west toward Franklin and the Mart and all the shadowed alleys under the El tracks and along the river. I wanted to bring in some extra troops to help me search, but the way I was driving I didn't dare take my hands off the wheel to feel under my seat for the radio Sunny had loaned me, and there was no way I could dial a number on my cellular. I needed to cover every block, every side street and every alley I could reach in the next few minutes.

Federov was tidying up and Patrick Vega was a loose end. He knew about Brooke. Maybe he could put Federov away. Had to be. Unless I found the van first, and I might already be too late, Patrick was history. A couple of slugs in the back of the head and they'd find pieces of him stuffed into a trash can or floating in the slime of the Chicago River.

I skidded to a stop under the El tracks.

A stooped and bald-headed Black guy selling *Streetwise* appeared from the shadows as I tried to figure which direction to go. The river was no more than three blocks away. If I remembered right, I was in the crotch of the Y the river makes just west of the Merchandise Mart. I could go straight or right and still hit it.

"Help a homeless man?" The newspaper vendor called. He kept his distance from the car.

"Did you see a brown van go by here a few minutes ago? White guy driving?"

"Ran through the light, almost hit me. Yeah, I saw it."

"Which way?"

He thrust his arm out to the right. "Gonna give him a ticket?"

"More than that, brother," I muttered.

The streetlights became scarce. I drew the Kahr out of my jacket and shoved it under my right leg, grip out. This was warehouse country. The broad outlines of darkened buildings crawled up either side of the street, which was bisected by a long-unused rail spur. I wished for a spotlight. I made do with the flashlight from the glove box. I flashed it into every crevice I passed. If the goons saw it, maybe they'd risk a shot at me and that would give Patrick Vega a tiny last chance to get away.

I hoped and feared the cops would stop me to ask what I was doing. Maybe I could convince them to help. More likely, I'd spend what little time Patrick had left trying to explain my fool's errand.

I rolled all the windows down and hoped. I think I even prayed a bit.

My optimism died, probably at the same instant Patrick Vega did. Two gunshots up and off to my left made me slam my foot down on the accelerator. I grabbed the little automatic with my right and steered wildly with my left, grunting as a couple of potholes nearly put my head through the canvas top.

The brown van was nosed into space that had once been a railroad siding between two brick warehouses, a half block from the river. I almost missed it.

I shot past the entrance, nearly put the brake pedal through the floor, and yanked the gearshift into reverse. The tires squealed and smoked. Just as I spun the wheel, I saw a flash and then heard the flat bark of a third gunshot echo off the bricks.

My headlights illuminated three figures on the right side of the van. Two up, one down. The two still standing moved. The one on the ground didn't.

It's damned hard to do a bootleg turn in a narrow alley, but I gave the brakes another workout and whipped the wheel hard left. The back end of the car slid around. More gunshots erupted, so close together the sound blended into one massive BOOM.

I scrabbled for the door handle while I slapped the gearshift into park with my gun hand. Before I could get the transmission safely notched, though, the car clipped the side of the building and crunched to a stop about 25 yards from the van. The door popped open and I fell out.

I was on my knees, instantly.

My dad's voice snapped in my brain, *"Show 'em you got firepower!"*

Through the passenger side window, I saw the two guys rushing at me. I lifted the Kahr in both hands, double tapped, and dropped again, sliding back so the engine compartment and two tires were between me and them. Slugs slapped into the Mustang. I heard the almost musical "Zz-zing" a bullet makes when it nearly parts your hair. Like a bee, some say. More like a spinning chunk of lead traveling with enough velocity to rip apart your vital organs.

I took a breath.

Suddenly, no more shots.

My nose felt like it had been used for target practice. I tasted blood. I imagined the two Russians advancing toward me in the dark.

"Shoot, damn it! Keep their heads down!" My dad's voice again.

I sprung up, loosed off another two shots, fell down behind cover. This time I thought I heard running footsteps. I risked another pop up. I saw two figures headed away from me, running toward the van. I fired twice more. One of my slugs whined off metal. The guy on the right stumbled, then lunged toward the passenger side door. The van's engine exploded to life before his feet completely cleared the ground.

The van roared into the street. I jumped into the Mustang and gunned it to where Patrick's body lay. I clicked the flashlight on, saw the fringe on his jacket. Two bullet holes were punched into his back. A pool of dark blood spread from his skull.

I sped from the alley, fishtailing slightly as I cranked the wheel in the direction the van had taken.

Brake lights flashed and disappeared ahead of me. I floored the accelerator again, cursing myself for not keeping the Mustang's engine in better condition. Where the hell was I? The Merchandise Mart loomed up on my left like some kind of huge monster born out of the goop in the water beyond. Next to it was the Mart Plaza and its Holiday Inn with rooms that fronted the river. I had gotten lost down here half a dozen times as a reporter covering events at the Mart and the hotel. The streets are a vague maze of dead ends and switchbacks into parking lots. Great.

Then again, the guys in the van were from Russia, for chrissakes. Just having pavement to drive on was probably confusing the hell out of them.

The van slowed as it bounced across some railroad tracks. I closed to within two car lengths, read the license plate, then dropped back. The guy on the passenger side didn't like that. He leaned out his window holding something long and cylindrical. There were suddenly pops and flashes and my windshield took two hits. I realized this was "Alias" without Jennifer Garner and with no guarantees I'd be around to have my contract picked up for next season.

We flew up a ramp. When the van reached the top, the driver whipped it in a turn so tight he risked rolling over. It stayed upright but skidded sideways across the street and bounced off a concrete retaining wall in a shower of sparks. I took the turn, too, and immediately recognized where I was. In his obviously panicked urge to get away, the van's driver had dead-ended them. The entrance to a parking garage lay straight ahead. The passenger pulled himself back inside just as the van blew through the turnstile and snapped off its plywood arm.

Terrific. Now maybe the director of this weird episode would jump out, yell "Cut!" and we could all go play grabass with the script girls.

No way.

Just inside the garage, the van sideswiped a parked Mercedes and slammed to a halt. The two guys bailed out, saw I wasn't backing off, and laid on the firepower again. I veered right to avoid entering the structure. The Mustang's windshield spider webbed and burst inward. The car jumped the sidewalk outside the garage entrance and slammed into the waist-high exterior wall. The front end buckled. The hood popped. The belt held me tight.

Two accidents in one day. Bye bye insurance.

I groped for the belt release. Slugs whined off the windshield frame and the hood and tufts of upholstery ripped loose from the seat next to me. Pieces of glass bit into my hand as I forced open the door. I hit the ground hard enough on my left shoulder that my teeth snapped together.

Two of them, I thought. Here I am squirming around on the ground with only the wall separating us. They both probably have Uzi's or Mac-10's or, hell, water-cooled .50 caliber helicopter door guns strapped to their backs.

"*Move, son. Now!*" Came my dad's voice. I scrabbled to the back of the car.

One of the Russians stuck his head and shoulders above the garage wall. Just feet away, the Mustang, still in gear, tried mightily to push itself through the concrete. The thug attempted to peer around the sprung hood toward the front of the car. He probably figured I was slumped behind the wheel, dazed from the impact of the collision. When he finally saw the empty seat, I watched his dumpy features register puzzlement. But only for a moment. Like a deer surprised in the woods, his head snapped up. Our eyes met and he grunted in surprise. He swung his automatic rifle toward me.

I didn't wait to hear my dad's voice.

I shot the Russian twice, as fast as I could pull the trigger. The Kahr's grip slammed against my palm with each recoil. Blood burst from the guy's nose and throat. He folded over backward and disappeared behind the wall.

We make our own luck, the saying goes. Remaining where I was wouldn't be a constructive part of that process.

Staying low, I darted forward several feet until I could hunker down against the wall and feel the concrete at my back. I gave it a three count and popped my head up fast with the gun. I tasted blood. My left hand was on fire from the glass and bits of gravel imbedded in it. Nothing moved inside the garage. The El clattered and screeched by a few blocks away, its noise blocking any other sound.

The shooters' van looked like it was leaning on the Mercedes and there was a pool of dark liquid streaming from underneath both vehicles. The guy I shot was sprawled on his back, arms and legs splayed out, like a kid making a snow angel.

The lower half of his face was missing and blood spurted from his neck where one of the Kahr's 9mm slugs had torn through his carotid artery.

Go, go, go. Instinct again, not Dad.

I squeezed over the wall into the garage, keeping as low a profile as I could. Nevertheless, I nearly bought the proverbial farm, pasture, horse barn and all.

The other Russian's automatic opened up. A spray of concrete chips stung the back of my neck.

"You never hear the one that kills you so you ain't dead yet," Dad sneered.

Someone screamed.

I dropped behind a beater Chevy and sneaked a look toward the sound.

Two women were backing away from the dead shooter. One had her hand over her mouth and the other was trying to hustle her along. A bank of elevators was behind them. The one who looked ready to throw up started to wobble. Her friend caught her under the arm and half-dragged, half-carried her into an elevator. I let out a breath I hadn't realized I was holding.

A door banged open somewhere, then slammed shut. I shoved to my feet. The other Russian had run to the exit on the opposite side of the parking structure.

I pounded across the garage floor, the Kahr in my right hand at eye level, and kicked open the door.

I was across from the Merchandise Mart on Kinzie Street. The Russian ran down Kinzie, sticking as close as he could to the shadows near construction scaffolding that climbed up about two floors of the Mart's exterior. I hustled in pursuit.

He stayed close to the maze of scaffolding for about a block, until he reached an open roll up door that led into the building's lower level and ducked inside. Almost immediately, I heard a yell and then a burst of automatic rifle fire. Fear punched me in the heart.

I reached the door he'd gone through and sagged against the wall next to it. Caught my breath. Listened. Heard running feet. Counted to five. Swiveled around the door frame, gun ready.

A uniformed security guy sprawled outside a small guard shack a couple of feet from the entrance. Bullet wounds stitched him from groin to face. There were holes in the wall of the shed, too. His sidearm lay on the ground next to his hand, barely out of its holster.

I ducked back, took one more deep breath.

"The shooter, dammit! Find the shooter!" My dad demanded. I dropped lower and risked another look.

It was a staging and delivery area with high ceilings and just enough overhead light to display a haphazard collection of vehicles from cars to forklifts. Railroad spur tracks cut into the concrete floor began at a loading dock, snaked around a corner and headed west under the building toward the river. I caught movement along the tracks about 30 yards away.

The Russian, running.

I charged through the doorway, holding my fire in case anyone else was nearby. The Russian squeezed off a burst that probably burned through an entire clip. I dove forward and hit the ground rolling until I slammed into the wheel of a crane truck. Bullets pounded the crap out of a pile of building materials and paint cans on a pallet behind me. A light fixture on the ceiling crackled, snapped and went out. More darkness. Not necessarily a bad thing. I crawled behind a forklift and waited until I heard the crunch of feet hitting gravel. When I could tell he was on the move again, I jogged in pursuit. In the gloom of the remaining light fixtures, I could see only a shadowed form moving away from me, his footfalls amplified in the hollowness of the huge space.

The near-darkness seemed to stretch for blocks and the light decreased the farther I ran. We were under the Apparel Center now. My shoulder ached from all the falling I'd done and the stress of keeping the gun extended in front of me. I was breathing raggedly, mouth dry as I sucked in as much air as I could and then gasped it out. I felt like I had a set of bongos beating in my chest.

Electronic sirens wailed in the distance.

I heard a Metra train headed into Northwestern station. More light ahead. I realized I was looking at an exit about 50 yards in front of me that was barred by a chain link fence and gate. Beyond that had to be the river.

The Russian ducked to his left, stumbled across the tracks, and disappeared into the blackness. I sidestepped to the right and nearly collided with a pickup truck on cement blocks. Two-by-fours jutted over its tailgate. A couple of Cushman carts sat beyond it and then there was no cover at all.

Now where had the son of a bitch gone?

Suddenly terrified that I was in his sights, I dropped flat, then crawled to where I could see through the blocks and under the truck. The sirens died. The train finished rattling around the bend in the river. It got very quiet again.

I waited. The bongo rhythm increased. I waited longer, the Kahr aimed where I'd last seen the Russian. Dust tickled the back of my throat. I swallowed several times to squelch a cough. I waited.

He flinched first.

He eeled around a cherry-picker and made for the exit. I fired twice, rolled hard right, and tried to wedge myself into the ground.

He surprised me. No return fire. As I steadied the Kahr for another try, he took a running leap at the fence. He'd scaled chain-link before. In three quick moves, he was up, sliding over the top and then dropping clear on the other side. I fired twice more. Saw both bullets spark as they spanged off a ventilation shaft at ceiling level well short of my target.

Gone again.

He would either take off running or wait somewhere out there to kill me as I emerged. Either way, I had to get over that fence.

Reaching the exit, I saw he wasn't waiting in ambush. He was headed across a small paved parking area toward the upright iron skeleton that was the abandoned Wolf Point railroad bridge. Beyond that lay the river. The mercury vapor streetlights on the far shore made the water look like a rain-slick highway. If he kept going, past the bridge, he could follow the driveway back out onto Kinzie where he might hurt someone else.

Dropped the Kahr into my jacket pocket. Took two steps. Vaulted onto the fence and felt the twisted tops of chain link digging into my fingers. Hauled myself up. Sharp little spears tore my shirt. I twisted and caught myself to keep from falling. Managed to land upright.

The moment I landed, a car engine roared to life off to my left and sent my heart into triple rhythm. A BMW convertible with a guy behind the wheel rounded the corner from the Apparel Center parking lot and caught the running Russian in the glare of its headlights. The driver braked, obviously startled. The Russian pointed his rifle at the front windshield.

I sprinted around the back of the car to draw his fire and lifted my gun.

The Russian yelled at the Beemer's driver to stop. Brake lights flashed, then glowed steadily as the driver attempted to comply.

Furious, I squeezed off two rounds. The BMW rolled forward. Gutsy driver. I had a clear view of the Russian over my front sight. I fired again, and again.

The BMW rocketed out of the lot and screeched onto Kinzie.

The Russian dropped his rifle, stumbled backward, turned, and seemed to throw himself toward the old bridge. I tracked him with the Kahr. He fell onto the bottom of a flight of stairs that climbed the side of the bridge to the tender's tower. From 15 feet away, I pointed the Kahr at the center of his chest.

"That's it. It's over," I wheezed.

His eyes locked with mine. Wordlessly, using his elbows and butt, he hauled himself up another rung. Another. A third.

"Give it up, man," I pleaded.

"Fuck. You." He sagged against the rusted railing, face in shadow.

I took another step. "Let me see your hands. Put 'em in your lap. I have a cell phone. I'll call an ambulance."

He suddenly leaned back and grinned at me through awful teeth. "*Nyet!*" he sneered. Then damned if he didn't shove himself up yet another rung.

This was fucking ridiculous.

"Damn it, hold on! Just…"

Metal screeched. He jerked forward, grin disappearing. In slow motion, the old stairs sheared off from the top of the frame. He seemed to hang for a moment, then dropped butt-first through the opening and down the far side of the embankment.

I ran forward.

The Russian gunman lay on his back just shy of the water's edge. Two thick pieces of rebar about an inch apart protruded like exclamation points from his chest.

I heard shouts and somebody threw a spotlight on us from across the river. In its glare, his eyes locked open. His mouth opened, closed, opened again.

Then the light blinked out.

My hand holding the Kahr dropped to my side.

CHAPTER 16

▼

Shock and exhaustion pushed me to my hands and knees. I was breathing in tight, hard rasps. Couldn't seem to get beyond that. My throat felt like I'd swallowed a wad of phlegm that was stuck halfway down and wouldn't let air past.

"Concentrate!" I thought. A feeling of lightheadedness came over me and I wanted to lie down right where I was.

Sirens again. Really close, this time. I needed to go.

First, however, I climbed down the embankment and knelt next to the dead man. There was a long, nasty, bullet-sized gash along the side of his head and a hole in his thigh. Neither would have been fatal. The two metal dowels sticking out from next to his heart had killed him.

His eyes and mouth were open wide, shocked. On the ground, partially covered by his big right hand, was a little Colt .25 automatic. I was glad he was the one who died in surprise and not me.

I went through his pockets, feeling like a grave robber out of Dickens. A thick wallet was stuffed into the side pocket of his jumpsuit. No ID, but a nice wad of fifties and hundreds. I left it alone, put the wallet on the ground, stretched my sleeve down to cover my hand and wiped the slimy leather on the grass before stowing it back in his pocket. I didn't touch the gun.

I'm sure it violates some journalistic ethic to get caught kneeling over a dead man with a gun stuck in your waistband, so I fought my way up the slope to the parking lot. My list of options wasn't long. The Mustang wasn't in shape to be driven and was likely surrounded by cops. I'd never make it back there anyway. Kinzie Street would be swarming with copmobiles.

Instead, I followed the curve of the river around to the Apparel Center's own parking garage, then found a door that opened into a labyrinth of hallways. No one in sight. More importantly, no security cameras. I ducked into a rest room and checked myself in the mirror.

I looked like a squirrel who's been trying to hide a cache of nuts. Blood caked my mustache and again seeped from my nose. My jacket was torn in enough places to make me wonder if I hadn't taken a round or two and just hadn't noticed the pain.

My eyes belonged to a killer. Black and emotionless. They scared me. So did the clammy, hung over sensation and the shakes, an electrical buzz that I couldn't control any more than a Parkinson's patient can stop his tremors.

I cleaned up the best I could, using towels and tepid water from the faucets. Took off my sport coat and folded it around the Kahr.

The Kahr people were relatively new to the gun business. I wondered if this one was the first of their line to kill anyone. The thought made me put my hands on either side of the sink and wait until the acid roiling in my stomach and up my throat began to subside.

The coat was a bulky package but as long as I was reasonably clean and presentable, I didn't think anyone other than a cop would question it. I left it on the counter while I tried to get a signal on my cell. It wasn't happening so I picked up the coat and left the rest room in search of a pay phone. The shakes were getting worse and so was the clamminess. I needed help.

Sunny has several telephone lines but only one she answers after she's gone to bed. She calls it the Bat-phone. I needed to lean against a wall while I dialed the number. She answered on the second ring, alert, but annoyed.

"I just shot and killed a guy in a parking lot across from the Merchandise Mart. Another guy's dead, too." My voice cracked. "Damn. Now that I think about it, one more and I would have had the hat trick."

I might be going into shock but she wasn't.

"Where are you?" she snapped.

I hoped her Israeli guy was as good at detecting and defeating phone taps as she believed him to be. I told her where I was and where I planned to be, if I stayed conscious long enough.

"Got it," and she was gone.

I headed for the lounge on the mezzanine level of the Holiday Inn Mart Plaza. It's above the registration desk. There was some kind of contractors' convention in the hotel. That was good. I'd try to blend with the builders when the cops made their sweep.

I walked off the elevator with all the focus of a drunk trying to toe the line for a trooper's field sobriety test. The lobby was busy and loud. Some of the conventioneers had evidently checked out the bar before checking in to their rooms. I fit right in.

In the lounge, I found a discarded newspaper and made like I was reading it. I felt as obvious as Inspector Clouseau. Next thing I knew, Sunny was shaking me awake.

"I've checked us in," she said.

I saw two of her at first and I gasped, suddenly overcome by a paranoia so intense I could feel my nails digging into my palms. She leaned over and looked into my eyes. Anyone watching would figure I was about to get kissed. She put her hand under my arm.

"The only way to the room is back through the lobby. Feel up to the walk?" She wore a U of I sweatshirt and jeans with a ball cap pulled low over her forehead.

I hoisted to my feet and let her lead me to the elevators. She chattered away through the whole jaunt. Three uniformed cops and two guys whose ragamuffin outfits screamed *tactical squad* pushed through the lobby and approached the front desk as we disappeared down the hall.

Nobody got on the elevator with us so I slumped against the wall and talked. She didn't react until she warned me to shush as we reached our floor. I tried a smile. From her tight expression, it must have been ghastly.

She took some gear out of a battered gym bag as I lay down gratefully on one of the twin beds in the room. Then she went to wash her hands. I was asleep by the time she came back. Her hand on my shoulder roused me.

When I opened my eyes, the only light in the room came from a lamp with a towel thrown over it.

"What's the date today?" she asked. I told her. She ran through a couple of other questions: President's name, Mayor's name, my home address, my mother's name. I breezed through them.

"Talk to me some more." Her voice sounded far away until she put her face right into mine. A nice face.

Light stabbed my right eye, went away, attacked the left one.

Squinting, I asked, "What do you want me to say?"

"Whatever you're thinking."

"You learned how to do the light-into-the-eyes thing from watching E.R. didn't you?"

"Sometimes it helps to know how to fix things that get broken," she said. I could tell I was the only one who'd be answering questions.

Her hand slid to my wrist, paused while she took my pulse, and then released. She reached into her bag and removed a blood pressure cuff, which she attached to my upper arm. All the conveniences of a hospital right there in the Holiday Inn. I wonder if that would work as a marketing gimmick. Maybe not.

"Where do you hurt the most?" she asked.

"Back of my neck. My head. My nose. This." I lifted my left hand.

She let loose of the bulb and slid the cuff off.

"Hold still."

Digging into her bag again, she came out with an oversized tweezers and picked glass shards and pieces of gravel out of my palm. Next, she sprayed my hand with Bactine and bandaged it. Her fragrance mixed with the medicinal smell. It was nice. It was distracting, too.

"Are you still dizzy?"

I sat up and swung my feet over the edge of the bed. By the time I struggled upright she was beside me with her hand on my shoulder.

"OK, slugger, I wasn't looking for a demonstration. Lie back down."

"Dizziness is gone," I said. "I must be cured."

"Sure you are. Your pressure's at stroke level. Your pulse is way up. And that nose. You like leaving a blood trail wherever you go?"

She worked for a few minutes, during which I closed my eyes. I felt one small jab of pain, but then the nose-throb began to diminish. She threw the gauze wrappings and her tools back into her bag and went to wash up once more.

I dozed again. When I awoke she was sitting cross-legged on the other bed and looking at me.

"How do you feel? About killing a man?"

"Not sure. Haven't thought about it much."

"Get sure. Do you have a lawyer?"

I shrugged. "Never needed a criminal attorney before."

"Barney Tanner is a friend." Barnett Tanner. Hmm. Sunny kept surprising me. She looked at her watch. "It's not too late to call him, either."

"You mean he's not doing Larry King tonight? Court TV? Chatting with Kurtis on A and E?"

"If he is, we'll interrupt him."

I considered that for a moment.

"Let me find out where I stand first." I pulled my cell phone from my jacket and dialed Vinnie Seamans' number from memory. He'd be in the middle of things, probably at the garage where I'd wrecked my car. And shot the Russian.

"Yeah," he said after two rings.

"It's Reno."

"Your ears musta been burning. Where are you? You hurt?"

"I'm fine. As for where I am, I think I'll keep that to myself for the moment."

"You think you can play fast and loose with this? It looks like you killed at least one guy over here. The dicks are talking to my people about drawing up charges right now."

"For what?"

"Aggravated mopery, what'd you think? It's a murder beef. I'm not kidding, son. I'll come get you but you need to talk to some people about this."

He was calling me "son" so he had an audience. But he was also using his "we can work this out" tone. I had room to maneuver.

"Tell me something. Do they have the E.T.'s over there? Crime lab? The usual setup?"

"What do you think? They've been picking up brass for three blocks."

"Both those guys had automatic weapons, Vinnie. Did you happen to notice all the exterior work they did on my car?

"Hang on a minute, will you? Do *not* hang up."

I heard a scraping noise as though he was holding the phone against his chest. I looked across the room at Sunny and winked. A car door slammed.

"Okay," Vinnie grunted. "Had the 18th District Commander in the car with me. What'd you get yourself into here?"

I described what happened as completely as I remembered it, careful to emphasize all the shooting they did and how little of the gunfire I'd returned. A couple of times he told me to slow down. He was taking notes.

"Where'd the gun come from?"

"Got it from a friend," I said.

"No. No, that's not gonna fly." I thought he was accusing me of lying. When he paused, though, I realized lying was what he *wanted* me to do.

"What's the history on the piece? Legit or…Christ! It wasn't that PPK of your dad's, was it?"

"No." It was my turn to mute the phone. I asked Sunny where she'd gotten the Kahr.

"Street."

"It's clean." I told Vinnie.

"Okay. This'll work. Your story is, the kid had it. The one they killed, this Patrick. He had the piece. Listen to me on this. You came up right after they did him. Right *after*. You heard the shots; you were checking to see if you could help him. They came back, saw you, and started blasting. You grabbed *his* gun to shoot back and defend yourself. You got that?"

For a guy who had started the conversation saying something about not playing fast and loose, he certainly was tap dancing to his own tune, now.

This, more than anything, was what Vinnie had spent his whole career learning to do. It was what he'd done for my dad numerous times. Covered. Manipulated.

Who was I to argue? Especially if choosing to tell the truth would land me in a cell.

"I got it," I said.

"You had no choice. There you are, trying to see if the poor kid needs an ambulance and the Russians come back and try to clean your clock. What else could you do? That clears you on the gun charge. You know the law on that. U.U.W. means Gun Court, no exception."

He seldom got as animated as when he was trying to work a deal. My Uncle Vinnie. The Fixer. I remembered what Sela said about how Talmadge got angry if his scams didn't turn out the way he intended. Vinnie was the same way. Cranky.

"Now, on the rest. Man, you gotta come in. There's no way around that. You got a lawyer? You want me to get you one?"

"I've got one."

"Who is it?"

"How about I show up at Area Three in the morning at 9? That work okay with you?"

He sighed in exasperation. "Is this lawyer any good? He does criminal work, right?"

"How good does he have to be to just keep repeating 'self-defense?'"

"Look, Reno, you may think this is a skate for you but there are a few things you got to factor in. You haven't exactly been the poster boy for cooperation with law enforcement the last few days. Want me to tell you who I've got hanging around? The Superintendent is here. The DEA's agent in charge is here. The FBI's agent in charge is here, along with some heavy hitters from Washington…"

"Terrorist Task Force. I've met them."

"Then shut up and hear me out. You look okay on this with my people but that doesn't guarantee no free pass. If you haven't gotten the word, this isn't just cops and mobsters. The Feds have a little image problem and they're putting a lot of resources into this Russian thing to help straighten that out. You understand what I'm saying?"

"Heroic G-Men take down the Russian mob? Pretty soon they'll be putting their pictures on baseball cards, too."

His voice got lower and more urgent. "You get between these federal people and their political goals, Reno and they're gonna bury you in a cell in Missoula, Montana, or someplace and tell any lawyer who asks that they don't even know your name. I am *not* making this up. This is a terrorist case. You know what that lets them do."

"They're not going to fuck with a reporter like that."

"Maybe not somebody who's on TV every day, no. I hate to tell you, Reno, you aren't that guy anymore."

His tone was flat and certain. For once I didn't have a response.

"Nine tomorrow morning at Area Three," he said. "And you better not bring some ambulance chaser."

*   *   *   *

When I hung up, Sunny was finishing a call to room service. She asked if I wanted her to call Tanner. I thought about it for longer than the idea deserved and then told her to go ahead.

The last attorney I used was the one who renegotiated my contract with the radio station. A portly, smiling man with perfect teeth and an impeccable hairpiece, he'd once been a TV host. I still think he cut a side deal for himself with the New York owners. Not exactly the guy I wanted fronting for me in a case that could send me to prison.

She used her cell to call Barnett Tanner. While she was on with him, I had another idea. I punched up Paul's number. He wasn't as quick to answer as Vinnic had been and, when he did pick up, I heard jazz in the background and the buzz of voices. He sounded a little buzzed himself.

"Reno, goddamn, man! Where are you? Tracy Petrakis from CPD News Affairs called me an hour ago and said they have a flash alert out on the citywide channels to have you picked up. What the hell happened?"

"I tried to keep a guy alive and wound up getting used for target practice instead."

"You okay? Need anything? You want me to take you in like Russ Ewing used to do?"

I pictured Paul as Russ Ewing, a TV reporter who specialized in being the middle man between fugitives and the law. I imagined Paul and me walking a gauntlet between rows of cops. Smiled.

"I got it covered. Thanks. I need…"

"Guess who's called me about half a dozen times since the Witting story broke? Her little chickie. She's scared shitless that the paper is going to 'out' her as Witting's girlfriend."

"Does anyone at the paper know about her?"

"Are you kidding? They're scrambling around trying to get an obit together, not do an investigation into 'Licia's lifestyle. Although, her party-hearty reputation is probably going to surface anyway. You know the troopers found Ecstasy in her luggage, right?"

"I've been sort of focused on other things and I wanted to…"

"She had a plastic bag of pills, couple of them tested out as 'X.' They've asked the M.E.'s office to look for signs of it in her blood when they do the toxicology. That might explain a lot."

Except why she'd taken it in the first place if she'd known she would be driving a car. I sighed and gave in.

"What's the girlfriend have to say about her?"

"She never went back to bed after we left. Paced the room, cried a bit. The girlfriend kept trying to reassure her everything was going to be okay. She didn't hear what we were talking about so she didn't know why 'Licia was so upset. She kept trying to get it out of me."

"Did Alicia give her any indication she was going to kill herself?"

"She worried about that, but she says on toward morning, like six or so, 'Licia seemed to figure something out. She went from crying to sort of an up-mood in the space of about a half-hour. Apparently she decided going to the gym would make her feel better."

"Right there it sounds like she ingested some kind of chemical. The mood swing."

"Maybe. The girlfriend says no. But she says 'Licia got obsessive about going to work out."

"You planning to talk to her again?"

"Probably. She says I'm the only one who knows about their relationship. You'd think she'd be crying and shit but she's up for a promotion and afraid this'll hurt her chances. Go figure."

"See if she overheard anything else, particularly any names Alicia might have mentioned. People she talked to while she was in town."

"Sure." He paused. "Are you really okay? Did you kill that guy like Petrakis says?"

"Ah, let's just say…"

"OK, OK, never mind. I know that tone of voice. Get back to me when you can. And if you need anything…"

Sunny was still on the phone when I signed off with Paul and she gave me her cell so I could answer some of the lawyer's questions. A former U.S. Attorney for the Northern District of Illinois, Barnett Tanner is one of Chicago's top criminal defenders. He spends so much time on television as a star consultant, I always wonder when he has the time to handle cases.

We'd never met, but he walked me through my story on the phone so effortlessly, his questions so precise, that it took less than half an hour to give him not only what had just happened but most everything I knew about the case all the way back to Brooke's murder. He agreed to drive me to Area Three in the morning so there wouldn't be any doubt I had come in voluntarily to be questioned.

Sunny took the phone back. I headed for the bathroom and took a quick shower. When I came out, she was just closing the door on the room service waiter. She brought the cart in herself, like a good bodyguard.

"All this and you find me a lawyer, too. You're an impressive person, you know that?"

"For years, yep. You're just noticing?"

It was half-past midnight. The guy I'd shot in the parking garage had been dead for about three and a half-hours and his partner for fifteen or twenty minutes less than that. I, however, was alive. A little glassy-eyed and fuzzy, still stiff from the stress of nearly being killed, but the pains were receding. Alive. That was the operative word.

I was alive. They were dead.

We had turkey club sandwiches with fries. A glass of wine for her and hot chocolate for me. I bit into the sandwich. It tasted marvelous. I dipped each french fry into a puddle I created with six of those little packets of ketchup they give you and chewed them carefully. I finished the hot chocolate by savoring every sip and letting the marshmallows stick to my tongue.

I didn't know the name of either Russian or anything about them except that they were both lousy shots, but seemed to enjoy the shooting. I knew that they were cold-blooded enough to take a guy off the street, drive him to a dark place and put two rounds in his back and then an extra one in his head just to be sure. I didn't know, but could reasonably assume, that the second thug hadn't thought twice about offing the security guard.

I was alive. They were dead.

"What's that look for?" Sunny asked. She was at the desk where she had set up her laptop, one hand poised over her keyboard and the other holding the glass of wine. She had the all-knowing, all-seeing eyes of a cat, that woman.

"Pretty good sandwich for a Holiday Inn," I said. "How's your wine?"

$$* \quad * \quad * \quad *$$

I fell asleep about two minutes later. Awoke as she lifted the remnants of my sandwich from my hand and put it on the plate that she took off my chest. She wore a t-shirt and jogging shorts. Her breath smelled of Listerine. She looked marvelous. I struggled to sit up.

She said, "You know what shock can do, right? Sometimes you can sleep it off. It looks like you may have. Your pulse is down and you're breathing better but I'm not a doc and I'm not going to leave here until I see you up and moving in the morning."

"What about your shift, my shift, whatever. The station?"

"See what I mean about shock? Tomorrow's Saturday, chowder head."

I closed my eyes and heard her moving around the room. She muttered into the Motorola. There was a muted response.

When she climbed into the other bed. I opened my eyes. The room was so dark it made me think of an underground hotel I stayed at once in the Australian outback. The blackness so dense you felt you could reach out and grab a handful.

I wondered if I'd encounter my whispering friend in my dreams again. I wished I'd rolled over in time to see his face before it disappeared into the ozone. Then again, maybe he wouldn't have had a face. Or, like something out of Dean Koontz, he would have been all slime and goo.

I didn't dream at all.

I was up, showered again, and clear headed by 7 a.m. One of Sunny's colleagues brought me a change of clothes. At eight she walked me down to the front of the hotel where Barnett Tanner sat behind the wheel of a Lincoln LS in the driveway. He stepped out when we approached.

Tanner was big and barrel chested and not a cheap dresser. I bet that his suit wore a Chipp of New York label on the inside pocket and that his shirt and crisp Guards tie had also been hand-made to his exact specifications. The Berluti shoes too, maybe. The A. Lange & Sohne on his wrist wasn't custom built, but it had cost him $12,000. Or maybe it had been a gift from a recently-found-not-guilty client. The thought cheered me until I realized it also could have come from a guilty client who had no other way to pay his fee.

Sunny took off. I gave the Kahr in my rolled up jacket to Tanner. He put it in the trunk and we eased out into Saturday traffic.

"You can relax," he said with a grin, as we rolled toward the expressway. "I talked to the Assistant State's Attorney who caught the case. They're not going to prosecute. We're just going over to 35th and Michigan to get your story on the record."

"What happened to meeting at Area Three?"

"The case is being run out of the Chief of Detectives office."

"OK, so if the state isn't going to file, what do you expect from the Feds?"

He adjusted the rear-view mirror and thought about his answer.

"I suspect you know the government. Surprises R Us. They may be waiting with a warrant, or they may just be there to watch."

"What charge would they use?"

"Interfering with a Federal Investigation would be the easiest. Maybe something under one of Ashcroft's anti-terrorism statutes. Frankly, I don't see the grounds for anything like that but they may."

So I couldn't relax all the way. Vinnie Seamans isn't known to give meaningless warnings. If he shouts fire, something is burning. Just how brightly, I suspected, I was about to find out.

Unlike the old police headquarters building at 11th and State where a portion of the parking lot lay beneath the El tracks and even the brass occasionally had to clean bird crap off their windshields, the new building looks like the home office for an insurance company. The parking lot takes up the better portion of an iron-fenced square block that is nearly free of train trestles. The lobby is more spacious and open than the one at the old place, too, with only the reception desk and the metal detectors plunked down between the entrance and the elevators to tell you you're entering a high-security environment.

The desk officer looked at Tanner's driver's license and bar association card, and at my driver's license, and signaled two guys who'd been standing near the metal detectors. Neither wore jackets. Both had automatics clipped to their belts and police ID hanging from their shirt pockets. They watched with boredom as the desk man walked us through the metal detectors, and then they took over as guides and led the way to the elevators. Neither said a word. I'd never made it this far inside The Building, only to the room where they held news conferences on the public side of the barrier. I'd heard most cops hadn't gotten past the security perimeter, either. The word was, if you hadn't been summoned for serious business in The Building, it was off limits. No tours, even for sworn personnel.

There was a rumor on the street that a patrolman from one of the Districts had been caught working out with a friend in the Building's gym and that both officers were handed written reprimands and a non-paid day off.

So, here I was, gliding in silence up to the third floor, wondering if I would walk out with Tanner or in handcuffs with Special Agent Dark.

The corridor was quiet but I could hear and see activity through office doors on either side. We passed the office of the Chief of Detectives and went into a small conference room just beyond it. Dark was there, looking very Hooverish in a grey pants suit and white blouse, a blue, laminated CPD visitor tag with the number 17 stamped on it clipped to her jacket lapel.

Two detectives I hadn't seen before regarded me with the universal cop expression of disinterest. The tallest of the pair leaned against the wall, reading something in a file folder. He'd shaved his bald pate down to nearly nothing and wore black-rimmed glasses. He looked crisp and fresh in shirt sleeves and suspenders, not at all the sort to wear a pistol hanging from his belt without a jacket to cover it. His partner was less than snappy in an out of season, one-size too small corduroy sport coat and a tie that had what appeared to be a splotch of white paint, or maybe correction fluid, on it. The longish-haired guy wearing a brown suit with cat hair clinging to it had to be from the State's Attorneys office. He'd already sat down behind a small pile of documents.

Tanner shook hands all around. No one offered to shake hands with me. I wasn't offended. At least it wasn't the interrogation room with the ring bolts on the wall at Area Three.

"Mr. McCarthy, I'm Detective Piper, this is Detective Maridosa," the tall detective said.

"You know Agent Dark and that's Assistant State's Attorney Bunnell. If you'll take a seat, we'll get started. Mr. Tanner, we'd like to videotape this interview if that's okay with you?" As I sat, the camera lens was at eye level on the wall across from me. Tanner looked at me. I shrugged.

Piper read me my rights and explained that I would be questioned about the events surrounding the deaths of two individuals the night before in the area of the Merchandise Mart. He read off the addresses involved and the time the 9-1-1 call had been received. Like a trained chimp, Bunnell chimed in to say that the State's Attorneys office had reviewed the reports of the investigators and crime scene technicians and decided there was no apparent basis for the filing of any charges but that this should be still be considered a custodial interrogation. I should, he advised solemnly, consult with my attorney prior to answering any questions. If I felt the need to do so.

"My client understands the Chicago Police Department is seeking information to close the investigation into last night's unfortunate incidents," said Tanner. "But we're curious as to why the Terrorist Task Force is represented here." We all looked at Dark.

She stepped away from where she'd been leaning on the wall with her arms folded.

"Just observing."

"I'm sorry, I'm not clear on this," Tanner said mildly. "By 'just observing' do you mean you're here to learn the interrogation techniques used by these two detectives? Or because you believe the information Mr. McCarthy provides may be relevant to some current federal investigation?"

"Mr. McCarthy is a possible witness in one of our cases."

"A witness to…?" Tanner smiled and spread his hands, palms-up, in a "go on" gesture.

"We believe he may have certain facts about an ongoing investigation."

"Yes, that's usually why someone is considered a witness. Please enlighten us further, Agent Dark."

She blushed but quickly figured out what J. Edgar would have done in her situation. "I'm…I'm not prepared to do so at this time."

"May I take that as an assurance you're also not prepared to slap the cuffs on him and lead him into federal detention as soon as we're finished?"

She blinked as though he'd just given her the Three Stooges eye poke. "I'm really…that's not what…"

"Because if this meeting was called for the sole purpose of allowing you to take my client into federal custody, I assure you I'll have the Attorney General himself on the phone before you reach the elevators."

"That's not my intention, sir," Dark said, but everyone knew from the anger in her voice that she would have liked nothing better.

Tanner kept his eyes fixed on her for another ten seconds or so, then swivelled back to the table and nodded toward Piper.

It took the detective a moment to react because, like kids in a classroom when the teacher explodes at another student, he, Maridosa, and Bunnell had been watching the byplay between the lawyer and Dark.

When Piper realized he had the floor again, he asked me to tell what I'd seen and done the night before. I followed Vinnie's script about the gun to a "T."

Then I finished speaking, the room was silent except for the sound of Bunnell's pen as he scribbled on a legal pad.

Then Maridosa asked, "Where did you say you got the gun, again?"

"From underneath Patrick Vega's body."

"You reached under him and found it?"

I was ready for that one. "No. I could see the grip sticking out when I knelt down next to him."

"Did you see the two men approaching before or after you picked up the weapon?" Piper asked.

"I picked it up when the van turned into the alley."

"Did they fire at you first or did you fire at them?"

"One of them fired at me. I heard the rounds hit my car and saw the muzzle flashes."

"Pretty convenient to find a weapon right there to use to defend yourself, wasn't it?" Maridosa pushed.

"Very fortunate, yes."

"Why do you suppose the shooters didn't see it? If it was right out in front of him like that, it must have fallen out of his belt, no?"

"Beats me. I wasn't there when they shot him."

"It was dark in the alley, wasn't it, Mr. McCarthy?" Piper this time.

"Yes."

"Were you holding a flashlight or…"

"I had left the door of my car open. There wasn't much light but I could see, yes."

"You're saying these two men murdered Mr. Vega, left the scene, and then came back to find you leaning over his body? I hate to tell you this but killers like these guys, and we think both of them had done this kind of thing before, very seldom come back to see if their victims are still dead."

"Maybe they saw me pull into the alley…"

"You could have been a cop! Don't you think it's a little odd that they'd risk getting caught just to see who was following them?"

Tanner jumped in, earning his money again. "That question calls for my client to be a mind reader, Detective."

"Did you have a cell phone with you last night?" Maridosa asked.

"Yes."

"Did you call 9-1-1 to report finding a murder victim?"

"No."

"Or to report your conclusion that Mr. Vega had been abducted in the first place?"

"There wasn't time…"

"Why were you looking for Mr. Vega?"

"I thought he might have information about the Talmadge murder."

"So you think whoever sent the two mopes to kill Vega also ordered the hit on the Talmadge girl?" For the first time, Piper's expression changed and he showed real interest in hearing my answer.

"I'm not convinced of that, no."

"Really? You think two different agendas are being served here?"

"Possibly. The tip I got indicated that Patrick Vega might have information about the Russian *mafiya,* as well as personal information about Brooke Talmadge. Her friends, that sort of thing."

Bunnell glanced to where Dark was standing near the door off my left shoulder. Before I could check to see if some sort of signal passed between them, Bunnell leaned over and whispered into Piper's ear. Piper got a sour look on his face but nodded.

"So it's clear for the record," he said, "you were conducting an unauthorized private investigation into Brooke Talmadge's murder?"

Tanner put his hand on my arm. "Don't have to answer that, Reno."

"No, this one's okay. I'm a reporter, Detective Piper. Reporters gather information."

"That reminds me," Piper held out a hand. "Your press pass."

I'd anticipated that. City ordinance says the cops have the right to yank it back any time for "just cause." I took it out of the pocket of my jacket, where I'd transferred it from my wallet earlier that morning, and slid it across to him.

I was sorry to see it go. Not because it granted me any magical powers. Media credentials are, after all, just ID cards, not permission slips. Losing it was just one more indication of where my career was headed. Even in the midst of everything else, it stung.

Piper and Maridosa spent another thirty minutes cross-checking my story. They came back several times to the part about finding the gun. I was offering a variation of the old "I found it on the street" routine that they doubtless heard from every creep they picked up carrying a Saturday night special. It was the obvious weak point in my tale.

The problem for them was, they couldn't do anything about it unless I broke down and confessed. I gradually began to realize they were following a script. My lie, their lame questions, and even the routine with the media card, were all part of what good ol' Ed Sullivan used to call "the reeeally big shew."

I figured out the plot of the "shew" as we bumped along, the cops pulling their punches and me bobbing and weaving like a stunt man in a John Wayne movie. This is how I thought it went:

Neither the city, nor the Feds, wanted it known that the Russian *mafiya* had gained a foothold in Chicago and was now in a shooting war with the street gangs. That made sense. Chicago was just beginning to live down its reputation as home to ratt-a-tatt Al Capone and a long succession of his buddies.

If the planners of multi-million dollar trade shows, seminars and conventions learned that the Uzi had replaced the Tommy gun and blood could be spilled in touristy River North just as easily as on the West or South sides, they would be less likely to set up shop here. As for the Feds, they didn't want people thinking that the Russians slipped past them. Why? Because they're still trying to put the screw-ups of 9/11 behind them.

The problem was that the Government, in its arrogance, had marched into town and declared its own version of martial law. While that was all fine and well before the shooting started, now that bodies and parts were piling up, the Chicago cops were starting to get a little pissy about being treated like Barney Fife on their own turf.

Or so I imagined.

I suspected the cops had moved my interview to 35th and Michigan to underscore its "importance." They had gone through the motions of hammering me with questions. They'd taken away my media credentials. They'd invited the Feds to be present to see they were coming down as hard as they could on the dumb ass reporter who kept sticking his nose where it didn't belong.

"Too bad we couldn't file charges on the fellow," Their actions appeared to say. "Just not enough evidence." In effect, their message to the Feds was, "We've done all we can...now you guys take your best shot."

Of course, if the Feds did something really stupid, the Chicago cops wouldn't have to take the heat.

Under the expanded anti-terror statutes, as Vinnie had noted, Dark and Mohler could make me disappear for a good long while by tagging me as a material witness and filing the right paperwork under a judge's seal. And they could do it. The Feds used exactly that tactic against a group of people detained after 9/11, some of them American citizens, too.

Since I was technically out of the news business, who would put up a stink if I was suddenly not around? I had no job, no family. Examining my lifestyle, they probably convinced themselves I couldn't afford much of a lawyer and whoever I got wouldn't know how to fight the kind of court order they would get. Dark must have been very surprised when I walked into the room with Barney Tanner.

Close. Really close.

I didn't realize I was shaking until I reached for the pitcher in front of me to pour a cup of water.

Instead of slopping it all over the table, I just left it alone and folded my hands on the table. I could feel the trembling all the way up my arm. I took a deep breath and let it out in time to hear Piper say he was finished and did Tanner or I have any questions?

"Have you identified the two dead men?" I asked.

"No ID on them and the van was stolen. Big surprise." He paused, as though working out whether to share any more.

"The ATF traced the MAC-10's they were using, though. Part of a shipment that went to the old Soviet Union ten years ago. To the KGB. We're running their prints through Interpol."

Tanner and I stood up to leave an hour after we walked in the door of the Chief of Detectives' conference room.

This time, I got in on the handshakes, although Dark had slipped out before the meeting ended.

I felt pretty good as we walked down the corridor toward the elevators, this time with Piper as our guide. He and an evidence technician were going to tag along and pick up the gun I had left in Tanner's trunk. We ran into Dark and Mohler at the elevators. Talk about spoiling a mood. They didn't look our way but neither did they move. Tanner broke away from our group and went over to stand so close to Dark he probably should have given her an engagement ring first. He bent to speak to her as the elevator arrived and the doors opened.

The three of us got on, but the two agents chose to wait for another car.

I pointed at Mohler's feet. "New shoes?" I asked as the doors closed.

Piper glanced at Tanner. "What was that about?"

"I just told her if I suddenly can't find Reno on any day between now and when they start indicting Russian mobsters, his picture is going to appear on so many newscasts, and so often, people will think he's running for office."

"Dick brains. All of 'em," Piper growled.

We collected the evidence tech in the lobby and strolled to Tanner's car. He opened the trunk and produced the Kahr. The tech took them, bagged and tagged each, and gave me a receipt.

Tanner got behind the wheel. I started around to the passenger side.

The tech walked away, but Piper put his foot up on the Continental's bumper as though to tie his shoe. When the tech was out of earshot, Piper said, very quietly, "Kinsella's still looking for the kid. Said to tell you good shooting. Oh, and the prints came back from Interpol. They belong to two guys who died five years ago."

CHAPTER 17

▼

Tanner drove me to the city's vehicle impoundment lot on Lower Wacker near the river to find the Mustang. The one-armed attendant confirmed my doubts that it would be drivable when he shuffled me out to where the tow driver had left it. The hood was sprung and the front grill shoved back so far that it cracked the radiator. I counted five bullet holes in the hood and four in the passenger side. The windshield was a maze of starred cracks and the front passenger seat looked like a child's plush toy with the stuffing oozing out.

"You drive that outta here this afternoon, Bud, and I got some water in the shack there you can turn to wine, you get my drift."

"Can I pull some stuff out of it?"

"Ain't spozed to let you til you pay the tow bill but, hey, I used to watch you on TV all the time. Can't see no harm innit."

All I was after was the Motorola radio Sunny had given me that I'd ditched under the front seat. I figured the cops had seized it when they did their inventory search after towing the car but I climbed behind the wheel and fished for it anyway. I felt something jammed up against the seat springs. I got out, pushed the seat forward, and went at it from the back, finally drawing out the radio.

"Jeez, somebody sure didn't do much looking around, did they?" the attendant sneered. "Glad that wasn't a gun. Or a body part."

I said I'd make arrangements to reclaim the car, and went back to where Tanner was waiting in the Lincoln.

"Want to buy a classic Mustang?" I asked, sliding inside.

"That bad, huh?" he asked.

"It wasn't in the best shape to start with. I was sort of thinking about making a change anyway but I don't like seeing it shot to death."

"Know the feeling. A friend from college and I rebuilt an old XKE the year before we started law school. I let him drive it to Colorado. Big mistake. He wrapped it around a tree one night after a frat party." He shook his head. "Of course with Ford-building the Jaguars now…"

We talked Mustangs until he dropped me off at the Hertz office in the Loop with the admonition for me or Sunny to call him if the Feds made any moves that were in the least threatening.

I had turned to walk away when he called my name and leaned across the seat to talk to me through the open passenger window.

"I could pass a message to the U.S. Attorney that you're getting out of it. You'd probably save yourself a load of grief if you did."

"I might've taken that advice before last night," I said. "Not now."

He gave a wave and let his LS glide into traffic. I turned to go into the Hertz office, then realized I was just a block from Petey's Gym where Alicia Witting had thought she would be able to work off the fear and anxiety from my late night visit. I crossed the street and ducked into the carpeted foyer.

It had been a men's athletic club before the Petey's chain took it over and gave it a facelift. Now, the cement walls held contemporary paintings and the high ceilings had been dropped and acoustically tiled. A busty brunette and a bald but muscular guy behind the front desk showed the benefits regular workouts could bring. Signs advertised the "Herb and Sprouts Cafe" and urged members to attend a Tai Chi demo class that night. I chose to speak to the brunette who was as much a walking advertisement for Lycra spandex as she was for doing stomach crunches and upper body weights.

"Help you, sir?" Her eyes registered the Motorola in my hand and she was instantly wary.

"A woman by the name of Alicia Witting worked out here yesterday…"

"We've already talked to you people." The bald fellow's tone suggested the topic would interrupt the flow of his Chi for the day. "What else you need?"

"Just routine follow up," I said. People expect cops to say "routine." "Were you here when she came by?"

The guy crooked a finger for me to follow him down the counter and away from the brunette. "She didn't work out. She wasn't a member and she didn't want a guest card. I told the other guys this, the state troopers or whatever. They said she was in a wreck or something?"

I smiled and ignored his question. "Sometimes it takes awhile for us to get it right, all the coffee we drink with those donuts. What was she here for if she didn't want to work out?"

"Oh, she *wanted* to work out. Had some story about how some chick set it up for her to use the chick's membership whenever she was in town and blah, blah, blah. Asked for Elaine, the manager. I told her Elaine was outta town and we don't let two people work out on one card."

"How did she take that?"

"She got pissed. Sat around, tried to get me to call Elaine."

"You didn't want to do that?"

He snorted. "You kidding? Elaine's in Seattle with her sick dad. I'm gonna call long distance on her cell 'cause some bimbo wants to throw her weight around?"

"So she identified herself?"

"Secretary to some congressman or something? Didn't mean dick to me, dude. We get all kindsa people in here all day long. If they pay, they get in the locker room. If they don't, they hit the bricks."

"What did she do when you refused to call the manager?"

"Offered money. A hundred bucks! She coulda worked out all day for half that. I told her, for fifty I'll give you your own locker, your own towel, whatever. But she said this other chick set it up. I finally had to tell her to get lost. A real mouth, you know?"

"She got upset?"

"She flat freaked. Cissy, the chick I was working with, wanted to call the cops. I don't like doing that. No offense but, it looks bad, I can't handle a chick, you know?"

"Sure. You remember the name of the woman whose membership she wanted to use?"

"I remembered it yesterday when your buddies were here." He thought for a moment then made a face. "Nah. Gone now. Which is what I got to be, dude. We're getting busy."

"One quick one, then. When's Elaine coming back?"

"Back in town? Tomorrow. Already have a message for her to call the other guys. You want her to call you, too?"

"That's okay. Let's see if they can handle it themselves this time."

*   *   *   *

The smiling, heavyset woman behind the Hertz counter rented me a lime green Taurus station wagon. She paused every few moments during the paperwork process to grin at me over the tops of her red-framed glasses as though we'd shared a joke. When she finished writing, she told me she loved my work on TV.

"It must be fun," she said. "More fun than this, anyway."

Why correct her? "Sometimes," I said.

As I was on my way out the door she grinned again. "I'll be watching you!"

I headed for home my usual way along the Drive but, unlike most times, I took no pleasure in looking at the swimmers and boaters and the girls blading their way along the lakeshore.

No question, I was glad to be out from under a possible indictment for killing the Russian. It felt strange, though, to have put two bullets into the guy and still not know who he was. Guilt wasn't a factor. I would not forget the total lack of expression in his eyes as he surveyed my wrecked Mustang, waiting to shoot me. I could still see Patrick Vega's lifeless body there in the alley, too. In the fringe jacket Brooke had given him.

I considered Vega for a moment. Would he still be alive if I hadn't started nosing around? I had a hard time believing he had been killed to keep him from talking to me. It was far more likely Federov was shedding liabilities and hadn't wanted Vega around to talk to the Terrorist Task Force. Remembering Sela made me dig out the cell and call her. If she hadn't heard about Patrick, she needed to.

By the time her phone rang seven times, I was starting to get nervous. By ten, I had to consciously loosen my grip before I hurt either myself or my cellular. She picked up three rings later, out of breath and laughing. I only told her Vega had been killed; she didn't need the whole story. She took it well. I made sure she was with her parents and suggested she come up with something to tell them so they made sure to lock their doors and take more than casual security precautions. I felt better when she said their summer home was in a gated area, patrolled by security.

"If you see anything out of the ordinary…" I began.

"I'll be okay, Mr. McCarthy. Talking to you yesterday, that helped me. I'm feeling better about everything, basically. I needed to tell somebody that stuff, I guess."

My next call went to Sunny so she would know I was a free man again. The relief in her voice was good to hear.

"Anything new I should know about?" I asked.

"Not really. I've got Russ and Amelia doing a physical rundown on this Jerome Belzer. I've been looking at him online, too. Nothing that connects him to Federov except that one building and that's through a management company. He's a patent attorney. He's married, lives here in Skokie. He owns his home. He's not much of a joiner. They own two of the smaller Toyotas. Bought the house for a couple of hundred thousand three years ago. If he's a gangster, you sure wouldn't know it to read his financial profile. The firm isn't high-dollar and it doesn't look like he is either."

"What's a patent lawyer doing representing a management company? And what's he doing taking calls from Alicia Witting?" I asked.

"Funny how those answers didn't just jump right out at us. How're you feeling?"

I took a look at the lake as I made the curve that turns the Drive into Hollywood Avenue. It was crystal blue again, mirroring the sky.

"It's a beautiful day and I'm not in jail for killing a guy," I said. "But the more I hear about Federov, the more I want to catch the little fucker by surprise and ask him if he killed Brooke."

"Oh—kayy," she said. Did she figure I was so totally exhausted I didn't know what I was saying?

"I'm serious. I want us to figure out a way to get me in to see him one-on-one. Office or home, I don't care. No scheduled appointment. I want him off guard and I want to see the look on his face when he realizes it's me."

That brought a moment of silence, either out of respect for my audacity or worry about my sanity.

"So confronting him will be your version of those interviews where you shove a camera in a guy's face in the rest room or wherever and ask him how long he's been beating his wife."

"Let me first go on the record as saying I *never* bushwhacked anybody coming out of a john." I joked. She didn't respond in kind.

"You think this is a wise move? Even though his people have tried to kill you? Twice?"

"The first time the guy had a personal beef with me. The second, well, hell. It's not like Federov ordered them to take me out. I caught them killing Vega."

She grunted. "Yeah, and if you wait by your phone, I'm sure he'll call and apologize for their rude behavior. Did you take a knock on the head last night that you didn't tell me about? This *mano a mano* idea of yours is nuts."

"You think he'll consent to a meeting if I call him up? Maybe go through his secretary? Two or three levels of junior-grade flacks?"

"Have you tried?" she snapped.

"I don't want his image talking. I want the man. It sounds to me like he may have had a real relationship with Brooke. If that's the case, and he didn't order her killed, I wonder how he's taking her death. He's for damn sure not offering his opinions to the cops."

"Reno…," frustrated, she started again. "He doesn't need to offer his opinions to anybody. Hello? He has professional killers working for him. If he knows who murdered Brooke…"

"If." I said. "If he knows."

                    *   *   *   *

Something like 25 voice mails and one cranky and very hungry cat awaited me when I got home. I unlocked the door, scooped Socks off his perch at the front window and let him sniff my face to be sure I wasn't just some intruder in a Reno mask. Thirty minutes later, after feeding both of us and taking a shower as hot as I could make it, I sat in my office with the air conditioning blowing on me and zipped quickly through my messages. They were all pretty much what I expected.

Marisa Langdon, very formal, wanting to know about my involvement in last night's shooting near the Merchandise Mart. Time-stamped 20 minutes after her call came one from Frank Hanratty, asking the same question with a lot more heat. Assignment editors from channels 2, 5, 7, 9, 32 and CNN all left requests that I phone them back as soon as possible.

Nope. Not going to happen.

I debated for a couple of minutes whether to call Hanratty. It was pretty damn clear to me that any chance I had of ever working in television again was as dead as the Russian guy I shot. A DUI, a drug possession charge or beating one's wife might bring a suspension, maybe even a strong suggestion that the reporter seek counseling. I'd never heard of a reporter killing someone and staying in the business. Not even urban legends.

In the end, though, I found myself dialing Frank's number.

He told me he was just getting home and would call back in five minutes. The phone rang in six.

"What the hell did you get your ass into last night?" he growled.

"I'm not going to talk about it, Frank."

"The *hell* you say!"

"Can't do it. Advice of my attorney." Tanner hadn't given me any such advice, of course. I simply saw no point in helping Channel 14 get the story I wanted to put together.

"Do you realize what a jerk you sound like? And, by the way, you told me you were going to just ride out that suspension and go back to work. What happened to that?"

"People started dying."

"Yeah, and if this involves what I think it does, you could die, too. Jesus Christ, man, for once use some sense. You're a news guy, not the goddamn Man of LaMancha."

"I'll keep that in mind." I wondered why I had bothered to call him. I'd known this was coming.

"Yeah, and you're an asshole, too. I don't want to see you hurt, Reno. That's all I'm saying."

He sounded sincere, but Hanratty had been cajoling information from reluctant sources since before I got to junior high school. To most journalists, those working the crime beat especially, sincerity is something to be worn, or taken off, just like a coat and tie. His reporter was on the verge of breaking a major story. I was the dot they needed to connect Brooke's murder to the Russian mob. Why wouldn't he play the friendship card?

I kept my mouth shut.

"Ok, just tell me this," he said, his tone becoming conciliatory. "No questions about last night, nothing involving you. Something easy. Do the cops know who killed the Talmadge girl?"

"If they do they haven't told me." I wasn't lying. Some thought they knew, but I wasn't aware of any pending indictments.

"We're off the record now. Does that work? For my ears only?"

"Frank, if you remember, we've had a few disagreements about exactly what that 'off the record' stuff means."

"Never thought I'd see the fucking day. Reno McCarthy turns into a fucking suit. I must be living *The Invasion of the Body Snatchers*."

A click and he was gone. Probably better for both of us. I wasn't tracking too well and he was getting more frustrated with every question he asked. Or, rather, with each of the questions he asked that I chose not to answer.

Another message was from Paul. He was at the airport, heading for California. He left a number for me to call later, if I wanted. It was a little ironic, I thought, that both of us would leave the business at the same time. Of course, he was going willingly. I leaned over and put my elbows on the desk, rubbing my eyes with the heels of my palms.

The sound you hear, I thought, is your career disintegrating.

I wondered if I would end up teaching. Yeah, that was real likely. The Killer Prof. Maybe I could do the farm report or read weather for some small station out West. I'd have to use a phony name, probably. Bib Tucker with the news. Yee-ha.

I had a couple of options for spending the rest of the afternoon. Most tempting was to mow the lawn, then crank on the sprinkler and sit in a chair under my favorite tree until I dozed off. Nope. Couldn't do that. I still needed to find Alan Talmadge and I couldn't count on him dropping by to help me with the yard work.

I made a couple of calls, finding out only where he wasn't. He wasn't home. He also wasn't on the links.

Alan Talmadge drove a Beemer. I had written down the plate out of habit the night Brooke was murdered. I called the guy who was the media liaison in the Secretary of State's office. Running registration checks is a courtesy the SOS offers reporters. My contact was reluctant, having seen the news that I was being questioned in connection with a homicide. He also knew me well enough that he finally gave in. I hoped the address on the plate would be different from the house on Woodley Road or the apartment in Rogers Park. If Alan had been letting his sister use the one apartment, there was a chance he might have another.

"You know Glen Grove Country Club?" my SOS buddy asked. "They must have rooms or apartments for their members right there on the grounds. Anyway, that's the address listed."

It figured. He could live at home but sack out at the club if he was in no condition to drive.

Now the dilemma. I could call ahead to see if he was there or I could drive up and check in person. If he was hiding out, the club operator wouldn't tell me anything. Ergo, I'd have to go take a look.

I was headed out the door with car keys in hand when I stopped, suddenly apprehensive.

My ankle felt very bare.

I hadn't wanted to carry the damn Kahr when Sunny offered it to me and now I felt uncomfortable without it. Not just a little uncomfortable, either, I realized, as I felt my right hand begin to shake at the thought of being unarmed. It shook so furiously that when I held it up in front of my face, I thought of a plate wobbling at the end of a juggler's stick right before it falls off and shatters.

I took a deep breath and let it out slowly. I was standing in the foyer at the front door where an oval pane of glass allows a shaft of sunlight to poke in on nice afternoons. Sunshine was streaming in, and the beveled edges of the cutout picked up little sparkling pieces of light and made them dance right across my field of vision. Almost like the way the gunshots had winked at me from out of the darkness…

I went to the closet where I kept my dad's Walther. Lifted it, worked the action. I dropped the clip and used my thumb to pop out each of the rounds and inspect them. It held seven nice, new .380's. It fitted with perfect balance in my hand. Less stopping power than a 9mm, but lighter weight and slightly less recoil.

After reloading the clip with rounds fresh from the box, I jacked one of them into the chamber and added another to the clip in its place. Seven plus one, they call it. Finally, I took a rubber band out of my desk drawer and wrapped it around the wooden grip, then slipped the gun into the waistband of my slacks at the small of my back. The rubber band keeps the gun from sliding around.

I put my sport coat on to cover the gun and left the house to go look for Alan Talmadge.

I struck out at the Club. His Beemer wasn't in the large, and now mostly full, parking lot adjacent to the clubhouse. I thought about finding a spot to wait and watch for a couple of hours, but the sight of one of the caddies I'd seen the other day trudging out from the pro shop toward a weather-beaten Toyota gave me another idea. I cruised up beside him and rolled down my window.

"Bet those bags get heavy after a couple of rounds, don't they?"

The kid looked curiously at me. "Try five rounds since seven this morning."

"Alan Talmadge play today?"

"Sure did. First foursome of the day." He grinned and then touched his nose. "You were looking for him before, right?"

"Just can't keep track of the guy. You wouldn't happen to know if he's staying in a room here, would you?"

He rolled his eyes. "Yeah, he is. Second floor—220. Told me to haul his bag up there for him after his round. You a cop? I mean, with his sister and all."

"No, but I need to ask him a few questions and I don't see his car. Did he say where he was headed this afternoon?"

"I don't…no wait. They were talking about some kind of party. Who was having it, though? Man, my brain is fried. I'm sorry."

He brightened suddenly. "You could call the people he was playing with. Earl and Claire Nordstrom or Jennifer Prokop. I think he may be dating that Jennifer. She's hot."

"Got their numbers?"

"They'd have 'em in the shop…"

I used a folded twenty to persuade him to get the numbers for me. He ducked back inside for a few minutes. When he emerged and trotted over, he handed me a scorecard with the numbers scrawled across its face.

"Just a thought? That Jennifer is hot like I said? But she's also kinda rude to people. If I was calling anybody, it'd be Earl. He kinda likes his beer and he's probably had a few by now. I mean, it's just a thought."

One of the things I've found about the news business is that sometimes you get really lucky and the streak holds for the rest of the day. Other times, you think you're about to nail down an interview or a fact and it slips away from you.

Earl Nordstrom had a loud, brash voice and a nasty laugh.

"You're looking for Al? Al and Jenn just left, sorry to say. They were here most of the afternoon swimming. You just missed 'em by twenty minutes. Al, I can take or leave heh, heh, heh, but always sorry to see Jenn go, if you know what I mean."

He lowered his voice. "Best damn tatas in six states heh, heh, heh. Hey, you can probably catch him on his cellular."

"Damn, I must've left the number at the office," I said.

"Then again, I think they were headed to her place for a little of the horizontal scramble. The way she was acting, well, you know what I mean. She was in need, my man."

"So, can you give me his cell phone number?" I asked.

"Nah, nah, nah. We aren't going there. How do I know you aren't one of those Roooshin bastards coming after him? If you know Al, you know his cell phone number. Who is this anyway?"

"My name's Reno McCarthy."

"Oh yeah? The reporter who came to the club and was hassling him the day after his sister was murdered? Yeah, like I'm telling you anything, you fuckhead."

That click again. Hung up on twice within two hours. I really felt like I was back in the news business now.

On my way through the club's foyer, there were fifty or sixty people milling about, all in summer formal wear. Off to my left, a sun porch with a nice view of the eighteenth green was set up with a wet bar and, beyond that, I could see white-coated waiters and busboys arranging tables and a buffet in the dining room. There was no one at the reception desk.

I grabbed the phone as I stepped behind the counter. Punching in the numbers two-two-zero, I let it ring unanswered while I looked for the place where they kept room keys. If they used modern key-cards that were programmed as needed, I'd be out of luck.

Fortunately, the club hadn't moved into the 21st Century. I found a row of hotel-type mailboxes behind a small sliding door on the wall and reached into the one marked "220." One key with the old-style "Drop in Any Mailbox" tag on it.

Stairs led upward behind the reception area. I took them two at a time and found myself in a bland hallway that looked like it came right out of a hotel in the tropics. Ceiling fans turned slowly every few feet and each of the room doors was louvered. I half-expected to see a guy in a panama hat with a patch over one eye and a parrot on his shoulder coming toward me. Nobody showed. I couldn't even hear the sounds of the party from one floor away.

Talmadge's room was the second one on my right. I knocked and waited before slipping the key into the lock. Too late, I remembered the automatic under my jacket. Let's see now. I was breaking and entering, while armed. Last night I had killed a guy. This was sure turning into one hell of a lawless weekend for me. I'd have to find a liquor store or White Hen Pantry to knock over on my way home.

I've only seen pictures of the rooms where seminarians and cloistered monks live but this one didn't appear to be much different. A single bed, unmade, sat against the far wall of a space perhaps twice the size of a jail cell. Instead of Jesus on a cross over the bed, there was a picture of a bulldog in knee-length pants standing on two legs and leaning against a golf cart while another bulldog in similar attire lined up a putt. A table and chair faced a window and next to that was an easy chair that probably had been there since Ben Hogan was a boy. Talmadge's golf bag lay next to the bed. There was a closed suitcase partially covered by the bed linens. I unsnapped the locks and rifled through it. Underwear, socks, two soiled golf shirts, two condoms, a sealed pint of Jack Daniels and an eight by ten manila envelope that held a picture. I slid it out.

Ever look at something that's meant to arouse and get a greasy, queasy feeling instead?

Staring back at me was Brooke Talmadge, topless. She was sitting up in bed as though she had been startled awake. A professional shot. The lighting and staging were both first rate, as was the sensual expression she wore. Equally innocent and wanton. Part little girl, part seductress. I turned it over to return it to the envelope. It had her measurements on the back: 34-21-38, written in a feminine hand. What I didn't recognize was the name printed just as carefully underneath: Rebecca Tarnower. I wondered if that was another of her street names and then realized it was probably the alias she planned to use when she moved to California.

But, what the hell was a photo like that doing in her brother's suitcase?

On impulse, I kept the envelope and left a piece of paper with my name and phone number in its place. Shake 'em up, I'd said to Sunny about Federov. Why not rock Talmadge's world, too? I used my handkerchief to wipe the room key and tossed it into the suitcase, then got out of there. No one was in the hall when I walked out and no one hailed me as I passed through the lobby. Outside I looked up the number the caddy had given me for Jennifer Prokop. It rang five times before triggering an answering machine.

"This is Reno McCarthy, Alan. Why do you have a naked picture of your sister?" I waited. Nothing. The phone disconnected. I called back, recited my cell number for the tape and waited again. Same thing happened.

I was less than ten minutes from Sunny's office. I drove over there, thinking I'd use her reverse directory to get Prokop's address and then go stake her place out for awhile. Russ opened the door before I could hit the buzzer. He grinned when we shook hands.

"Good timing. I just got back from walking Belzer's neighborhood. You're gonna want to hear this."

*   *   *   *

Sunny sat behind her desk with Russ, another bail agent named Angela Stein and me, all spread in front of her like a good poker hand. She held several digital photos Russ and Angela had surreptitiously taken of Belzer and wife. I'd looked at them before we sat down. Belzer was a balding, fleshy fellow in his mid-forties with too-thick glasses and one major honker of a nose. His wife could have been his sister just as easily, though she probably outweighed him by twenty pounds and had a little more hair, color courtesy of Clairol. She also had the start of a pretty good mustache. Neither of them looked dangerous. I mentioned that and got a grim smile from Angela.

"Those who do not appear dangerous are the ones who get in close to use a knife," she said. "Or who walk unnoticed into the market, as though they are shopping, and explode a suicide bomb."

Angela grew up in Israel. She has the intensity of someone who has watched people close to her suffer and an attitude that suggests she won't allow it to happen again. About five-four, she is powerfully built, with hands large enough to hold a big Desert Eagle automatic, her chosen sidearm.

"We spoke to many of their neighbors. Most in that area are immigrant Jews. As you might expect, they are reluctant to talk to strangers. We used a cover that we were looking for a Jewish man preying on other Jews, a thief fleeing the law. It was helpful, I think, that I am fluent in Hebrew.

"Our progress, initially, was slow. Then Russ located an individual at the end of the street who provided us with just the information we sought. Why Jerome Belzer is working for this Mikhail Federov."

Sunny grinned. "Do tell."

"He was quite talkative. He is retired and has no family. He belongs to the Neighborhood Watch. He listens to the police radio and keeps binoculars next to his chair which he has placed at his second floor bedroom window."

"Your traditional nosey neighbor," Russ interjected. Angela frowned at him.

"He is quite well informed," she acknowledged. "He told us that Belzer is a second generation Russian Jew, as is his wife, Elena. His parents died a number of years ago. Her father is dead, as well. Elena's mother returned to Moscow several years ago to take care of Elena's aunt who was ill. The aunt has since died. The mother has remained there.

"I think it is because of his wife's mother that he does what Federov wants him to do."

She paused and locked her gaze on me. "Sunny tells me you know of the *organizatsiya*," she said. "Then you know they are like any other group of thugs. They take advantage where they can find it. Their weapon is fear."

"Not to be disrespectful," I said, "And not that we need absolute proof. But you've made quite a jump from Elena Belzer having a mother back in the old country to her mother being held hostage."

"The Belzers are not wealthy but they have enough money to be comfortable. By all accounts, she is a devoted daughter. Why would she not have traveled to see her mother and her aunt in the past five years? If for no other reason than to attend her aunt's funeral last year? And, of course, why has Elena's mother not returned?"

"How do we know Elena's so devoted to her family?"

"Our nosy neighbor. He suggested we talk to their rabbi," Russ put in. "Rabbi says mom and daughter were inseparable. Always came to temple together, did their charity work together. He says he's asked a couple of times why momma hasn't come back. Never gotten a real good answer. I think he figures something isn't right, too, but that's where he clammed up. I mentioned the mob and he all of a sudden found something else he had to do."

"Is the mother an American citizen?" I wondered.

Sunny chimed in. "I'll check with Immigration, Monday."

I turned to Russ and Angela.

"What's the word on Belzer? Asshole lawyer, attitude, nice guy? What?"

Russ shrugged. "Keeps to himself when he's home. Neighbor says that started a few years ago. Used to be a pretty friendly, over-the-back-fence guy. Nowadays, he says, Belzer hardly even waves to anyone. He also goes out maybe one or two Saturday nights a month, about nine or so, sometimes doesn't come back 'til two or three in the morning. Always looks tired when he rolls in."

I raised an eyebrow at that. "This neighbor camp on the Belzer's front porch or what?"

Russ stretched both arms above his head and grinned. "Hey. Mr. Nosey should get himself a private dick's license, come to work for us doing surveillance. And, he's got decent binoculars. Checked 'em myself."

"Speaking of surveillance," I said.

"Already planning on it," Sunny said. "I'll take tonight and get Mark to help."

I stuck around after Russ and Angela left. Sunny checked both on-line and in the Polk's directory to see if Jennifer Prokop's phone number popped up displaying an address. There was no listing anywhere. I sighed and flopped back on the couch.

She ducked into her mini refrigerator and came up with a Dr. Pepper which she offered to me. I declined. Caffeine wasn't going to solve my problem. I lifted Alan Talmadge's envelope and displayed the photo. Sunny pursed her lips in distaste and frowned when I told her where I'd found it.

"Now that's something even my smutty mind didn't imagine," she said. "The brother hot for his sister? You suppose he killed her?"

"Not a chance. After I saw them together, I watched him drive away in the opposite direction. There wasn't enough time for him to make it around to the alley behind the building, park, run up the stairs, go in through the apartment's back door and do it."

She drank some of her Dr. Pepper and leaned back, making her chair squeak.

"Mommy and Daddy sure raised a couple of well-adjusted kids in Alan and Brooke Talmadge, huh? Were they trying for depraved, you think?"

"I don't know, Sunshine. Brooke…" I shook my head. "You know, everyone I've talked to has said basically the same thing. She was on a mission to screw her old man for what he did to her boyfriend and his father. I could see her going through a year of that, maybe two. But she was out there for four years, getting in deeper and deeper."

"Talmadge is lucky she wasn't a guy. She probably would have shot him. You know us girls. We like to take our time with revenge. It's that whole Mars and Venus thing."

"What was she trying to accomplish? Get word toTalmadge she was a slut? I think he already had that part figured out."

"Girls know their daddies don't like to think of them growing up at all, much less growing up and sleeping around. But having sex with their fathers' contemporaries?" she snorted. "In some cultures, they still stone young women for doing that. It's more taboo than adultery. Brooke knew it would enrage her father more than anything else she could have done, especially if he had any sexual feelings for her. Which I'm imagining he did. I bet she knew it, too. And her behavior was something he couldn't control. It made him look like a moron."

"She figured all that out when she was nineteen?" I said.

"Some of it was probably instinct. She had a master of manipulation in the family, didn't she? This way she turns her skill around and focuses it on the guy who trained her to be the way she is."

"Giving him a motive to kill her."

"Well." The blue eyes blinked and she inclined her head. "You think so? He sure waited for the wrong time if that's the case. Why would he kill her right after he set up Ferguson? You and Paul think he's the one who tipped Ferguson's wife to the affair, right? Talmadge had to know if the affair comes to light there's no way he can keep Brooke's murder under the rug. Ferguson just resigns without comment, it'll probably stay that way. If it gets to the press that she was Ferguson's mistress for the benefit of the Russian mob, hoo-boy. Then her murder becomes one big hairy deal and all her background with her loving daddy will come out. You know it will."

I didn't want to admit it but I felt my head bobbing anyway. When Sunny cranks that computer brain on, it's hard not to appreciate what tumbles out. If Talmadge had just built a path his man could use to walk into the U.S. Senate, he wouldn't want to do anything to risk that.

It looked at my watch. It was almost six. I could feel a headache circling in the vicinity and asking for landing instructions. I needed about ten hours of uninterrupted sleep followed by breakfast, followed by a two-hour nap. I stood up.

"You okay to drive?" Sunny asked. "All of a sudden your eyes look like they're going to roll back up into your head."

"Yes, Mother," I said. "I'll brush *and* floss, too, ok?"

"See that you do, young man."

*   *   *   *

When I got home, Socks was perched on top of the cat tree I keep for him in my living room. I could see him watching me as I approached the front door. He sat perfectly still, paws together, looking more than ever like he wore a tuxedo. He didn't move an inch when I came in and started for the stairs. Two birds on the porch railing outside proved to be far more fascinating than his sometime roommate.

I tried Kinsella once again before I climbed into bed.

"We just got the kid." he growled.

"What happened?"

I heard him suck in a breath.

"His homeys were hiding him out in a flop on South Michigan. Couple of tactical guys heard from a couple hookers about four of the Lords being up in two rooms and armed to the teeth, so they take a couple other tac teams and stake out the joint. They know not to move in or nuthing and they know to keep what they're doing quiet, not tell any supervisors, just make like it's all routine. Everything was all fine and dandy until about two hours ago when a uniform sergeant goes up into the place with some babe he's been banging. Her room is on the same fucking floor. Can you believe that?"

He sighed. "This sergeant gets into some kinda shouting match with one'a the assholes who's bodyguarding Mookie, and Mookie sticks his dumbass head out to see what's going on. The Sarge recognizes him from the bulletins and that just sets everything off."

I slumped back into my pillows and switched the phone to my other ear. "How many dead this time?"

Now the frustration in Kinsella's voice turned to disgust. "Oh no. You don't just get the totals. I got to take you through the whole thing. I mean because this is just so fucking brilliant. The Sarge figures he's got the world by the ass on this one 'cause he's got his radio with him right? He follows his chick into her room, tells her to shut the fuck up and calls in a ten-one, officer needs assistance, he's found the suspect the Area guys and the Bureau want to talk to."

"What happened to land lines or cell phones?"

The Chicago Police department's radio frequencies have enough listeners they should be rated by Arbitron and sell advertising time. *This burglary-in-progress call is brought to you by Jake's Pawnshop...*

"She doesn't have a land line and his phone was in the car. So he calls it in, the guys across the hall have a scanner, realize they've just lost their hideout, and they try to blow outta Dodge, right? But, the brilliant Sarge has his chick peeking out, watching the hall. The bad guys see the door cracked. I guess they get scared, and they put about a million rounds into the broad. The Sarge takes a couple in his vest and both legs but blows away one of the bangers with a lucky shot of his own. The other three hop on out into the street and split."

I nodded, knowing what the bad news was even before he finished telling the story.

"Mookie's dead?"

"Oh, yeah. Yeah. Naturally. Could it have gone any other way? Sarge fires through the wall, hits him square in the back of the head. DRT."

Dead-Right-There.

"I don't suppose he wrote the license number from the Jag in blood before he expired."

Kinsella made a rude sound.

"He mighta twitched once or twice when he hit the carpet but that's about it. We got nothing. That fucking asshole sergeant probably'll get a case of caviar and another one of vodka for the favor he did the Russians."

"I suppose it's a stupid question, but is there a chance what he did was intentional?"

"I thought about that, but nope. People I talked to who were at the scene say this guy had to have help tying his shoes but he was straight arrow. If anybody'd offered him money to take out a witness, he would've pissed his pants getting to the bosses to tell them and then stood around like a puppy waiting for his head to be rubbed."

"Shit," I said.

"Change of subject," he said wearily. "Piper treat you decent?"

"Tried to pull my balls up my throat, but yeah. I didn't take it personally."

"Just so you know the Feebs wanted to listen to your interview from another room so you wouldn't know they were there. Piper wouldn't let 'em. Chief of Detectives backed him up."

"You put in a good word for me?"

"Right. If I'd opened my mouth at all they'd probably have you in Pontiac already."

He pushed for me to join him for a late dinner. I begged off and put the phone back where it belonged. I'd left a James Galway CD in the player across the room and fumbled for the remote to switch it on so it could lull me to sleep.

As exhausted as I was, it felt odd to be in bed while the sun was still out. The sounds of children at play reached me through the hum of the air conditioner. I wasn't totally sure if I was hearing them in the present, or as echoes from the past. I strained to listen, to hear their words, but the harder I tried the more remote they became.

Strange adult voices woke me six hours and change later. Fortunately, no one was in my room but the sounds weren't just in my head either. I'd forgotten to turn off the Motorola I'd brought in from the car.

As the ether I'd been traveling in cleared, I realized I was hearing Sunny and someone else. They were talking in the clipped yet comfortable manner of two people used to spending nights on the street, connected in electronic intimacy by an encrypted two-way radio unable to be monitored by outsiders.

> "...exiting the lot now..."
> "Does he have company?"
> "Nobody behind him. You can pick him up at Sawyer if you want. Looks like he's headed for Location Adam."
> "I'll keep the parallel for a few blocks just to be sure."
> "Mercedes that dropped him off is westbound toward the tollway ramp. Two occupants."
> "Descriptions?"
> "Big and ugly. Otherwise, too far in bad light."
> "Thanks, Mark."
> "I'm sliding out to the street now. He's two blocks ahead at the light."
> "'K. I'll come up from Waukegan northbound and catch him when he clears."

They were talking about Belzer, that he'd been out for the evening and was now returning home. I thought about coming up on the radio to ask for a briefing then realized Socks was asleep at my feet and I'd have to move to grab the Motorola. I left it where it was and just listened as Sunny followed Belzer toward home. A couple of minutes later, though, Socks must have sensed my edginess because he poked his head up. Before I could tell him to go back to sleep, he jumped off the bed and padded out of the room.

"What's going on?" I asked on the radio.

"You're supposed to be asleep," Sunny came back.

"Guess we know I'm not."

"I'm about to tuck Jerome in for the night."

"Where's he been?"

"Mark, I've got him. Let me go first and we'll leapfrog him."

"10-4, Sunny. Hey Reno."

Sunny said, *"Went to this Russian nightclub in Des Plaines. The minute he was inside, Mark figured something was up. Next thing we knew a van was headed out to the highway from the alley in back. Didn't follow. I figured it's better they don't know we're on to him. If they're playing games like that you can figure they're expecting surveillance."*

I swung my legs out of bed. "Let's brace him when he gets home."

"How do you plan to do that?"

"Same way I did with Witting. Go up and knock on his door."

Sunny didn't answer. I started to get dressed. I could almost hear her thinking, *"And Witting worked out so well for you."*

She would never say it, of course. But I imagined it was taking a great deal of control for her not to snap something else at me.

When my phone rang, I was expecting it.

"You have bad dreams or something?"

"I'm hoping this conversation isn't going to be one."

"I'm not just running errands for you here, Reno. I know how to do this. Jumping in the guy's face in the middle of the night might make for great TV but it's a lousy way to get information."

"I want to talk to him right now, when he's looking over his shoulder a little bit anyway. We'll hit him with everything we know and go for broke."

She was silent for a moment. "He's a lawyer. He'll know…"

"He's a patent lawyer for crying out loud. And he'll know how much he has to lose if we put even what we have now on the air."

"On what air?"

"Oh. Did I forget to say we might have to lie a little?"

CHAPTER 18

▼

The Belzers lived in an airplane bungalow with a nice front porch and cobble-
stones in the foundation and up the chimney. Sunny's quick, silent reconnais-
sance before I got there showed lights still on around the back. We agreed I
would go in alone. She and Mark would loiter close to make sure Belzer didn't
blow me away.

It was comforting to know they'd be there to turn him in if he did. They'd
also be watching the street, just in case.

I looked at my watch. It was 1:30 a.m. as I tapped on the back door. I stood in
the light from a backyard flood, making myself a perfect target, and kept my
hands in plain view. I was betting he'd answer the door without a second
thought, figuring his midnight play pals had come a'calling again.

Belzer had a round face with close-set eyes and wore wire-frame glasses that
made him look a little like the actor who played the Gestapo agent in *Raiders of
the Lost Ark*. One hand came up to push them back a bit on his nose as he opened
the door. He growled something in Russian.

"Speak English," I said.

I saw a spark of fear in his eyes.

"What is it? Alex assured me no one would ever come to the house."

"I'm not one of Federov's goons," I said.

It's always handy to keep business cards from past jobs just in case you might
need one some day. I handed him one with the Channel 14 logo and the words
"Investigations Unit" prominently displayed.

"I'm getting ready to do a story about you and your wife and Russian organized crime. I'm required to give you a chance to respond before it airs."

The "required" is a nice, overbearing touch. I've gotten various reactions to that kind of announcement over the years. Often it's outrage, as with Alicia Witting, and the door slams in my face. Sometimes fear turns an otherwise healthy complexion gray. Occasionally, I've seen what cops and ME investigators see. Tears.

I expected lawyerly condescension or outright anger that I would dare disturb him at that hour of the morning. He just blinked at me as though I'd spoken Urdu.

"Elena? Why?"

"I'd like to come in and talk to you about that."

"I'm not required to speak with you, you know. In fact, if I were advising a client, I'd insist that he say 'no comment.'" He spoke the way many people do who have learned English as a second language. As though he were considering the rightness of each word.

"No comment doesn't get your side of the story told, though, does it?"

"You assume I wish to tell 'my side.'"

"Alicia Witting chose not to. Look what happened to her."

His lips lifted to display a nothing smile.

"Do you have a camera focused on me at this moment? Is this conversation being recorded?"

"No, it's not. My cameraman's waiting down the block."

"You certainly didn't come prepared, did you? Suppose I had decided to confess everything to you the moment you handed me your card? What then? A significant moment of history would have passed unrecorded."

I wondered if his evening had included just a shade too much to drink, or if Sunny's people had made a drastic error and this guy was playing for time until I told him he was on World's Funniest Home Videos. I was trying to think of something to say when he pushed the door open.

There was a florescent light on in the small kitchen. He'd apparently been in the midst of fixing himself a sandwich. Several slices of turkey and a piece of cheese were laid out on a tiled counter next to the refrigerator. He stopped there for a moment to wrap them in some aluminum foil and store them away.

He moved as though oblivious to me but, when he picked up a knife, I pushed my back against the door and watched until he dropped it in the sink. I took note of workingman's hands with thick fingers and chewed nails, a couple of them even showing a little blood.

Without turning to look at me, he said, "I was going to drink some herbal tea. Can I offer you some?"

"Sure."

He brought two porcelain cups out of a glass front cupboard and put them on the table in the middle of the room, then set a kettle to boiling on the stove.

"My wife likes the microwave," he explained. "I prefer the old fashioned way. I believe the young people refer to that as 'retro.'"

I realized neither of us was making an effort to speak quietly.

"Is Mrs. Belzer sleeping?" I asked.

His head dipped slightly. "No. My wife is in the hospital."

He gestured for me to take one of the two wooden chairs drawn up to the table. "Elena has lung cancer, Mr. McCarthy. I see by your expression that's not something you learned during your investigation of us."

"No. I'm sorry."

"Smoking," he sighed. "We certainly should have known better. Our parents worked in factories all of their lives. They smoked as well. If you know Russian cigarettes you know that was like putting guns to their heads. Each of them had cancer, of course, as did our grandparents. And yet Elena and I both smoked. I stopped two years ago. They don't allow it in the building where I work. Elena, at home all day…"

The kettle began to whistle and he brought it over to pour water for both of us. "Sugar? Cream?"

"No, thanks."

"Ah. A purist."

He finished topping off our cups and returned the kettle then took the chair opposite me. We tasted our tea carefully.

"You are surprised," he observed after a moment. "You did not expect me to invite you in for tea at one in the morning, did you?"

I had to smile. "I wasn't sure what to expect. This is exceptional tea, by the way."

"Remind me to give you several bags to take with you. Elena and I found it at a store in Chinatown over the winter."

"What do the doctors say?"

"Oh. They are not optimistic, of course. They told us a month ago she might have one or two months of relative comfort, but she already requires more medication for the pain than they expected. I spend mornings with her and go to the office in the afternoon. Not that I am able to accomplish much. My billable hours have been abysmal the past few months, I'm afraid."

"Is her illness the reason she never went to visit her mother?"

He smiled. "You ask that so casually, like we are old friends. No. She did not go to Russia because it is not safe. If she had visited…she would be there still."

"Federov?"

"Not him specifically, no. Others like him. You know how it works?"

"Blackmail's pretty universal."

"Oh, yes."

"How long has the organization had its hooks in you?"

"Three years? Four? Time flies, as they say. You should know I am not unique. They are excellent list-keepers, these *vor v zakonye*. What you would call 'thieves-in-law' or perhaps 'godfathers.' Those of us who emigrate and leave family behind are always at risk. If the *mafiya* believe we can be useful in some fashion they will approach us. Very few turn them down."

"Other than the fact you didn't want your mother-in-law harmed, why did they choose you?"

"Partly because my father always spoke out against them. Look through the back issues of enough Russian-language newspapers and you'll see the editorials he wrote. Andrei Nikolaevich denounced the underworld at every opportunity! And now his son is corrupted by the same forces he fought so hard against. They love the irony of that. They feel it is fitting punishment."

He lifted off his glasses and rubbed his eyes as though the light was suddenly painful.

"Isn't your father dead?"

"Yes. Many years. To them, however, death makes no difference. They are just as pleased to take vengeance against his family."

He ran his finger along the rim of his cup.

"Another reason they chose me is that I was very politically active at the time. I knew many people and circulated easily. My firm encourages giving back to the community. I embraced that concept. I had no idea it would make me a target. Now, when I attend community functions and political events, it is to gather intelligence for Misha."

"Misha?"

"A pet name Mikhail encourages those close to him to use. He likes to think of us as his extended family."

I was about to ask another question when the radio in my pocket burped.

"Reno?" Sunny said.

"I'm fine. No problems," I said.

"It's clear out here, too."

"Is that your private detective friend?" Belzer must have seen my surprise because he gave a small smile.

"Oh yes, I know you cannot be preparing a news story about us. I read the newspapers, watch television. They have few facts, and often get them wrong, but...I have managed to keep up."

"So why are we sitting here?"

"Because you are not the police, not a federal agent. You have no official standing and yet you appear to be a competent investigator. Perhaps because I know you will use what I tell you to get under Misha's skin. I would like that. He views himself as untouchable. I would enjoy it if you would disrupt his life as he has disrupted others."

He had been playing with his glasses and now he slipped them back on and peered through them at me, as though seeing me for the first time.

"Aren't you worried about comebacks?"

He bit a nail, glanced up. "Retribution? I think about it. Of course. You must understand, however, that Elena's cancer has taught me there are more important things to worry about than protecting myself. I am fifty-seven. I have been performing various illegal acts for people my father despised for several years. Speaking to you is the cowardly way I choose to atone for that."

"Cowardly?"

"Were I truly courageous I would stand up and denounce Misha in court. For all the world to see. That is truly a risk I cannot take. Elena needs me. I will not allow her to die alone."

He stared at me, as though weighing what he was going to say next.

"I remember you from the television news, Mr. McCarthy. You took risks, did you not? You protected sources. Yet, you put people in jail. Yes, I did my own little investigation of your background after I read of your involvement with Brooke's death. You are, I think, a responsible man. Perhaps we can use each other."

"You realize I've got a very limited agenda," I said. "I'm not Eliot Ness. All I care about is whether Federov killed Brooke Talmadge. Not bringing down the Russian mob."

"But if you discovered he killed her, what would you do?"

"I can't say until I get to that point."

"Would you kill him?"

"Not willingly."

"You are so sure?"

"If you read the papers, you know I killed someone last night. One is my bag limit for this lifetime."

"You may have to eliminate him. Misha is a fearsome enemy when he's angry."

I wanted to get off that subject.

"Was he angry at Brooke?"

He leaned back and considered the question. "More...at the situation, I think, than at Brooke. Perhaps even at himself for placing her in that kind of jeopardy."

"He cared for her then."

"Oh yes. I knew him for about a year before they met. He would use prostitutes the way some people order meals. His relationship with Brooke Talmadge was quite different. He controls two complete wings of Lake Point Tower, but had never shared the space with anyone except his bodyguards. They live in the units one floor below. He allowed her to move in with him, and then have full access inside his 'secure zone.' I was shocked."

"And since her death?" I asked.

"I have not seen or talked to him. I have regular meetings with another man. Alexi. He may be the only person Misha has spoken to. Alexi tells me it devastated him. He now apparently believes he was wrong to rekindle the relationship between Brooke and Senator Ferguson when there was already an asset in place."

"Meaning Alicia Witting."

"Yes. He used Alicia's lifestyle against her. She was sexually promiscuous and a drug abuser. The irony is that she had begun to, how do you say it? 'Straighten it out?' by the time Misha reached out to her. That didn't matter to him. He had enough proof of earlier transgressions to ruin her career. To be certain, he gave her certain tasks to perform for him. She provided top secret information using her standing in the Senator's office."

"If he could get all that from her, why add Brooke to the mix?"

"After World Trade Center attack, Alicia could only provide certain kinds of information without arousing suspicion. Misha anticipated Brooke could attain access to the Senator's personal thoughts and feelings. She would be able to discuss matters of greater scope, directly with him. She would know his intentions. Such intelligence could then be sold to any entity willing to pay for it."

"Makes for better blackmail, too. Ferguson could honestly deny he knew Alicia was a spy. He could claim he didn't know about Brooke, either, but he'd look like an ignoramus. A spy sharing his bed."

"Exactly. At first, there was consideration given to removing him from office entirely and orchestrating the ascension of someone more...susceptible to influence. Misha changed his mind when the Talmadge girl told him of their previous affair."

"Was Brooke's father involved in the scheme?"

"In a minor way, yes. He had someone in mind to take over Ferguson's seat, if the Senator was displaced. That was all."

"His deal with Federov fell through?"

"Yes. Misha agreed with me that Red Talmadge's reputation precluded trusting him."

"Even so, did anybody tell him his daughter would be part of the plan?"

"I…" He gave it some thought. "That I don't know."

I smiled to encourage him. "You know a lot. I'm surprised Federov trusts you the way he does. After all, he drafted you. You didn't enlist."

"Ah. An apt way to phrase it. One could say I created an identity for myself. I made myself trustworthy. Useful and trustworthy. And…"

His face clouded. "There's the matter of the money."

"Money?"

"When you do his bidding, Misha is quite generous. To refuse payment would be as dangerous as stealing from him."

Bad cops put it the same way: "If you don't take, your partners think you're a rat." I nodded.

"Of course, once I accepted the money, there was no salvaging my reputation. He has documented everything I've done. He mentions that, from time to time. He makes a little joke of it but…his point is very clear. If I ever claim that he forced me to work for him, that record will refute anything I say. And I have the money for my wife's treatments that insurance doesn't cover."

"Federov sounds like a cagey guy."

"He enjoys puzzles, Mr. McCarthy. He's been given the city as a giant game and told he can make up his own rules. His only directive is to seize the drug business away from 'the amateurs' as he calls them. Most people would regard that as insanity. He accepts it as a wonderful challenge. In his eyes, he cannot fail."

"Is he one of these godfathers you mentioned?"

"No. He is what is called *smotryashchiy*. What you would think of as a manager or supervisor. A regional manager, perhaps. Do not be fooled by the title, however. Or by his manners, if you should ever meet him. He is the essence of evil. He carries tremendous weight."

"What exactly do you do for him? Besides managing one of his apartment buildings?"

"You know about that, do you?"

He shrugged, nibbled a nail.

"What can I say? The building wasn't Misha's to begin with. It belonged to a friend of mine, another emigre, another of those with loved ones left behind. Gregor was the only one in his family to leave Russia. His brother and sisters are all back there. They all owned property in Kiev or Odessa, so it was natural for him to again buy real estate when he moved to Chicago. He bought the building. It started to do well. There was a surge of business. Most of his renters up until then had been Hungarian, Polish. He suddenly found himself signing contracts with one Russian after another. Many of them worked for the taxi company. More wanted to move in. Several he recognized from his old neighborhood. They were thugs, some even *bezopasnosti*, the enforcers. Leg-breakers. He went to the owner of the taxi company to tell them he had no more apartments available. The next thing that happened, Federov's people were shoving him around, blindfolding him. He heard a pistol clip being snapped into place. They told him what his new business plan would be."

His eyes were locked on his tea cup.

"I was already doing legal work for Gregor, as favor. That is what drew them to me, unfortunately. I was told to continue. Then I was given other tasks to do, once they checked into my background. Mostly political things. Research. I am a conduit."

"You helped with Alicia Witting."

"I passed messages, yes. From time to time they would ask me what I thought about doing this or that regarding other situations. Political things only," he stressed. "No violence."

"You said Federov regarded you as 'family'…"

"I have visited his home. We have shared meals. Now it is only meetings with Alexi Voronin. He is *bezopasnosti*. That is where I was tonight." He chewed a fingernail, realized what he was doing and put his hand down on the table.

"If I am found in ditch with bullet in my head, Alexi will have pulled the trigger. Each time I go with him, I wonder if it is to be the last time."

"You and your wife could have gotten out. Witness protection…"

He had lifted his finger to his mouth again but pulled it away and snapped, "What kind of life would that have been? No. I do not run. Ever! I will give information about some of Misha's other business. I have lists of people who are helping him. I will help you investigate him…"

"Not me. Like I said, if he didn't kill Brooke or order it done, bringing him down is someone else's job. I know a Chicago cop you can talk to about that."

*   *   *   *

I asked him about Federov, then thought of something and called for Sunny to join us. She came in through the back door. When Belzer stood up in a gentlemanly way and offered her tea, she looked a little stunned and politely declined. Belzer disappeared into another room and came back a moment later carrying a chair for her.

"Tell us about Federov's place at Lake Point Tower," I said.

"It is magnificent! What would you expect of someone who has millions to spend? He has a full wing on the 71st floor for his residence and another, one floor below, for offices and his bodyguards. Neither property is in his name, of course. No one knows when he comes and goes. He uses few of the amenities, never dines in the restaurant. He occasionally swims in the indoor pool."

"That's a valet parking and doorman building. How does he stay invisible?" Sunny asked.

"There is an elevator from the basement of parking garage. His car is never driven by an attendant. He once told me he pays $125,000 a year for the privilege of having his bodyguards drive him into the garage and bypass the valet. The windows of his vehicles are darkened. No one knows if he is in the car or if it is merely bodyguards or staff."

"How do people get in to see him?" I asked.

Belzer smiled. "Few do. No one just 'drops by.' He has alarms and video surveillance. His bodyguards are armed with automatic weapons."

Sunny sat forward, curious. This was her territory, after all. "He's hooked into the building's video system?"

"Yes. He has monitors in his office and bedroom for every camera, including those in the elevators, the shafts and the maintenance areas. I am sure he has security people watching those monitors twenty-four hours a day. There are cameras in other areas, too, that his people have installed."

"Sweet." She nodded approvingly and looked at me.

"I did a security assessment for someone who was considering moving in there. I'll give this Federov jerk credit. Patching into Lake Point's cameras took professional techs and a lot of patience. Given the construction of the building, how old it is, I'll bet adding new equipment wasn't easy, either. All wireless probably, especially in the elevator shafts."

"He watches everything," Belzer said. "It is obsession, I think. I have seen him staring at the lobby monitor the way a child looks at a favorite cartoon. He can even watch from his home the people in his bank offices across the river."

Sunny nodded again. "Microwave or infrared. As long as he's line of sight, no problem."

"And the guards?" I prompted.

"There is one just inside the door that leads to the elevator common area. There have always been two others in his residence when I have been there. I don't know how many below."

"So when you get off the elevator you see…a guy with a machine gun?"

"No." He closed his eyes. "There is a door to Misha's wing immediately to the right. It is closed but there is a camera above it. The guard sits on the other side of the door. There is a corridor behind him and the doors at the end of it open into Misha's home."

We talked about the layout for awhile, trying to figure a way to get inside. I wanted in badly but I was beginning to think even a SWAT team might have trouble getting past those doors.

Always tougher to take an opponent who has a fixed position I thought, remembering the line from a class on military history. Not to mention the high ground. Maybe I should go back and read *The Art of War*. Ol' Sun Tzu had an answer for everything.

It was past three when we left Belzer in his kitchen, still sipping tea and biting his nails. Sunny and I didn't say much on the way to our cars except that we would talk later in the afternoon. The moment I got behind the wheel, I felt the exhaustion of the past few days bearing down on me like a rogue wave. I drove home and went back to bed.

I slept without dreams until noon. Would have gone well into the afternoon if it had not been for Socks jumping onto my chest and snorting his displeasure at my laziness. I got up, flipped on the local cable station and watched the latest news loop as I fed him.

No progress reported on the drive-by killings of three Russian men on the West Side. The breaking story was about shotgun blasts "out of the night" that left a man and his wife dead in bed in their upscale condo on the south side. The husband had a long record as a gangbanger, although his lawyer was quoted as saying he most recently had become an activist who regularly lectured kids on the evils of gang life. The lawyer also said the husband was considering a run for the City Council.

Yeah, no doubt. Although with his experience stealing, maiming and back shooting, he'd be well qualified. Unofficial sources were quoted as saying the guy never moved out of the gang life but rather up a level or two that took him off the street and into 'management.'

The only connection made between that double murder and the other recent gang violence was by the anchor who grouped the stories together because it allowed for a nice segue. I sat down at my computer and checked the newspapers online. No connecting of the dots there, either, not even by the brighter columnists. If any other reporter was seeing the sudden spike in gang-related shootings as the beginning of a war, they were keeping silent about it.

I switched over to Channel 14's Web page. Nothing there, either. The lead article said temperatures were expected to be back in the nineties and the city was opening its cooling facilities to anyone without air conditioning.

I glanced at the thermometer which hangs in the backyard. 89 degrees. Perfect for a run. I needed to stir up the endorphins and see if they could clear out cobwebs brought on by too much stress and too little sleep. I put on shorts and a t-shirt, dug a fanny pack out of the back of my closet and slipped the Walther into it, then headed out.

It was the kind of heat that causes you to break a sweat even if you're exerting no more effort than lifting a lemonade glass. I did my pre-run stretches against an oak tree in the front yard, long slow ones that let my leg muscles know they were about to see some action. Across the street and two houses down, my neighbor mowed his lawn. He had a towel wrapped around his neck and I knew he would stop in a few minutes and soak it with a hose. I could hear kids howling in delight as they splashed in another neighbor's backyard pool. A late-model Beemer SUV passed the house and moved slowly down the block. I thought of Alan Talmadge. He hadn't responded to the note I'd left for him.

I finished my stretches and walked down to the end of the driveway, considering what route my jog would take. Two miles to the lake, another mile up through the Northwestern campus, staying close to the water where it would be cooler, then three miles back. A respectable distance.

Thought some more about Alan Talmadge and how I didn't want to play phone tag with him. I turned, intending to go back inside and grab the cell to carry with me in case he called. As I did, two things happened simultaneously. A fellow the size of an NFL linebacker came loping around the garage toward me, and the sport utility I'd seen just a couple of moments before slid to the curb at the end of the driveway.

There are fanny packs for guys who have to carry guns all the time. They have a nice Velcro fastener that allows you to rip the front panel down with one hand while you yank the weapon loose with the other. Mine wasn't that combat ready. It had been styled to hold nothing more threatening than wallets, car keys and maybe a pair of sunglasses. Even so, I managed to get the damn thing unzipped. I had the Walther out and swinging up toward the guy coming at me from the backyard when he suddenly stopped, threw both arms out to his sides and curved his lips into a nasty 'gotcha' grin.

CHAPTER 19

▼

"If you shoot him, I will shoot you."

Keeping the Walther aimed in a two-handed grip, I glanced over my shoulder.

The SUV's passenger door was open and there sat Yevgeny Olokoff, the guy I'd sucker punched after he confronted Brooke in the Holiday Inn parking lot. He was holding what looked like an assault rifle with a sound suppressor. Though he kept it low and out of sight behind the door, there was no question where it pointed. Beyond him, the SUV's driver was an indistinct blur.

Oddly, I thought of an old comedy routine from the Fifties. A mugger confronts Jack Benny and, at gunpoint, demands, "Your money or your life." The old skinflint goes into his trademark pose, one arm across his chest, the other hand cupping his chin. After a lengthy pause, Benny replies in that droll way of his, "I'm thinking it over!"

I was thinking it over, too, but nobody was laughing.

I lowered the Walther. Olokoff snapped something in Russian. The refugee from the NFL's linebacker draft came forward, took the gun and tossed it over his shoulder into the bushes by the porch. Then he grabbed my arm and walked me toward the SUV.

Olokoff got out sans rifle and opened the back door.

"Get in," he said. He grinned as I passed him, and when I stepped up to hoist myself through the opening he spun and drove a hard fist into my testicles. It wasn't unexpected, and I managed to turn slightly when I saw his shoulder drop so I took most of the force on the outside of the thigh, but a punch to the nuts is a punch to the nuts. A fearful sick pain made my world go white and I tumbled sideways into the truck, hands coming up too late in the universal gesture of protection.

Olokoff laughed.

I felt my legs lifted out of the way of the door and heard it bang shut. I wasn't going to black out and I knew the pain would subside, but for the moment I was paralyzed. The other back door opened and Olokoff's partner got in beside me while Olokoff slid into the front and the SUV began moving.

"Sit up!" Olokoff demanded.

When I didn't comply, rough hands grabbed me by the armpits and dragged me off the floor and into the seat. My stomach rolled. I swallowed and took a short breath.

Olokoff leaned around in his seat and glared at me. "How you like it now, eh?"

"That," I began, felt my throat seize, gasped through it, "your best shot?"

The driver nudged him and said something in Russian. The guy sitting beside me slapped the side of my head. I fell against the back door and covered up. All three of them laughed.

"I give you best shot later, pussy." Olokoff smirked. "You never forget best shot."

The sport utility accelerated, pressing me into the seat. I felt the barrel of a pistol probe my left ear. Suddenly, every pain they had caused disappeared and they had my complete attention.

"You listen, pussy," Olokoff said and then rattled something at the driver that sounded angry.

"My friend says you sit quietly or my other friend will shoot you and put you out into traffic," the driver said. He was easier to understand, even sounded a little amused. "We are taking you somewhere to be spoken to. If you give us no reason to harm you, you will not be hurt again."

"Where...are we...going?" It was a struggle to talk.

The driver met my eyes in the rear view mirror. "I'll tell you what, Mr. Reporter Man. So, you need to know everything, eh? Look at this!"

Olokoff either understood English better than he spoke it or he sensed the driver was about to let something out that I shouldn't hear. He pointed a finger and snapped, "*Nyet!*"

I got that part.

"Where are we going?" I demanded, just to keep the conversational ball rolling.

This time Olokoff surged around the front seat, eyes wide, and slammed me in the forehead with the heel of his hand. "Shut UP!"

I was lucky he didn't aim for my nose. It was a pretty good shot, nonetheless.

Dazed, I don't remember any of the ride until we hit Lake Shore Drive. The pain actually brought me around. My ears rung and my head and nose played off each other to see which could hurt worse. The first thing I saw was the exit sign for LaSalle Street.

Minimize the pain window. Maximize the thinking window.

Had my neighbor seen what happened to me? If so, did he describe the vehicle to the police? Probably not. Sunny would try to reach me eventually. She knew I sometimes turned my radio and phone off, though. So how quickly would she start to worry? When she did, would she assume my disappearance was the work of the government or Federov? The gun in the yard would tell her. If she found it.

We rolled under the Drive at Grand Avenue toward the Navy Pier arch. I started to panic. Who knew what would happen if I let them take me up to Federov's place? That was undeniably where we were headed. If they could get me there unseen, what was to say they couldn't drag my body out of there without alarming any witnesses, too?

Ironic. Wasn't I the one who had wanted to sneak in and surprise the guy? Some surprise.

We passed the rear of Lake Point Tower. Off to my right and across a stretch of grass, were the locks where the Chicago River empties into Lake Michigan. Frequently, there's a police boat in that area. As the driver slowed to make the U-turn that would lead us to the front entrance to Lake Point, I slammed my hand down on the handle next to me and the door popped open.

The thug next to me must have felt me tense to make the move. He had one big arm wrapped around my neck before I could even clear the opening. I saw surprise on the faces of several people walking along the sidewalk that leads to Navy Pier. Then the door slammed shut and the barrel of my seat mate's gun drilled into my side so hard I gasped.

"You think we care if we have to shoot you, Mr. Reporter Man?" The driver asked, his voice reflecting no affect whatsoever.

"We shoot you. We drive away. We leave body in alley."

The sport utility slid around the corner. The entrance to Navy Pier flashed by. Kids ran down the sidewalk past the shooting water sculpture. We drove underneath the Lake Point Tower overhang and into the parking garage. A red-jacketed valet waved and went back to his Sunday paper. Down one level, past rows of parking spaces that had probably cost their owners more than the cars that were in them. We stopped in a corner and both the driver and Olokoff turned to look at me.

"We walk to elevator and go up, 'kay?" The driver said. "Simple? No problem? 'Kay?"

I nodded. It hurt to do so, but less than it would have ten minutes before. The pain was now just a bell-ringing headache.

The driver smiled. He was the smallest of the three men, with a pronounced widow's peak and a faint scar that joined both eyebrows. His teeth looked as though he'd been chewing rocks.

"If you call out to anyone? We kill you. We kill person you involve. 'Kay?"

"That'd be really stupid," I said, worried about the effort it took to get the words out.

Another smile. "For you, yes, stupid. You understand now?"

"Yeah, yeah," I said.

The basement felt damp and clammy. I had the sense of thousands of tons of mass above me and water on all sides held back by layers of concrete. Claustrophobia grabbed me. I thought of being underground permanently. I wondered how near to death I might be.

I moved as slowly as possible getting out of the SUV and over to the elevator. I wanted someone else to see me. Not that I would try to get help. I wanted a witness to the fact I had been in the building. Just in case. Also, my knees were shaking so badly I was afraid to try and walk faster for fear I'd just drop and my escorts would put me out of my misery.

Olokoff and his sizeable friend each held an arm for the ride up to the 71st floor. I suppose they didn't want me to fall in view of any of the building employees who might be monitoring the video camera mounted in the elevator. I wondered if the building kept tapes from each camera. If so, I'd have my witness. Somehow that wasn't as comforting a thought as it might have been. The driver carried a thick briefcase that looked heavy. I thought about that and supposed he probably had folded the stock of Olokoff's MAC-10 and stuffed it in there.

There was no one in the foyer of the 71st floor. A camera was mounted above the door that led to Federov's quarters. The door opened as we approached it. Belzer was correct about the guard, right about the machine gun, too. It lay across the Coleman chair parked in the hallway behind him. I fantasized about lunging for it as we swept past but at that point they were nearly carrying me. I wondered if Federov was watching our progress. I wondered if the boys knew the boss had his eyes on them and were hustling me along to impress him.

Another chunky guy, this one in black jeans and a black t-shirt and with arms like a longshoreman's, ushered us into the apartment. He had two tattoos in Cyrillic letters, one on his left forearm and the other on the back of his right hand. His face was surprisingly soft and vaguely reminded me of that comedian who used to play the character Pee Wee Herman.

Olokoff took the briefcase from the driver and disappeared down a carpeted hallway. The other two left. Pee Wee looked at me.

"Are you hurt?"

"I've felt better."

He grunted. "Could be dead."

"There is that."

"This way."

I followed him down the hall where Olokoff had disappeared. We passed one closed door and then entered a living room of startling size and depth and with such an incredible panoramic view that, for a moment, I thought there were no windows. I felt suspended in mid-air, almost the sensation I've gotten when lifting off in a helicopter. It made me dizzy enough I had to put out a hand and touch the wall to steady myself.

The glass stretched floor to ceiling and wall-to-wall for about thirty-five feet. Displayed as though on a screen were Navy Pier and the lakefront to way down past the museum complex. I could see Grant Park and a nice portion of South Michigan Avenue, too, and the tops of most of the Loop's buildings. It was a bright shiny Chicago summer day without a hint of haze and no clouds unless they were ones I seemed to be standing on. The lake was so crowded with sailboats and power boats and lunch-liners and WaveRunners and Jet Skis that if I imagined them all to be cars on the Kennedy expressway, the traffic jam would be endless.

A helicopter hovered near the water intake cribs and the old lighthouse on the breakwater. Closer in, the Odyssey cruise ship maneuvered into its mooring on the Pier. I let my eyes wander, imagining I could see the restaurant table at Riva where all this had begun, where Hanratty had bought my lunch four days ago.

"You're welcome to sit down if you're feeling lightheaded."

I'd been so drawn into the view that I hadn't heard Federov approach. Or was the room so acoustically tight, the carpet so thick, that it deadened the sound of his footfalls?

He looked younger and leaner than the pictures I'd seen. Part of it was the difference between a man with a thick mustache and heavy shoulders posing for the camera in a $1,000 tailored Armani suit and the same guy relaxing at home in

$500 Armani sweats and $300 Nikes. All the casual elegance couldn't chase away the drawn features or the way his right fist wrapped so tightly around a tennis ball that the muscles jumped in his forearm.

He underhanded the ball into a deep-cushioned couch as he crossed the room to introduce himself. An accent emerged only as he pronounced his given name. He had jet black hair, combed back and perfectly barbered, possibly moments before he stepped into the room. His eyes were remarkable. As shrewd as a psychiatrist's, they also conveyed a warmth and good humor that surprised me.

"Did one of my employees give you that bruise on your forehead?"

"No, I fell into a Mack truck."

He went to a wet bar discreetly molded into a corner away from the windows and used tongs to lift several ice cubes into a towel. He offered it to me.

"Here. You're going to look like a unicorn otherwise."

I took the compress and used it. He poured tap water into a glass and then dropped a couple of tablets into it that made it bubble.

"Nervous stomach," he explained. "Can I get you anything?"

"How about an explanation of why you had me kidnaped?"

That made him smile. He downed his Alka Seltzer, or whatever it was, and poured himself another tap water over ice to carry with him as he wandered to the windows.

"My orders didn't include having you hurt. I allow my colleagues certain latitude in how they perform their tasks. I'll be honest, as you Americans like to say. I thought having you brought here, rather than picking up the phone and simply inviting you, would make a stronger impression."

"Consider it made. Punched in the balls, punched in the head. No one knows where I am. I'm unarmed. Not exactly dressed for the occasion. I'd say the advantage is yours."

He nodded. "Do you think I'm going to have you killed?" Still conversational.

"You tell me."

Trying to appear unconcerned, I abandoned the superb view for a moment and took in the furnishings. What wasn't oversized and custom built with thick cushions and muted tones was formal, but still looked comfortable. A couple of 1940's French chairs faced a couch with a wide ottoman. Two Saarinen side tables were arranged on either side of the couch and a library table behind it held an ugly silver samovar. An ebonized Lacewood stereo cabinet sat under a portrait of a man with Federov's features wearing a Russian Army uniform complete with black cross belt. He sat astride a white horse and was turned slightly, left hand resting on a riding crop that lay across his left thigh, his right hand holding the reins.

I gestured toward the painting. "A striking man."

"My father."

"His expression suggests he used the crop on more than just his horse."

"He seldom used it on his horse, in fact. He holds animals in very high esteem. People, on the other hand…yes, he believes pain can be quite a useful stimulant in certain situations. That's not to suggest he's a sadist, of course."

"Depends on one's point of view, I suppose. Is he alive?"

"Oh, yes. Arthritic to the point he has to use special tools to manipulate the keys, but he's become quite an Internet researcher. He tells me he'll sit at the computer for hours jumping from one site to another. He has contacts all over the world."

"Still running the family business?" I asked, politely.

"Do you know how some entrepreneurs will begin a new venture when they retire from another? My father devised one of the most successful methods of obtaining credit card information from secured sites. He is the envy of the younger hackers working with him. They all use his same basic methods now."

"He's a good thief in other words."

"One of the best," Federov said without expression. "You find that abhorrent?"

"Maybe it's the cultural difference. Around our house, we celebrated when my dad won a police league bowling tournament."

He didn't react to my sarcasm.

"My father's computer creativity is merely a hobby for him. His passion is something else entirely." He picked up a honey-colored amulet from an end-table and handed it to me. It had what appeared to be a beetle suspended inside.

"Are you familiar with amber, Mr. McCarthy?"

"Not really."

"It's a semi-precious stone created from the resin of certain kinds of trees. Sap. Trees produce it to protect themselves from such things as boring insects or the loss of a branch to a storm."

He touched the amulet. "Insects such as these are trapped and fossilize when the resin hardens. In the 18th Century, the King of Prussia presented a series of amber-inlaid panels to Peter the Great. They were eventually installed in a room in Yekaterinsky palace outside St. Petersburg where they remained until the Germans stole the room during World War Two."

"Stole the room?" I asked.

Federov motioned for me to follow him farther into the apartment. He led me to a closed door at the end of the hallway.

"The Amber room was absolutely magnificent," he said, eyes shining as though he was seeing it, reveling in it, as he spoke.

"The panels covered an area of eleven yards square. Each was inlaid with Baltic amber, all pristine quality, carved by craftsmen. There were also mosaics made of other stones, quartz and jade and onyx. It was essentially a jewel box built to human dimensions."

He removed a key from his pocket.

"Hitler's troops overran the palace, and dismantled the panels. They shipped twenty-eight crates in a convoy of trucks to what is now Kaliningrad on the Baltic Coast and from there…"

He snapped his fingers. "Into the air. Or so the story goes."

He unlocked the door and pushed it open. Blackout drapes covered the windows and the darkness of the room looked impenetrable.

"Some believe the panels are at the bottom of the ocean, others that they burned up when the Allies bombed a castle where they were stored. My father thought differently. He emerged from the war as a Colonel in *Glavnoye Razvedy-vatelnoye Upravlenie*, Russian Military Intelligence or GRU. He convinced his superiors that the panels could be found. The loss of the Amber Room was not only a cultural tragedy but a political disaster. The government provided him with an unlimited budget and assigned him to mount a search.

"My father committed himself to the effort, Mr. McCarthy. His methods were unique, really. More those of a man well-versed in ferreting out spies and traitors. No one cared. He re-interviewed people reported to have last seen the panels and the mosaics. He found one of the investigators who told of finding a room fragment after that air raid I spoke of. He interrogated many, many individuals. Some of them didn't survive his questioning. He was good with his hands, riding crop or not. It was said that he generally received the information he sought."

Federov flipped a switch.

The room lights came up with a comforting glow like candle wicks catching flame. The highly polished surfaces of the tables and built-in shelving gleamed. It reminded me of stepping into a church sanctuary and seeing stained glass gather the harsh daylight glare and gentle it into something soft and reverential.

The intricately carved panel set into the wall opposite the door was a honey-color that seemed to glow with increasing intensity the longer I looked, until it dazzled my eyes and made them hurt.

I didn't blink.

Obviously broken from a larger work, it was a view of what appeared to be a courtyard and a wall and maybe a raised arm in front of what might have been a tree limb.

It was exquisite.

Federov stood next to me.

"My father left the GRU and joined the KGB in the late 1950's. He had not completed his mission. He was assigned to a special commission searching for the Amber Room. Twenty years after that, he was still searching. It was a time of great upheaval in the Soviet Union. He chose to leave the KGB and serve another master, as it were. He never gave up looking for the Amber Room, Mr. McCarthy. Impressive tenacity and dedication, wouldn't you say?"

"Yeah." Other stones set in the amber panel gleamed but couldn't match the amber's thrilling depth of color.

"My father discovered that the Germans split up the crates shipped from Yekaterinsky palace, what you would call Catherine's Palace. They were all sent to the same destination but by various routes, doubtless for security. Some were opened and the panels used as target practice by those who guarded them along the way. A very few arrived safely."

He paused.

"Ten years ago, my father found where the Germans hid our Amber Room. In a cave, if you can believe it!" he laughed.

"What you see here is a part of what first caught his eye as his team opened the crates. It was his gift to me when I was given the opportunity to come to America."

I almost forgot where I was, and how I had arrived. "It's...it's magnificent."

Federov said nothing but I sensed him nodding.

"The color just rips your heart out," I said.

"Perhaps it doesn't surprise you that Brooke wept when I first showed her this room." His voice had gone slightly hoarse. "Afterward, she requested I give her a key, so she could visit whenever she wished."

"I believe it."

He touched my arm. "Come. We have business." The catch in his voice was gone.

I let him guide me back into the hall. When I turned to take another look at the amber mosaic, I found he had already shut off the lights and was closing the door. I was surprised to feel cheated. He keyed the lock and faced me.

"My father has since found other pieces, some larger, some smaller. There are experts working to restore them. I am hoping to eventually have the complete panel."

He walked ahead of me toward the living room.

"Unfortunately, some other sections surfaced in Germany. They are included in a project to re-create the Amber Room at the State Museum at *Tsarskoe Selo*, on the grounds of Catherine's palace."

"Sounds like you'll have a hole in your masterpiece."

His shoulders lifted in what I thought was a shrug of resignation, but when he turned he was smiling. It would have been a pleasant expression, had it reached his eyes. Never made it.

"I'm told that many craftsmen work for the pure joy of restoring a magnificent artifact. But I ask you this. How many of them would sacrifice their loved ones for their art?"

I said nothing. He continued into the living room. Pee Wee waited there, holding out a cup and saucer which Federov accepted.

"Of course, there is also the matter of security at the museum. Despite the state's grand desire to bring the Amber Room full circle, it pays the security staff only a minimal salary. A few rubles in the right hands, heads turned away at a critical moment and I will have what I need to complete my 'masterpiece,' as you put it."

"Okay, so you've got the world by the ass," I said. "Did you bring me here just to show me your toys?"

He clapped his hands. "Mr. McCarthy, you behave just as I expected! In my business, conversations must be oblique. You are refreshingly direct."

"Good that one of us is."

He took a sip from the cup. "Thank you, Alexi. Would you like coffee, Mr. McCarthy? It is from Uzbekistan. Uzbeki coffee is quite strong."

Under other conditions, I might have accepted. Not with my raging paranoia. Strong coffee can cover the taste of about anything that can be added to it. My face must have revealed my thinking because Federov said something to Pee Wee who laughed and took a seat.

Federov sank into the overstuffed couch. I stayed where I was, up against the wall, facing the windows.

This time the view didn't unhinge me.

"All right. We get to the reason you are here." He drank some more coffee and put the cup on the table in front of him. Something like a cloud crossed his features.

"I did not kill Brooke Talmadge. Not only did I not kill her myself, I did not direct it done.

"Of course, you have no way to know if I am telling you the truth. All I can offer in my defense, frankly, is that her death has changed my life. I assure you. I did not do this thing."

There it was again. The slight catch in his voice. Only this time, if I hadn't been listening with extra-special intensity, I might have missed it. If he was lying, he was pretty good. Then again, why wouldn't he be? Most sociopaths have no trouble emulating the emotions the rest of us expect to see.

"What difference does it make if I believe you? It's not like I have proof you have to refute."

"I want her killer found. I think you can do this. It seems you have made it your mission to find this individual, just as my father made it his mission to find the Amber Room. However, you will not be able to find the real killer if you continue to consider me your number one suspect."

"You had the motive. You had the opportunity. You haven't been shy about ordering people killed. Patrick Vega, for example."

"One of the reasons you are here, Mr. McCarthy, is the way you dealt with Leonid and Tash. Do you know they were both KGB? I certainly don't appreciate losing valued employees but I must say the manner in which you dispatched them...most impressive for an amateur."

My anger gave me certain bravado.

"Yeah, you don't like to lose your employees and I don't like to see an unarmed man gunned down."

He sat forward in his chair.

"If someone attempted to blackmail you, what would you do? Eh? He had the audacity to call here, on a private line I set up for Brooke to use. Do you know, I heard it ring and I actually thought...for just a moment...I thought she had survived. Perhaps someone else had died in her place. Your American movies with their saccharine endings are undoubtedly having an effect on me.

"He called me, this little faggot. Demanded I provide one hundred thousand dollars and he would keep silent about Brooke's work 'on my behalf.' A ridiculous figure from a foolish little man. It took nothing to discover his current occupation and where he could be found."

He put his hands up to either side of his face, creating a tunnel he looked at me through. "Block everything else. Consider it completely from a business standpoint. You will understand."

"Consider me unconvinced. About Patrick or about Brooke."

"There was nothing in the world Brooke could have done that would have persuaded me to have her killed! Nothing she knew, nothing she would say to anyone. Mr. McCarthy, had she gone to the FBI and told them everything she knew about me, I would still love her. Her death…" he stopped speaking for a moment and looked into the distance.

"I would strangle her killer with my own hands. I have never committed murder, but if the opportunity presented itself for me to look in this man's eyes and squeeze the life out of him, I would do it in an instant."

"Didn't O.J. say something like that?"

"Let me tell you this. I can only offer a certain kind of proof. It is not the kind that would be helpful in court but between us, as men, I believe it is worthwhile."

"What's that?"

He had a short conversation with Alexi who nodded and went out.

Federov said, "I know of your conversation with Jerome Belzer early this morning. We have been concerned about him for some time. He was not the strongest individual and his wife's hospitalization weakened him considerably."

A little of the queasiness I'd felt before ran through me, but I made a conscious effort to tamp it down. I knew I had been clean going over there and was sure nothing Sunny had done had drawn any attention to her. She was as competent at surveillance, and anti-surveillance, as anyone and probably more so than most.

Federov went on, as though he had wiretapped my thoughts.

"Some time ago, we installed audio monitoring equipment in his home. When I learned that you wished to confront me, I took the initiative. We needed to have this conversation on my terms."

"Why?"

"So I could offer the only proof I have that I did not kill Brooke. I will allow you to leave when we finish this conversation, Mr. McCarthy. We will not detain or harm you in any way. In fact, I'll have Alexi drive you home if you like. Even as I am aware that you now know enough about my business practices and activities that you could seriously compromise me, you may walk free. You have my personal guarantee. I want you looking for Brooke's murderer. And I will help you."

"What you really mean is, enough people know that I'm in your shorts that killing me would be a pretty obvious."

Alexi returned to the room carrying the briefcase Olokoff's driver had carried into the apartment. He set it down at Federov's feet and returned to his chair. Federov bent and opened it.

I suddenly wanted out of there.

"Please. If I felt it necessary, you would be dead already. This you should know. My father taught me there is no risk too great if one has a mission to complete. I have always believed that to be so. I did not kill Brooke, Mr. McCarthy. And I have no reason to kill you. This, however, was necessary."

When he reached into the bag, I suddenly knew what he would withdraw.

I began to retch before I even saw what it was because I knew, Jesus, I knew what he was lifting, and then it was free and he was holding it by the hair and I felt a burning in the back of my throat and I swallowed once and I averted my eyes from the sightless ones that stared at me and I gagged and felt Alexi next to me, taking my arm, asking me to come with him to a bathroom about six steps from where I'd been sitting.

I bent toward the commode, put my hand on the sink and coughed a couple of times. Belzer's fish-belly white face and terrified expression were superimposed on everything and there was a roaring in my ears that overwhelmed all other sounds.

I didn't throw up.

I leaned against the bathroom wall, however, and sucked in horrible gasping breaths until the pictures disappeared and I could stand and look into the mirror and not see them.

"Jesus," I said. "Jesus, Jesus…"

"Take it easy man. Just stand easy there. He's put it away." Alexi was far more Americanized than his boss. He sounded like he was from Brooklyn. Maybe he was. He handed me a wet towel. These people were damn solicitous after the fact.

"What the hell?" I said and my voice shook.

"If Jerome would speak so candidly with you, who else might he feel compelled to contact?" Federov said from the bathroom doorway.

I snapped my head toward him but his hands were empty except for the disposable wipe he was using to clean them, slowly, one finger at a time.

"You now have my admission to two murders. I hope you appreciate my candor."

I turned. The rage I telegraphed caused Alexi to slap a restraining hand firmly on my shoulder.

"You're a fucking lunatic,"

Federov shook his head. "Jerome's death might not have been required except for one thing. Something we could not control but which would have caused him to become even more reckless. His wife died in the hospital about two hours after you left him. Natural causes. Absolutely not our doing," he added.

"None of these deaths mean anything to you, do they?"

"Brooke's death meant everything. The others? As I say, it is the way I do business. It is the way I will accomplish my mission. Do you understand now why I am allowing you to live?"

"That's the most ludicrous excuse for murder I've ever heard. 'It's just *business*?'" My head felt like it was going to split down the middle. I tasted blood and looked in the mirror to see it dripping from my nose. I used the towel I'd been given to swipe it away.

"You're a fucking monster."

I started for him. Startled by my advance, Federov took a step back into the living room. I followed him, ready to smash that aristocratic face. Alexi's hand clamped onto my arm and he pressed a gun to the back of my head.

"You think you know who killed Brooke?" I snarled. "Maybe have a couple of suspects in mind? Why not just kill 'em all? That'll solve your problem."

Those obsidian eyes of his narrowed and seemed to glow.

"Rest assured, Mr. McCarthy. Rest assured. When you identify the guilty party, he will die. There is no question of that. I could do as you say. Wipe the board. In this case, however, it is necessary I know the specific person responsible. When you have calmed down sufficiently, I will tell you who I think it is. We will discuss it like gentlemen and then I will allow you to go. You will find out if I am correct and I will then deal with him when I choose."

He resumed his finger wiping.

*　　　*　　　*　　　*

A homicide detective once told me over a few beers, "Consider the true nature of evil, Reno. The devil is among us, there's no question. You won't see the horns or the pointed tail. You may not see a gun or a knife. He'll be wearing a business suit or the hard hat or the doctor's caduceus or maybe just the jeans and blouse of a soccer mom. But he's here and he's hard at work every damn day."

Or Armani sweats, I thought.

I will tell you who I think it is.

I was focusing on that, taking deep and even breaths, when somebody down the hall shouted something in Russian. I had no idea what it meant, but it sounded sharp, fearful, and a lot like a warning.

We turned in that direction. Something flashed outside the huge living room windows.

Hovering there, not twenty yards from the building, was the helicopter I'd figured was ferrying tourists. A door along its belly slid back. I glimpsed a gun barrel and dove for the floor.

The apartment windows imploded.

Bullets stitched the living room wall in tune to the thump of a heavy machine gun. Pieces of the ugly samovar flew into the air. I rolled to my right, trying for the cover of the hallway. A marble-topped table exploded and collapsed on top of me. Something dropped on top of that and jammed my shoulders to the floor.

The 'whucka-whucka' of the rotors intensified and I had the sudden terrifying thought that the chopper had caromed into the building and was going to fly right through, pulverizing everything in its path. I yanked loose of the oppressive weight but stayed flat to the carpet.

More explosions. More glass shattered. I was nearly in the hallway but still in the line of fire.

Without warning, the helicopter bucked and I saw the gunner thrown backward. Gunshots sounded and bullets pocked the side of the chopper. Somebody was firing at it from the apartment.

I scrambled to one knee, about to make a lunge for the cover of the hall. In that instant, however, I checked over my shoulder. And saw Federov.

He lay, face-up on the remains of the table. I thought his left arm was curled under him until I saw the red-frothed chunk of meat where his elbow had been. Ruined nerves leapt as though electrical current ran through them. There was a bullet hole the size of a quarter low in the right front of his sweatshirt.

His eyes opened. Jesus, he was alive!

I looked quickly toward the chopper. It had disappeared from view but I could still hear the hammering of its rotors.

I scrambled toward Federov and dropped to my knees. His lips moved. He wheezed.

From the other room, the automatic rifle opened up again, answered by the pounding from the machine gun on the helicopter.

I leaned toward Federov's face.

"I…didn't…kill…her." He forced the words out, grabbing my arm with his remaining hand.

"Look close to…" he said. Then his grip relaxed and his hand fell away.

"You FUCKER!"

The shout came from the other side of the living room, followed by a stream of curses. Olokoff stood there, feeding shells into the breech of a Streetsweeper shotgun. Even from where I squatted, I could see heat rising from the barrel.

I stood to run. The gun came up in one smooth motion.

Four shots that sounded like cannon fire erupted from just over my right shoulder. Olokoff took a step as though he had been shoved hard in the chest. Red bloomed on his shirt and his shotgun discharged into the ceiling. He fell backward.

A hand slammed me between the shoulder blades.

I saw the helicopter ascending to block the sun.

Alexi shouted "Go!"

I was hunched over and running when the guy sitting in the chopper's doorway opened up again. A volley of shots from the building answered. As I fought to unlock the front door, all the sounds of gunfire melded together.

✻   ✻   ✻   ✻

I remember two things from my run down the corridor to the elevators. The walls on either side of me were chopped to pieces by bullets, the way walls always are when you look at televised scenes of street fighting in a war zone. The guard who had been on duty there as I was brought in was sitting in the folding Coleman chair with his hand to his neck. He looked puzzled.

Blood geysered in spurts from his carotid artery. He'd been hit by a slug channeling through the wall behind him. As I approached, his eyes met mine like he was about to ask me what happened. He opened his mouth, blinked once…then his eyes went blank, though his expression didn't change. The last I saw him, he was still sitting there, hand to his neck, eyes staring.

I pounded the "Down" button and was startled to find Alexi standing next to me. He still had the gun in his hand and kept it pointed back down the hall. I wondered if he thought the guys from the helicopter were going to jump through the window and come after us.

The elevator doors slid open. Two guys with MAC-10's stared at us wild-eyed over the barrels. I had a moment when I didn't breathe. Alexi snapped a command and the two guys lay the weapons on the floor outside the door and got back on the elevator with the two of us. From somewhere outside the building I heard a low rumble that could have been an explosion and the car shook slightly. Alexi hit the button for the lobby.

When we arrived, the cops were waiting.

CHAPTER 20

▼

An hour later, the lobby had become a combination medical triage area and clearinghouse. Security doors were propped open, the elevator banks were guarded by H-B-T cops in black fatigues with MP5 machine guns slung across their chests, and there was more brass than you'd find in a fern restaurant. Chiefs and Deputy Superintendents huddled with FBI supervisors, and rumpled looking assistant State's Attorneys drank coffee with guys from the U.S. Attorney's office while harried paramedics split their attention among the wounded and the emotionally fragile.

They pronounced me in mild shock, wrapped a blanket around my shoulders and encouraged me to drink water and not touch the coffee a Metro Canteen guy was handing out. Like I would have, anyway. The Canteen folks are great but you could scour rust from a pipe with their coffee.

One of the paramedics handed me a release form and a pen.

"You able to do any good upstairs?" I asked.

"Some. The M.E.'s people will have a jigsaw puzzle to put together, though." The look in his eyes made me add a few years to my estimate of his age. "Even in Kosovo we didn't leave 'em mangled that bad."

His older partner looked over from where he was bandaging an arm. "Hey Eddie, we're not supposed to talk to him."

"Shut up, Fitz." Eddie shoved the handles of his responder kit together. "You were up there, right? If it's any consolation, the chopper took a couple of good hits and the rotor blew. It went down inside the breakwater. They're fishing it out now."

I leaned back against the marble wall and felt its cold hardness through the blanket and my t-shirt. The paramedics moved away. I thought I saw Kinsella walk through the foyer but he didn't approach me. I closed my eyes. Maybe just a little standing-up nap, I thought. Put all of this out of my head for a couple of minutes or so...

"Don't go getting too comfortable, son," a familiar voice growled next to my ear.

Vinnie Seamans and a guy with a commander's insignia on his uniform were staring at me. Behind them was my buddy Stinson from the Task Force. There wasn't a hint of a smile in the bunch. The cop pointed his two chins at me. His eyes were so small they could have been raisins.

"This the fella you was talking about?"

"Unfortunately." The tone Vinnie used had pissed me off when I heard it from my dad and it pissed me off now.

"Is there anything that happens that you don't know about?" I snarled.

"Very goddamn little. Especially when it's on every news station in the city, not to mention CNN and God-knows where else."

His eyes were warning signs. I was being told to play it very carefully and very straight.

"What happened here, Reno?"

I looked past him and indicated Stinson. "I won't talk to the Feds without my attorney present," I said.

"Be smart here, pal. Do yourself a favor..." the police commander began. Vinnie put a hand on his arm.

"Give us a minute, gentlemen?"

The commander nodded and stepped away. Stinson said, "You think your jurisdiction supersedes ours?"

Wrong move, I thought.

Vinnie turned and I didn't need to see his face to know, he was in a countdown to going nuclear.

"Before you start a pissing contest, you might want to talk to Director Blumenthal at the Bureau." He offered Stinson a cellular phone. "Push number 6 on speed dial. His secretary is Susan Lang. If you use my name, she'll put you right through."

Stinson held his ground for a moment, then walked off toward the Metro Canteen truck parked in the turnaround beyond the lobby windows.

"Number Six," I said. "That's your dry cleaner, right?"

He swung his head back to face me. I thought I'd get a wink but I was wrong.

"Nathan Blumenthal, Director of the FBI," he said. This wasn't Uncle Vinnie. This was the street cop who had seen everything, manipulated everyone and had contacts at levels that still surprised me.

"Come along," he said. I left the blanket behind as he pointed the way to an elevator I hadn't seen before. We got on, alone, and he pressed the button for the second floor. On the way up he looked at the gold paneling.

"One time in my life I thought this was the way to live," he said. "Corporate law, nice office about as far from the street as I could get. A million dollar condo. Hot and cold running women."

"Dad would never have let you live that down."

"You got that right. He used all the right words. He introduced me to a couple of State's Attorneys who had gone on to private practice. Not one of them was any happier. I went ahead and got the degree anyway." He shrugged.

"Maybe one of these days I'll write wills for old ladies in my spare time."

It was something I'd heard him say more than a few times.

The elevator doors slid open. The cops had apparently taken over the building offices on this floor as a command center. Detectives used secretary's desks as they talked to witnesses and residents.

Vinnie guided me to an empty conference room and closed the door behind us. The chairs were leather and swivelled. We sat like a couple of executives schmoosing after a board meeting.

I told him about the kidnaping. Halfway through, I asked him to call Sunny and let her know I was okay. I listened to him talking to her.

She had guessed what happened and was on her way. He told her not to bother trying to crack the police line; he'd bring me home. She must have snapped something at him to contradict that because he looked startled, as he sometimes does when he hears Sunny curse. He told her he'd arrange for her to join us when she arrived.

I finished my story. He leaned back in his chair, put his hands behind his head and gazed at the ceiling.

"They won't be able to cover it up now," he said after a time.

"The G will still try." I said.

"Yeah. City will, too. Never happen, though. Be seeing a slight decline in those tourist dollars for awhile, I think. Can't keep the Russian mob out of the papers this time."

I hadn't wanted to ask but I did.

"How bad was it?"

He glanced my way with a sigh. "Eight dead, not including whoever was in the chopper. May have more by the time they go through all the floors. The hitters used explosive rounds. Got a co-ed and an old man. They just looked out their windows at the wrong time. Your man Federov. Five mopes who worked for him. Although it looks like one of them took a couple of rounds from inside the apartment. You wouldn't know anything about that, would you?"

I'd left out the part about Alexi saving my life. I just shook my head. "I didn't see anything except that chopper door opening. After that I was either face first into the carpet or headed for the elevators."

"So if somebody did a gunshot residue test on your hands?"

I held them up, palms outward. "Have at it."

"Figured as much."

A few moments passed. It was quiet in the room. Eventually, he said, "What we've been seeing so far between the Russians and the gangs have been little skirmishes compared to what's gonna happen now. Now it's the Russian Winter."

"Or the Russians back off and let the 'bangers keep the dope."

"Never happen," he snorted.

Then, in a lecturing tone I could remember from riding along with him when I was still in high school, he said, "1942, the Germans were banging on Moscow's door. The Red Army didn't have the training or expertise but they still kicked serious German butt. They mobilized, got the weapons and support they needed. Hitler's troops weren't ready for the cold. Ran 'em right out of town. Killed a bunch, too. No. Russians won't wimp out." Vinnie, the military history buff.

"Where'd the helicopter come from?" I asked.

"The tail number registered to some outfit in Will County," he said. "Feds are tracking it. My guess is they'll find it was a dummy company, prob'ly with some offshore ownership. Bloods and Crips in LA have been operating that way for years."

The steady rush of air from the elevator shaft behind one conference room wall provided white noise that kept us from hearing anything except each other.

"Intelligence says the gangs are all backing one big play. Black, Hispanic, maybe even some Vietnamese, all joining up. Those guys found themselves a helicopter, so now the Russians'll think they need Stinger missiles. That's how it's going to go. One escalation after another."

I remembered Polo Tony's lesson about the gang leaders who went into the military to get training. I remembered O'Meara's story about the submarine. I felt my back grow cold.

"Russians are going to have to regroup. 'Spect they'll import more man-power." Vinnie added. "You watch. The homicide rate is bad now? We're gonna be wading in bodies in another month. The Twenties, Capone, all that shit? This will wash it right out of the history books. Keep an eye on the news. A month or two, you come and tell me how right I was."

"I'll pass. I'm finished with the Russians."

"That's what I wanted to hear. Got your murderer. You're all done."

"Nope. Nobody up there killed Brooke," I said.

As much as I regarded Federov as a walking obscenity who deserved each moment of the agony he'd experienced, I believed his dying declaration.

I told Vinnie about that now. It won me a frown and a shake of the head. "Con job."

"Why would he go to the trouble? He justified two murders as his way of doing business. If he'd considered me a threat, I'd be dead, too. He was in the middle of a gang war! What's another body?"

Vinnie's eyes told me he understood my logic but he kept shaking his head, doggedly unwilling to concede the point.

"He wanted me for his personal gumshoe." I continued. "I'd finger the killer and he'd take it from there."

"Yeah, well, whatever. It don't matter now. What happened up there closed the file on the Talmadge girl. You know why, too. She had an important daddy and some very high-end clients, one of whom just got blown away. The End."

"You're saying nobody goes down for Brooke?"

"Far as my boss is concerned her killer's down, bagged and tagged. You don't like that? Tough. The good guys all have to line up on one side and the bad guys all with their hands in the air on the other for you to be happy? C'mon, son. You been around a long time. How often you seen it work that way?"

"Talmadge wouldn't have enough clout to close down an investigation like this," I mused. "The only one who could do that would be Ferguson. Ferguson slammed the door on Brooke's murder, didn't he? Or got somebody else to do it, acting on his behalf."

I nodded to myself. On a roll now. "Quinn. Your boss. What'd he get? Help in a re-election campaign? Or is he going to run for governor when the dominos start to fall?"

Vinnie gave me the cop fisheye and then put one thick finger to his lips and shook his head.

"No. I'm not letting this happen." I surged out of my chair.

"Sit your ass back down!"

I started for the exit. I'd almost reached it when he called after me.

"You want to know how it's going to play, you go out there with a mad on? By now, Stinson's got hold of his people in Washington. They've told him to keep it in his pants, but he's got a material witness warrant drawn up with your name on it. Didn't know that, did you? You think they won't use it if you go being a loose cannon about this?"

"Tanner will have a field day with that," I said.

"Tanner won't have nothing. He signed a National Security oath when he was U.S. Attorney. He's been reminded of that. Washington *let him* pull those Feds off you yesterday because the Russian angle had to stay under wraps. That doesn't count any more." He shrugged.

"You said it yourself, Reno. There's a man who's got Power with a capital P. I'm not claiming he's a good man or even a wise one. He's sure not very bright, comes to women, that's for sure. But he wants to keep his job. Other people want him left in place, too. You, on the other hand," he flicked a pencil and sent it spinning across the lacquered top of the conference table. It fell out of sight. "You don't have squat. You can be handled."

I felt the room shrinking around me. I peered into the face of my father's oldest friend. And, I'd thought, mine.

"You're not just buying into all of this, are you? You're the one who stitched it together for them."

He spread his hands. "You know the kinds of stuff that *one* senator has in his head? The contacts? The personal credibility and negotiating power? You have any idea what will happen to U.S. foreign policy if he takes a fall from grace?"

"Vinnie, for chrissakes. We're talking about letting a murderer walk." Then a second hard thought banged into my brain. "Wait a minute. Are you trying to tell me somebody thinks Ferguson killed Brooke?"

He waved that away. "No, no, no. He had nothing to do…that's not even a slight possibility." Leaning forward, tapping on the table to make his point. "Look at it. If this murder investigation stays open, it's gonna come out that the country's most important senator tripped over his dick. He let not one but *two* Russian mob assets get next to him. And he was sleeping with one of them! That gets out, he goes away, everything he could do for the country goes with him. Arms control. Maybe dismantling nuclear weapons in North Korea. Who knows what else."

"Jesus," I said. He probably thought the flag waving had gotten to me but it was more the fact that he was the one waving it and with the fury of a zealot, too. Uncle Vinnie, I thought. When did you become one of the pod people?

He started to stand. Maybe to put a fatherly hand on my arm or to touch my shoulder. Commiserating with my frustration. Halfway to his feet, however, he must've thought better of it. He sank back into the comfortable leather chair. He didn't look at all comfy, though. Sweat streamed off of him like he'd just walked out of a steam room. I'd never seen the guy like this. If he'd been white, I imagined his face would have resembled a cherry tomato. Instead, it was just an unhealthy gray.

"For once in your life give it up, Reno. I'm asking. Please. Let it go."

I just stood there, biting back what I wanted to say hard enough I thought my jaw might snap. If he couldn't read my posture and the look in my eyes, then he wasn't the intelligence expert everyone always gave him credit for being.

✴   ✴   ✴   ✴

I didn't disappear into Federal clutches.

Vinnie left me in the conference room for several minutes. When he came back, he was trailed by a slender black woman with a Chicago Police star on her belt and a 9mm Glock backing it up. She introduced herself as Sergeant LeFort and, without interrupting once, she let me tell her everything I'd seen, heard and done from the time I left my house. When I finished, she took me through the experience one more time with her questions. They were intelligent and thoughtful and she weighed each answer with the gravity of a polygraph examiner before proceeding to the next.

Vinnie left after the first telling. I assume it was to let the Dark Empire know I'd be going home with my tail between my legs and they could slap somebody else in the cell they were holding open for me in Bumfuck, Montana. He came back with Sunny. LeFort looked like she was a little ticked he'd done that, and even more so that he dismissed her with a wave of his hand when she probably had more questions to ask. She went, though. Vinnie has that kind of presence.

He walked us out through the lobby to Sunny's car in the turnaround in front of the entrance. Sunny took my hand, perhaps fearful that the Feds were waiting to snatch me up. Across the street I could see six TV microwave trucks and CNN's satellite unit pulled up on the grass parkway next to the Water Reclamation Plant. No fewer than a dozen cameras pointed our way. I glanced at my watch. It was just three o'clock. It felt like it should have been at least eight. Good response from the stations and the networks, I thought. Especially on a Sunday.

I wondered if Marisa Langdon was out there somewhere, about to use everything she'd gathered over the past few weeks. It's what I would have done. If a breaking story comes along while you're preparing your exclusive, just tie the stuff you already have into it and try to let it sound like you were on top of things all along. It's the TV version of saying, "I knew that!" It's what they mean when they tell you a reporter "sounds authoritative." Most of the time, the viewers won't know the difference. They either won't care or they'll think you're a reporting god.

Levering myself into Sunny's Ford Expedition wasn't the least painful thing I'd done in the past 24 hours but it beat sticking around the carnage on the 71st floor. Or in the second floor conference room, for that matter. She got us away from there fast, the way she usually drives her other car, which is a four-year-old Porsche. I couldn't see all the cameras swiveling to track our departure but I imagine they did. I was glad for the tinted windows.

We were on the Drive before she said anything and then it was in a very small voice.

"A guy named Roy Carnahan was supposed to be watching your house. He called in with food poisoning. I tried to get Russ but he wasn't available."

I touched her hand. "It's okay, Sunshine."

"It is not OK! This is my *business*, Reno. I should have made him stay until I got there. I should have called you and told you to stay inside until I got there. I messed up."

"They would have spotted him, or you. It wouldn't have stopped them."

"You could have died." She brushed at her face so fast I could never swear I saw a tear leak from her right eye.

"I don't dispute that, but what were you going to do? Put a sniper on my roof?"

"I thought of doing that. For tonight. I really did."

"Let it go. I'm fine."

"Yeah. This time."

"There isn't going to be a next time. We're finished with the Russians. They aren't the ones who killed Brooke."

I got a quick glance for that. "How do you figure?"

"Federov tried to set me up as his stalking horse. He didn't kill Brooke but he thought he knew who did. You can give me the raised eyebrows all you want but I believe him. His bodyguard kept me alive because Federov told him I was supposed to leave there in one piece."

Alexi had said as much during our elevator ride. Something else left out of my statement to Vinnie. No doubt I was going to burn in hell for that but, damn it, I saw no reason to give the guy up. I told Sunny the entire story.

When we reached the house, my lawn-mowing buddy across the street was nowhere in sight. I'd have to remember his keen powers of observation if I ever wanted to start a Neighborhood Watch. I collected the Walther from the yard and Sunny came inside with me. While she fixed sandwiches, I ducked upstairs to shower. I let the water run until the temperature started to drop then got out and toweled dry. With everyone else's blood scrubbed off, I felt cleaner but a gradual numbness began to overtake me. Once dressed, I had to resist a strong urge to sit on the floor and stare at the walls. If Sunny hadn't been waiting, I might have done just that.

As I crossed the room, I stopped next to a picture of my dad and Vinnie on the wall next to the door. Dad smiled into the lens and it was a real smile, not a just-take-the-freaking-picture-willya grin. In others, snapped with Mom or me, the set of his mouth stopped short of expressing real pleasure. I'd never figured out what that meant. Uncertainty, perhaps. With Vinnie, though, with his partner, it was a full-out smile. Vinnie's matched it. Friends forever.

We took Sunny's sandwiches and sat on chairs in the middle of the backyard, under the maple tree with leaf-growth so dense that by August the grass underneath it has given up trying to survive. Now, though, it was as plush as the rest of the lawn. Socks emerged from under the porch and circled us until we each gave him a strip of bacon. When he got what he wanted he sank to his belly next to my chair and fell asleep. I envied him.

"We're back to the beginning," Sunny said. "Since you believe Federov, who's your next logical suspect, Holmes?"

I drank a little of my summer beverage. It's something a favorite aunt of mine made for us when I still carried a Mattel cap gun on each hip, but I've never been exactly able to duplicate the recipe. The difference between a ten-year-old's taste buds and those of a guy in his forties, I guess. Iced tea, fresh orange juice, fresh lemonade.

"Well, for starters, I'm betting he wasn't a pro."

"Why?"

"It was hands on. Almost...I don't know. Personal? Close, anyway. Vinnie even said it might have been an accident. He grabs her in a choke hold to stop the screaming and maybe he overdoes it."

I let my eyes roam too much when people are talking to me. Sunny is a good listener. Hers just fasten on you and when she nods, it's not just from habit. It means she's understanding, or at least processing, what you're saying.

"And then think about what he did to me," I said. "No knife or gun. He hit me in the face with a telephone."

"And left you alive, too."

"Exactly. What if I'd seen him? Even a glimpse. A pro would assume the worst. He might use the first thing he could reach to knock me down but once I was out, he'd finish it."

"Keep going."

"I looked at the layout in the back of her building. Somebody who knew what he was doing would never cramp himself by parking back there. The alley's too narrow. Suppose he kills Brooke, takes off, and finds somebody's visiting grandmother has him blocked? What's he going to do? Clip her with a phone and take her wheels? But one witness puts somebody running to a car parked in the alley right after all the commotion in her apartment."

"How did he make entry?"

"Through the back door. Real high security. A knob lock a kid could snap."

"And he broke her neck?"

"Strangled her. Accidentally, maybe."

"If it was a pro, it wouldn't be accidental. He'd either be there to warn her off the blackmail, or kill her. A pro would walk before he'd do something he wasn't being paid for. He wouldn't wait for trouble. If he heard noise at the front, he'd go out the back. And you're right. He'd have planned a cleaner getaway." She sounded like she absolutely knew what she was talking about. It was a little unnerving, her knowing so much about how a professional killer might operate.

"How do you know this stuff?" I asked.

"Clean living and I read a lot," she answered crisply. "So, if it wasn't a pro, maybe you've eliminated one potential suspect."

I had considered that. "Sure. Ferguson goes. As ex-FBI, he'd probably know how to pull it off himself, but there's no way he'd chance being seen in the neighborhood. He would have brought in muscle. The cops have ruled him out, too."

"How about Brooke's father?"

"I'm thinking about him. Actually I'm thinking about the goon with a gun he has working for him. Teddy Case."

Sunny scribbled the name in her notebook. "This is the bodyguard Talmadge hired because he was playing games with friend Federov?"

"Thug might be a more accurate term. The problem for me is that Talmadge knows all about blackmail. He wouldn't let somebody have that kind of leverage over him. Unless he planned an accident for that somebody. The other problem I have is motive. Why would he want his daughter dead?"

"I'll run a background on Case. What other suspects do we have?"

"Whoever else Brooke was shaking down. That could have been one person or a dozen. My guess is there were a handful of guys because she was trying to get enough cash to start her life over again."

"And from what you've said, Alan Talmadge is the one person who would know the names of those guys."

I went inside and came out again with a portable phone and the notebook with the phone number for Alan Talmadge's girlfriend. I called, got the answering machine.

"This is Reno McCarthy. I've got this pretty well put together, Alan, and it's looking like you're a candidate for a material-witness warrant. Cops don't like it when you hold out on them. You want the option of staying in the daylight instead of living in a cell, call me back. This offer is only good today. Tomorrow, I take what I know to the cops."

"You didn't mention that the killer is probably looking for him, too," Sunny said.

"I think he knows that. It's probably why he's moving around so much."

"He won't be difficult to find as long as he stays local. We'll find the girl-friend's address, put someone on that. Won't be tough to cover his other friends. It'll just take some legwork."

I nodded. It was time to bring everything we had into locating the kid, if for no other reason than his own protection. The killer had gotten lucky when Patrick Vega ended up on Federov's hit list. That left Alan Talmadge as the one witness against him. If, indeed, Alan had been helping his sister.

I lifted the phone again and punched in Kinsella's number. He grunted a mean hello after almost ten rings.

"I need your help," I said.

"Yeah, right. My ass," he snapped. "Hold on a minute."

He barked a muffled order to someone and then I heard the ding, ding, ding a car door makes when it's opened while the key is in the ignition.

"If you were a leper before, you're the fucking Ebola virus now. You have any idea how seriously you've pissed everybody off? From the Superintendent to the U.S. Government? Probably the dogcatcher, too."

"Joe Pulitzer said something about how a reporter isn't supposed to have any friends. I guess he was right." I winked at Sunny. That wasn't the exact quote, but it sounded good.

"Yeah, well, to me that just means you're onto something. So spill it."

"You said you didn't find a john book in Brooke's apartment. Is that still true?"

"Yep. Docking station for a computer but no computer, no notebook, files, nothing." He paused. I heard his lighter flick and was glad I wasn't in range to smell what resulted. "I got the evidence list, you want to go through it."

"What I really want to do…" I began and then the call waiting beeped and I saw the name 'A. Talmadge' flash on Caller ID.

"Let me call you back," I said and then switched over and said hello. Silence.

I said hello again and heard a hard sniffle and then a listless voice said, "What the fuck were you doing in my room?"

"Alan?"

"I asked you a question, man. I wanna know…I wanna know what right you think you have…" He was loaded, no doubt about it.

"You know who killed your sister, don't you?" I said.

"I'm gonna…you don't got *no* right to go searching through my stuff, man. I want that picture back."

"Alan, listen to me."

I heard the phone drop. When it was picked up, an older, sterner voice that had probably wowed them on the floor of the statehouse snapped, "Who is this?"

"Reno McCarthy."

"Ah! The man who can't leave well enough alone."

"The man who wants to find your daughter's killer. I'd think you'd support that effort."

"I support the authorities, Mr. McCarthy. They have the proper role in the investigation. Not a cashiered reporter." The phone clicked in my ear.

As I put it down, Sunny smiled. "I take it Alan ran home to daddy?"

"Yeah. I'm just trying to figure out why."

"Duh? Because that's where he feels safe?"

I stood up and stretched, feeling every twist and turn my body had taken over the past three days.

"But why did Daddy take him in?" I wondered. "He's got to know the cops are looking for him. Why does Talmadge want to be in the middle of that? With all he's got to hide?"

"Arrogance. With his money and his lawyers, he probably figures he can hold off the cops indefinitely."

"No," I said and stood absolutely still as an idea came to me. "Sunny, where's Brooke's mother?"

She looked confused for only a second. "We figured she's institutionalized but we haven't found out where."

"Exactly. I'm guessing Talmadge is probably going to drop Alan in the same hole. You up for taking a real fast drive?"

CHAPTER 21

▼

There was a lawn gala underway next door to Talmadge's Winnetka home.

I couldn't smell the smoke from the barbecue grills but I could see it curling ghostlike through the trees until the sun turned it to lace and it trailed off into the sky. Woodley Road was too narrow for parking, but the red-suited valets had managed to leave a couple of cars jammed up along the edges anyway. I suppose they had been told that everyone from the neighborhood would be at the party and wouldn't be complaining to the cops that they couldn't navigate into their homes.

The closer we got the more I believed that to be true. Beneath three huge tents, women in summer frocks and men wearing patchwork golf slacks and blazers in blue and green milled about carrying glasses and sometimes holding hands. I saw the reflection of a swimming pool beyond the canvas and imagined the younger generation was cavorting there.

On a Fourth of July when I was maybe eight or nine, my dad had been hired to work security for a similar event. The guy throwing it had been a ward boss or some other political type and told my dad and the other off-duty cops to bring their kids. I remembered how a nice grandmotherly sort of woman marshaled everyone under the age of about 14 into a line and then, with the snap of a drill instructor, had sent us marching across the lawn blowing on kazoos and waving American flags. I think I kept that flag well into high school.

Talmadge's front drive was empty, the crunch of the Expedition's tires loud even at the fringe of noise from the party. As we got out, I could hear a trumpet player suddenly let loose and I stopped walking, transfixed. We were easily 200 yards from where the band was set up and couldn't even see it but there was no mistaking that sound. Sunny looked over at me in the same instant and, from the slow smile that spread across her face, I knew she recognized the tune and the player.

"No way," she breathed.

"*Blue Birdland*," I said.

"Somebody who sounds like him?"

"Nah. That's Maynard. C'mon, this is the North Shore."

"Maynard Ferguson. No freaking way. Working a yard party, no less."

I grinned back at her. We've both been fans for years. I was so focused on his screaming horn, in fact, that I didn't notice Red Talmadge open his front door and step out into the driveway. Sunny took a step away from me and let her hand slip back toward her right hip under the sand-colored jacket she wore.

She'd seen Talmadge's man Case come out with him, jacket off, heavy automatic butt forward in a cross-draw holster.

"Cowboy," Sunny muttered.

Maynard ended his riff and the applause was what you might expect from a crowd of people who all had one hand wrapped around a cocktail glass. I continued up the drive. Sunny stayed in a defensive position off to my left, just as nonchalant as she could be.

"He's magnificent, isn't he?" Talmadge asked. "Teddy and I have been sitting on the porch listening. He's quite mesmerizing."

"I'm surprised you're not over there, mingling," I said.

"You're so predictable, Mr. McCarthy. And I presume this is the talented Miss DeAngelis? I knew when I hung up the phone you wouldn't be able to resist driving out to see Alan. I decided I should be here when you arrived. To give you the bad news."

Damn it. We'd missed him.

Talmadge had the look of a funeral director describing the embalming process.

"I'm sure you're aware that Alan has a terrible drinking problem. We both decided that now is the time for him to begin confronting it. Elaine has made such good progress in her treatment she felt he could benefit from the same program. I'm really quite proud of both of them."

"You had the white coats waiting for him when he came home, didn't you?"

He chuckled. "Well, I'm not quite that prescient. But, yes, I took advantage of the clinic's outreach and intervention services. Sometimes the only time to convince someone they need help is when they're in the midst of a crisis."

"Or when people who want information from them are about to knock on the door."

Talmadge spread his hands. "Alan knows nothing of his sister's death."

"Alan was Brooke's bagman, Senator. He may not be able to name the murderer but he knows the likely candidates."

"Bagman!" He laughed. "Let me assure you. If Alan had any information relative to his sister's death, I wouldn't hesitate to have him speak to the appropriate authorities. What he *has* is a chronic illness and he's finally going to get help."

"Hiding Mrs. Talmadge worked so well you figured you'd go the same route with Alan, is that it?"

"Why on earth would I want to 'hide' my ex-wife? You're quite delusional. You need to see a doctor. I felt it was partly my fault Elaine began drinking so heavily. The pressures I put on her when I was in public life. She actually might have been able to come home this week but for what happened to her daughter."

"Altruism? That won't wash. You want both of them where the cops can't pick their brains."

All I had was the accusation and he knew it. He shook his head slowly, a man not understanding why he's so misunderstood.

"Excuse me?" Sunny took a step forward. *'His sister?' 'Her' daughter?* What's that all about, Mr. Talmadge?"

"I'm not sure I follow."

"You refer to Brooke like she wasn't related to you."

He frowned. "Brooke and I drifted apart. That's old news, as your friend there might say. Many fathers and daughters have conflicts."

"Most fathers don't arrange the death of their daughter's boyfriend."

"My God! That story again. I haven't heard that in years. Total fabrication of course. You spread that rumor and I'll have your license lifted."

I was pretty sure Sunny was rattling his cage because his attitude pissed her off, but what she'd said caused a couple of ideas that had been banging around in my head to suddenly collide.

"Who would have started a vicious rumor like that?" I asked. "A fellow club member who considered you a fraud back then, too? That wouldn't have been Brian Ferguson would it? The 'older man' your daughter was sleeping with? The guy whose wife mysteriously found out about their affair a few weeks ago?"

"Brooke never had good taste in men. No doubt that's what killed her. I think we're finished here."

He could have been calling the end to a news conference. Case eased backward and opened the front door, watching us as though we might rush the house. If I'd thought Alan Talmadge was in there, I might have done just that. I figured, though, that Talmadge was telling the truth. He couldn't have known whether he'd be facing us or the cops, and cops would have insisted on checking inside.

The door closed and Sunny and I stood there in the driveway looking at each other and listening to Maynard Ferguson working his way up the musical scale to double C again.

"Talk about anger management skills," I teased.

"Like you have room to criticize, Mr Objective TV Guy. I thought the top of your head was going to catch fire when you started in with the stuff about Ferguson. Where did all that come from?"

I took her arm and guided her away from the house, conscious of microphones and cameras.

"It makes a kind of twisted sense. Sela Grauman says Ferguson was the guy who tipped Brooke that Talmadge had connections with the INS. Then Brooke, while she's still a teenager, hooks up with Ferguson and breaks away from Daddy's control. What Talmadge perceived as his happy family life started to unravel. Had to have pissed him off, don't you think?"

Sunny stared at me and her smile reappeared. "Go ahead. Tell it."

"Talmadge could have snitched Ferguson off back then, sleeping with a high school girl. Maybe he tried. Maybe Ferguson's FBI friends deflected it. Who knows? So we fast forward to a couple of months ago. It's five years, six years later. Ferguson is extremely vulnerable now. His goody-goody reputation is solidly established. Talmadge finds out Brooke's gone back to him. Here's another chance for payback. Payback to both Ferguson and his own daughter who's been embarrassing him for all that time. What's he got to lose? It's just an anonymous phone call."

"Something to gain for sure if he opens up a Senate seat," she finished. "What's all this hypothesizing get us?"

I was still working that out as we got back into the Expedition. She took her time rolling out the drive and down Woodley Road. This time we left our windows open and paused in front of the house where the party was being held. Maynard headed into "Maria" from *West Side Story*. Sunny let the truck idle there until a uniformed security guard came up to us and, very politely, asked us to move.

"Socking Alan into treatment just confirms he has a bunch of names in his head that Talmadge doesn't want him telling anybody about," I said.

"He doesn't want his political friends questioned by the cops."

"Exactly."

"Even to catch his daughter's killer? I agree on the revenge angle, but that part's a little harsh."

"C'mon Sunny! You think Red Talmadge in there gives a rats' ass about his daughter's murder, other than how he can benefit from it? Here's a scenario for you. We assume Brooke's clients are pretty much all guys in power positions, right? They were all sleeping with…"

She finished my sentence "…a Russian mob boss's girlfriend."

"They were sharing a mistress with a mob boss. Shades of Jack Kennedy. If Ferguson goes down for his affair, the media's going to be hunting for the rest of Brooke's clients. Talmadge holds the key. He can parlay his silence into a lot of favors, I bet. If Ferguson doesn't go down, Talmadge's candidate loses his shot at buying the Senate seat but, as the consolation prize, Talmadge still owns a bunch of people. Anybody whose name is linked to Federov is going to be terrified after what happened today. Talmadge will tell them their secret is safe with him. For a price."

"He wins either way. You think maybe that's what Brooke told them, too? Maybe she brought Federov's name into it. Or maybe not his name, just the fact her boyfriend was mobbed up. If she was that desperate for cash, why wouldn't she have used all the pressure she could?"

"Son of a bitch." I hadn't stretched it out that far but I knew she was right. I slumped back in my seat and wrapped my arms around the headrest.

"We need that list, Sunshine. If we can't get to Alan, we need to come up with her johns' names some other way. The killer's one of them. No question."

"You know, if we go back to the office," she said. "I have that rundown of Talmadge's clients I got from the Board of Elections. Bridges was on there. We could start with that."

I was getting ready to tell her it was a good idea when my phone rang. It was Kinsella.

"You forget about me?"

"Huh?"

"Yeah, I thought so. We were talking about the evidence inventory. I believe the last thing you mumbled was something about what you'd really like to do?"

I'd left him hanging after Alan Talmadge returned my call.

"Sorry about that. I thought we had a line on finding Talmadge's kid."

"And?"

"The old man put him into a clinic somewhere to dry out. And to hide him."

"Yeah, well, he's spending money he don't need to. Last I heard we're shitcan-ning your big case by calling it solved. They even threw it back at me as investigator of record with a nice letter of commendation for my hard work. Told me no follow up necessary. Translated, a'course, that means don't fucking touch it or we'll have your ass."

"You agree with closing it?"

"I don't know. Are we still off the record with this?"

"Charley, you were never *on* the record. I'm just a curious citizen now. No more reporter powers."

Sunny glanced over, raised her eyebrows at me, and muttered, "Reporter powers?"

I smiled and pointed at the road. She mouthed the word, "Dork" and turned back to driving.

Kinsella said, "I think it's a load of crap. Your boy Federov didn't do her himself. That idea was never righteous, far as I'm concerned. Closing the case means the killer walks."

"Unless you come up with good reason to reopen it, right? Like a suspect?"

"What? You find the guys driving the Jag?"

"I was thinking we might go back over to the apartment and try to come up with Brooke's john list."

"Shit. That's been tried, remember? Besides the place isn't a crime scene anymore. It's plain old private property. Keys are locked up with the case file."

"You suppose the super knows the CPD doesn't have right-of-access any more?"

He didn't answer right away and I could almost see him sitting in his car, working out the pros and cons. Problem was, it was a long shot. If I could have guaranteed him there was evidence to be had, he wouldn't have hesitated. As it stood, all I could offer was a chance to go in a direction he'd already rejected as the wrong way to solve the case.

Hell. If he said no, I was ready to go over later anyway, by myself, and break in. Yeah the best evidence techs and investigators of the Chicago Police Department had probably scoured every inch of the place but I hadn't had a shot yet. Might as well try.

"Fuck it," he snapped. "Meet me there."

"Give me 45 minutes."

*   *   *   *

Sunny dropped me at my place to get my car, made me promise to call her or Russ on the radio if Kinsella and I had to split up, and then shot over to her office to see if she could pluck anything useful from the Board of Elections list. I drove down to Brooke's apartment and found a spot for the Taurus a half-block from where Kinsella had bumped his car over the curb in a fire lane.

He waved for me to join him going through the foyer door. I felt a moment of light-headedness as we passed the threshold, almost as though taking that step I'd gone over the edge of some high place and was now poised to either fall or fly. Appropriately enough, my nose began to throb. The inner door that had been blocked open by a phone book the night of the murder was now closed and sported a heavy duty lock.

Kinsella rang the bell marked "Manager—M. Post." After a moment, a tinny voice asked us our business.

"Chicago Police," Kinsella said. I thought I heard a muttered "shit" as the manager rang us in.

M. Post was a skinny buzzard in black socks, Bermuda shorts to his knees and a t-shirt. His head drooped from bony shoulders. Kinsella showed him his ID wallet.

"Just a few more questions."

Post backed up into his apartment. He had a slight limp.

"Good Jesus, you people think I got all the time in the world or something?" The innards of what looked like a garbage disposal unit were spread out on a newspaper across his kitchen table while WFMT played classical music from a small radio on the counter top.

Kinsella took it all in with a casual glance. "Been a couple of days. We were wondering if any of the tenants have been talking. Theories, whatever."

"Sure they been talking. Have I paid any mind? No. I gotta fix what they break." He gestured at the jumble of parts.

"I was just thinking, maybe someone else mentioned seeing something that night. It might help us. Anything at all."

Post shook his head. "I got this disposal unit here. I got another one under the table comes next. I got two crappers won't flush up on three. What I don't got is time for listening to these people squawk on 'bout that girl. You want to know what they're saying, be my fucking guest." He made a sharp gesture toward the ceiling with his right hand.

"You were home that night?"

He shook his head. Exasperated.

"Jesus Christ! I was home. I had the air on. It was raining. I didn't see nuthin or hear nuthin. Now that's gotta be the tenth time I told you people about all this."

"Say, Mr. Post? We'll let you get back to your shitty toilets if you'll just give us a key to get into the apartment. That work for you?"

M. Post turned without a word and rooted in one of the drawers behind him. The apartment key hung from a ring with a square of cardboard that had her apartment number written on it. Kinsella snatched it and headed for the door. Post was muttering again as we let ourselves out into the hallway.

The living room where Brooke had died was as I remembered it, more or less. Stepping inside and closing the door behind me didn't send me into a sudden fit of recovered memory as it might have if we'd been on a police TV drama. I just took it all in, thinking about that night and what I'd seen and where I'd fallen.

Couch along the wall to my right. A table and lamp between two chairs underneath a window that looked out over the balcony and into the alley. The door where the killer had entered. All the shades were drawn and the light in the room had a dirty yellow quality. To my left was the kitchen where I'd fallen. There were traces of black fingerprint powder on the refrigerator and the cabinet doors and on the drawers next to the sink. I stared at the carpet where Brooke had died. It was a tight Berber weave. If there was blood, I couldn't see it.

Kinsella withdrew some papers from his jacket pocket and handed them to me, then hesitated. "I got pictures, too."

I waved it all away and wandered down the hall to the bedroom. The drawn blinds made this room darker than the living room. I snapped on the overhead light. There were no pictures on the walls. I expected to find mostly Alan's stuff but he had apparently taken what was his and left Brooke's belongings for another time. I wondered who would collect them now.

A tired wooden desk under the window offered up the docking station Kinsella had mentioned, but the laptop had failed to magically reappear from another dimension. I brushed fingerprint powder off the drawers and quickly went through them. A user manual for a Dell laptop. A user manual for a miniature Sony camcorder. I felt suddenly foolish about this whole escapade. The cops knew how to conduct a decent crime scene search. What was I looking for? A microdot with Brooke's john list on it wrapped inside a dust bunny?

I could hear Kinsella in the kitchen, moving pots and pans. Restless, I prowled the room. Peered at the bookshelves on one wall. Brooke or Alan, or both, had apparently been working their way through the self-help manuals. Dr. Phil. Chopra. John Gray.

I tugged another, more familiar, book from the stack. A guide to accessing public records and information put out by Investigative Reporters and Editors. I had the same edition at home and this one looked just as well-thumbed. Next to it sat Gould's *Illinois Criminal Law and Procedure* and an Illinois Attorney-General's handbook on the Open Records Act. I opened that one and a small Legislative Directory for the most recent session of the General Assembly fell out. I had a brief flare of hope as I opened it that I'd find names circled with arrows pointing to them and the notation "Client." No such luck. Not even one dog-eared page.

I looked some more. Jammed into a space at the back of the top shelf were two manuals on setting up camera surveillance and a video tape on the same subject, all the kind of thing you find in ads in the back of *Soldier of Fortune* magazine. I paged through them. They showed how to place cameras so they wouldn't be seen by "the subject," evaluated different camera and film options and even reviewed how computer-linked, micro-digital cameras could send images of a covered space secretly over a secure web page. It made the back of my neck prickle to read that and I spent another few minutes looking through the room for hidden lenses without success.

A sense of something teased me and flitted away, just enough to make me angry. Then part of it came to me. I turned back to a page with pictures of several different cameras. One of them was similar to one I'd seen resting on top of the headboard on the porno movie set in Eddie Marn's house.

I went back out to the living room. Kinsella looked at me expectantly, turning away when I shook my head. There was a framed print on the wall above the couch of a couple holding hands as they walked in a wintry Lincoln Park, high-rises behind them. I lifted it away from the wall. Nothing. There were no clues lurking in the TV/stereo cabinet or in the drawers of the table near the window. Kinsella leaned against the kitchen counter and looked bemused.

I sat on the couch and took a deep breath. Let it out in a sigh. "Let me see all of it," I said, holding out my hand for the files.

The pictures were digitally crisp 5 by 7's taken from every conceivable angle in the room. I carefully placed the close-ups of Brooke's body upside down on the coffee table in front of me, concentrating on the others instead.

I arranged the photos in a layout that showed most of the room and compared what was in them to what I saw before me. There had been some disarray that night. I remembered the suitcases of clothes, gone now, that had been on the living room floor. A TV tray lay smashed next to the couch. The telephone used to break my nose was outlined in chalk. I could see my blood on its base.

I leaned back on the couch. If I closed my eyes now, the night of the murder would return. I didn't want that. I wanted the hard reality of what was in front of me, not memories. I took it all in. What caught my attention were the pictures of the coffee table itself. Shuffling them out of the array, I put them side by side.

On the night of the murder there had been a TV Guide on it, a remote for the TV, a fancy hand mirror. I looked closer at the photos. A bent straw lay on the floor, partially obscured by the table edge. OK, a straw and mirror made a quick and easy setup for snorting a line or two of the kind of snow that's in season all year.

"Charley?" I said, leafing quickly through the evidence sheets.

He cleared his throat. "What?"

"Do you remember if they found any snortable drug residue on the mirror that's shown in these pictures? From here on the table?"

He came into the room and stood looking down at me. "No drug residue, no drugs at all. Why?"

I pointed. "How about on the straw on the floor?"

"Maybe. Lab reports weren't done by the time they yanked me."

"I don't recall anyone saying Brooke was into dope, though, do you?"

He shrugged. "Her brother might have been."

The mirror looked to be brass and had Brooke's initials in the handle. OK, I thought. Maybe she liked to sit out here and watch TV and sneak peeks at herself in the mirror, comb her hair. I looked around the room. No wall mirror. Comb or brush her hair before she goes out.

"Assume the mirror's not here for cutting dope," I said. "What was the straw for?"

"Takeout?"

"Find any takeout cartons or cups?"

He retrieved the evidence logs and began looking through them.

"No," he said after a moment.

Basic Criminal Investigations handbooks all say the same thing: in every homicide, the suspect either removes something from the scene or leaves something behind. Maybe something microscopic, like fibers or dirt. Fingerprints if you're lucky and he's really stupid. In one case I'd covered years ago, the killer left his fire department-issued paramedic's helmet, with his name inside, next to the body. You never know.

I went into the kitchen and rummaged around the cabinets. No boxes of straws. Back to the bedroom and then a quick trip through the bathroom just to be sure. The straw hadn't come from the apartment. I walked the length of the living room and back and paused next to the couch, then paced back to the door. Kinsella regarded me curiously.

"All you need is the hat and the pipe, Sherlock."

I rocked to a halt, afraid if I moved I'd shake apart the puzzle that had suddenly come together in my head. I could hear the drone of the air conditioners that were cooling the neighbors' apartments and, muffled, the voice of a woman calling to a child to come inside. Somewhere above us, someone dropped something to a hardwood floor.

"What?" Kinsella said. "It's a crime scene thing. We got guys pacing like you, we tell 'em they're doing the Sherlock. 'Cept you need the pipe."

I waved him off. He went silent instantly and I knew he'd seen the look on my face.

A steel band was squeezing my chest. I couldn't believe the conclusion I'd just reached.

"Show me again how you think he killed her."

He got behind me and encircled my neck with his arm. He told me to tap him if I needed to be released.

"You get the neck in the crook of your arm, right here. Do it fast enough and you're not going to get any resistance. You can twist, turn, and cut off the carotid artery."

"This's a wrestling hold isn't it?

"Yeah. Not one they're allowed to use. Do it wrong, you could kill the other guy."

"Charley. Can you get the name?"

I realized what I wanted was in my briefcase in the Taurus.

"What name?"

"Come on," I said, grabbing the evidence file and thrusting it at him.

"What the hell, Reno?"

"We're done here. I'll meet you at the car."

I didn't wait for him to answer or respond. I didn't want to talk, or hear anyone talking, until I worked through what had emerged from the place my brain stores unrelated data until I'm ready to use it.

I left him to lock up and I retraced, in reverse, the route I'd taken the night Brooke was killed. I had my keys in my hand and had to skirt a young, trendily-dressed couple in the foyer. I only vaguely heard the "Hey!" when I failed to hold open the security door for them. Then I was running down the walk like a man fleeing a fire. Or chasing after a killer.

I unlocked the door to the Taurus and prayed the document I was looking for was where I thought I'd left it. I'm not the best keeper of paperwork, as most anyone who's worked with me would know. If they were smart, they made sure they kept the original and gave me the copy.

It was there, stuffed into the outside pocket of my briefcase. I withdrew it, scanned the information and stuffed the paper into my jacket pocket. Kinsella was just coming outside and I waved to him as I headed down the street at a jog.

"Hurry up!" I snapped. He was breathing heavily when he joined me in the foyer of the apartment building next door to where Brooke had died. The place had the same layout but the security door stood open.

"I don't...get to the...fucking gym enough," he said, face scarlet. I noticed he had his hand inside his jacket on the butt of his automatic.

"We aren't going to need that," I said. "But I hope you have your phone."

Mine was back in the car, battery dead. I led the way upstairs to apartment 4K and knocked on the door.

The guy who opened it looked expectant, a smile forming on his lips. He wore jeans and a yellow cashmere sweater with the sleeves rolled up and was barefoot. Candles glowed from a small table next to a couch in the living room behind him. His smile dimmed by about 40 watts when he saw us. "Yes?" he said.

"Police," I said, before Kinsella could even get his wallet open. "At least he is. Are you Eldon Lazzar?"

"Yes?"

"The night of the murder down the street, police interviewed you? And you gave a statement about what you'd seen?"

He nodded and looked thoroughly puzzled. I wasn't surprised. I was talking way too fast. I took a breath, smiled back at him.

"You told the officer about a car. What make and model was that, do you recall?"

"Of course. A Jaguar. Perhaps black, but as I told the officer it was dark and I couldn't be sure."

"But you're sure it was a Jaguar? No question?"

He brushed at the corner of his mouth with a fingertip.

"Well, I guess I'm not really. I mean, not really sure *now*. I was the other night but..."

"How's that?" I took another breath, held it.

"Well, I was talking with my friend yesterday and he asked me the same thing. He watches *Law and Order* and *CSI* and all those programs? 'You have to be sure, Eldon,' he said. 'A woman was killed you know.' So I told him I *was* sure but then he told me that Ford makes the Jaguars now and that there's a Lincoln model that closely resembles one of the Jaguars, the low-end one. My friend is on his way over and he said we'd go online and he'd show me what he meant. I don't really know cars that well but the Jaguar, well, the *name*, you know? They've always been so sleek."

I was glancing at my watch. It was after ten o'clock.

"How soon do you expect your friend?"

"Oh, he should be here now, actually. I'm sure it won't be more than a few minutes."

It took another ten for the friend to arrive, during which time Kinsella took Lazzar through his statement again. When the friend showed up, he wore shorts, a polo shirt that showed off nice pecs and had a cashmere sweater of his own, light blue, fashionably thrown over his shoulder. Lazzar took him by the arm as though to make sure we didn't grab him away.

"Ken, these are police officers. They're asking the same question you did. About the car."

"Of course they are!" Ken said and smiled, dazzlingly. He opened a magazine he carried under his arm.

"I think we can answer it for them, too. This," he pointed to one picture, "is a Jaguar X-type," he said.

"And this," he flipped forward several pages, "is a Lincoln LS. To my mind they don't look anything alike but for people like you, who think a Mini Cooper is Gary Cooper's son, you get the idea."

We all watched Lazzar compare one to the other.

"Oh, my goodness," Lazzar said and put a hand over his mouth. "They do look so much alike, don't they? In the middle of the night, with the rain, I just can't say for sure."

He eyed Kinsella and then me. "That's okay, right? I mean, I'm not causing a problem for you, am I?"

"Not at all. Thanks for your help," I said.

I headed down the stairs, gesturing for Kinsella to follow. Outside the building he grabbed my arm, as though afraid I was going to take off and start running again.

"Goddamn it, McCarthy. Slow down a minute. You're gonna give me a fucking cardiac. What the fuck was that all about?"

I looked skyward for a moment. I wasn't looking for Divine Intervention, although the thought crossed my mind. I was trying to clear my head and find the words to explain my theory.

"If you can bear with me while I make a couple of phone calls, I think I'll be able to tell you who killed Brooke Talmadge."

*   *   *   *

I remembered the number I needed to call without looking it up. It was a pager. Its owner called me back within two minutes. Asking the questions and getting the answers took a little longer and involved some anguish when the guy realized what I was trying to establish. I told him to keep his mouth shut, punched the button to end the call, then dialed another one on its heels.

Elise Bascomb Hanratty answered.

The wife of my former boss didn't sound happy to hear from me.

"Frank's not here," she snapped.

"You know where I can find him, Elise? It's important."

"Why?"

Surprised by her ferocity, I didn't answer right away.

"What's going on, Reno? What are you doing calling Frank this late at night?"

Carefully, I said, "I'm not sure I understand."

Panic now joined the anger.

"Goddamn it, Reno! I'm not speaking a foreign language. Tell me what's going on."

"What's he told you?"

"Oh, yes, of course. You think the big macho newsman ever talks to his wife? Someone called him an hour ago, ok? I was standing in front of him when he answered. I thought he was going to have a stroke. He went absolutely white. I think he would have fallen if he hadn't had a chair right by him where he could sit down."

Kinsella was staring expectantly at me. I held up a finger.

"What did he say when he finished the call?"

"Nothing. Nothing. He just walked through the house muttering and then locked himself in the study. I tried to get him to come out but when he did he just walked right past me out the door."

"How long ago?"

"A half-hour. Tell me what's happening!"

"Where did he go?"

"God DAMN you. I don't know! Usually…usually when we have a fight he'll either go to the station or out to the boat. I…called my father and asked him to check the station. I haven't heard from him."

She began crying. "What's Frank involved in now, Reno? Just tell me. I can handle anything but I don't want to be the last to know. Just give me that, okay?"

"I'm trying to find out, Elise, just bear with me," I said. "Was he carrying anything when he left?"

"No, but he had on his windbreaker. I asked him if he was going to the boat but he just kept walking." She suddenly began speaking in a very low, nasty way. "Is he fucking that little tramp now? Is that what it is?"

"Who are you talking about?"

"Like you have no idea. She took your place, you know. You were his son when you worked for him but then she came along and all of a sudden he had a daughter. That would be a sort of incest, wouldn't it?"

I rubbed the heel of my hand against my forehead and spoke with the careful patience you'd use if someone was threatening to take a header off a bridge.

"No. No, I don't think..."

"I even walked in on them once. Right in his study. I caught them. He had his arm around her from behind. You should have seen the look I got. 'Teaching her a wrestling hold,' he says to me. Like I'm a gullible little twelve year old."

"I don't think Frank's having an affair with Marisa," I finished. "That's not the problem."

"Like I could ever believe you. You're probably both doing her. Is it good for you too, Reno?"

I told her I'd check on him and broke the connection before she could say anything else. I realized the hair on the back of my neck was standing up. Kinsella put out a surprisingly gentle hand and pushed the phone down.

"Who you think it is?"

I took a deep breath and pushed the sound of Elise's voice out of my head.

"My old boss at Channel 14, Frank Hanratty. He brought me into this. He drives a Lincoln LS. He got Brooke's address from a producer at the station about two hours before she was killed. He's a former wrestler. Both high school and college."

Kinsella's face twisted in puzzlement.

"Your boss? How the fuck did *he* know her?"

"I have no idea. But wait a minute." I went on to tell him about Frank filling his briar as we sat on Navy Pier, then fiddling with the pipe cleaner, twisting it into contorted shapes. I remembered countless nights in restaurants and bars, Frank stirring his iced tea with a straw and then absently playing with the plastic the same way, keeping his hands busy and his mind off ordering a drink. I also remembered his odd manner the last two times we'd talked, his near begging me to get off the case. For my own good, he'd said.

"Come on, McCarthy," Kinsella said. "They don't indict people for playing with straws or for driving Lincolns. What else you got?"

"The car," I shook my head in amazement. "That's the key. A friend at the station told me his wife bought it for him after he totaled his old one. Ran into some girl. Funny thing is, that friend of Brooke's told me Brooke been in a crash, too. She broke her ankle in fact. I'm guessing it was about the same time."

"What you're saying is, you don't got dick for facts."

"Winnetka might still have the report on his accident."

"If they do, our computer should be able to dig it out, too." He spent some time schmoozing with someone at the 9-1-1 Center then asked for a records check on both Hanratty and Brooke. He listened for about two minutes, nodding impatiently, then closed his eyes and lowered his head as he let the phone drop into his lap.

"Praise the Lord," he said. "The two of 'em woulda met on July 22, last year, at 3:20 p.m. He ran a stop sign and broadsided her. And maybe true love blossomed."

CHAPTER 22

▼

I rode with Kinsella. Unlike the last time I'd been in his car, I didn't notice the fetid smell from his cigarettes or even the stop-start-hit-the-horn-punch-the-siren way he drove. My thoughts foundered elsewhere.

Frank Hanratty had brought me to Chicago and given me all the freedom I needed to get the I-team going. He'd backed me when decisions had to be made and argued with the lawyers and Chazz Bascomb when something I did poked their noses out of joint. I had spent hours in that office of his, or in the newsroom, or in the back of the Billy Goat or any number of other downtown dives plotting story strategy and throwing out ideas for skirting informational roadblocks.

Frank was the tactician who always knew how we felt because he'd been there dozens of times himself during his newspaper career. Frequently, sources he developed were crucial in helping us turn a corner when nothing else worked. He knew the state's Open Records Act as well as I knew the Gettysburg Address in seventh grade. I'd watched him fill out a Freedom of Information request, properly worded, in the middle of Michigan Avenue during a blizzard.

I shook my head. The guy was a classic Chicago news hound. You almost expected to see him wearing a fedora with a press card in the band and chomping on a cigar while he talked out the corner of his mouth. He'd come to journalism after picking up an undergrad degree from a city college and then a graduate degree from Northwestern. And he'd been a wrestler. Along with the politico pics on his walls there were several of him holding trophies he'd won. For about a week he'd even had two showing him in clinches with opponents. He'd taken them down at the insistence of an HR geek who found photos of a young Frank in tight shorts offensive.

A wrestler. Goddamn if he hadn't been. Four years in high school and then four in college. In fact, his favorite expression as we approached deadline on a piece and looked to him for guidance whether to take it all the way had always been, "If you think you've got the moves, take 'em to the mat, boys and girls."

I tried to visualize him with Brooke and couldn't. My imagination just wouldn't bring me there. I could, however, see how easily he might have laid a thick forearm across her throat in the darkness of her apartment. Funny where a creative mind allows you to go sometimes.

Frank Hanratty ran on fury. Countless times I'd seen him storm into his office and break something when a story crapped out or we got beaten by the competition. He yelled at someone at least once every day I worked at Channel 14. Frequently it was me. Once, when the Arbitrons came back showing us flat for the second sweeps in a row, the newsroom shook with a crash that brought everyone surging to Frank's office. He stood there, desk upended in front of him, papers fluttering to the floor like confetti. The moment we all began to appear, however, he walked around the mess and slammed the door. No contrition. No attempt to apologize for startling all of us.

Goddamn you, Frank.

Kinsella made a couple of calls to have guys he knew in the Marine Unit check Monroe Harbor for Hanratty's boat and determine if he was aboard. He also tried to get an 18th District tactical car meet us at Channel 14, but grimaced when the answer came back. Every available plainclothes unit was tied up on a protection detail at one of the major hotels or was down the street at Lake Point still doing interviews.

"Can't make an official call for backup 'cause officially I am not doing this," he said. "Might be able to get a uniform to ride over and sit in front but I sure as hell don't want to bring them inside."

"Lemme have the phone and I'll call Sunny…"

He shook his head. "Nah. I'll handle it. Just taking one civilian along will be enough to get me busted down to Traffic in the Loop. Bringing a bounty hunter…no way I'm doing that. Any way to get into the building without advertising we're there?"

Channel 14 did a half hour of "Nightside" News at nine, choosing to compete against WGN and the Fox station rather than go up against the network affiliates. After 9:30, the station emptied out, especially on Sunday nights, and even the late shift mini-cam crews went off duty.

"Used to be half a dozen security guys working overnights and making regular sweeps but who knows if they're still around? Probably one guy at the desk in the lobby and maybe one monitoring the cameras in the security room in the basement. A couple of engineers."

"How about the newsroom or wherever this guy has his office?"

"Maybe a desk assistant monitoring cop calls."

We slid to the curb in front of the station a few moments later. Hanratty's black Lincoln LS was parked in a spot opposite the front door. I found a Winnetka village sticker attached to the front window. I wondered why he'd parked on the street when he had a reserved spot inside the garage.

The street was uncharacteristically deserted for a summer night. Usually, even past eleven, tourists would be out strolling to and from Navy Pier four blocks to the east. It looked like the Pier was experiencing a pronounced loss of visitors. I was surprised. You'd think an aerial gunfight and helicopter crash would have brought them out in droves, cameras clicking and whirring.

"Lookee there, Bertha! They got body bags just like on *CSI!*"

From where we sat, we could see the reflection of both red and yellow strobes bouncing off the buildings, indicative of fire and other city crews still on the scene. I wondered if they'd managed to bring up the helicopter.

The overhead doors blocking Channel 14's parking ramp were down and no light shone in the attendant's cubicle.

"I'm going to break the law. Don't watch," I said and scrambled out of the car.

Normal video surveillance procedure is to put a camera at every entrance to your building. The fact he'd added card-key access however, made me think Chazz wouldn't go the camera route. His argument would be that no one could break through a big, heavy door like that without causing enough commotion to alert a passing cop and, besides, the door itself was hooked into the building's alarm system.

I glanced around. No one nearby. I shattered the glass in the door to the cubicle with my elbow and reached inside. The little rocker switch was right where I thought it would be below the counter. I punched it and watched the doors roll slowly upward. I looked around quickly. No cameras tracked my movements. Good ol' penny-pinching Chazz. I waved at Kinsella. He drove the Crown Vic up the ramp and I closed the door behind us.

A nearly new Audi sat in Frank's NEWS DIRECTOR slot. One of the new, compact Cadillacs was nosed in next to it, in the space marked MR. BASCOMB. There were two other cars parked across the garage near the mini-cam trucks.

One was a battered Chevrolet. When I'd worked there, only the night engineers and brass were allowed to use the garage. I went over and peered in the Audi's window. A pair of women's running shoes sat on the passenger seat and the back held a Chicago and Vicinity map book. Pristine otherwise. I felt the hood. No warmth. Frank had always told me I was welcome to use his parking spot after hours. I guessed the Audi belonged to Marisa Langdon.

A key-card reader in the process of construction sat next to the elevators. Chazz's penny-pinching had its benefits. On the ride up to the newsroom floor, Kinsella said nothing but reached back and took out his automatic, slipping it into the side pocket of his jacket.

The newsroom lights were on. Six TV monitors on the wall showed Channel 14 and the programming from ABC, CBS, Fox, WGN and CNN. Scanners murmured and crackled and the screen on one of the computers displayed the logo of the AP's Electronic News Production System. Someone had probably been using it within the last twenty minutes or so. A black shoulder bag lay on the desk with Marisa Langdon's station ID clipped to the strap. I glanced across the room. Hanratty's office was open and the lights inside were on. I pointed to it. Kinsella put a hand in his pocket and moved to peer inside. He shook his head.

Looking for signs of human habitation, I went down a short corridor and glanced in each of the four editing bays. In all but one, video equipment hummed but displayed blank screens. In the fourth, the monitor showed a freeze frame of the front of Lake Point Tower. An empty Styrofoam coffee cup with lipstick on the rim sat next to the computer keyboard. That's a big no-no around the expensive gear but it told me Marisa must have been working there. Was she in the break room on the next floor getting another coffee? Bathroom? Or, did she go to Chazz's office? His car was here and that was the logical place for him to be. Were Frank and Marisa up there in conference?

I picked up the nearest phone, hesitated and then punched in an extension. Looking around the newsroom, I had a strong sense of deja vu. Except for the tension coursing through me, this could have been any night I'd stayed late working the phones or doing some last minute editing on a story after everyone had gone home.

The phone rang and rang. Nobody answered Chazz's private line. Nobody returned to the newsroom.

My shoulder muscles felt like they'd been fastened to one long board. On one of the overhead monitors, Bruce Willis shot at some guys in an airport terminal and they fired back with machine guns. Brrrrrrrrrrrp. I flashed back to Federov's living room and was overcome by one of the most sustained feelings of dread I'd ever experienced.

"Something's wrong," I said to Kinsella and gestured with the phone. "Hanratty's father-in-law owns the station. He should be here or upstairs and I'm not getting an answer up there. Somebody's been using an editing bay and hasn't shut it down. Hanratty's car is downstairs. That means he's somewhere in the building, too."

"Let's check the boss's office," he said. He took out his ID case and affixed it to the breast pocket of his jacket so his star showed. Then he removed the automatic from his pocket and held it down along the side of his leg.

"You got another one of those?" I asked.

He snorted. "Yeah, that's what I'm all about, McCarthy. Giving a civilian a gun so he can back me up searching a building where I have no right to be. This ain't *Law and Order.*" Just stay behind me and be ready to duck. And let's take the stairs to where we're going and not the elevator. I don't wanna play pop-up target for this fool."

Before we climbed four flights, I paused long enough to open the women's restroom door and call out, "Anybody home?" No response.

We pushed into the eighth floor corridor, both of us breathing heavily, with Kinsella in the lead. It's the only carpeted hallway in the building. The overhead fluorescents were off, in keeping with Chazz's well-known effort toward energy conservation. The exit lights glowed red, providing eerie illumination.

Chazz Bascomb's office suite sat at the east end of the hall. Kinsella and I both paused to listen, then walked into the foyer. The oak-paneled double doors to the inner sanctum were closed but light shone from beneath them.

Kinsella flattened against the wall on one side of the door and motioned me to the other side. He tried the knob. It turned. I realized I was holding my breath. How goofy would we look if we charged into the middle of some routine meeting on property where neither of us should legally be, him waving a gun, me trailing behind, smiling like a maniac?

Kinsella rolled off the wall and shoved open the door. I went after him. If Hanratty was in there with a gun he'd have two targets. No waiting.

He wasn't, but I didn't feel the least bit goofy.

The only meeting Chazz Bascomb would be taking from now on was with his Maker.

He had probably been standing behind his nice, big, cherry wood desk when the shotgun blast hit him just below his sternum. Fired from about where we stood, it lifted him off his feet and shoved his body backward. He sprawled face-up across the top of a credenza, head lolling against a floor to ceiling window that displayed a magnificent view of Lake Point Tower, Navy Pier and the lake. The thick glass was pockmarked with blood spatter. Pieces of intestine bubbled from the wound.

Kinsella lowered his gun.

"Fuck me to tears," he said, disgusted in a way that only a homicide detective seeing fresh kill can be.

Neither of us moved. Kinsella gave the room a preliminary once-over. He was the one who'd be expected to remember it all in some future trial. I, on the other hand, strained mightily to hear any sound that would indicate that Frank remained nearby and was about to open fire on us. The only thing I could hear, though, was blood dripping from the credenza to papers scattered on the floor.

Thap, thap, thap.

Kinsella turned and pointed toward the door to the hall. I thought he was ordering me out to preserve the crime scene, but he followed and then took the lead. We paused just beyond the foyer. He spoke softly.

"Any hiding places up here?"

"Not unless he has keys to these other offices."

It felt like we were talking inside a church. Or a funeral home. I looked up, my attention drawn to the floor status light above the elevator. It showed two cars on "L" but the third was stopped on four, the newsroom floor. I lifted my chin toward the display. He trotted for the stairs with me in his wake. Halfway down he stopped and tugged out his phone and handed it over.

"Punch nine for Communications. Tell 'em what we've got and that a plain-clothes officer is on scene. Stress that, willya? I'm gonna go ahead and check the newsroom again."

"I'm right behind you."

"Fuck that," he hissed. "This ain't a news story anymore, McCarthy. That guy up there hasn't been dead more than ten, fifteen minutes. Just make the call and stay here. Tell 'em I want a Plan One for the extra manpower on the perimeter and a full H-B-T response."

I held up the phone to show him the display. It read "NO SERVICE."

"We're in the middle of a concrete and metal building," I said. "Look, Frank knows me. I think I can talk to him. If he sees you alone, he's liable to go apeshit. You want to kill him or have half a chance to take him alive?"

He weighed that, using his left arm to blot his forehead. Finally, he said, "I see why he fired you. You're an asshole."

*   *   *   *

"Die Hard" still played on one of the monitors overhead, but it had an audience of sorts now. Through the open door to his office I could see Frank at his desk, hand outstretched as though in the middle of making a gesture to someone. He looked up in surprise as we swung into the newsroom and his hand dropped slowly. Kinsella was in point-shoulder position with his automatic aimed straight at him.

Frank looked horrible. Flushed of face, he had the eyes you get after knocking back too much bourbon in too many smoke-filled taverns. From where I stood, they didn't seem to focus on us but somewhere above our heads. He put both hands on his desktop and rose slowly.

"Reno," he said. Something clogged his throat and he cleared it.

"Chicago Police," Kinsella snapped.

I stepped away from him, careful to keep out of his line of fire but also staying where I could still see Hanratty through the door.

"Sir, I want you to do a couple of things for me," Kinsella continued in a reasonable tone. "I want you to keep your hands where I can see them at all times. You got that?"

Frank looked down at his hands as though he had just realized where they were. They made small tents on the desktop as he balanced himself.

"Very good," Kinsella continued. "Now I want you to step very slowly around to the front of your desk. Hands out in front like they are now."

"You don't understand."

"Sir? Step to the front of the desk with your hands in plain sight. Do it now."

I glanced quickly around the newsroom. No sign of anyone else. Where was Marisa?

Frank wore a blue windbreaker with the station logo on the front. There might have been a gun bulge under it but I couldn't tell. I wondered if Kinsella could.

"Come around the front of the desk, sir." Kinsella prompted.

Frank didn't move. He brought his eyes down from the ceiling and locked them on mine.

"You had to keep after it, didn't you?" he said.

"Sir, step to the front..."

"I'm trying to have a conversation with Mr. McCarthy, Detective," Frank said. "Could you give us a minute?"

As if dismissing a pesky waiter.

"Frank, you want to do what Charley says..." I began.

"Relax and do exactly as the nice policeman tells you? That's the punch line to a dirty joke isn't it? Speaking of dirty jokes? Red Talmadge called me a couple of hours ago."

I opened my mouth to respond but this time Kinsella cut me off.

"Mr. Hanratty, we don't have all night here. You want to converse, you come out of the office like I told you. Very slowly. Do it now," he repeated.

"What are you going do if I want to talk from here? Tell me that. I taught this girl, and your buddy there, to always question authority. So I'm questioning you. You going shoot me for standing behind my desk?"

So Marisa was in his office with him. Great. He'd either mentioned that in passing or to make it clear he held a potential hostage.

Marisa said, "Frank. For God's sake."

"Talmadge knew. He told me he was going to tell Chazz what I did. Said I'd better run and hide. Did he figure it all out or did you tell him, Reno? He said you were just at his home."

"I didn't tell him anything, Frank." I felt very tired. "Maybe his kid."

"Of course. Alan. I knew someone was watching when I dropped off the money. I assumed it was Brooke. But she was afraid of me. I loved her, Reno. I would have done anything for her and she was *afraid* of me."

"What scared her?"

"She was my lifeline! Good God, you know better than most how Elise and I go at it. Brooke was quiet, smart. God, was she ever smart. She wanted to learn. She wanted to learn from me, not criticize everything I said and did."

He stopped suddenly, voice breaking. "She'd been mistreated her whole life. I think the concept of someone caring about her...she couldn't handle it."

We weren't getting anywhere. "Frank, c'mon out of the office. We can talk about this in a few minutes."

"We'll talk about it now! I think the officer there is going to get tired of holding that gun and he's either going to put it down or shoot me. If he shoots me, Marisa has a great story, don't you, hon?"

He moved his eyes slightly to his left and then they came back to me.

"So, Reno, have you been to up to Chazz's office? He came in here ranting and raving. We had a nice visit. I told him everything. He was quite attentive. Especially when I told him what a bitch his daughter turned out to be."

"Why did you send me to the break room, Frank? What did you do?" Marisa asked.

Under his breath, Kinsella murmured, "Son of a bitch. Get him out of there, Reno."

"Just something I've wanted to do for years. Haven't you wanted to kill him a time or two yourself?" He glanced back at me. "How about you, Reno? He ruined your career. Didn't you want to pop him?"

"Sure. More than once."

"More than once! I imagined it every time I saw the miserable son of a bitch." He took a deep breath. Staying put, hands on his desk, was obviously a strain and it was beginning to show.

"All along, he wanted to nail me for marrying his little girl. Wanted me out of the family. Lately, he was after me to divorce her. Said I'd given her enough heartache. How about that? She's riding my ass every day and I'm the one giving *her* heartache."

"Tell me more about Brooke," I said.

"Ah, God. You believe, I never knew what she was? Until she socked me with it a month or so ago. She said she was a model who wanted to get into broadcasting. Into news. I never knew she was a fucking hooker."

"I believe you."

"Yeah, sure you do. She started using me the minute we met. The minute she found out who I was, she wanted me to help her with her big project. Me, on the other hand, I fell for her. Who wouldn't? Reno, she was beautiful. You saw her."

"Sir!" Kinsella snapped.

"I told myself I had to stop. I even threw away her number. You know how it is when you try so hard to forget something and it imprints in your memory instead? I couldn't get her number out of my mind. She said it was fine that I kept calling. She liked that I was so much older. She liked what I could teach her. That was what really nailed me. You know what it's like to have a young girl wanting to *learn* from you? She pulled every string I got. I fell for it all."

"Maybe it wasn't all an act, Frank."

"Of course it was!" His expression turned patronizing.

"Jesus Christ, man. When I'd told her how I felt about her, you know what she told me? 'You old men are all the same. Somebody makes your dick hard, you think you're in love.' The next thing she does is tell me the magic number is 50 G. Like I had it in my wallet. Like I had some easy way to get it without hitting Elise's trust fund. Brooke says I don't come up with the money, she tells Elise I'd been banging her for a year!"

He dropped his head, then brought his eyes back up to mine.

"I couldn't let her do that. Chazz was just looking for one little thing. We've been getting pretty consistent good ratings. He couldn't fire me over that, over anything connected with work. If he found out I was cheating on his daughter, Jesus! And with a...that would have been the end."

"I remember how that goes," I said dryly.

"Yeah. Like it was for you. So, I was supposed to let Brooke Talmadge ruin my life? I knew she'd do it, too. She was planning to ruin her own old man. She didn't care who else got hurt. I had to...stop her."

Beside me, a sound came from Kinsella, somewhere between a grunt and a sigh. A confession was good. But now Frank had nothing to lose from anything that happened going forward.

"See, Elise has been wanting a Porsche," he said. "She's had her eye on the 911. That's a hundred G, new. So I told her I had a buddy who could find us one, get a great deal. It was the only way to get the money up front. I thought she was going to run it past Daddy first but she just said fine, took it out of her trust fund herself. If I hadn't gotten the cash back, I don't know how I would have explained it later, spending the money and not coming up with a car. That's why I needed Brooke's address, Reno. I couldn't just give her the 50G and walk away, could I?"

Slowly Frank closed his eyes and opened them again. His left hand came off the desk, fluttered a moment. He used two fingers to squeeze the bridge of his nose before dropping the hand back to the desktop.

"I figured if I could just see her I could convince her to give it back. That's all I wanted to do. Talk to her."

Kinsella shifted position slightly. "Hey buddy. At least let the girl come outta there. Why make this tough on her?"

Frank ignored him. "The hitch was, I didn't know where Brooke lived. Couldn't find a listing and she would never agree to see me after she demanded the money. I don't have the connections anymore to root around the city looking for her. I knew you could, though. My man, Reno. Finder of Missing Persons."

I sighed. "When I called Andy Nunez to have him track down her pager information, you were in the editing room with him."

"The only luck I've had all along," Frank said, but there was no glee attached. "I made sure he followed it up right away for you."

"Yeah. Thanks a bunch, buddy."

"I sat there on her couch. The back door was easy to break through. Really shitty security in that neighborhood."

He glanced again at Marisa. "Probably worth a sidebar story if you think about it."

"Frank…" I heard her say, but he wasn't about to stop. His eyes gleamed as though he was imparting some kind of special wisdom and we should be his grateful recipients.

"When Brooke came in? I grabbed her. She started to scream and it was as if…I don't know. I remembered all the moves. It was automatic. She knew it was me. It wasn't like I was trying to hide it from her. She began that god-awful screaming and bit me! What the hell was I supposed to do?"

He looked right at me then, but it felt as though his eyes were staring through my skull and into a world beyond either of us.

"I didn't know you were there, by the way. Had no idea. When you kicked that door, I thought it was, I don't know, the fucking boyfriend she'd never admit she had. By then, God, I'd done it. I felt her fighting me and then…she stopped. All of a sudden."

He suddenly pushed off from the desk, stood straight, and lifted his right hand to his face.

Kinsella took two steps. "Freeze fuckhead."

Frank put his hands out in front of him like a kid showing his mom they were clean.

"You're saying if I reach for my belt, you're going to kill me? In front of two witnesses? You still don't know if I have a gun."

"What I want to know, Frank," I interjected, allowing a little heat into my voice, going for distraction as well as an answer, "Is when you decided I was expendable. You had to know people would remember I'd been asking about her. You had to know the cops would come after me. You set me up. Care to tell me why?"

He glanced from me to Kinsella and back again. Slowly, a smile began to form on his lips, if not in his eyes. He pointed at me. "Always with the questions."

He looked to where Marisa was sitting. "How many times have I told you? 'The question you don't ask is the answer you don't get,' right? Reno always has another question. Well the answer this time, my friend, is…nothing personal you understand…you were convenient. If there was anyone who would accept the notion that Chazz ordered me to run a story it was you. You believed me because you wanted to believe. You knew what a prick he was. I had no idea you would be…right outside the door. You've got to believe me on that."

What had been almost a lighthearted tone faded as the spark left his eyes.

"And as for you, Detective. Maybe I'm ready to die but just don't want to do it myself. Suicide by cop."

"Fuck suicide. You either come out of there or I'm going to come in and yank your face off," Kinsella snapped and took another step. His body blocked my view of the door. "You got to the count of...shit!"

I didn't see what happened next. We both rushed forward. All I heard was a scream and the sounds of a struggle. Kinsella suddenly yanked his gun off target, toward the ceiling, and stopped as though he'd walked into an invisible barrier at Frank's office door.

"Shit!" he said again and lowered his gun into firing position. The way his finger curled around the trigger I braced myself for the shot.

Marisa was half-sprawled across the desktop and Frank had her by the hair with the Beretta from the gun case in his study pressed against the side of her head.

"Back up!" he shouted. Now his voice had the same snap of command that Kinsella had used a moment before.

"Back!" he said.

"Go on, go on, go on. You too, Reno. Back across the newsroom. You know I don't want to hurt her. I'll only do it if you make me. Go on, move back farther. You're Kinsella aren't you? Yeah, I've heard about you. Get back across the room, goddamnit. Move."

The look on Kinsella's face was pure rage, even more so than I'd seen the night of Brooke's murder when he'd been ordered to let me leave the station. He'd fucked up in one of the worst ways possible and allowed a murder suspect to gain a hostage. I knew that was exactly what was going through his mind and I knew in that same instant that he would kill Frank Hanratty if Frank gave him the slightest opportunity.

On the other hand, Frank's expression was damn near peaceful as he pushed Marisa off the desk and turned her so she preceded him through the doorway and into the newsroom.

"Drop the gun, Detective," Frank said. "Drop it right there on the floor and back away."

"Not happening." Kinsella rasped.

They were about twenty feet apart now, Frank's head on Marissa's shoulder, clear for the shot if you were an expert marksman or didn't much care about hitting her. I felt my backside hit the edge of a desk. I was moving so fast the force of the contact nearly bent me backward.

"This isn't the way..." I gasped.

Frank said, "Get over by the detective, Reno. I want to be able to see both of you. Then back out into the hall."

I scuttled around the desk and joined Kinsella at the door. Just before we stepped into the hall he said in a low voice, "Distract him and he's mine. Just get the gun off her."

"The acoustics in this room are funny, Detective. I heard that," Frank said and pushed the gun hard enough into the side of Marisa's head she winced in pain. Her nose was bloody, probably from going after him across the desk. This guy was hell on noses. Friends' noses especially.

He ordered us farther down the hall and we went. For every step forward he dragged her, Kinsella and I shuffled backward. Kinsella never took his gun off Frank and Frank never moved the barrel of his so much as an inch. Marisa's face was screwed up in pain.

We all paused by the elevators. Kinsella was breathing rapidly and his nostrils flared like a horse that's about to lose the Preakness by a hair. I was wound so tight that if someone dropped a pin two floors down I was going to hear it. My insides jumped when Frank punched the elevator call button and the doors slid open.

"There are more cops waiting downstairs by now," Kinsella said.

"Yeah yeah. Think they want her to die any more than you do?" Frank said. He stepped to the side and over the threshold of the elevator door. He looked at me again.

"I didn't want it to happen this way, Reno," he said and the elevator doors closed.

Kinsella moved faster than I would have thought possible, having seen him wheezing after our short run earlier. I followed him down the stairs. On the third floor, he ducked into the hall, checked the elevator signal and gasped, "Garage!" The exertion had cost him. He wasn't looking good as he took the stairs down again. He stumbled when he got to the garage level and had to grab the handrail to keep from falling. I nearly fell over him.

We both heard the rumble of the overhead door.

"Cocksucker," Kinsella snarled and pushed off, gun in both hands as he burst into the garage with me two steps behind. The overhead was just coming down. Marisa leaned against the wall at the top of the ramp. We ran toward her.

"I'm okay," she shouted and then gestured toward the door. Frank had opened it, then punched the button and let it drop back down as he ducked underneath. Now he was on the street and we were stuck for the long moment it took me to reach the button and slam it with my fist. I made up my mind what I was going to do and rolled under the door before Kinsella could react.

The night was cooler than I'd expected or maybe it was the sweat drying on my back that gave me instant chills. I saw a car ease from a parking space a half-block down to my right. Its headlights illuminated Frank who stood in the street, halfway to his car, facing the building. As I emerged, he fired one shot that spanged off the metal door well over my head.

"Goddamnit, Reno. Back off!" He turned and ran for his car.

Kinsella appeared beside me and, even as he swung up his gun, he fired. Glass shattered. I started forward, this time into his line of fire. He swore, grabbed for me. I turned as I felt the tug and shoved him.

"Give me a chance with him. One chance!" I snapped, then spun back to cross the street.

The car to my right suddenly accelerated, startling me and preventing Kinsella from getting off another shot. I saw Frank fumbling with his keys and then the car rolled between us. There were two people in the front seat, features lost in shadow. A relay clicked and a memory tried to kick to the surface.

I had only the time it took me to realize that the moving car looked a lot like Frank's parked car before I heard five pops in quick succession, so fast I had to think afterward how many there had actually been. Then the car accelerated and Kinsella was shouting and firing at it.

Frank turned back to face us. He seemed to be wondering where we'd gone. I heard Marisa gasp behind me and felt her hand touch my back. Kinsella brought his gun down with both hands. Frank dropped the keys and the gun he was holding and took a step, hands rising as though he had suddenly decided to give up. Then his knees buckled and he pitched forward and down without doing anything to break his fall.

The car. The fucking car had been a Jaguar. The cheap one.

Marisa brushed past me. I followed her to Frank's side.

"Oh God!" she screamed and reached for his shoulder. Moaning, she turned him over and dropped to her knees. Before I could stop her, she did the "Look, Listen and Feel" they teach you in CPR, hooking her hand under his neck to tilt his head back and open his airway. Blood soaked her hands, and then her blouse, but she didn't appear to notice.

I looked at Frank's eyes as I tugged her away. They were open. I remembered one time in seventh grade when I came home from school and found my dad passed out on the couch. His eyes had been open like that. It had scared me. I'd gone up to him, peered close and asked, "Hey, Dad. You in there?"

Hey Frank, you in there?

Just enough light spilled onto his face to give me the answer. His pupils were black and the size of quarters. He didn't blink. Blood ran sideways off his face from an exit wound that had punched through the top of his scalp. I had no doubt there were more in his torso but didn't want to look.

I put my arm around Marisa's shoulders and turned her away from Frank's body. She was crying. I looked across the street to where Kinsella was bent over and gasping for breath. The three of us stayed like that until the first of the squad cars pulled up between us.

CHAPTER 23

▼

You watch a man get shot to death in this town and you can pretty well figure on it screwing up any plans you have for at least the next several hours. Watch a well-known TV news director get killed after he's offed his boss/father-in-law in the penthouse of the television station and you might as well haul out the camping gear and a soft pillow before you call the cops.

I got to revisit the same Area Three interview room where Kinsella and I had danced the night of Brooke's murder. This time my waltz partners were a guy I'd never met before, Detective Sheila Yount, acting as though she could now, finally, get even for me sending her to Gang Crimes' buddies to jail, and a sergeant who spelled the two of them when they yelled themselves hoarse. They weren't really looking for information because they knew Kinsella was giving someone else the official story of what had happened at Channel 14. Maybe he was even telling somebody down at The Building. Maybe even the Superintendent himself.

It was an opportunity for them, and anyone else who wanted to stop by, to rip off a piece of my ass. Two lieutenants stuck their two cents in, as did the Assistant Deputy Superintendent who rides the streets at night as the highest ranking officer on duty in the department. I thought they might start allowing the janitors and then maybe some of the drunks in the holding cells downstairs to take their shots next.

Sometime before dawn, though, almost like the eye of a hurricane had swept over the building, the yelling and the questions ended. There was a commotion in the squad room. Raised voices. Yount pushed away from where she was holding up the wall and went to open the door. I peeked over her shoulder.

Barnett Tanner stood in the middle of the room, toe to toe with the Area Three Detective Commander. Two other detectives looked on from nearby desks but weren't making any effort to intervene. One of them had a hand over his mouth and from his eyes you could tell he was trying not to laugh. Tanner's face was tight. Two steps behind him, Sunny had her arms crossed as though daring any of the other cops in the room to step up and challenge her right to be there.

"Shit," Yount said. Her partner joined her in the doorway.

"Hey, you're blocking my view," I said.

At the sound of my voice, heads turned. Sunny smiled.

Tanner said, "Yeah, I thought so," in a disgusted voice. The commander joined the first and middle fingers of his right hand and pointed them at my two minders, then snapped them back at himself in a pissed off 'come here' gesture. The Muttrina and Jeff of Violent Crimes left me behind and joined him for a conference.

"You okay?" Tanner asked.

"Butt's a little sore," I said.

"We would have been here sooner but there was some confusion," he stared back at the boss detective who folded his arms, "as to where you were being held. Come on."

"He needs to sign a release form," the commander said peevishly.

"Shove it up your ass," Tanner snapped.

At that, the cop with the hand over his mouth made a gasping noise and got up and headed for the door. I could see his shoulders shaking. A laugh riot. We passed him in the hall getting a drink of water. He gave a thumbs up without glancing our way.

"Where'd they send you?" I asked as we started down the flight of metal stairs to the first floor.

"Area Four. The 1st District. Then the 18th," Sunny said. Area Four and the 1st District are out on the South side and the 18th District station house is near Cabrini Green. Tanner had probably logged about 25 miles looking for me. I'd heard of cops playing that kind of prisoner shuffle in New York and LA but it wasn't something that happened often in Chicago.

We were halfway across the lobby and headed for the front door when Vinnie Seamans appeared from a corner conference room and lumbered into our path. Tanner puffed up to object but Vinnie waved it away.

"State's Attorney says he'd personally appreciate it if I could have a couple of moments alone with your client. No hassle, no charges. Everything off the record."

Tanner turned to me. He was frowning hard. I guessed the idea didn't sit well with him.

"Reno?"

"I don't know. You got the FBI or CIA hiding in there?" I asked.

Vinnie took a breath. "No."

I shrugged and followed him into a room often used for news conferences. It had the look of a small theatre with a raised stage at the far end and long tables with folding chairs set up to one side and an American and a Chicago flag hanging limp from their stands on the other. The thick brick walls and low lights made it feel like the back corner of a castle, the place where the real decisions about who lives and who dies in the kingdom are made.

Vinnie crossed to where four Styrofoam cups sat on one of the tables. Steam still rose from two of them. I wondered what had been going on in here and who had been taking part.

Vinnie straddled one of the chairs and leaned his crossed arms on the back piece. "You wanna sit?"

"Not particularly. Anybody make any progress tracking down the shooters?"

He didn't answer right away. Then he nodded briefly, as though he'd decided something for himself.

"Found a Jag abandoned, double parked, up on Goethe. Bullet holes in the trunk caught some beat cop's eye. Looks like one of Kinsella's shots may have gone all the way through. There was blood on the passenger-side front seat and some expended brass."

"Fingerprints?"

"Don't matter. They carjacked a cab dropping a fare a couple of blocks away. Freelance TV cameraman who lives in the neighborhood was just leaving his place, saw what was happening and followed 'em. He'd heard everything going down on a scanner and called Communications. Couple of guys working transit detail picked up on the cab. By the time the marked units pulled it over, the one who caught Kinsella's round was dead. The other one popped a couple shots at the coppers. Bad move. She ate about nine rounds."

"She?"

"Uh-huh. Interpol had a record on her and her boyfriend going back about ten years. Turn on your TV when you get home. That cameraman got the whole thing on tape."

"Names?" I wondered whether the guy had been Alexi.

"I had my hands kinda full this morning, Reno. Trying to keep your ass out of jail."

"Just think. About twelve hours ago you were ready to help the Feds put me in one."

"CPD's pretty pissed. You've been a bigger pain in the butt than the '68 riots. They're beginning to think the FOP brought you in to jack up the overtime budget."

"Funny."

"They wanted to charge you. The boss said no. Again."

"Charge me with what? Aggravated Having a Hunch? Accompanying a Police Officer in Performance of His Duties?"

He brushed that aside. "He figures you've got plenty of information to share, now. He says to drop by in the next day or two. He'll take you out to lunch."

"What information is he talking about?"

"Something led you to Hanratty. That suggests you've seen some files the old man would be…interested in."

"Kinsella was with me the whole time we were in that apartment," I said slowly.

"See, Reno, Kinsella is the one mentioned it. He says you came up with some ideas that didn't exactly make sense to him. The impression he got was maybe he was watching a show."

I wanted to laugh. Wait until I tell this to Sunny, I thought. Brooke's murder had become a shell game and now everyone thought I was hiding the peanut.

"No," I said. "I haven't seen Brooke's trick book or computer or anything else. I came up with Hanratty's name because I knew his habits. That's all. Actually one little thing got me thinking."

"The straw."

"You look through his car, you'll probably find a mess of drive-through cups without straws. Or bent straws like the one in the apartment. He had to keep his hands busy. It was an easy trademark to spot."

He tried to stare me down. I waited him out.

"I'm not buying it, Reno," he said. "Wasn't anything in that car. Pristine, just came out of a car wash."

I shrugged. "Not my problem. I don't have what you want. Talk to Talmadge."

"He denies even knowing what his daughter was involved in."

"Sucks to be you then, huh?"

"Just 'cause the cops let you go now, don't mean you'll be walking around out there this time tomorrow."

I tried to look past his cop's bland expression for some sign of my Uncle Vinnie. His real self had either disappeared or was hidden so well he was likely to forget where he put it.

"What's that mean?" I asked. "What are you gonna do? Approve a charge of criminal trespass? Or what, maybe I get a grand jury subpoena? I don't think so. I think me being in this place, the cops yelling at me, even this conversation, is all for show. Your boss doesn't want to draw up criminal complaints. He wants to know who Brooke's tricks were. That's why he went along with the idea of closing this investigation. He wants her files and an affidavit from me, something he can stick in a cabinet somewhere. Maybe he'll share with the US Attorney and win some points, maybe not. Maybe he'll just make everybody on that list sweat awhile. You charge me with something, the whole thing comes out in court. Talmadge and his connections. How you, the Feds, the cops all are hiding just how much influence the Russian mob has in Chicago." I shook my head.

"Not happening," I said. "And don't tell me the G's ready to send me to Montana now, either. What would be the point?"

"You got a chance to make some real friends here, boy. What's it going to hurt? You owe the people on that list something or what?"

"You really don't know the answer to that, do you? Tell me something. When you look in a mirror do you see your own face looking back? Or is it some cartoon version of you with puppet strings attached?"

He flinched. It was a reaction I'd never seen. I suddenly remembered my mom's face when they came to tell us what Dad had done in the small park across the street from our house. As stoic as Dad, she wiped at a tear that tumbled from the corner of her eye, then seemed to wither in front of me. Vinnie shed no tear but he suddenly looked older and far more tired.

He didn't move out of the chair. Maybe he expected me to apologize. He wasn't the same man my father had known. Or maybe he was and I was the one getting the education. For the second time in twelve hours, I had nothing to say to him.

Before I left with Tanner and Sunny, I asked the desk officer about Marisa. He stopped tapping computer keys long enough to tell me somebody from Channel 14 had come to get her. When I inquired where I might reach Kinsella, however, I didn't get an answer.

*   *   *   *

Tanner took Sunny and me back to my car but she lifted the keys from my hand and drove the rest of the way to my place. She didn't say much. I could tell she was brooding again.

I thought for awhile about Frank Hanratty. My friend, my boss. The guy who gave me a lift in the career back when I'd been looking to move up from Kansas City.

"Look close…" Federov had muttered as he lay dying. I wondered if he'd meant to say, "Look close *to you*. If Hanratty was the one Federov suspected all along. I wondered how and why that might have been. Frustrating. I'd never know for sure.

It was fully daylight by then, birds chirping and a steady breeze coming off the lake. The day felt like Spring. My shoulders and neck ached and I felt hung over, distant, ready for sleep that would last a couple of days if I could ever get the courage to close my eyes. I didn't want to do that, though. There were too many images ready to jump into my dreams.

I sat at the table in the kitchen and watched Sunny prepare her signature breakfast of huevos rancheros. Socks came in and she let him sniff a green pepper. He squinted, shook his head and took off for the windowsill in the study. I let my hand slide along his back and up his tail as he passed me.

"What'd you tell Rudy to get the morning off?"

"Emergency," she said and looked over her shoulder at me.

"And he said?"

"City News was already running the story about what happened at Channel 14. He knew where I was going. He huffed and puffed a little. Settled down when I said I'd be back tomorrow. I think he was going to give Roderick a chance." Roderick was an assistant producer eager for an opportunity to get on the air.

"The Next Generation," I said. I wondered if Frank had ever thought of me in that way. New kid on the block. Following in his footsteps. I must have dozed for a couple of minutes in my chair, because the next thing I knew Sunny was touching my shoulder and pointing at the plate she'd set in front of me.

"Eat. Let's think out loud for a minute. I'll start." She handed me a fork.

I ignored the way the eggs burned my mouth and began shoveling them down. Plucked a piece of toast, slathered it with orange marmalade and finished it in two bites. She sat down across from me with a glass of juice and a notebook which she opened and laid on the table.

"I've been thinking about Brooke. I was going through the list from the Elections office. There were way too many names. I just had to try and guess which of her father's clients she might have been seeing. It's a good thing you came up with Hanratty. I could have put the names up on the wall and thrown darts at them for all the luck I was having."

"Yeah, the Elections list was a long shot," I agreed.

"While I was guessing, I got to wondering. How did she choose one guy over the next? Did she have any criteria? Maybe a reason to believe one would have been hornier, or an easier mark than another? I looked some of them up on line." She took a sip of juice.

"If looks did it for her, I couldn't see a pattern. They're all ages. Some are bald, some look fat, a few are hotties. Pretty much a cross-section of male humanity. Most of them are fairly high profile, too. I found a lot of them in the society pages with their wives. Maybe just the fact they had all known and done business with her father was good enough. You know, to rub his nose in it. But then I'm looking at all these pictures in the newspaper and I thought of something you'd said. You made the point several times and it all of a sudden jumped up and hit me. Hey?"

I glanced at her. "What?" I said. She smiled and pointed at my lip. I wiped my mouth and dove back into the eggs.

She continued. "What was the most consistent thing people told you about Brooke?"

"Um." I met her eyes again, fork paused in mid-air. "She kept to herself."

Sunny nodded. "Yes. She was very low profile. And she had no relationship, no contact with her father."

"Right."

"Now, I know how guys like to thump their chests when they make a conquest but do you suppose these guys, people who have very public reputations, would brag about visiting someone like her? Even to their locker room buddies? If she was into bondage and discipline and whatever else, I'll bet that was the last thing they'd do. I can't see any one of these CEO/lawyer/banker types wanting all his colleagues knowing he likes being tied up and whipped. Might make things a little frosty at board meetings, don't you think?" She raised her eyebrows.

"So if she wasn't talking, and her johns weren't talking..." I began.

"...how was Talmadge supposed to find out she was screwing all his friends?"

I got up and took my plates to the sink. Both were empty. Heavy thinking makes me hungry. "Alan said his father knew about Brooke and Federov."

"So? If her scheme was to embarrass him by her promiscuity with his clients, why wasn't she going out of her way to let him know about *all* of them? And if she *was* telling daddy about all of her little adventures, why didn't Talmadge stop her? It wouldn't have been hard. All he would've had to do was tip a friendly cop. He sets her up, she's busted. Talmadge could have made that happen, right? But she kept on for years."

A tingle of anticipation felt like electrical current right in the center of my chest. "Maybe her intention was the opposite of what we thought it was. Maybe she was trying to hide her adventures, not advertise them." I said.

"Yes," she smiled. "Yes, that makes much more sense."

We looked at each other for a moment. Sunny asked, "So what did she plan to accomplish? Sneaking around and sleeping with people who knew her father? And more importantly, people who knew her father's business?"

I thought about the bookshelves in the bedroom at the apartment. The investigative reporting texts and the resource manuals for prying information out of the government. I leaned against the sink and tried to dredge up what had bothered me about that at the time. What had Alan told me about her first year in college? She'd slept with a journalism professor. And of course, there had been Hanratty who, if I remembered right, had said something about her wanting his help with "her big project." But the surveillance manuals? The references on cameras? Those hadn't come from any classroom.

"When your eyes go out of focus like that it tells me you're either getting ready to faint or you're thinking brilliant thoughts," Sunny teased, lifting me out of my reverie.

"She claimed she wanted to get into the dirty movie business," I mused.

"Claimed?"

"It didn't make sense, though. Eddie Marn was too jumpy about it. I should have known then. He told me Brooke came to him three years ago looking for a job and he blew her off 'cause she didn't look young enough for the kind of stuff he was doing. C'mon. You've seen her picture. Made up the right way, she could have easily passed for a teenager." I stabbed the air with a finger.

"The Russians bankrolled him. He came right out and admitted it. What's to say they didn't have him doing all sorts of errands for them on the side? He knew the action around town, knew the players. It wasn't like he was new to that part of the movie business. The Russians moved in, took over his action because he was turning a profit but they also bought his expertise. He was the one who shot the video for their blackmail schemes. Asa told me that. He even named Eddie as the one who got him in trouble."

Sunny looked up from taking notes.

"Blackmail," she said. "Interesting concept."

"I saw his studio. He was shooting all voyeur stuff. Mock hidden cameras. How easy would it have been to jump from that to the real thing?

"Could have been inspired by the real thing."

I nodded. "Brooke must have known what he was doing. That's why she picked him. She asked Lynn Robinette for help finding someone who knew about surveillance stuff. Lynn sent her to Marn." I thought some more.

"Son of a bitch. Marn didn't want to admit he'd worked with Brooke, or even knew her that well, because she'd gone on to become Federov's mistress. That's why my coming around scared him so badly. He wasn't about to tell me anything that would bring any heat down on her. He knew Federov would take it out on him."

Sunny put down her pen and ran both hands through her hair, closing her eyes for a moment. When she opened them, she put what we were both thinking into words.

"Brooke was getting ready to blackmail her father. She was using his clients to get information about him."

"Maybe blackmail. More likely, angry as she was, I'm thinking she just wanted to ruin him. Turn everything she'd learned over to someone. Newspaper, TV station. Maybe even give it to Hanratty. That would have been some irony."

I gave her a rueful smile. "We should have figured her motives way before this."

"Well. Not necessarily. I mean, the Russians were a pretty big distraction."

"Damn," I said and smacked my fist lightly against the sink. "It's so obvious when you look at her background. I never gave her credit for being smart, even though everyone I talked to about her said she was exceptionally bright."

"So, what do we do now?"

For the first time since talking to Hanratty over lunch at Navy Pier, I could feel the tightness between my shoulder blades loosening. "I think we should finish what she started. If she put together that kind of information about Talmadge and his dirty deals, I want to find those files. Should make for pretty interesting reading."

"You said the killer took everything."

"Cops think so. To them, killer is one of her johns, he takes the computer to keep from being identified. Or, killer is a home invader and takes the computer because it's there. But if she was really doing an investigation of her old man, and it meant that much to her, I'm thinking she'd keep copies of everything somewhere, wouldn't she?"

"I would. In fact, we do. All of our sensitive case files are backed up off-site."

Sunny suddenly laughed. "There's that glassy-eyed expression again. You know just where to start looking, don't you?"

*   *   *   *

It took four long days, dozens of phone calls and, in the end, came together only because we stole the key evidence.

Sunny accomplished that small felony, virtually under the noses of two state troopers who were as unable to do what she did as I was. Who knows if they even would have thought of it. They didn't have quite the same goals and motivation that we did.

I spent awhile talking to Paul in California and then to people he recommended both in Washington and at Tribune Tower. Deal making. I talked to lawyers and to a politician. Sunny and I both spent some time with a woman who became nearly hysterical when she saw me at her door. Sunny calmed her down and convinced her to claim ownership of the recently liberated property. It wouldn't have worked out as well without her. I had lunch with John Gennaro.

I visited Marisa Langdon. I talked to Andy Nunez and spent time in conference with their new boss, Irv Bolton. Irv was a guy I'd always gotten along with at Channel 14. Now he was sitting behind Frank Hanratty's desk and, as he told me in confidence, unwillingly running the show. He popped antacids and kept running a hand through his thinning hair all the way through our chat.

Channel 14 was a station in chaos. Bolton and Marisa helped me carry a couple of ideas upstairs to where Elise Bascomb Hanratty and a squad of lawyers were attempting to mitigate the sudden death of her father and the void it left in the ownership of the TV station. Chazz Bascomb had apparently never believed he was going to die. He left no plans for succession of leadership.

That worked in my favor. Her father had been murdered by her husband. Her husband had been killed by mobsters. My scheme to set things right became a cause for Elise while she mourned. Gave her something to focus on. A way to bring order back to her life.

On the afternoon of the fourth day, Sunny and I took a drive to Winnetka. We knew former State Senator R. Edwin Talmadge was in residence because Russ Traynor had been keeping an eye on him for us. The neighborhood looked much the same as our last visit except that Maynard Ferguson and the crowd of party goers next door had been replaced by a couple of guys wielding chain saws who were attacking a diseased oak tree. They paid no attention to us as we crunched up the driveway to the porticoed entrance of Talmadge's place and parked.

I felt and looked pretty spiffy. Gabardine suit, British regimental tie, nicely polished wingtips. Sunny was stunning in fine cotton slacks, jewel-neck pullover and a matching suit jacket that was cut just right to conceal the off-the-rack holster and upscale 9mm automatic on her right hip. She carried the briefcase.

I counted on Case coming to the door when I rang and he did. He snickered when he saw me. I kept my expression bland and watched my lips move in the reflection of his sunglasses.

"Is he home?"

"Like he wants to see you two."

I pointed past him. "Just a minute sir," I called.

Case glanced in the direction I'd pointed, realized he'd been had, and snapped his head back toward me. I stepped into him and brought my elbow around, hard. There was a satisfying thump as my elbow connected with his face. It's a great way to hit someone if you don't want to break your hand.

He sagged against the door frame but surprised me with a grab for his pistol. I thumbed him in the throat. His mouth made a wet sound and I snagged the gun as he toppled backward into the foyer. I pressed the barrel into his cheek.

"You're out of it, understand? We're doing you a favor. You don't want to be here when the shit hits the fan."

He stared, hating me but frightened, too. Sunny had run his background through Lexis. He had reason to be. The gun felt a little theatrical so I lifted it away.

"He's not paying you enough, brother. Trust me. Go."

We waited a moment while Case decided whether to fight or flee.

"My piece," he cawed.

"You've got to be kidding," Sunny said. "Your boss may feel safe letting an ex-con pack a piece around his house but we don't. Yeah, we know about your visit to Joliet. Five years, car-jacking, wasn't it? It's 3:30 p.m. Does your parole officer know where you are?"

"Get moving," I said. "Last chance."

Case got to his feet, holding his neck. He glanced once toward the rear of the house and then back at us. "Who are you people?"

"Spider Man and Wonder Woman." I jerked my thumb toward the driveway.

Talmadge was sitting at the same table on the sun porch as he had been when we first talked, except this time his back was turned. So he could gaze out over his lush lawn, I guessed. A glass of orange juice sat at his elbow and papers were spread across the table's surface. I opened the French doors and went through them.

"What did they want?" he asked in a bored voice. He didn't look up.

"They want to see you squirm," I said.

Talmadge swung around in his chair, so startled that he upset his glass of juice.

"What the hell?"

I gestured to the table. "Your stuff's getting wet."

He looked back, swore, and thrust out a hand to move some papers away from the sticky flood. By the time he looked at us again, we'd split up. Sunny took the couch to his right and put her briefcase on the coffee table. I leaned against the wall where I could easily see into the living room or look out into the yard. I heard an engine start near the house and the sound of a car backing up.

"What the hell are you two doing here? Where's Teddy? Teddy, Goddamn it!"

"If you look through the trees you can see his car just hitting the road," I said. "He bailed. I have a feeling a lot of people around you are going to be doing that."

It didn't surprise me that his political aplomb returned almost immediately. Nobody had ever accused Red Talmadge of being slow in a clinch. He scooted his chair halfway around and peered at both of us over the tops of half-frame glasses.

"My God, you're fools. All I have to do is push the button on that white remote on the desk and a silent alarm will summon the police. Are you completely out of your minds? This is a burglary and at the very least an assault…"

"Yeah, yeah, yeah. Go ahead and push it, Senator. We're not shy, are we, Sunny?"

"Not even a little bit."

"We might be able to overlook some of your faults. The payoffs," I waggled my hand. "Ehhh, somebody's gotta do that, keep the wheels of government greased. Tipping Ferguson's wife to his affair with your daughter, now that was nasty. But I can see why you needed to do it. But, the bottom line is, you're a lousy father."

"Yeah, you pretty much suck at being a daddy," Sunny added.

"And setting up people to be killed, including Frank Hanratty, who was a friend of mine by the way, definitely makes you a scumbag."

"I did no such thing!"

I looked over at Sunny. "Want to start with that?"

"Sure. An excellent beginning."

She withdrew a sheet of paper from her briefcase. "SBC shows an incoming call from this house to Frank Hanratty's private number at home, placed just before he left there on Sunday evening."

"Oh, please. You obtained that illegally and it wouldn't convince a jury of anything," Talmadge scoffed.

"Elise Hanratty actually 'obtained' her husband's records from the phone company and, by the way? You're looking at the only jury you need to care about right now. We'd vote guilty," I said.

Sunny held up a video cassette and several papers.

"Here's something even more fun. Does the name Winston Monet sound familiar? He's now a regional supervisor for the Immigration and Naturalization Service. He was a district manager in Chicago when you knew him five years ago. On this tape, he tells your daughter how he arranged for the visas of David Tobarro and his father to be lifted so that they would be sent back to El Salvador. Oh, and how you managed to pull a string or two so Monet would get a nice bump in grade. He was pretty proud of that."

I jumped in before Talmadge could respond.

"Your fellow club member and political nemesis, Brian Ferguson, got Brooke started asking questions. That was back before she had professional help taping her sessions, but every word recorded just the same. Is that why you went after him and told his wife he was having an affair with your daughter?"

"Victor Childress," Sunny rattled another tape in the air. "Senator Mark Twoomey. A scheme to funnel money into the Governor's re-election campaign through a couple of phony companies. No mention of you there except that the Secretary of State's office lists you as owner of one of the companies. Oh, now here's Mitch Dubois from the Governor's staff. He's a hottie. He's not what you'd call a stud in bed but he sure chatters on about how he and a few other people got their regular state pay even though they worked full-time on the Governor's last campaign. And channeled some of it to you for getting them the jobs."

"I don't know what you're talking about," he huffed.

I said, "Of course not. Wink, wink, right? You don't want to admit anything because this room is miked, isn't it? You have it set up so casually, people figure, 'this isn't his office, I can talk freely.' But this is the room where you do all your business so, somewhere, there's a microphone and tape."

Sunny spoke up. "Probably has it wired to a hard drive, Reno. Tons more recording time that way. Microphone's in the fan, right above the table." She pointed to where a small nub punched out the side of the ceiling fan. "Another one in the lamp on the side table. It's a video camera, too."

"No wonder Brooke figured out how to keep good records of her conversations. She learned from you, right here."

"Are you finished?" Talmadge snapped.

"Nope. Show him the other one," I told Sunny, and gestured at the television and VCR in one corner of the airy room.

He started up from his seat. "I don't have any desire to…"

I stepped in and blocked his movement. I was close enough to him I could see some tiny gray nose hairs that his barber had missed. I put a hand on his shoulder and squeezed in a fraternal way.

"Oh sure you do," I said. "This one's all about you, Talmadge."

After a moment, he sat down.

The shot opened as a naked Brooke Talmadge scrambled under the covers of a very large bed in a suite at the Four Seasons. She snuggled next to Mikhail Federov. The rustling of the sheets suggested a microphone placed on or near the headboard but the low light level didn't show where it might have been.

"Now you see why I insisted on bringing you here?" Brooke teased. "I knew you would be this way if there was no one nearby who could hear you. You animal."

"There's no one listening to us at the apartment. I would have them shot!" Federov laughed as he picked a glass off the side table and took a sip.

"I also like coming here because…this hotel is where you and my father first met isn't it? In the bar?"

Federov put his glass to Brooke's lips and she drank some. "You must stop with this fixation on your father. It is not healthy."

Brooke kissed Federov's ear and apparently let a little of the liquid from the glass trickle there. He laughed again and playfully pushed her away. I looked at Talmadge. His face was stone, but he was watching.

"I'm not fixated," his daughter said on the screen. "I just think it's funny. You being his client and then blowing him off for being so small time. I think it's hilarious."

"Your father is what he is. A political functionary. He was useful when we needed him to assist in giving the bank certain legitimacy, but then he felt we owed him something beyond merely paying his exorbitant bill. I think not. In Russia, someone such as that would know their place. Here, he believes he is one of the…intelligentsia. He actually tried to…what is that expression? To court favor?"

"Lobby. That's what he is basically. A lobbyist."

"Yes. He tried to lobby me to help him buy a Senate seat for one of his friends. That Bascomb person. What a fool your father is."

"You just say that because you know how it turns me on." Brooke said.

She grabbed Federov's face and kissed him hungrily. "Turns me on just like taking pictures of us turns me on."

Brooke lifted a camera from her lap and pointed it at him.

Sunny snapped off the tape.

Talmadge looked at each of us, suddenly breaking into a condescending smile. He gestured to the television.

"That proves absolutely nothing. I don't know what you think you have with those other tapes, either. As broadcasters, surely you know that Illinois is a two-party consent state for audio recordings. Unless my daughter had a judge's order, anything anyone said to her in front of a hidden microphone is totally inadmissible."

Sunny lifted the tape out of the machine and slipped it back into its sleeve. "You know, Reno, the man *is* a lawyer. What he says is completely true. Completely."

"Sad, isn't it?" I said and sighed. "All those tapes. All that great potential evidence."

She nodded solemnly. Then she suddenly snapped her fingers.

"Except Brooke got consent! On every one of those tapes, every single one, there's another camera in the picture. You saw her holding it, didn't you? Want me to run that back for you?"

Talmadge's jaw rippled but he said nothing.

Sunny snapped her briefcase closed. "Sometimes she's holding the camera. Other times it's on a tripod. And on every single tape, just like the one we showed you, the person either doesn't object or encourages her to do whatever she wants. As long as *he* gets to keep the tape. The tape he knows about, that is. Guys are so easy when it comes to homemade porn."

I said, "Check the statutes. We did. There's no law against multiple recordings. You consent, that's it. Besides. Brooke was a smart girl. She documented everything she could."

"What are you talking about?"

"The paper trail of course."

I took a letter out of my pocket and handed it to him. Signed by his daughter, it was a perfectly worded Freedom of Information request for somebody's expense records from the Secretary of State's office.

"She was better at this stuff than most reporters and producers I know. For sure better than me. Then again, she had some pretty good instructors. And an awful lot of incentive."

"She might not have graduated from college but she sure made it through Bedroom University," I said. "Her major was Paying Back Daddy. Let's see now. For law, Professor and Judge Charles Bridges. Political Science, Professor and Senator Brian Ferguson. Investigative Reporting, Professor and News Director Frank Hanratty. Those were the full professors. There are some assistants and adjuncts in her tape collection, too. I'd say she got full value from her education."

"Some education," he said. "It killed her."

"Yeah, and from the sound of your voice, you must be all done mourning, huh? Sure, Brooke's dead. But you can think of all those tapes as the Ghosts of Christmas Past. Believe me. They're going to haunt you." I let that hang in the quiet room.

He bowed his head and smoothed a hand across the letter I'd given him. When he looked up, I could see fury mixed with political cunning in his eyes.

"How much do you want? That's what this is all about, isn't it? How much?"

Sunny glanced at her watch. "Ten seconds," she said. "I win."

"Damn," I said to Talmadge. "I bet you'd go at least a half a minute before you tried the bribe. I just lost five bucks."

"What does that mean?"

He looked from Sunny back to me. No sense of humor.

"It means if there are two people in the world who don't want your money, it's us."

"If you use those tapes, I'll ruin you."

I bent at the waist so I was eye to eye with him, the way you might address a small child.

"I saw your daughter dead, Talmadge. I had a guy try to mash me into the side of a building. I've been shot at and beaten up. I've watched a man I respected very much shot to death in front of me, and a kid I didn't know executed. And I've killed a man. Now you tell me. You got anything to put up against that? Because if you make a threat and you don't deliver, some day very soon I'm going to come back to this room and I'm going to beat you to death."

I had tried to arrange my features into an expression of calm self assurance. Sunny said later that, by the time I finished speaking, I looked ready to reach into Talmadge's chest and squeeze his heart until it stopped.

That wasn't what I was thinking about.

I was concentrating on his eyes, waiting, the way early man probably waited with a stone-tipped spear, watching the entrance to a cave for prey that was bigger and stronger than he was. I wasn't sure what to expect until I saw it and then, oddly, I wasn't surprised. A little flicker of movement, way back there in the dark where the fearful child in all of us resides.

Talmadge looked away.

CHAPTER 24

▼

We emerged from the house into an afternoon that looked far different to me than it had when we entered.

The sky was still cloudless and blue, the birds continued to chirp, and the guys with the chainsaws worked mightily to chop up the diseased tree next door. The difference was, I knew Red Talmadge's world was in the process of lurching to a halt. I might have taken pleasure in that, but I could remember only too well what it felt like when the same kind of thing happened to me. I wouldn't be doing any gloating.

The first car up the drive as we approached Sunny's Expedition was occupied by Special Agent Jesse Dark and her partner, the ever unpleasant Special Agent Mohler. In exchange for turning over Brooke's tapes and documents, I'd hammered out a deal with my now-best buddy, Supervisory Agent Stinson. He, a couple of guys from the FBI's political corruption unit and some Assistant U.S. Attorneys all agreed to let me see how much I could rattle Talmadge before they picked him up for questioning.

Mohler got out and walked past without acknowledging our presence. Still pouting about the dog crap, no doubt. I hated to help the two of them look good but they were the assigned case agents on what the Feds now called REDMOB and seemed to be the designated heroes of the day. Works out like that sometimes. They'd probably both be promoted and I'd never even see a Thank You card.

From what Gennaro told me the day before, as soon as the Bureau's supervisors and U.S. Attorneys had gotten a look at the tapes we'd brought them, they'd

- 407 -

decided to land on Talmadge with the full weight of the government and see what squirted out.

"Too many people on those tapes referred to him and Federov doing business, even Federov himself," Gennaro said, using a shot glass of Bushmills to doctor his cup of coffee.

We sat in the rear of a Loop tavern, two blocks from the Federal Building. It was a lawyer-and-politician kind of place. High-backed booths with padding thick enough to absorb whatever kind of secrets might get spilled. Every so often he'd nod and smile at other patrons, shaking a hand here and a sharing a quick joke there. I wondered if he was running for office.

"'Ol Red made himself too visible, licking Federov's boots like that. Like a mob wannabe or something," he said.

"So they'll question him and then what?" I asked.

"For a mope, the guy still carries some weight. Even the bosses in Washington know that. They're walkingon tippy-toes, trying to decide whether to indict him or give him an out. He flips, he probably could nail half the state government and a few congressmen and senators, too. I mean what are we talking? You got your campaign fraud, money laundering, extortion, bribery." He ran out of possibilities and took a sip of his coffee, decided it wasn't strong enough and added another teardrop of booze.

"In fact, and you didn't get this from me, one of the corruption squads looking at our good governor's finances has been sniffing around Talmadge for a couple of months. His daughter's tapes give us what's officially referred to within your government as 'a woodie'."

"'Us?'"

"Now, now. Don't be assuming nothing. Kind of hard to get out of the 'we' n 'us' habit after twenty-some years."

"Sure, John."

"Hey, you don't go asking questions about me, I won't get into the real story of how you stumbled upon those very incriminating tapes and files."

"Nothing secret there. Turns out Alicia Witting and Brooke Talmadge got to be pretty good friends in the short time they knew each other. After all, Federov was playing them both to get next to Ferguson. They had some common gripes."

"Not like they had anybody else's shoulder to cry on."

"Brooke apparently spent some time snooping through Federov's stuff while she lived with him. She found the tapes and some documents Federov had used to get a hammer on Alicia. It all provided evidence of blackmail. Brooke stuck all that into the file she'd been compiling on her father. It looks like even before Ferguson's wife found out about her affair, Brooke had decided to skip out on Federov, start a new life."

"Fine," Gennaro interrupted impatiently. "I heard all this. Then she and Witting get to be such *good buddies* she tells Witting she's been putting together these files and where to find them if she suddenly disappears or dies or gets struck by lightning or whatever."

"Yup."

"So when Brooke gets whacked, Witting comes to Chicago, somehow gets hold of them, and gives them to her lesbo girlfriend, whatsername. Gwen? After which, Witting manages to kill herself by driving into a bridge at 70 miles an hour. You want to tell me why she did that exactly?"

"Sounds like you've been reading some confidential Bureau reports, John," I grinned.

"Whatever. I got friends just like you do. And, speaking of your friends, how did you get so cozy with this Gwen that she'd dial you up first thing after she conveniently comes into possession of these red hot materials?"

"She thought I'd know the right thing to do with them."

He waggled a finger at me. "Kiss my rosy red rectum. My guess is *you* figured out where Brooke kept her stash and then you sweet-talked the young lady into stepping up and saying it was her found 'em instead. C'mon Reno. If Witting had hold of the shit that's in there, why'd she need to kill herself? Everything I read makes her out to be just a patsy."

"I seem to recall reading somewhere she was flying on X."

"Cute. 'Read it somewhere'. Yeah, in the M.E.'s report, which hasn't been made public yet. Don't avoid the question, my friend. You found Brooke's Daddy Dearest File, didn't you? Off the record and between friends."

I made a face.

"How would I do that? And why?"

"I gotcha there, smart ass. The gym." He pointed his finger again and settled back against the wall of the booth with a self-satisfied look.

"Gym?"

"Yeah, go ahead, play dumb. Troopers following up the accident found an application for Petey's Gym in Witting's briefcase. There's a Petey's right across from the car rental office. Witting was in there the day she died trying to use someone else's membership and their locker. We find out who the woman was and, whoa, guess what? Picture in the club's records looks a little like Brooke Talmadge. But by the time the troopers think to let us know about it, we get in to take a look at the contents of her locker, nada. All gone."

"You're saying I snuck into a women's locker room and stole the tapes?"

He stared at me, nodding. "Sure, Reno. Yeah, that's just what I'm saying. Those legs, I can see you in a dress. No, you goof. That hot private eye you hang out with got in there somehow. What I want to know is how you figured where to look."

"I'll show you mine if you show me yours," I said.

"Shit," he said.

He thought about it while he took another sip of his fortified coffee.

"Okay. You wanna know what it's like these days? I'm retired. I'm doing favors. That's my new life's work. Like, I let certain people know to stay off your back. *Capische*? You think the Bureau and U.S. Attorney took those files from you and agreed to your deal on Talmadge because they love you now? Au contraire. A certain suit from D.C. wanted your body in a meat locker and your head on his wall. I convinced him you'd make him look good."

He glanced around and then burned his eyes into mine.

"Oh, and while I'm on the topic of knives in the back? Stay away from Vincent Seamans. The man is *le notizie cattive*, bad news, in case you hadn't noticed. You want to know why the Bureau was playing games with you in the first place? His idea. He told 'em if they riled you enough you'd go right out and cause Mikhail so much grief he'd try a whack job. They had you covered just in case, but still."

"They had me 'covered?'"

"Told you they were watching, didn't I? I just didn't know the whole story. You were their staked goat, buddy boy."

Three strikes Vinnie, I thought. I felt the same hollowness of spirit I'd experienced in the conference room at Lake Point Tower. Steering by remote control, my "uncle" had aimed me right into the middle of a gang war. He'd known me well enough to understand that, as long as people ordered me to back off, I'd charge right ahead. Come to think of it, Hanratty had known me pretty well too. Although, as it turned out, not well enough.

I settled back in the booth and gave Gennaro part of what he was asking to hear.

"Brooke Talmadge wasn't just using her promiscuity with his clients to embarrass her father. She turned hooker so she could target people who knew specific details of his illegal deal making. She was doing what amounted to investigative research."

He snorted. "More fun than going to the library I guess."

"Not even close. I think her choice was between prostituting herself and killing him. She was that angry. You saw the material she put together about the guy from INS?"

"Who's been suspended, I hear. Yeah. I'm up to speed on the death of the boyfriend. You're telling me she carried this grudge for five years? Sounds like she was related to Polo Tony not Red Talmadge."

"I paged through her journal. It was in one of the files. She grew up watching her father making deals. She heard the rumors from other kids, kids whose mommies he screwed or whose daddies he set up and then slammed for campaign contributions or no-show jobs or whatever. She was already curious about a lot of things. Very sexual, too. Daddy was fed up with that. In her journal, she hints he might have had some not very appropriate interest in her. Who knows? He wasn't happy with her promiscuity, anyway. He waited until she found one she really cared about. He had the power to get rid of David Tobarro and he used it."

"I saw the audio cassette in her collection. What did she do, tape her old man's phone calls?"

He motioned to the waitress who brought more coffee. She pointed to my cup but I waved her off.

"Ferguson knew Talmadge, knew he was slime. He suggested Brooke check to see if he had his office wired. She found the tape of the phone call where good old dad talked to his buddy at INS."

"Ferguson puts her onto her old man and then Federov puts her on to Ferguson. Wonder if the good Senator knows his little hoochie mama was setting him up?"

"I tried a couple of different approaches to get an appointment and ask him. I was told he's not dodging questions. He's just on vacation."

"Tell me about it. Even the White House is in on this, 'least the way I hear the story. Doing damage control. The U.S. Attorney is trying the soft approach to get him to come in and talk. I mean, he could use a subpoena, get ol' Fergie before a Grand Jury, but Jesus! The most powerful guy in Congress? And in the same political party? The USA begged him to just talk to a couple of agents and tell his side, but it's not happening."

His scowl darkened. "You know, Hoover had a saying that's still gospel. Makes sense, too. 'Don't Embarrass the Bureau.' You'd think a guy like Ferguson would remember."

"Ferguson showed Brooke how easy it was to get information on her father. Could be he even mentioned other people who would know useful things. She decided that making Talmadge pay for the Tobarro's was going to be her full time job. A friend sent her to Eddie Marn. I originally thought she wanted to become a porn queen. Marn even told me she tried to get him to hook her up. I think he lied about that. I think she just wanted someone who could teach her how to document the 'interviews' she was doing and Marn was one of the best at playing with hidden cameras."

"Hang on a minute. I remember this guy. Marn would have only helped her if he could have helped himself at the same time."

"I'm thinking she got him to show her what she needed to do. She would never have invited him along. She was smart enough to know he would have used the tapes himself."

"Didn't I see she'd done a couple of bondage videos?" Gennaro asked.

I nodded. "Minor league. Web-only stuff and it was part of the scam. She invented herself as an S and M freak to keep the escort services from trying too hard to recruit her. She came across way too wild for most of them. She could act the part but, my guess is, it was all for show. She wouldn't take clients who didn't fit her profile."

I sighed and drank some of my tea. The place had a great orange rind tea.

"It took her five years to get the kind of information she wanted on her old man. But that's how she did it. She unraveled his life one piece of yarn at a time. She'd find one guy, she'd get what she could from him, he'd point her toward another one. Or give her enough information about one scam or another that she could do a document search and see the rest. Not too different from the way you or I would work it."

"Yeah, except where we'd interrogate the *idiota* to try and get him to snitch, she'd fuck him silly. How's Witting fit into your little drama?"

"One of Sunny's people had her under surveillance when she left the hotel. We thought she'd meet with Federov, or at least one of his cutouts. She went directly to the health club and tried to get in."

"How did you manage to find out the membership name the Talmadge girl used and get into her locker?"

I shrugged, smiled.

"We're pretty good friends, John, but that might be admitting to complicity in a couple of felonies."

Gennaro made a rude noise but I wasn't about to point a finger at Sunny as a computer hacker, burglar and thief. In truth, I didn't know how she'd come up with Brooke's CD files and some 25 video tapes. All I could have told him was that the combination to the locker had been in our hands for several days and we hadn't realized it. It was the series of numbers written on the picture I'd found in

Alan Talmadge's suitcase. Until Sunny saw them and burst out laughing, I'd thought they were Brooke's measurements. The hotshot investigator revealed as a perv. Maybe I could spend my retirement wearing a long raincoat and flashing women on the El.

"So Witting offed herself because the people at the club wouldn't let her in to get to the locker and the documents?"

"Gwen told us Witting thought she was going to be indicted as a spy. She intended to get Brooke's file, drive up to Wisconsin and make Ferguson look at it. She wanted him on her side before she turned herself in. When she couldn't get the file, I'm guessing, panic and whatever pills she'd taken made her suicidal. She had my card in her hand at the time. I can only see that as a pretty clear message that I'd left her no choice."

"Musta been a good Catholic girl," Gennaro said. "Spreading the guilt like that."

I recalled those words as I stood in Talmadge's driveway, watching Dark, Mohler and a second team of agents go up to his door and ring the bell. I wondered if any of them would claim afterward that they had seen a look of guilt pass across his face when they showed their credentials and told him what they were there to do. I doubted they'd actually see anything of the sort. A small amused smile, perhaps, as he realized the system he had flim-flammed so many times was finally coming to take a hard look at him. Guilt? Hard to imagine. He and Federov could have been twins in that regard.

Sunny touched my arm and inclined her head toward the road. Leon, my favorite Channel 14 camera guy, was set up just beyond Talmadge's property, long lens pointed at the house. I looked back to where he was no doubt focused. Watched the door open and Agents Dark and Mohler flashing their badge wallets like a well-practiced drill. Watched Talmadge invite them inside and close the door behind them.

"You know, Reno, Brooke's going to get what she wanted," Sunny observed. "Probably more than she could have expected."

"She'll bring down her old man. A good number of his buddies. And, depending on how the White House wants to handle it, I think Ferguson's going to take a fall, too. Brooke's journal doesn't pull any punches."

"That's kind of ironic, isn't it? Since he's the one who started her on her little odyssey."

I shrugged, thinking about something else. "I guess she didn't need a superhero to come along and avenge her after all."

"Oh. Do you know one of those?" Sunny asked mischievously.

"A couple of them. Present company included."

She touched my arm again. It felt pretty good. I debated taking her hand as we walked down to the road. With the camera there, I decided it might spoil her professional image.

Marisa Langdon stood near a live truck parked out of sight of the house behind some trees at the end of the driveway. Its mast was extended and I knew Leon's shot of the *federales* arriving to interview a celebrated former state senator had been used live on Channel 14's News at Four. Neither Supervisory Agent Stinson, nor Agent Dark had been consulted about that. I knew they wouldn't approve. I didn't care.

"Is he here?" I asked Marisa. She smiled and nodded.

That morning, Irv Bolton had begged to go back to being second in command and she'd been named Interim News Director, a promotion she wasn't expecting and one that still had her looking a little stunned. Probably awestruck, too. She was now the youngest female TV news director in Chicago and, as far as I knew, the youngest in any major television market in the country.

I suspected most of the rationale behind Elise Bascomb Hanratty's decision was based on the overall respect Marisa had garnered amongst her colleagues since coming to the city, and the classy, respectful way she'd presented her eyewitness report of Frank's confession and subsequent murder. There was also the consideration that all of the networks had been hammering at her agent's door for the past three days and Elise had known she needed to act quickly or lose her best talent.

I stepped past and looked into the rear of the truck where banks of monitors captured the view of Talmadge's house. Leon held the shot tight, waiting to see if the agents would come out with Talmadge in tow. I suspected they would. Charley Kinsella sat in a swivel chair next to the producer who was running the live broadcast. I grinned when I saw him.

"I thought the suburbs were the Dark Territory to you."

"Yeah, the air's pretty rare up here but when I got your message I figured it was probably worth the drive. Once. As long as you're the one buying dinner."

"You doing okay with the Department?"

"Ah, fuck 'em. Internal Affairs ruled the shooting justifiable then docked me two days for firing into a moving vehicle. My commander, the dickhead, tried to get them to nail me for conducting an unauthorized investigation until my lawyer brought up how I'd cleared a couple murders."

The live truck technician leaned toward me. "About two minutes, Reno." He handed over a small IFB earpiece which would allow me to hear the anchors talking. I snapped the clip to my collar and let the device dangle.

"Gonna get interviewed huh?"

"Something like that," I said. "Stick around."

Marisa put her hand on my shoulder and looked up at me.

"Think you remember how?"

"I'll wing it, see if it comes back."

Sunny looked from Marisa to me, concerned. "You think it's wise for you to be talking about all this without Barney Tanner around?"

"Just watch for a bit," I said.

"Reno? I know that look. You're up to something."

I grinned at her, feeling like a little kid about to climb on a Ferris wheel for the first time, or a teenager about to drive a Ferrari. There was one aspect to all of this I hadn't shared with her, more out of superstition that if I talked about it, it might not happen. I walked to where Leon had his camera set up. Marisa came with me part of the way but when Leon handed me the microphone with the Channel 14 logo on it, she paused and I went forward by myself.

"Reno?" Sunny said with a funny inflection. I think it was at that precise moment that she understood.

I stepped around in front of the camera and slipped in the earpiece.

EXCERPT FROM "CHANNEL 14'S NEWS AT FOUR"

Anchor: *As we've been reporting since the top of this newscast, Federal authorities in Chicago are launching a brand new investigation into political corruption. Channel 14's Investigative Unit has learned one person the Joint Terrorism Task Force wants to question is former State Senator R. Edwin Talmadge. A couple of minutes ago, we showed you federal agents arriving at Talmadge's North Shore home. Now, we welcome Reno McCarthy to Channel 14 after an absence of several years. He's outside the Talmadge home and will help us understand just what's going on. Reno, it's good to have you back. What can you tell us?*

McCarthy: *It's great to be back, Ben.*

For years, Red Talmadge has wielded secret power both in Springfield and in Washington. Now, some startling documents and video tapes obtained by the I-Team tell a sordid story of kickbacks, bribes, campaign fraud, and even an attempt to unseat the U.S. Senator who some in government refer to as 'the most important man in Congress,' Senator Brian Fahy Ferguson.

The paper and video tape trail of lies and political manipulation is even more remarkable because it was put together over five years by Talmadge's own daughter, Brooke Talmadge. We've presented the Talmadge File to federal authorities. U.S. Attorney Robert Clary tells us they've found it compelling enough to initiate their own investigation. In this newscast, and in newscasts during the next several days, we're going to highlight some of the deals documented by Brooke Talmadge's investigation of her father. We're going to show how our own investigation in recent days links Talmadge to Russian Organized Crime, specifically to it's Chicago boss, Mikhail Federov, who was gunned down Sunday.

Ben, as you see behind me right now, federal agents are leaving the Talmadge home and escorting the former state senator to their car. Sources tell us those agents will take him to the Dirksen Federal Building, where the questioning will begin, focusing first, we're told, on ghost pay rolling in the Governor's office, then moving on to allegations of ties with the Russian mob or so called "Red Mafiya..."

BREAKING NEWS REPORT, CCN NETWORK NEWS:

Anchor: *Welcome Back to CCN Center in Washington, I'm Ramsey Kyle.*

Word is just reaching us of a plane crash in the Nicolet National Forest in Northern Wisconsin. That's not far from the Michigan state border. First reports from the scene indicate the plane that went down was a business jet. It carried a pilot, co-pilot and four passengers, all of whom perished in the accident. Sources say that aircraft was owned by the family of U.S. Senator Brian Fahy Ferguson of Illinois.

Now, we caution you: there is no confirmation the Senator was aboard.

As you can see from the graphic on your screens, this area is about 370 miles north of Chicago, perhaps 250 miles from Minneapolis-St. Paul. The aircraft took off from a small airfield in Woodruff, Wisconsin, about fifteen minutes prior to when area residents claim to have heard an explosion and to have seen a bright flash. This all tak-

ing place about 9 p.m. Central Daylight Time or approximately ninety minutes ago. We have—just a moment. Oh I'm being told now—CCN's White House Correspondent Jordan Hayes joins us live from the East Lawn. Jordan what can you tell us about this tragic accident? Was Senator Ferguson aboard?

Hayes: *Ramsey, that plane crash in the woods in Northern Wisconsin is sure to have repercussions around the world. White House Spokesman Brittany Owens has just announced that the passengers on the ill-fated flight were Senate Foreign Relations Committee Chairman Brian Fahy Ferguson, along with his wife and two longtime aides. It appears Senator Ferguson and his wife had been vacationing at their summer home in Northern Wisconsin and had departed this evening to return to Washington for the funeral of another aide who was killed in a car crash in Chicago last weekend. As you can imagine, this news has stunned President Barker, who has sent his condolences to the Senator's family. He has ordered that flags on all government buildings be flown at half-mast...*

0-595-29359-X